Phantom Ships

The Author

Photo: Gilles Savoie

Claude Le Bouthillier has published seven novels and one book of poetry. His eighth novel and second collection of poetry are both slated for publication in fall 2004. He has won several major literary prizes, including the Pascal-Poirier Prize (2000) from the province of New Brunswick, an award of excellence bestowed for an author's life's work. For *Phantom Ships*, originally published in French as *Le Feu du Mauvais Temps*, he received the Champlain Prize (1989) and the France-Acadie Prize (1990).

Born in New Brunswick, Claude Le Bouthillier studied psychology at the University of Moncton and the university Paris-X-Nanterre. He has worked in educational and university settings, in a clinic, and in his own practice. At present, his office is in Caraquet. For the past thirty years, he has devoted a great deal of his time and energy to writing and to promoting literary activities and reading. From 1989 to 1991, he chaired the Public Lending Rights Commission. Claude Le Bouthillier represents Acadian writers on the Board of Directors of the New Brunswick Arts Council and chairs the Acadian Poetry Festival held every fall.

The Translator

Photo: Joel Ouriou

Susan Ouriou translates fiction from French and Spanish and writes fiction in English. She has been nominated twice for the Governor General's Literary Award for Translation (2003, 1995). She is the founding editor of *TransLit*, a bi-annual anthology of literary translation, and still serves on its editing collective twelve years later. Her first novel, *Damselfish*, was published by XYZ in 2003 and was a finalist for the 2004 Alberta Book Awards Georges Bugnet Award for Novel and the City of Calgary W.O. Mitchell Book Prize. Susan Ouriou lives in Calgary and works as a simultaneous interpreter.

Phantom Ships

a novel by

Claude Le Bouthillier

translated by Susan Ouriou

XYZ
Publishing

Originally published as *Le Feu du Mauvais Temps* by Québec Amérique
© 1989 by Claude Le Bouthillier and Québec Amérique
English translation © 2004 by Susan Ouriou and XYZ Publishing

National Library of Canada Cataloguing in Publication

Le Bouthillier, Claude

[Feu du mauvais temps. English]

Phantom ships: a novel

Translation of: Le feu du mauvais temps

ISBN 1-894852-09-5

I. Ouriou, Susan. II. Title. III. Title: Feu du mauvais temps. English.

PS8573.E336F4813 2004   C843'.54   C2004-940464-4
PS9573.E336F4813 2004

Legal Deposit: Second quarter 2004
National Library of Canada
Bibliothèque nationale du Québec

XYZ Publishing acknowledges the financial support our publishing program receives from the Canada Council for the Arts, the Book Publishing Industry Development Program (BPIDP) of the Department of Canadian Heritage, the ministère de la Culture et des Communications du Québec, and the Société de développement des entreprises culturelles.

Editor: Rhonda Bailey
Layout: Édiscript enr.
Cover design: Zirval Design
Cover painting: Joseph Turner, *Typhoon Approaching*, 1840
Map of ancient Acadie (p. vi): Victoria Tico Thibault

Set in Caslon 12 on 14.
Printed and bound in Canada by Transcontinental Imprimerie Gagné (Louiseville, Québec, Canada) in April 2004.

XYZ Publishing
1781 Saint Hubert Street
Montreal, Quebec H2L 3Z1
Tel: (514) 525-2170
Fax: (514) 525-7537
E-mail: info@xyzedit.qc.ca
Web site: www.xyzedit.qc.ca

Distributed by: Fitzhenry & Whiteside
195 Allstate Parkway
Markham, ON L3R 4T8
Customer Service, tel: (905) 477-9700
Toll free ordering, tel: 1-800-387-9776
Fax: 1-800-260-9777
E-mail: bookinfo@fitzhenry.ca

For my mother… and for my family,
both close and extended, guardians of the seeds
that sprouted through my imagination
into this novel

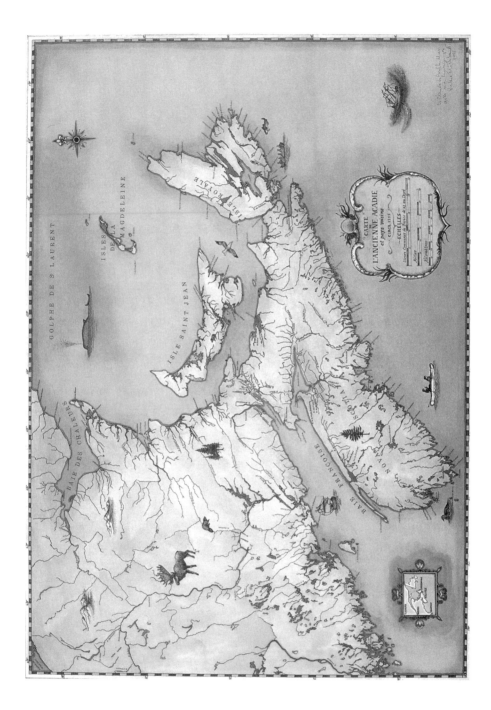

CARTE
de
L'ANCIENNE ACADIE
et pays voisins
CIRCA 1755
—ECHELLES—

GOLPHE DE S.T LAURENT

ISLES DE LA MAGDELEINE

ISLE ROYALE

ISLE SAINT JEAN

BAIE DES CHALEURS

BAIE FRANÇOISE

NOUVELLE ECOSSE

Chapter 1

The land we have seen on the south side of this gulf is as fertile and as beautiful as anything we have ever seen, with its stunning countryside and prairies as flat as a lake. The land to the north is a highland with tall mountains covered in forests and many varieties of tall, thick trees. Among others, there are beautiful cedars and pine trees as far as the eye can see, tall enough to make masts for ships of over three hundred tons...

...The heat in this region is more temperate than in Spain.

     – Jacques Cartier in the Baye des Chaleurs, 1534

At the entrance to the Baye des Chaleurs[1] in the spring of the year of grace seventeen hundred and forty under the reign of Louis XV, Captain Hyacinthe, an old Breton seadog, his beard white, his face weathered by the salt of the sea, scanned the horizon, a pipe clenched in his teeth. The trip from Quebec[2] had been made without incident, and favourable winds had pushed *L'Ensorceleuse* down the St. Lawrence River[3] and past Gaspeg[4]. Some ten Atlantic crossings had made of Hyacinthe an experienced seaman, and his men – thirty-sixers

---

1. Natives called it "Ktan metjéoé" or "sea teeming with fish."
2. In the native language, "Quebec" means "narrow passage" or "river opening."
3. Natives called it "the path that walks."
4. Also called "Honguedo," which means "earth's end." Today's Gaspé.

for the most part (since they had signed up for thirty-six months) – respected him as much for his strict discipline as for his sense of justice.

Joseph was leaning on the ship's rail, lost in thought. Tall and fair with pearl-grey eyes, a slender nose, a bushy brown beard with auburn-coloured streaks, and long brown hair held back off his face, he had an aura of nobility about him, of grandeur and generosity. His wiry muscles hinted at great strength; he walked with a wave's fluid grace, and his fine, knotted hands held both a worker's strength and a violinist's sensitivity. His origins, however, were a mystery. His adoptive parents were already in their forties when he arrived as a present from France. Their love for him was all the greater because they themselves were unable to have children. Joseph grew up on Rue Sault-au-Matelot, in the heart of Place Royale, where Champlain founded Quebec. He spent his childhood just down the street from the royal battery, right next to the warehouses and docks, the place of transit for merchandise between the two continents. His father Pierre initiated him at an early age into the secrets of the smithy: the iron, the fire, the sparks. The mysterious, unpredictable dance of the flame keeping time to the blows of the hammer on the anvil instilled an adventurer's spirit in him.

As an adolescent, Joseph worked in the smithy and helped his father on Quebec's fortifications; each spring, the powder magazine and walls damaged from the winter freeze needed repair. While working on those same damp ramparts, his father was felled by influenza. Joseph was barely out of adolescence. His sorrow lessened over time, and he remembered his father as a good, hard-working man. He still had his mother, Jacqueline Vandandaigne, of Flemish origin, an affectionate woman, who had a love of life, good food, and the things of this earth. He adored her. Nevertheless, he left her and set sail in mid-April, just shy of his twenty-fifth birthday...

Joseph's daydreaming was cut short at the sight of an island silhouetted against the setting sun. The heart-shaped island disappeared then reappeared as the ship rode the waves. An island from another galaxy, another time. Its giant spruce trees, blackened by the savagery of this country of drizzle, seemed to tap the clouds for their sap, and the tall white birch trees stood out against the arc of the heavens like royalty banished amongst the commoners. The wild coast rose several leagues away, and when the captain spied a small cape, he decided to drop anchor at low tide for the crew to repair a leak. He barked his orders and *L'Ensorceleuse* sprang to life; men ran across the bridge, shimmied up the masts, and furled the sail. Calm was restored to the ship, and Joseph took out his violin; as he fiddled, glaciers marched past to the north of the island, like the wise men following the Star.

Miscou: the island that guarded a continent, dotted with cedars, spruce, and birch trees, its green and white sentries draped in magic and fog. Miscou: a name chosen by the Mi'kmaq to describe the low, marshy ground, a land haunted by the legendary giant, the terrible Gougou they called Koukhu. As tall as a ship's mast, the monster, with a hideous female face, was known for her shrieks and for the prisoners it was rumoured she kept in her huge pocket for snacks. Was it not said that come nightfall, surrounded by peat bogs and the wild wheat of the heath, a furious parade of Mi'kmaq souls made pacts with the evil Gougou in order to take revenge on the white men who had invaded their land, profaned their sanctuaries, raped their women, and spread deadly diseases among their people? Was it not said as well that the sons of Eric the Red, those hulking bearded Vikings, had travelled these bays long before the end of the first millennium? The carved dragon that decorated the prow of a longship run aground on the point of the island seemed to confirm that fact. The ship was still visible at high tide, miraculously conserved, probably due to a special coating, like a blue whale poised to swim out to sea. But in truth, what didn't one say when the fog enveloped Ile Miscou in its cottony cocoon pierced by the loon's cry?

Joseph had no time for the rumours that haunted the crew that night because the two seagulls whose appearance announced the approach of land and the languorous notes of the violin brought to mind his fiancée, the charming Emilie, more beautiful than Miscou's wild raspberry bushes, Emilie who had mysteriously disappeared, gone God knew where, vanished into thin air… It was said that a merchant ship had taken her to a distant country, but how to know for sure? With Emilie gone, living in Quebec had become a form of torture for Joseph. The sea breeze blowing up the St. Lawrence reminded him of the scent of her skin. The churchbells at Notre-Dame-des-Victoires carried the memory of one May evening, a gentle thrill; their first kiss, in the dark, next to the confessional. It was as though, even then, their love had been placed under a holy sign. When he walked through the narrow streets up high on Cap Diamant, he imagined he could see her dancing there, in rhythm with the breeze that stirred her long chestnut hair, and he seemed to hear, above the noise of the city, her laughter, which had brought him such joy.

In Quebec, Joseph had sunk into despair, confronted as he was with his sorrow at every turn. Then he heard the news of Isle Royale. Word came of a fortress built in honour of King Louis, with towers so high the Sun King's sons could see them from Versailles; stonecutters were needed for the fortress, as they had been for the road to Berthier. The prospect of adventure made him smile. To set sail… the wide horizon, space, oblivion. The decision came easily. In an attempt to banish his fiancée from his mind, he let himself be drawn by the lure of adventure, encouraged by the stories of Sinbad the Sailor, which had been the stuff of his childhood daydreams. *The British colonies of Boston will be kept in line*, was his consoling thought.

L'Ensorceleuse set sail once more at dawn. As the ship cleaved through the waves with each gust of wind in its sails, they finally attempted an entry into the Baye des Chaleurs. *Jacques Cartier must have had a vivid imagination to give this frigid bay the name "chaleur!"* Joseph thought. *One would expect orange, grapefruit, and coconut trees with a name like "chaleur." Of course, he did arrive during a heat wave.*

L'Ensorceleuse tacked from one gust to another as they sailed into headwinds. A school of porpoises frolicked in its wake. The sky was a deep blue, almost purple, and a few

Northern Gannet, large white birds with black spots on the tips of their wings and their tails, dove for herring. Joseph was captivated by the spectacle as the ship arrived within view of a small crescent-shaped island baptized Caraquet[5], which protected the bay.

"That's just what the map shows," he murmured. "The Indian camp must not be very far off."

The ship rounded a long dune at the point of Caraquet, an island measuring three to four leagues and crowned with wild rose and raspberry bushes that came to life in the springtime. On the coast nearby, a native village sat along the banks of a stream. They were Souriquois, or Mi'kmaq, and the tribe was made up of some twenty families – children, grandparents, and other relatives – approximately two hundred people who lived in conical tents made of long poles attached at the top and covered with hides and birchbark. It was more like a camp than a village because in the wintertime, several Mi'kmaq travelled south to the region of the Poquemouche or Miramichi rivers to hunt. There was a great bustle of activity along the coast. Thick white smoke billowed skyward. Herring, eel, and salmon were being smoked. Beaver, mink, otter, and silver fox pelts were being prepared to adorn members of the perfumed classes of Europe's courts. Joseph felt nothing but scorn for certain nobles who arrived from Europe wearing their lace ruffles to establish their summer home. With their haughty airs, they were much more preoccupied with their curls than with the colony's inhabitants. Joseph was even more disgusted after meeting during the crossing the pedantic marquis who was on *L'Ensorceleuse* with them, and who treated anyone trying to make his acquaintance with arrogance.

A few Mi'kmaq began shooting their rifles in the air in the general jubilation characterized by shouting and a joyous commotion. Others left the crabs, clams, and mussels they were gathering to jump into their canoes. Those seal-hunting at the point of Caraquet headed for the ship as well. Hyacinthe, who had often invited Joseph to dine at his table,

---

5. Caraquet means "located at the mouth of two rivers" in Mi'kmaq.

loaned him his telescope. Surprise deepened the furrow in Joseph's brow when he saw a white-bearded man wearing native clothes standing by one of the tents.

"That's a white man," he exclaimed.

The captain immediately replied. "That's Gabriel Giraud, known as Saint-Jean. He's always been a wily one, that one. It's said he escaped from the galleys where he was serving a life sentence for counterfeit."

"How long ago was that?" Joseph asked.

"Around 1711. The Mi'kmaq found him half-dead. They took care of him. He became a fur trader in the Miramichi. In 1730, he came here to the stream that now bears his name."

Saint-Jean climbed into a canoe.

"They adopted him as their chief. He's the one who settles their disputes and distributes the product of the hunt," Hyacinthe added. "He's their sagamo, their captain, the one who leads because of his prestige and wisdom."

The canoes were fast approaching the ship, which had dropped anchor a few cables' length from shore. The kneeling Mi'kmaq paddled rhythmically; despite the crisp spring air, some wore nothing but a breechcloth, a simple strip of cloth passed between their legs. They boarded the ship with enthusiasm, their curiosity seemingly boundless. Most had no beards. Their bodies gave off an acrid odour, and their hair was greased with thick animal fat that protected them from the cold and the mosquitoes. Joseph was fascinated by the many drawings that decorated their skin, telling of their exploits or representing their totem. After the usual brief formalities, Saint-Jean began the fur-trading negotiations. The Mi'kmaq asked for new rifles, powder, fabric, iron pots, and, of course, jugs of brandy, mirrors, and glass beads. Since Hyacinthe knew Saint-Jean, he knew he wouldn't be able to satisfy him with shoddy goods and a few ancient muskets.

Once trading was concluded, Saint-Jean announced, "Two Mi'kmaq arrived from Port-Royal[6] yesterday claiming the British in Boston are awaiting a large military fleet."

---

6. Annapolis Royal.

"How did they come by that information?" Hyacinthe asked.

"You know that the British from New England use Iroquois to fight the Acadians and the Mi'kmaq. An Iroquois relayed the message."

"That could be bad news," the old seadog remarked.

There was a heavy silence.

"If you should see a British fleet off Miscou, would you be able to send a messenger to Quebec in time?" he asked finally.

"Yes, it would be possible. One would have to canoe to the Restigouche[7] post at the Baye des Chaleurs then up the Matapedia[8] River to Rimouski[9], and from there up the St. Lawrence to Quebec."

The captain said nothing, as though waiting for an offer.

"But I can't leave the camp right now. You'll have to leave me a few men," Saint-Jean proposed.

"That's impossible," the captain retorted. "If there are any storms during the crossing, we won't have enough hands on deck."

Joseph was not sure what came over him. He heard himself say, "I'm willing to stay until fall."

7. Native word meaning "a five-fingered hand." Today's Campbellton.
8. Algonquin word meaning "dog's land."
9. Mi'kmaq word meaning "the junction of two rivers."

Chapter 2

On October 31, 1603, the French admiral Montmorency
delivered a commission to Pierre du Gua, Sieur de
Monts, a Protestant gentleman of the court of France.
The commission, a vice-admiralty commission, covered
"all the maritime Seas, Coasts, Islands, Harbours &
lands found near the said province and region of
Lacadie... and "the lands he shall discover and inhabit
henceforth."
... In making him the King's lieutenant-governor on
November 8, Henry IV bestowed on him authority to
grant seigneuries for all lands located between the 46th
and the 40th parallel as well as a ten-year monopoly over
trading with the savages on the Atlantic coast, in the
Gaspé peninsula, and along both shores of the St.
Lawrence River... lastly, in the first year, he will be
responsible for transporting to Acadia one hundred people, including any vagabonds he is able to conscript.
— Marcel Trudel, *Histoire de la Nouvelle France,*
Le comptoir, 1604-1627

Joseph settled into a simple existence in a small hut in the
camp at the point where the Saint-Jean Creek – Ruisseau –
flowed into the sea. As a man of action used to making decisions without hesitation, he had no intention of remaining
inactive while waiting for a hypothetical English fleet. So he
restarted the small smithy that Saint-Jean had neglected in
order to focus on the fur trade. It was as though the fire from

the smithy was the only thing that could compensate for the pain of losing Emilie, the hammer on the anvil giving birth to objects born of his pain. The bellows fired up the embers, sparks danced with each blow of the hammer on the red-hot rods, incandescent metal was dropped hissing into cold water to be cleansed, all to the accompaniment of Joseph's laboured breathing and the sweat trickling down his body. Hatchets, irons, nails, arrow tips, hardware, and even horseshoes piled up, for he knew one day there would be horses in Ruisseau.

He did not notice her until the third day. She was slender, bare of torso, dark, proudly wearing a wampum necklace – beads of seashells on a string used both as currency and symbolic decoration. Her necklace drew attention to her breasts. She wore a skirt cinched tight at the waist by an embroidered belt studded with loon feathers. Her earrings were carved out of golden seashells. The magnificent young woman was Angélique, Saint-Jean's daughter. Her mother, a Mi'kmaq who had taken the very French name of Madeleine, had been married to the Norman captain Alfred Roussi of Rouen. A daughter, Françoise, now living in Gaspeg, was born of that first marriage. On her husband's death, Madeleine married Gabriel Giraud, known as Saint-Jean. Angélique had never known Madeleine because she was only a year old when her mother died giving birth to her brother Jean-Baptiste. Angélique imagined her mother through her father's words, then carried on the family tradition by developing her own talent with medicinal herbs and learning the midwife's art herself.

This was Joseph's first contact with native customs. *I would never see half-naked young women like this in oh-so-Catholic Quebec, even less so in Notre-Dame-Des-Victoires Church. Not women of such innocence and purity. My God, she is beautiful!*

Lost for words, he couldn't tear his gaze away. *How can an Indian – Métis or no – have such long golden hair to her waist?* he wondered, noting she was even more blonde than her father. Her hybrid beauty fascinated him.

Every day, Angélique came and sat at the entrance to the smithy, mesmerized by the tall, taciturn, bearded man who struck the anvil so furiously. By the seventh day, Joseph and

Angélique still had exchanged only a few words. That day, after bringing him a drink of sugar, ginger, and cold water, Angélique decided to break the silence. "Why did you come here?" she asked.

"I was supposed to go to work on the Louisbourg fortifications, but I have to stay here until the water freezes over to warn the Quebec garrison if the British come up the river," Joseph replied.

"The never-ending wars. I don't understand your Christian principles one bit."

"Believe it or not, I have a hard time understanding them myself," Joseph confessed with a hint of irony.

Not satisfied with his brief response, Angélique insisted, "Why did you leave Quebec?"

Joseph decided to confide in her, "During a trapping expedition out by the St. Maurice[1] smithies, where cannons are manufactured for the Quebec fortress, I was badly hurt and the Algonquins cared for me. I spent the winter half-delirious and amnesiac. By spring, when I returned to Quebec, my fiancée had taken me for dead, and left. I tried to find her but in vain. Emilie had flown off to other climes. Louisiana, the West Indies, Europe?… So I decided to leave and make a new life elsewhere…"

Angélique said nothing, but her expression showed she wished she could comfort him, rub salve on the wound. "You'll forget," she finally said.

Joseph thought he heard, "I'll help you forget…" He, too, had questions he was dying to ask.

"How is it that you're so blonde?" he ventured at last.

"They say that shortly before the French came here, a strange boat with a carved prow appeared off Miscou; they were Vikings come from a great island in the North, an island with volcanoes and geysers. The Mi'kmaq welcomed them like lost gods, and bonds of affection were woven between our two peoples on beds of moss. As you can see, they left their traces!" she said with pride. "There are many other legends… When

---

1. Trois-Rivières.

the moon rises, the southwester breeze murmurs that Jacques Cartier was welcomed in Ruisseau by the chief of the Mi'kmaq, who offered him his daughter as a token of his friendship."

"If the rumour is true, then an explorer's trade doesn't just involve planting crosses!" Joseph exclaimed.

Although Angélique spoke French, her voice held the intonations characteristic of the Mi'kmaq language, which sounded sweet to Joseph's ears.

"But my son has no European features."

Joseph had trouble imagining her as a mother. "You have a son? But you seem so young!"

"I had a baby when I was sixteen. His father died over two years ago, carried away by one of the white man's diseases. I didn't turn to the forge to forget my pain, though, I turned to plants, herbs, and flowers."

A seagull soared overhead, clouds filled the sky, time slowed to a languorous pace. Time for pleasure. His deep-seated fascination with this woman seemed to show the way to a new life.

Day after day at the fiery forge[2], Joseph exorcized his pain and sense of loss by striking the anvil again and again. On the tenth day, his rage surfaced. The forge blazed, resembling the hell shown in the missionaries' pictures. *After all, she could have left behind a letter, a note, a word, a message, to explain her actions… Contacted my family… Unless she had something to hide, unless she left with another man… Will I ever see her again? Will I ever get to the bottom of this?* he wondered furiously.

Another wave of anger engulfed him at the thought that Emilie could have betrayed him, that she might be honeymooning somewhere right now. Angélique had been watching him and was forced to take a step back as the flames took on apocalyptic proportions.

On the fourteenth day, it seemed to Joseph that Angélique's bared breasts were in the way of an offering. Saint-Jean watched their little dance with amusement.

---

2. Charcoal came from Ile de Pokesudie, which means "narrow passage between rocks."

Membertou, Angélique's son, had started to sulk. Although Joseph slid under the beaver pelts every night, he did not need them for warmth. By the second week after his arrival, his entire being, like the forge, was a bed of glowing embers.

* * *

All night long, the tribe celebrated along the shores of the Poquemouche, which looked like a raging river in places. By resin torches that lit up the night, the natives used their fish spears resembling tridents to harpoon eels and throw them in with the other eels squirming in baskets. Joseph was introduced to the sport. Angélique served as his guide. He was bewitched by the woman, by her powerful magnetism. He felt a growing passion as the stars danced in the sky and the moon disappeared. As the sun rose, he felt as though even the leaves on the trees had begun intertwining. But he couldn't quell a feeling of unease. Not brought about by the memory of Emilie, but by the thought of Angélique, her origins, and the child who was not his. And yet... Angélique symbolized the vitality of this continent steeped in the humus of its First Nations and its forty centuries of history. Born through her mother of a people that had incarnated the age of Enlightenment well before Louis XIV, when Europeans were massacring the Infidels to conquer Jerusalem in the name of the love of Christ, she was a breath of fresh air and mystery that he longed to touch.

"Come, I want to show you a quiet creek where I go to to be alone," she whispered.

She held out her hand to help him out of the canoe; he thrilled at her touch. He was torn between two passions: one inaccessible, the other near at hand... They sat together in a small moss-covered clearing under the shade of two giant birch trees. Angélique offered him some smoked salmon and wild strawberries she had brought with her. The intimate feast ended with fresh spring water after which he fell asleep. He woke to Angélique's eyes on him. Joseph stared back intently, as though her beauty might evaporate.

"I had a dream while you were sleeping," she confessed.

"About what?"

"You were lying dead on a bed of moss. You looked so fine, all surrounded by light."

"What does the dream mean?" Joseph asked, surprised.

"For us, it represents a sort of resurrection."

"Resurrection? Well, what do you know! That's what it would take for me to believe what I'm feeling right now," he thought out loud.

He knew the importance of dreams to her people. Her words gave him the courage to take her into his arms. He breathed in deeply. Time, space, and memory, like the sun overhead at its zenith, came to a halt. Mountains of clouds took shape, then vanished. The forest, the river, the creek all came alive. Slowly, his heart pounding, Joseph began to caress Angélique, who whispered her desire. Swiftly, Angélique shed her clothing. As they made love, Joseph felt as though he had merged with the trees of the forest, reaching higher and higher until he touched the clouds. This was what had been missing from his life – warmth, intimacy, and passion.

For Angélique, too, much time had passed since she last made love. For weeks now, from the moment she first set eyes on Joseph in Ruisseau, she had wanted to caress him, nestle against his body, lose herself in his scent, and feel his embrace. The love she'd felt from that first day grew even stronger as she witnessed his respectful gentleness; she wouldn't have waited any longer.

The shivers up and down her spine felt like a cloud of ocean spray. Her neck, her shoulders, and her breasts flushed with passion under his touch. Under his musician's hands, each chord of her body became part of a symphony. Her pleasure intensified to the point where it seemed for a second she would forget how to breathe.

In the birch tree overhead, a swallow sang for them alone.

* * *

And so they continued that summer. A jealous Membertou, six years old, kept his distance. In Joseph's presence, he showed nothing but indifference and spoke only Mi'kmaq. His attitude eventually enraged Joseph, especially since he had been trying so hard to win the boy over. Tough, undisciplined, always poking his nose where it shouldn't be, Membertou did exactly as he pleased: a real little savage in Joseph's eyes! Angélique tended to make excuses for him, she said his father had been a great warrior. The child spent his days wandering through the woods, eating in one tent or another, picking fights over nothing. There was no keeping track of all the mischief he got into. A week ago, as though inhabited by rage, he had hacked up a canoe. Then, to conceal the hut he built for himself in the forest, he stole several red fox hides from the storehouse. Saint-Jean, whose furs were more important to him than God, money, or women, had given his grandson a stern talking-to. Afterwards, Joseph insisted to Angélique that Membertou return the hides, but she hesitated, "With us, families are different," she explained. "There's no such thing as stealing. What belongs to one belongs to all. What children want is sacred. Children are given free rein and, when they grow up, they abide by the clan's rules. Do you understand?"

"Yes, I do. You let them live a carefree childhood for longer, but don't you think he's gone too far, even by your customs?"

Angélique did find that her son was going too far, but pride stopped her from saying so. Exasperated and sensing he had no role to play in Membertou's education, Joseph shouted, "You're his slave, you're not doing him a service."

"I'm waiting for him to grow up and realize for himself that other people have rights as well. Be patient, it will come… Maybe you're just jealous," Angélique said.

"That's quite possible," Joseph retorted, "but I still would like to see him bring the furs back."

Angélique was torn between her traditions and Joseph's request, which seemed more like a demand. Eventually, she gave in. Membertou threw a terrible fit. He screamed, he threw himself on the ground, he broke his bow and arrows, he cried, he sulked, and he made threats. Nevertheless he did bring the red fox furs back to the storehouse.

14

Joseph breathed easier; now it felt like he could play a role in Membertou's life. That evening, he lit a small fire in the centre of the big conical tent, spread pine branches on the ground to combat the humidity, and laid seal hides on top to make a bed. A bed for Membertou. Once the boy was asleep, Joseph took Angélique into his arms and forgot about having to become a father against his wishes. He was captivated by this woman who loved life, pleasure, beauty, and books. She was part-European after all, in love with the theatre, spending long hours as a child in the wild forests of Caraquet reading works by Molière, Corneille, and Racine brought in on French ships. She had been encouraged in her reading by her father who, as a youth, had shown an interest in the art of coin-making.

Membertou's troubles had made Joseph think. He did not want the boy to become an obstacle in his relationship with Angélique. Which was why he decided to keep his distance as well, to feign indifference and act as though Membertou was not part of his life and wait for the boy to take the first step. The ploy was starting to work: one morning as they were fishing for trout, Membertou ventured a question about Quebec. "Are tents in Quebec bigger than Ruisseau's?"

His question followed the sighting of large ships coming from Quebec, which were bigger than his people's canoes…

* * *

The Mi'kmaq camp was still asleep, and the sun was just peeking above the point of Ile Caraquet, yet Saint-Jean was already boiling his morning tea in front of his home. He lived off on his own, in a log house with a roof covered in slate from the Anse à l'Etang quarry in the Gaspé. Until it went bankrupt, the quarry had supplied the city of Quebec with shingles. Saint-Jean, whose heart was ailing, added a special potion prepared by Angélique to his wintergreen tea: rye ergot to help his arteries contract. He had aged prematurely, his ten years spent on the king's galleys having left their mark – wrinkled, cracked skin, hunched back, bald head, and long white beard.

His soul was in a state of permanent revolt against injustice, governments, and institutions, which explained why he chose to live far away from so-called civilization. When hatred welled up at thoughts of the fate of his companions in misfortune, he channelled it into engraving onto moose antlers the facts of daily life on the galleys. He had a dream, too, that helped him go on: to create in America a fur empire to outfit the courts of Europe. "I want to show those good-for-nothings that they need those of us who aren't as privileged as they are," he proclaimed to all and sundry.

The animals of the forest held no secrets for Saint-Jean, nor did the different stages of hide preparation: cleaning, degreasing, brushing, lustring… His great weaknesses were those of the gourmand, namely the food and wine brought by the French ships that put in at Ruisseau. He had given himself over to these pleasures often since his wife's death. But he'd been a gourmand since childhood, and his years of forced labour had only served to increase his appetite. He was obese, not a good thing given his health problems.

Joseph, too, had risen early. He pulled on a coarse linen shirt and baggy seaman's pants cinched at the knee. He took his knife from where it hung at the entrance to the tent and headed in the direction of the great birch tree next to Saint-Jean's house. Saint-Jean, whose survival had necessitated developing a biting sense of humour, called out, "Ready to make your getaway to Quebec?"

Pulled out of his revery, Joseph gave a start. "I want to write a letter to my mother, and mornings are my best time," he answered.

His mother had taught him to read and write using old books from Normandy that told stories of Joan of Arc and William the Conqueror. The books also told his favourite tales – the adventures of Sinbad the Sailor – carrying the whiff of perfume from the Orient. Having leafed through the yellowed pages of the books hundreds of times, he knew all the tales by heart.

"Do you plan on telling her about Angélique?" Saint-Jean asked casually.

He viewed the relationship between his daughter and Joseph favourably, but he wanted to make sure Joseph would not be clearing out at the first snowfall. Joseph would rather not talk about it, but he decided to be open with the old man.

"That's why I'm writing."

"If you're not sure, you should take some time to think about it."

Joseph felt great affection for Saint-Jean; another man might not have trusted him so easily.

"No, my mind is made up. Sometimes I miss my family and the excitement of life in Quebec, but I feel at home here. The surroundings are beautiful, the people hospitable… and I love your daughter and I've begun to connect with Membertou."

Satisfied, Saint-Jean lit his pipe and didn't push the matter further. Joseph headed toward the huge birch tree and tore off large strips of bark for his letter to his mother concerning his future.

Chapter 3

"Suffering," he said, "was nearly the sole occupation of
those poor people; they were stricken by illness, and
death took away many of them. Father du Marché had to
go back to France; Father Turgis resisted for a while,
comforting his small flock, listening to the confessions of
some, giving strength to others through the sacraments
of the Eucharist and Last Rites, burying those whom
death spirited away. But eventually the work and the
unhealthy air he breathed around the sickly felled him as
they had others. He fought until the last breath, though.
He had himself carried to the bedside of the sick and the
dying, he inspired them, gave them strength, encouraged
them, and after having buried the captain, the clerk, and
the surgeon, in other words all the other officers and
eight or nine other working people, he himself succumbed, leaving only one sick man to face death, whom
he accompanied to that point before breathing his last.

...He was the first of our Company to die of illness in
this land. He was sorely missed by the French and the
Savages who held him in high regard and loved him
dearly."

– "Account" of the Jesuits in Miscou in 1647, quoted by
W.F. Ganong in *The History of Miscou and Shippegan*

In late August, the Jesuit Ignace de la Transfiguration, wearing a tricorn hat with a wide, turned-up brim, arrived in
Ruisseau. The news spread like an autumn fire through a pile

of dead leaves. The missionary had devoted his life to bringing the gospel to the native peoples, and no weakness of the flesh had any hold over his asceticism. Not even a love for good food and drink. In fact, suffering made him happy, and mosquito bites replaced the hair shirt for God's greater glory. Come from Quebec by water, he navigated the St. Lawrence and the Matapedia rivers then, after a halt at the Restigouche post, he entered the Baye des Chaleurs. During the ten long days the journey took, the missionary meditated on the difficulties he encountered. *Only a few baptisms in ten years of evangelization. Why? How can I make them understand good and evil? As for transsubstantiation and the Trinity, the three persons of God, and the two natures of Christ, I'll never get that across...* he thought.

What the Jesuit did not realize was that even St. Peter would not have been able to teach the catechism, with its abstract concepts that had no connection with the daily concerns of the Mi'kmaq. "Black Robe has arrived! The patriarch is here!" Such were the names some used to designate the missionary. Several Mi'kmaq, without actually abandoning their own beliefs, had converted to Catholicism and venerated the priest, whom they saw as having magical powers. Not everyone did, however; several found his religion incompatible with their beliefs and maintained in front of the missionary that the laws of the Great Creator were written in the rivers, the trees, and the nature of human desire, which was pure... "You've made it into something evil!" They were surprised to see white men acting like rutting moose around native women when Black Robe was absent. The Mi'kmaqs' own sexual freedom meant they felt no need for such excess. "Your men desire our women so badly it makes one wonder whether they've never seen a woman before."

The shaman was among the priest's detractors. As the tribe's high priest and magician, he had a tacit agreement with Saint-Jean on authority regarding earthly matters. Saint-Jean always consulted him and gave him credit for provident decisions. As well, Angélique in her healer's role – a gift the shaman did not have – often called on him for healing rituals.

His nickname was Fiery Elouèzes because his eyes threw off sparks when he was angry. He harboured intense hatred for those he called "fat pigs covered in dirty hair"; to make matters worse, the missionary was also a competitor. The shaman's head was shaved bare except for one strip running from his forehead to the nape of his neck. His nose was painted a bright blue and his eyes were ringed with yellow ochre. He was careful to tend his terrifying look.

The shaman's faithful disciple was a giant, the warrior Foaming Bear, a strapping fellow: as dark as a crow, fierce, and impermeable to any influence from the whites and Catholics, whom he accused of destroying the Mi'kmaq way of life. At fifteen, on Anticosti Island, he had had to choose between dying under the claws of a huge white bear or slaying the monster with his tomahawk. He chose to fight, and the effort caused him to foam so wildly at the mouth that his hair turned white, earning him his nickname. "Those damn white men and the missionaries who represent them say we're poor and ignorant, faithless and lawless, like wild animals. They say their country is paradise. If so, why did they abandon their families and make the difficult ocean crossing to come to our snowbound lands to steal our worthless beaver pelts and eat nothing but cod morning, noon, and night? They waste their time accumulating useless things while we enjoy the seasons fishing and hunting. Paradise is here, and they want to turn it into hell," he proclaimed.

Fiery Elouèzes had just as many complaints. "Their beliefs are stupid: they eat the body and blood of their god and then accuse us of cannibalism. They claim the earth is the kingdom of darkness; yet if they just opened their eyes, they would see the sun and if they opened their ears, they would hear the rivers, trees, and animal spirits. Their idea of building log cabins that can't be moved is a trick to keep us in one spot and enslave us. What's more, the Black Robes aren't normal; they don't sleep with our women…"

The shaman could have gone on grumbling all day long, but he had an incantation session planned to neutralize the missionary's influence so he headed for his tent.

* * *

Ignace de la Transfiguration, who was not the most tolerant of
Jesuits, did not look favourably on the alliance of a white man
and a Métis woman. He had the usual prejudices of learned
Europeans, with their scorn and paternalism vis-à-vis the First
Nations.

"Have you thought this over, Joseph? The Indians are like
rude children who have trouble adapting to our religious
beliefs and customs."

"You're wrong, Father. Angélique is Métis. In any case,
the Indians are a devoted and pure people. They don't speak
with a forked tongue, they're hospitable, and they help me forget the white man's hypocrisy. Why should we strip them of
their traditions and change their way of life?"

The Jesuit refused to admit that good people could exist
outside the Church. The fact the Mi'kmaq had no word to
express concepts such as virtue, vice, temptation, angels, and
forgiveness led him to believe they were heathens. He was,
however, intrigued by the discovery in Acadia's forests of an
old moss-covered cross found by Champlain and Poutrincourt
in 1607. He had also read in a book by Lescarbot that during
their first contact with the white man, the Mi'kmaq peppered
their conversations with Hallelujahs, while those living in
Miramichi used the cross as a totem, a custom that predated
the arrival of the white man. In fact, that was why the whites
were called Crossbearers. Legend had it that after a terrible illness decimated the tribe, a handsome man carrying a cross
appeared to the wise elders and suggested they adopt the symbol to protect them from illness. This was done, and the illness
was conquered. Others claimed that Irish monks, including St.
Brendan and St. Colomban, ended up in the region prior to
the first millennium. The thought of the many legends made
Ignace de la Transfiguration dream of perpetuating the tradition of the cross and building an empire in America to the
greater glory of God…

His daydream was interrupted by Joseph, "She is white
on her father's side, and she loves me."

"Ah… my son, but her father belongs to that verminous race of Protestants," the Jesuit retorted.

Angélique arrived just in time to hear these startling words. "You have no right to pass judgment on your neighbour," she exclaimed.

"We hold the truth, and we are advisors to popes," the Jesuit said, haughtily.

The discussion had soured.

"I know your opinions on Indians. You decreed we are heathens, even though we believe in one God. Your civilization is the one that has brought us illness, alcohol, and evil through your religion that preaches nothing but fear and suffering…"

Angélique was beside herself. Joseph shared her opinion and thought it intolerable the way white men called the native people a race of lazy, immoral drunks and thieves. He took issue with the term "lazy." The natives lived according to nature's rhythm, which they respected, careful never to take more from nature than what they needed to survive. They could not be called "drunkards," either, for white men had introduced brandy to destroy the native way of life and obtain their furs at ridiculously low prices. In the native custom of sharing and hospitality, Joseph saw the opposite of "thieves," as some called them. *How can there be theft if everything belongs to the group?* he wondered.

As for the native notion of good and evil, he preferred it to the white man's view since their morality allowed ill-paired couples to look for happiness elsewhere. But Joseph was conscious of the immunity guaranteed by a Catholic marriage. The Jesuits had long arms, and excommunication was feared even more than leprosy. The excluded were banished from the body of the Church as unworthy members and deprived of prayers and sacraments. And of a Christian burial. Worse yet was the way other faithful were prohibited from speaking to or greeting the excommunicated, and were urged to flee them as though they carried the plague.

Who in such a tiny society can survive rejection? he thought. *Perhaps I could with my Indian friends, but why expose our children needlessly?*

Joseph realized he had to be seen to agree with the missionary, especially since the latter looked extremely upset. "Father," he said, "we sincerely admire the courage and faith that have led you to travel the breadth of huge countries and to suffer hunger, cold, slander, and rejection. Your knowledge of the Mi'kmaq language is a testimony to your perseverance... Angélique has what many Christians are without: a pure heart, simplicity, great honesty, and she will abide by the truth."

The word "truth" clearly lent itself to a number of different interpretations. Angélique understood Joseph's strategy, but she had no desire to deal with this priest she considered to be an instrument of white authority designed to destroy the Mi'kmaq way of life in order to better subjugate them. She was furious, but her love for Joseph ran deep. So a semblance of calm could be restored, she began playing with small stones in the sand, rearranging them and creating designs that reflected her agitation.

As for the missionary, he hated to admit to himself that he found this woman both exotic and beautiful and, for that reason, all the more threatening. *A non-submissive woman is the devil incarnate!* he thought.

"I'm not making myself understood very well," Angélique continued. "The Mi'kmaq believe in one God as well, but we have trouble understanding why we have to abandon our traditions. We leave profit, property, and material goods to the white man. When the colonies began, the Indians welcomed you with open arms; we helped you survive scurvy thanks to the healing powers of anneda..."

The missionary was openly touched by Angélique's mention of the sorry state of the new arrivals who died of scurvy during their first winters, and the miracle cure, the white cedar herbal tea the Indians brought for them.

"Yes, that was a gift from heaven," the priest admitted. "God certainly allowed the Indians to be His instruments to allow France to expand its empire... Will you respect the teachings of our Holy Mother the Church as promised on the day of your baptism?" he asked suddenly.

Angélique murmured assent.

So Ignace de la Transfiguration let them have their way.

After the wedding, Fiery Elouèzes opened the banquet by offering his red clay pipe to each of the spirits of the four directions then to the spirit of the sky before lowering his pipe to the spirit of the earth. He beat on his drum (two smooth hides stretched over a wooden hoop case containing stones) to give the signal for the feast to begin. Great bonfires burned both along the shore and in Ruisseau, and long pine tables covered in birchbark buckled under the weight of all the local and European food. Saint-Jean had dug into his stores. From a French ship that had stopped over in Ruisseau, he also bought goods meant for Quebec's high society. For his daughter's wedding, he had decided on French gastronomy and European-looking menus. As well as barrels of French wine and rum from Martinique, he had brought out truffles and chocolates from Rouen, ham from Mayence, oranges from Brazil, spices from the East Indies and Mocha coffee from Yemen. In his view, food was close to a religion, a rite he followed with art and sophistication.

The feast took on gargantuan proportions. An exceptionally late summer made it possible to gather all the fruits of the sea and the forest. On that September 1, 1740, on the Ruisseau beach, seafood was abundant. The wedding menu included red oyster soup seasoned with wild mint, clam chowder seasoned with wood garlic, smoked salmon with loon eggs. Clams, halibut, lobster, and crab were served, scallop and shrimp brochettes on cedar sticks, cod with mussel sauce, and trout seasoned with black mustard and seasalt wrapped in clay and cooked in the embers. The fruits of the land and the sky had their own place of honour: goose, teal, doves, caribou, and bear roasted on the spit (on a bed of blueberries, cranberries, and raspberries). Accompanying dishes were not forgotten either: wild rice, corn on the cob, and greens (watercress, wild leek, wood garlic, sorrel, fiddleheads[1], and dandelions) tossed in a birch sap vinaigrette. A few women prepared the desserts:

---

1. Ferns.

wild currants and juniper berries with moosemilk cream, pumpkin and maple nut pies, barley bread full of almonds and wild cherries. There were also all kinds of drinks: tea made of pine needles or the leaves of strawberries, raspberries, cherries or rosehip. However, the Mi'kmaq preferred either the cider from Ile d'Orléans, rum from the West Indies, the p'tit caribou[1], root beer, dandelion, and blackberry wine or the barrels of wine from Gascogne and Bordeaux with which to make merry.

Finally, they could eat no more. Some had overindulged on their traditional corn-based dish, called "migan" – corn either mashed and boiled with fish or grilled and ground, then mixed in with a meat and fish soup. Foaming Bear had stuffed himself on all kinds of game and had nearly finished off a quarter caribou by himself. Revved up by the rum vapours, he hovered around the missionary, just waiting for a pretext to warm the man's behind on the embers. But the shaman thought it better to temper Foaming Bear's enthusiasm. Fiery Elouèzes, proudly wearing around his neck a black and red medicinal stone carved into an oval shape, called on the Great Creator to ensure the missionary felt the evil effects of the talisman that had been found in evil Gougou's hideout.

Membertou was hiding behind some fat, still-steaming pumpkins that had been cooked in the embers. Armed with a slingshot, he shot small stones into the migan dishes. As for Ignace de la Transfiguration, he had not been able to resist the lure of the beaver tail dough dipped in maple syrup and cooked in a lilypad leaf. Slow, wild music enveloped the bay. The concert began with flutes made of elderwood and tam-tams. There were water drums[3] too, whose faint beat still managed to travel great distances. Other bigger drums on stands mimicked the beating of the heart and the vibrations of the earth in the four directions. Angélique began to dance, the stark sensuality of her slender body heightened by the crescendo of sounds rising to meet the rays of the setting sun.

---

2. A mixture of white alcohol and port wine.
3. So called because they were filled with water.

Father Ignace began to feel a prickling at the base of his spine. He had no idea the beaver tails he'd been eating were considered to be an aphrodisiac. Fiery Elouèzes could feel the Black Robe's growing consternation, which he attributed to the powers of his magic stone. Then the rhythm switched to a devilish cadence, and the dancers turned into shadow figures projected by the flames. The frenzied dancing gave off such sensuality that the missionary was obliged to walk alone farther down the shore to regain some semblance of composure.

Smoke from the fires and from the many tobacco pipes perfumed the heavens with their earthly aromas. The smoke wafting its way skyward mingled with the cries of those who, after their sauna in the sweat lodge, plunged into the creek. The missionary began dreaming about the French and Catholic empire of America, in which he would be God's right hand and the King's representative to this refractory people. But it was a disappointing time for him since many baptized natives refused *in extremis* a burial in the Catholic cemetery. It was not uncommon to see the families come for their dying family member to bury him or her in their ancestors' sacred sites.

Kings and popes fear us, he consoled himself, *but here we are faced with resistance not easily shaken by questions of right and wrong.*

His thoughts were interrupted by Joseph, who had come to join him. "What's the news of Quebec?" Joseph asked.

"The Canadiens are worried. The survival of the colony is not assured, and there's always the fear of an English victory. The colonies of Virginia and Boston are already twenty times more heavily populated."

With Angélique's scent still on his skin, Joseph felt far removed from such concerns. The mention of Quebec did not even stir up memories of Emilie for him… He was sufficiently alert, however, to notice that Black Robe did not mention the corruption of certain leaders, who were more interested in lining their own pockets than in fortifying New France.

Chapter 4

As of 1653, Nicolas Denys, nicknamed Grande Barbe, received from the Compagnie de Nouvelle France (established by Richelieu) a vast concession stretching from Canseau to the Baye des Chaleurs in Acadia. He organized the triple trade of lumber, fur, and fishing there with establishments in, among others, Miscou, Nipisiguit, and Miramichi. He was appointed governor of the territory and given the mission of settling eighty families there.

— The author

Five months had passed since Joseph's arrival in Ruisseau. The hot season was not yet over, and it was already time to begin preparations for winter. But the most urgent task was finding shelter since the newlyweds did not want to spend the winter in a tent. Joseph and Saint-Jean put the tribe to work digging a cellar, a lesson learned early in the colony's life when the first arrivals froze royally. Cedar trees grew abundantly in the wetlands upstream of Ruisseau, and Saint-Jean had cut several cords of cedar the preceding winter. The Mi'kmaq began squaring the wood with an axe from New England that was thicker and heavier than the trading axes manufactured in France. Notches were cut into the logs so they fit one on top of the other to form the walls. Pegs made of maple or larchwood helped reinforce the construction. The rest — the crossbeams and joists – was made of eastern white pine. White birchbark between the walls served to keep out the wind. In no time at all, the tribe had erected a one-room cabin measuring approximately fifteen feet by twenty-five. Little Membertou used his hatchet to chop off any knots that jutted out. Since the cabin was no Château de Versailles, the boy was allowed a few mistakes. Angélique and the women prepared the moss and clay to caulk the frame, while the rest of the tribe assembled embankments of dried seaweed to a height of approximately one foot to insulate the foundation properly. Finally, the sloping roof was covered with moss. With a stonecarver's enthusiasm, Joseph tackled building the hearth, a fireplace to be used for cooking, lighting, and heating purposes, although it mostly heated the great outdoors! He was euphoric as he worked, already imagining how, on nights when snow gently fell to the ground outside, he would be able to warm himself sitting on his bed of fur in front of the fire – the crackling wood knots, the scent of maple logs, the dancing sparks, and Angélique's gentle presence.

That fall the camp was invaded by mosquitoes. Joseph had to keep feeding the grass fire he'd lit in a metal barrel in his cabin; compared to mosquito bites, smoke was the lesser of two evils. Joseph was impressed by the Mi'kmaq spirit of ingenuity; for every problem there was a solution, for every season there was a form of entertainment. During the hot season, they built a sweat lodge. In a tent lying low to the ground, the Mi'kmaq arranged heated rocks in a circle in the centre, which were then covered with spruce leaves and sprinkled with a bit of cold water. Afterwards, the Mi'kmaq sat naked, shoulders touching, in a tight circle around the rocks. Sometimes, to feel the heat even more, they sang and tapped their heels. Then they ran outside and threw themselves into the creek. It was a ritual with therapeutic virtues since it facilitated the cleansing of the body.

But this was no time to dwell on fond memories of the good times in the hot season because there was still much that had to be done before winter set in: wood to cut, hay to gather, crops to store away, fish and meat to be smoked and cured.

Nothing could be neglected when everything had to be produced. Angélique prepared the flax with which she would make clothes, a lengthy operation that involved drying, crushing, carding, and spinning the flax. She also prepared the furs; she liked the beaver hides that she sewed together to make clothes or blankets. She still had to make soap; pick blueberries, wild strawberries, and raspberries; and bake apples. The work was exhausting, but she wouldn't have traded places with anyone. She soon forgot the long days once she was curled up in Joseph's arms, and the two of them drifted off to sleep in the warmth of their cabin.

The Mi'kmaq were more a trapping than a farming people, and therefore more nomadic than sedentary. But Angélique had insisted that next to the creek the clan clear a plot of land on which to raise a few oxen, sheep, hens, and one cow and to cultivate a small garden that produced turnips, squash, beans, corn, and other delicious vegetables for their table.

Saint-Jean had little to do with the farmwork. His passion was trapping, furs, and the forest. So he laid traps and, of course, kept up his weekly treks to his refuge on the island. Each week, he made the league-long trip in his sailboat. One fine morning that Indian summer, he invited Joseph along. At first, they said nothing. Finally, Saint-Jean confided, "Before I left France from the port of La Rochelle, I had to spend several months hiding out on the Ile de Ré nearby. The island's inhabitants saved my life. Since then, I've always wanted to have my own island, a sanctuary where I can rest and forget about the men who were on the galleys with me. I've built a fine observation tower there."

He had created a hideout at the western end of the island, at the top of a triangle formed by three huge spruce trees.

"What a wonderful view!" Joseph exclaimed.

They could see for great distances. The Gaspé coast was visible across the way as were, at the entrance to the Baye des Chaleurs, the Chipagan[1] and Miscou islands.

---

1. From the Mi'kmaq word "sepagunchiche" meaning "duck crossing."

"Cartier pinned his hopes on Miscou. He thought he would find a passage on the other side leading to the sought-after Indies," Saint-Jean said. "He believed so fervently that when he rounded the northwest point of Miscou, he named the point Cap de l'Espérance, Cape of Good Hope. As a sentinel guarding the entrance to the continent, the island has been witness, and sometimes even home, to many flags: Viking, Basque, French, English, Spanish, and Dutch as well as to pirates and buccaneers who, from the tales that are told, would stop off there to bury their loot and treasure."

Near the Mi'kmaq camp farther down the coast was a small island the Mi'kmaq called Pokesudie; it was a sacred site sometimes used for religious ceremonies.

"I often come to my hideout to sit and smoke my pipe… I watch the European ships sailing by. It's too late this year for the English fleet and the privateers: the frost is coming. You won't have to go to Quebec."

Deep down, Joseph was relieved. As much as he hoped for news of Emilie, he dreaded it, too. Sometimes, he wished he could close that chapter of his life and have done with it because he was happy with Angélique. She offered everything a man could ever want – beauty, warmth, generosity, intelligence, sensuality. Saint-Jean had lit his pipe and was reliving the past. "I've come a long way since my days on the galleys!"

He remembered his early years in Miramichi fur trading for the Comte de St. Pierre, who held trading rights between Ile Saint-Jean[2] and Miscou. He was on board the Count's ship that ran aground in the Caraquet region in 1723. The Count hadn't taken the loss of his furs well. Out of disgust with the Count's temper, Saint-Jean decided to settle down in Ruisseau… and work for himself!

Having reminisced enough, he turned to Joseph and said, "Some day I dream I will see along these coasts houses full of people, busy villages, tradespeople: carpenters, blacksmiths, locksmiths, ferriers, tailors, shoemakers…

---

2. Prince Edward Island today.

Joseph let himself be caught up in Saint-Jean's dream. "I think I can see husbandmen and vintners, too. I can hear seamen outfitting the ships."

"There will be goldsmiths, apothecaries, fishermen, barbers…" Saint-Jean continued.

"Men of the church," Joseph added.

"Not them," Saint-Jean exclaimed, irritated. "They ruin it all. The Indian customs are good enough for us."

Joseph understood the bitterness expressed by Saint-Jean, still hurting from past scars.

"I don't want any arquebusiers or gunners either," Saint-Jean continued, "but I'm afraid for the future. France isn't looking after us properly, and the most enterprising French who want to come to America, the Huguenots, have to settle in the colonies of Virginia, Boston, and Delaware. One fine day, the colonies won't put up with having a foreign empire on their doorstep anymore."

"But Pierre du Gua, one of Acadia's founders, was Protestant," Joseph pointed out.

"That's true, but that was a long time ago. I've even heard that Champlain had similar sympathies. But we won't change either the past or the politics of France."

Joseph could only concur with the wisdom expressed. Perched atop the spruce trees, the two men seemed as though suspended in time. After a lengthy pause, Joseph spoke. "Where does the word 'Kalaket' come from?"

"It's a Mi'kmaq word meaning 'at the mouth of two rivers.' The rivers run west of the creek named after me. But there's something peculiar about that word. The Normans who fish nearby on the Banc des Orphelins sail on big low-draft ships called 'calanques.' During storms, they seek shelter at the mouth of the two rivers… It's not a huge leap from 'calanque' to 'Kalaket,' perhaps that's what the Mi'kmaq did."

Silence again. As though in cycles: a few words, then a moment's truce to fully appreciate the serenity of the surroundings. Saint-Jean broke the silence, "Can you keep a secret? I have a hiding place that no one knows about. For years I've been stockpiling dried food, flour, and wine in a cave. I keep weapons and powder there too, in the event of a siege. If ever there's a raid along our coast, we could hide out there with Angélique and the children."

The word "children" reminded Joseph he had news for the old man. "Angélique is expecting," he whispered.

Saint-Jean wept tears of happiness.

* * *

Indian summer was drawing to a close. Opening his eyes one fine morning, Joseph realized that something was missing: all of a sudden, he felt horribly homesick. He thought of his mother, Quebec, the animated docks, the streets, the taverns, the meals with neighbours, and the great ships arriving from Europe and the West Indies.

Joseph spent all that day wandering through the camp, irritated by the sounds, the images, and the smells of Mi'kmaq life. He could no longer see the beauty and harmony, only ugliness and disorder and superstitions, like the one obliging menstruating women to keep to themselves in front of a tent. Nearby, a bear meat and fat concoction boiled in a pot: the meat had hung for too long, it was covered in hair and black from excessive cooking. The women ate greedily straight from the pot, wiping their fingers on the coats of the dogs that waited for scraps. The boiled beans doused with grease made him feel like vomiting.

Foaming Bear, who wanted Joseph as an ally, invited him into his hut – a large round, poorly vented tent that was full of smoke and too low to stand up in. Inside, some twenty people were seated by age and social rank, with the women next to the door to look after the chores! Strips of dried meat hung here and there, and the dogs roamed freely among the clay jars full of corn flour. An old man was eating his lice, not out of desire but to take his revenge on the lice. A horrific stench assailed Joseph's nostrils, chasing him away, back to Quebec, to his world, to his friends, to Emilie's perfume. At the risk of offending Foaming Bear, he slipped out. He headed toward the beach, to look for comfort by the sea.

On the beach, several women were sewing hides and birchbark to a pole structure. They were using pine roots as thread and sharpened bones as needles. Joseph was oblivious to their ingenuity, their hospitality and their respect for nature. He had forgotten that hygiene was just as bad in Quebec and that, actually, the stench was even more tenacious there: the stench of corruption given off by certain leaders, and the stench of superstitions and religious intolerance no amount of incense could mask. When he returned home in the same foul mood, Angélique asked, "What's bothering you?"

He hesitated, not wanting to hurt her feelings. "It's too quiet here. I miss Quebec."

Angélique was not at all surprised; she was accustomed to seeing many comings and goings in her tribe. "Why don't you build a schooner and go off on an adventure, starting with Quebec?" she suggested.

"That sounds like a very good idea. But I don't know if I can build a boat."

"You'll be able to with my father's help; he's had experience with shipbuilding."

He was genuinely pleased at the idea and let himself be won over by her suggestion. "We could sell our furs in Quebec for a profit, take merchants the oysters that have been piling up at Pointe-de-Roche[3], come back with tools, fabric, apples, cider. What a wonderful idea! Why didn't I think of it myself?"

He knew why; he was well aware that fear paralyzed him, a fear stronger than his desire to find out the truth about Emilie. *It might affect my happiness with Angélique*, he thought.

Guessing at the direction his thoughts had taken, Angélique said, "No matter how hard you try to hide it, I know she's still on your mind."

He had to confess there was some truth to her observation. "But that's only normal, after all. I don't know what has become of her; the mystery haunts me… But don't worry, I'm happy with you, and I have no intention of running away."

---

3. A point of land one league north of Ruisseau.

*　*　*

One fine November morning, Joseph saw a ball of fire racing across the sea off the island, changing its speed, shape, and direction as it went. Inside the fireball was a jet-black ship with large white sails and, on its bridge, seamen running.

"The phantom ship!" Saint-Jean exclaimed. "We'll have bad weather tomorrow."

"What is it?" Joseph asked.

"No one really knows; the closer you get, the farther away it moves. They say it's a phantom ship that belonged to a Portuguese explorer and that the Indians burned in revenge for a raid on their shores."

The weather was indeed terrible the next day. Northwesters raged furiously, making the trees facing the cape twist and groan; at one point, it seemed like the camp would take to the air. The next morning the shore reappeared, strewn with debris and flotsam. Lobsters and crabs clung to the tall grass along the shore. This manna from heaven meant Angélique was able to put up all the supplies needed for winter; the surplus would be used to fertilize the earth.

The winter promised to be fierce. Around late November, a huge white sheet blanketed the frozen bay in lacey creases. The sky looked as though it had been punched through with holes. Joseph and Angélique were at their happiest when storms raged over the Baye des Chaleurs. Stretched out on his bed of furs in front of the hearth, where embers burned under the ashes, and with the scent of Angélique in the air, Joseph felt a wave of serenity wash over him.

Angélique examined Joseph's lithe body. There was something she had often noticed – at the smithy, in the sweat lodge, as he built their house, or as they caressed each other outdoors or by the fire – on his chest above his heart, Joseph bore a skilfully wrought tattoo.

"I left Nantes in 1717 when I was two. My nursemaid died during the crossing… The tattoo must be an indication of my origins. I've always wondered about it, and I hate riddles…"

"It looks like a coat of arms, like the ones the nobles have. I've often thought you must be the bastard son of a king or prince," she said laughing.

"My parents must have been wealthy. When I arrived in Canada, a carefully wrapped violin was found in the trunks. Not just any violin either – a Stradivarius."

"Perfect, you'll be able to celebrate with a tune," Angélique murmured. "Because our baby in my womb is in a hurry to be born; I can feel it kicking."

Joseph laid his hand on the mound of Angélique's belly, which rippled with the stirrings of life.

"If it's a girl, we'll call her Geneviève," Angélique suggested.

"And if it's a boy, we'll baptize him René-Gabriel in your father's honor."

The cabin groaned as an especially strong gust of wind punctuated Joseph's wish.

"The weather doesn't get this bad in Quebec," Joseph complained.

"This is unusual. We expected a bad winter though, because of how high the bees built their hives in the trees. But it won't last; there'll be a lull in January, and we'll be able to go on the trapline."

"Do you trap the same animals found around Quebec?"

"I think so: mink, ermine, marten, red fox, muskrat, but mostly beaver. It pays, too. Before, the French – some of them anyway – gave worthless objects in exchange for our furs: mirrors, necklaces, alcohol to get the Indians drunk before robbing them. But ever since my father started looking after the trade, they've had to pay us with weapons, munitions, tools, fabric…"

Angélique spoke with feeling, proud to have a father who knew how to stand up for himself.

* * *

In February, Joseph went with Saint-Jean to the woods to choose two white pines for his schooner's masts. Before chopping them down, they waited for the waning phase of the moon, when the sap barely runs. Joseph spent the winter in a state of euphoria, revising almost daily his plans and calculations for his ship. His joy was all the greater with the swelling of Angélique's belly and the approaching birth.

In April's budding season, Geneviève was born, a rosy bundle of life like a dancing electrical storm off Pointe-de-Roche. That same evening, while the baby slept soundly, Joseph played his violin. In the melting snow, he danced on and on along the cliffs; he hadn't danced like this since Emilie had left him, a wild, crazy, exuberant dance, which led him to believe that in another time and place, someone in his family must have had a dancer's gift. Joseph was happy – a little girl for him, for Angélique, for the two of them. As for Membertou, he was a bit hesitant and jealous at first because of all the attention being lavished on the baby, but it didn't take long before he started helping his mother look after Geneviève.

In May, Saint-Jean traded furs with merchants from La Rochelle in exchange for ironwork, oakum, sails, pitch, Riga hemp, and other invaluable building material. They also took advantage of the opportunity to stock up on rum from Martinique, which made the work go by more agreeably. Saint-Jean already had a store of wood: logs had been soaking for a long time in a ditch at the mouth of Saint-Jean Creek since the sea water there made them exceptionally resistant. Pinewood for the bridge, oak and beechwood for the ribs, gunwales, and yards, and hemlock for the keel. He laid the wood out to dry for part of the summer and, by the fall of 1741, the schooner was beginning to take shape. This was Joseph's first boat, but he had spent so much time watching the shipbuilders in Quebec at the Cul-de-Sac shipyard that he felt capable of building a three-decker warship. What's more, his partner was an old hand. During his stay in convict prison, Saint-Jean had spent a great deal of time repairing galleys. Moreover, the Mi'kmaq were happy and eager to help. They showed them how to use the tools and do the caulking and the tarring. The sight of his two-master measuring sixty-two feet long from stem to stern and eighteen feet wide, with a draw of eleven feet, two decks, and a castle fore and aft, made Joseph feel as free as the cormorants that plied the bay.

The travel demon bit him, infecting him with a thirst for adventure. Excited by the prospect of setting out onto the high seas like his childhood hero Sinbad the Sailor, he baptized his ship the *Phantom Ship*. To the prow, he added the carved dragon that had decorated the Viking drakkar run aground not far off Miscou.

Chapter 5

Sedentary fishing is seen here as a guaranteed benefit.
– Intendant Jean Talon, November 2, 1671

In January 1742, Jean-Baptiste, Angélique's brother, returned like the prodigal son to Ruisseau after two years spent wandering. He had visited Quebec and Montreal, then spent time with the Odawas[1] in the region of Ottawa, an Algonquin name meaning "Father of Nations," a prophetic title for a future capital! He stayed long enough to learn to play lacrosse. Then he stopped off with the Hurons and the Eries in the Great Lakes region. On the Mississippi[2] he admired great canoes twelve metres long, pointed at both ends, paddled by fourteen men, fur traders who travelled as far as the Michillimackinac[3] post. Jean-Baptiste bore a scar on his forehead, a painful souvenir of his run-in with an Iroquois chief in an unusual battle, which, once fought, spared him from having to run between two rows of warriors armed with cherry tree branches. The young man had matured, his judgment grown more sound. He had discovered what he was looking for during his travels. His trips inland and in the Great Lakes region

---

1. Algonquin.
2. Which means "Father of Waters."
3. Today's Detroit.

had reminded him of his love for the sea and fishing; a rarity among the Mi'kmaq. Even before his travels, the Basque and Norman captains used to have him watch over the fishing gear they left in Ruisseau during the winter before picking it up again the next spring. They also asked him to supervise in Miscou and Chipagan the shabby canvas-covered huts that looters liked to ransack looking for hardware and nails. Huts in which the fishermen stayed after their day at sea, sleeping on dried herb mats laid out on rope beds.

Jean-Baptiste did not come home empty-handed. He made quite a stir when he brought out a powerful bow, four feet in length, that he had been given by the Abnaki. He brought back a pair of skates made of deerbone for Membertou, for his father delicious recipes from the Great Lakes, and for Angélique sacred masks used in healing rituals as well as a beaver-tail medicine bag. For Jeannette-Anne, the young Mi'kmaq who had caught his eye before his departure and had begun to haunt his dreams, he brought a game of dice called "waltestan," made by the Mi'kmaq of the Gaspé. He had not forgotten the other members of the tribe, to whom he distributed beaded tobacco pouches, decorated knife sheaths, and pipes of all kinds, including one called a tomahawk pipe because the peace pipe came with a tomahawk blade, of which Foaming Bear was the lucky recipient. Fiery Elouèzes received an amulet (a small bag covered in glass beads and containing the umbilical cord of a newborn child), which was to be hung over a child's cradle to guarantee long life to that child.

Jean-Baptiste's money bag bulged with gold French Louis, British guineas, and Spanish coins that he planned to use as a deposit on a cod business. *I'll be guaranteed a profit on the European, West Indies, and near East markets*, he thought. *Why there's even gold cod on the ceiling of New England's parliament building!* His dreams were made of gold, which worried his father since he didn't want to see his son become like the white man – a money hoarder. Jean-Baptiste was as dark as Angélique was fair, as solitary as she was sociable; his nose as pointed as hers was snub. It seemed as though his genes hadn't been touched by the white man. At twenty-two, he was as passionate about fishing as his father was about hunting. So he spent the winter months getting ready, gathering stores of salt and bait – smelt fished under the winter's ice and fresh spring herring – preparing the lines and hooks, and organizing the hold of the *Phantom Ship*. Joseph gave him a hand, as did Membertou. The boy had grown considerably over the past two years. At eight, he was no longer interested in making sandcastles and chasing whelks out of their shells on shore. He wanted to go on the trip instead. Angélique hesitated, worried about the rigours of fishing on the open seas. "He'll get seasick."

"Captain Hyacinthe told me an old trick: just put sand in his moccasins…"

But Jean-Baptiste and Joseph knew Angélique's arguments were only a pretext for keeping Membertou on land. Joseph tried to call on her pride. "It will make him into a man. What's more, his wanting to come along shows he's adopted me!"

Still worried, she implored, "Promise me you'll take good care of him; watch he doesn't catch cold."

She had her reasons for being afraid. Membertou had almost succumbed to a bad fever not that long after Joseph's arrival in Ruisseau. He owed his survival to the care he received from Angélique, who was skilled in the use of medicinal herbs to treat the sick. Several people said she had power in her hands – a fluid her hands gave off that speeded healing. Warm vibrations that made Joseph's skin prickle when she caressed him.

"You smell like a wild rose bush," he murmured, trying to reassure her and take her mind off her worries.

Angélique's only answer was to snuggle closer. She loved him, was still fascinated by his laughing eyes and the way they caressed life and those around him… with an ever-present hint of irony.

* * *

Jean-Baptiste's patience ran out. They were already well into the month of May and, because of the northeaster, the ice was stuck between Ile Caraquet and Ruisseau. Every morning, he watched the ice pack struggle to hold on to the shore. Every evening, he scanned the heavens to see if the stars were bright or pale, if the moon had lost its halo, or if the "puppets" were dancing. He was hoping for a southwester squall.

Finally, the time for their departure came. The Mi'kmaq came to bid the fishermen farewell. For the occasion, a proud Fiery Elouèzes wore his wampum belt decorated with symbols representing the great Mi'kmaq empire, which covered the districts of the Gaspé peninsula and the Maritimes, and those of Gaspé, Restigouche, Miscou, Poquemouche, and Miramichi. The *Phantom Ship* set off into the blue of the sea and sky. In the distance, the Gaspé coastline was tinged with hues of emerald and violet. The crystal crests of the waves held a hint of mystery, and the sea was still carpeted with a few glaciers doing a little jig: they were the hangers-on, loath to leave their cradle. Off Chipagan, the schooner crossed paths with a birch canoe outfitted with a small sail. Off Miscou, at the level of the Banc des Orphelins, they met up with several Norman and Basque ships arriving from Europe; some were of Nordic or Dutch design: bulging sides, flat struts, rounded shapes – heavy ships, like hookers and galiots, capable of transporting large cargo loads. Others, like Joseph's schooner or the Portuguese and Spanish caravels and pinnaces, had more delicate, streamlined hulls, square sterns, and struts that weren't quite as flat. Jean-Baptiste traded fresh rations in exchange for gold Louis from the European crews, who had been living off sea biscuits, salt beef, lard, peas, and beans for weeks on end.

There was an abundance of cod, and the crew of the *Phantom Ship* was forever pulling up lines weighted with three-pound lead and two fishhooks. Sometimes the schools of cod were so dense they seemed to buoy up the ship. There was one small problem, however; the hooks were too crooked. The cod swallowed them and then had to be slit open up so the hooks could be retrieved. The crew worked hard; they spent entire days fishing and preparing the cod. On deck, wearing his big leather apron, Jean-Baptiste had the cut-throat's job (he'd cut the fishes' throat and slice open their stomach) and Foaming Bear, the beheader's job (ripping out fish guts to work off his anger). He had to be sure to put into a separate barrel the livers, which, once filtered, would be used to make medicinal oils. The dresser's job, removing the cods' dorsal fin, was left to Seawolf, a young sea-loving Mi'kmaq, while Joseph's job was to cover each row of fish with a layer of salt to preserve the fish until the ship returned to Ruisseau, where they'd be cured; the process was called dry curing. Membertou was less active. In fact, he spent most of his time perched on the top mast table, drawing pictures on the sails of the white whales he saw off in the distance!

Jean-Baptiste thought he'd have to throw back any giant cod they caught since it didn't cure well, but he had the good fortune of crossing paths with a boat from St. Malo, which did prepare giant cod (by wet or green curing; the cod was slit open and salted but not dried), which the Parisians loved. A trade took place: two small cod for every big one. Jean-Baptiste began dreaming of the trip he would make to Quebec to sell his cargo of dried cod for fifteen livres[4] the hundredweight[5]. After three days at sea, the fishermen returned to Ruisseau with the schooner loaded as full as it could be; it was so heavy they risked running aground on the Banc des Orphelins! The tribe had not been idle during their absence. They had built what was called a scaffold[6] – a large floor topped by two gables and a roof covered with a ship's sail – where a cut-throat, a beheader, and a dresser could prepare the fish caught just off the coast. Attracted by the prospect of an effortless meal, a flock of seagulls was already circling the schooner. The Mi'kmaq had also upended rocks – called the cod-drying shore – on which to dry the cod. It was a delicate operation. So delicate, the whole enterprise just about ended up in disaster. They used too much salt, which burned the cod. Then when a heat wave coupled with high humidity hit the

---

4 Old French currency.
5. At that time, the hundredweight equalled one hundred pounds in weight.
6. In Port-Royal, the writer Marc Lescarbot spoke of the scaffold "that rose above the shore, like a theatre for comedy."

region, they didn't turn the cod on shore often enough. Eventually, they hit upon the proper dose of salt, sun, and wind. Jean-Baptiste could start to dream again about the gold coins that would soon jingle in his treasure chest.

* * *

Joseph had abandoned his schooner to bring in the hay at Pointe-de-Roche, where three rocks stood like sentinels beside the oyster flats. Angélique was there as well. She was particularly proud of her pumpkins; she had followed the native tradition of soaking the seeds in water before sowing them in birchbark boxes that she kept for a while in a warm spot. Transplanted into the vegetable garden, the orange pumpkins stood out against the backdrop of wild hay. Membertou chased after the wild rabbits for fun. Little Geneviève babbled in her hammock, while her mother, wearing a conical rainhat made of woven pine branches, hummed native lullabies as she sewed a red and blue fabric cross on her child's blanket to place her under heaven's protection.

"What's all this about?" Joseph asked, surprised.

"Maybe the missionaries are right. My happiness with you has helped me find forgiveness for the ones who hurt my father. I don't want to feel hatred and bitterness anymore."

Joseph, happy and at peace with himself, with nature, and with God, led her by the hand. The tide was low. The oysters lay soaking up the sun. Their delicious flesh-filled shells stretched as far as the eye could see.

"One day, when the French are firmly established in America, our grandchildren will trade with the motherland. They'll take crates of oysters to La Rochelle and bring back fine wine."

Angélique saw things differently. "I'm afraid our children will be faced with wars and occupation, just as Jean-Baptiste said the other day. France is neglecting our country too much. What will become of us?" she worried.

Joseph took her into his arms; his comforting warmth calmed her fears. Rocked by the scent of freshly cut hay and by the sea air, they stretched out at the foot of a small golden haystack. That was very likely the day that little Marie-Joseph, nicknamed Josette, was conceived.

Chapter 6

...Saying that the Sun, which they always recognized and adored as a God, created the whole of this wonderful Universe. The Sun immediately divided the Earth into several parts, each separated from the other by great lakes; in each part the Sun made a man and a woman to be born: they multiplied and lived for a very long time; but having grown cruel with their children, who set to killing each other, the Sun cried tears of grief, and the rain fell from the sky in such abundance that the water reached the summits of the highest, tallest rocks and mountains. The flood, which they say spread over all the earth, forced them to take to their birch canoes to save themselves from the furious depths of the general deluge; their effort was in vain, however, because a raging wind tumbled them over into the horrible abyss in which they were buried, all except a few old people and a few women who were the most virtuous and the best of all. God then came to comfort them for the loss of their relatives and friends, after which he let them live on earth in great, contented tranquility, giving them by the same token all the skill and ingenuity required to capture as many beaver and moose as they needed for their subsistence.

– Ancient legend of Canada, told in *Honguedo*

Sometimes Membertou accompanied his grandfather on his trips to Ile Caraquet. On those occasions, he slept up in the lookout in the tall trees. One such night he could not get to sleep. On top of his excitement over his coming journey to Quebec with Joseph, the geese and ducks flying overhead made a terrific noise. He climbed down from his perch as dawn was breaking over the point of the island and as the first rays of sunlight traced winged angels in the sky. At least that is what Membertou thought he saw. Enchanted by the images and distracted from daydreams about Quebec, he trotted off in the direction of the sun and almost disappeared in the tall grass. His grandfather had told him about evil Gougou, who lived in a cave on the northeast side of the island, on the side of a small hill covered in sea grass. This part of the island seemed strange to him. The colour of the soil was not the same. The vegetation, too, was different. He stopped short, noting with alarm that he was on Gougou's territory. He was panic-stricken. He could not budge. The winged angels had fled long before him. *Maybe Gougou's evil breath is what changes the colour of the soil*, he thought.

He gave a start when a pack of hares pursued by a silver fox ran by not far from him. Their antics captivated him and restored his calm. Suddenly, the hares vanished as though by magic. Membertou ran to the place where they seemed to have disappeared. Behind a grove of shrubs, he found an opening carved into the side of the hill. Curiosity got the better of him and he stepped inside. A weak light shone in the distance. On the shore side, the passage widened. Membertou penetrated into a grotto shining with a thousand fires. He wondered if he was dreaming. He glimpsed cave drawings that looked, with their yellow, brown, and red ochre, to be very ancient. To his left, a fresco showed a creature surrounded by light who looked like the Great Creator as depicted by the shaman. From the creature's breath grew a planet with vegetation unfamiliar to Membertou. He could make out strange animals and birds. He was stupefied, struck dumb with wonder. A second fresco showed a naked man and woman contemplating a garden of trees and flowers that Membertou did not recognize. This one reminded him of the stories the missionary told about the Garden of Eden. Farther on, he could make out a large canoe on which perched a bird, holding in its talons a tuft of grass. A gentle-looking animal, with one single horn growing out of its forehead, stood on a small promontory, almost submerged by the waves. Membertou stood for a long time gazing at the drawing. He would have liked to tame such a beautiful animal despite its haughty air as it defied the flood with its single horn as straight as an arrow. To his right, a painting represented a large ship with a carving of the god Odin on its prow. *That looks like the shipwreck on Ile Miscou*, Membertou thought. *The Mi'kmaq painted the Viking ship!*

He was reminded of his mother's blonde hair, a sign of the mingling of Mi'kmaq and Viking blood. He never tired of gazing on and stroking her wheat-coloured hair. He was not sure what to think anymore. He looked closely at the symbols painted beside the ship: twenty-four signs unlike the ones in the Eden paintings.

He kept exploring, discovering other, what seemed more recent, paintings. One scene struck him: a family, with a child in a birchbark cradle. He thought of Joseph, his new father, and Geneviève, the little sister he was learning to love. It hadn't been easy; he had been jealous for months after her birth. When she began to walk, he spent hours playing with her. He teased her, played tricks on her, made faces to make her cry; it was one way of showing the rancour he felt about this child taking his place. On the other hand, when Joseph lost his patience and scolded Geneviève, Membertou sprang into action. His tantrums were something to behold. He yelled and broke everything he could get his hands on. His rage exploded when he was punished (by Joseph, who did not always abide by Mi'kmaq customs) for hurting Geneviève or for egging her on when she was up to no good or using bad words. The sounds of the nearby waves rocked him, as though in celebration of a moment of closeness with his new family. Suddenly, a light above his head drew his gaze. In a crack in the grotto, a small polished metal chest lay on a dark blue rock. Intrigued, he drew nearer. He examined it. Opened it. A fountain of colours sprang out at him: the yellow, blue, red, and violet of gold and precious stones. What fascinated him above all was a gold cross with rubies on the ends. *This must be the paradise described by the shaman and the missionary*, he thought.

All the beauty had made him forget about evil Gougou. *I can't wait for Grandfather to explain all these enigmas to me.*

He closed the chest, left the cave, and walked out onto the beach. The sun was slowly rising above Miscou point. That was where he found Saint-Jean, who knew what had happened as soon as he saw Membertou on the beach.

"Where were you?" he shouted as Membertou emerged from the tall grass.

"Grandfather, I found a heavenly spot over there, in a cave," Membertou said, still under the spell of the special place.

It took Saint-Jean a minute to regain his composure and think of something to say. "I thought I told you not to wander over there. Now you must swear not to tell a soul."

"Fine, but tell me about what I saw in the cave."

"Not so fast… Sit down and listen. A long time ago, the Mi'kmaq discovered this site, and the cave paintings tell their story. They also painted the story of the creation of the world according to their beliefs. The legends are the same legends as the Catholics, with a Garden of Eden, the flood…"

"What was the flood?"

"Some say it was God's punishment for man's evil ways. Others say that, in ancient times, a moon fell to earth and provoked the catastrophe. The moon fell on a continent that had a flourishing civilization before it was submerged. It was called Atlantis. Its inhabitants had to flee from the earthquakes and volcanic eruptions. Several ended up in Persia and others in Egypt, where they built the great pyramids. The flood also covered the lowlands of Canada."

"Where did you learn all this?"

"I never told you about my early days in Rouen. My father was a printer and had a huge library where I learned all about lost civilizations. In the evening the Huguenot intellectuals of the city would often gather at our house. Hiding at the top of the big stone staircase, I listened to their conversations. The wars of religion were over, but my parents were still suffering from harassment. They were ruined because of their beliefs. They never got over the bankruptcy and died in poverty. I was twenty at the time, and my only thought was to seek revenge and reclaim our honour. So I began counterfeiting money to buy back the family property, but alas, I was caught and sentenced to the galleys."

Membertou had already heard about the galleys; now he was impatient for information about the next drawing. "I saw a superb animal inside the cave," Membertou remarked. "Does it exist somewhere?"

"The Ancients called it a unicorn. Legend has it that it was too proud to take refuge in the Great Canoe and so perished in the flood."

"That's unfair!" he cried. "Why doesn't the God of Creation protect his creatures?"

"No one knows God's plan," Saint-Jean said, with a hint of bitterness.

After a moment's silence, he said, "You must have noticed the Indian paintings showing the Vikings and their writing."

"Yes, and some funny drawings underneath the paintings…"

"They're called runes. The Vikings write them on small stone disks, which they use to predict the future."

"What about the ship with the carved figurehead? It looks like the shipwreck at Miscou."

"It's called a drakkar. The Vikings stayed for a while… In fact, your mother Angélique has certain features…"

"Are you the one who spread a rumour about evil Gougou to keep people away from this place?"

"Yes."

"So where does Gougou live?"

"It's thought she hides out on Ile Miscou, but there's no way of knowing for sure."

A heavy silence settled to mark the solemnity of the moment, as though they had been enveloped by Gougou's evil breath.

"My fear is that with the sea eating away at the cape year after year, soon there will be nothing left of the treasure," confessed old Saint-Jean.

At these words, Membertou gave a start. He'd been so caught up in the story he was hearing, he'd almost forgotten about "his" treasure. "I found a little chest full of precious stones and gold coins..."

"Aren't you the little gougou! I thought you had missed it. Well, I guess there's nothing for it but to tell you the whole story. More than twenty years ago, during the high tides of October, the carcass of a burned ship showed up not far from Miscou, on the shores of a small island I called Treasure Island. You remember the story of the cursed ship that the Mi'kmaq set fire to in order to take revenge for the raids... It's said that a certain Gaspar de Corte Real, from a family of Portuguese navigators, massacred Beothuk Indians in Newfoundland in the year 1500; it didn't take long for tribe members to repay him in kind. In 1502, his brother Miguel came looking for him and was killed on Ile aux Hérons by a young Mi'kmaq who accused him of seducing his fiancée. Legend has it that the explorer will return one day in a burning ship to take his revenge. You know, there may be a kernel of truth to the legend of the phantom ship... I found the chest in the ship's hold and brought it to the cave. I'm convinced that one day the treasure will come in handy, if not to ensure our prosperity, at least to barter with the English, who, I'm afraid, will soon be treating us like slaves. The treasure is sacred. We could use it to become rich, but we must touch it only in case of dire need. We must live like ordinary people, otherwise we'll become possessive and greedy. I was the only one who knew about this place. From now on, you will share my secret with me, my son."

Saint-Jean refused to say anything more. Proud of the trust being placed in him by his grandfather, Membertou did not ask any more questions.

Chapter 7

That which is called Carraquet is an island in front of
which lies a very large bay three leagues deep; there is a
river in the interior (Rivière du Sud)... I have visited the
bay from both sides of the north coast (Maisonnette and
Anse Bleue)... Next is Chipagan, which is nothing but a
large recess that goes from one sea to the other by way of
breaks that form islands; only small ships can pass by
rounding a point, rowboats go through a small pass
(between Ile de Pokesudie and terra firma) to enter the
bay called Chipagan; it forms another island that comes
to a point that runs alongside the bay deep into the sea;
this is called Miscou Point...

– Excerpted from the document on the
Chaleurs Abbey south of the St. Lawrence River.
Written in Louisbourg on the 19th day of August 1724
by Sieur L'Hermmitte, king's engineer

...a very tall rock, high on both sides...

– Champlain, within sight of Percé Rock

In late September, the *Phantom Ship* was ready to travel to
Quebec. Angélique brought down jars of pumpkin jam in a
small crate. Jean-Baptiste loaded the hold with dried cod.
Joseph piled up crates of oysters that had been gathered on the
Pointe-de-Roche sand bar.

Angélique took advantage of a small break from the task
at hand to open a few oysters, which she ate with Joseph.

"They're an aphrodisiac," she said softly. Joseph didn't need to be told twice, and her words were borne out...

When the sun was at its highest point, the ship skimmed past Miscou and its Breton, Basque, and Norman fishermen's huts. Across the way, on Ile Chipagan, traces could still be seen of Nicolas Denys' installations from the time the king had bestowed on him, by letter patent bearing a great green wax seal, the title of lieutenant-general and governor of coastal Acadia, and had entrusted him with setting up trading posts for fish and furs, the two income sources which motivated France to look after its colonies. Denys had criss-crossed the huge territory for close to fifty years, at a time when France's dreams for the continent were equal to its size.

"Denys was an important man," Joseph began thoughtfully.

"Who's that?" Membertou asked.

"He came over with the founders, Razilly and D'Aulnay. In your grandfather's library, you may have noticed the two books Denys wrote, both vigorous pleas for the development of our country. For more than fifty years, he fought in the king's interest; he even went to Versailles and offered the king the finest silver fox furs. To little avail, however."

Joseph's comment sparked Membertou's imagination. He had never understood why the French left their distant and wonderful country for Canada's snow and fog.

* * *

On the second evening, the *Phantom Ship* dropped anchor not far from Percé Rock. At dawn, Membertou began rowing his dory toward this marvel of nature, which stood like a sphinx pierced with two huge holes carved out by the sea. At high tide, small boats could pass through it, which Membertou did. Afterwards, at the risk of breaking his neck, he climbed the rock, knocking down fossils that were several thousand years old. Joseph forgave him his escapade because he brought back a delicious supply of eggs. Nearby, on Ile Bonaventure, Northern Gannet wove overhead as though making a roof to shelter him. There were so many of them – like snowflakes blocking the sun – that it felt like an actual snowstorm.

The next day, Joseph and his crew stopped at Gaspeg, known as the key to Canada because of its command of the river on the way to Quebec and its reputation as one of the safest harbours on the Atlantic coast.

"It was here in 1534 that Jacques Cartier claimed possession of the country," Joseph said. "With a cross measuring three toises[1] that bore a crest showing three fleurs-de-lys and the inscription VIVE LE ROY DE FRANCE, Long Live the King of France.

"Can we see it?" Membertou asked.

"It crumbled… in as sorry a state as New France is. If the king doesn't look after his spoils better than this, there will be nothing left," Joseph grumbled.

Saint-Jean had asked Joseph to give a certain Françoise a few bags of fine flour on his behalf. Françoise was the daughter of Madeleine, the widowed native woman who had married Saint-Jean after her husband died. Françoise never accepted her second family, and Saint-Jean never understood why. So the ties between Saint-Jean and his adopted daughter were those of business, nothing more. Françoise was responsible for the Gaspeg fur-trading post. She was self-disciplined and had a hermit's temperament, which one had to admire. In order to protect her privacy, she rarely confided in anyone, but that day she spoke to Joseph about her husband Pierre Le Vicaire, who was off fishing, and about her two youngest daughters, Anne and Marie, and about her desire to visit Quebec. Jean-Baptiste, who had never heard his stepsister express a personal longing, could not believe his ears.

"You're welcome to join us… we have enough room," Jean-Baptiste offered.

"Maybe some other time…"

Just when her guests were leaving, she even asked for news of Saint-Jean, leading Jean-Baptiste to believe she was finally having a change of heart!

---

1. A toise is equal to approximately two metres.

* * *

The *Phantom Ship* set sail up the St. Lawrence River, and a favourable wind soon brought it within sight of the Tadoussac coasts at the mouth of the Saguenay.

"Sieur de Roberval tried in vain to establish settlers in this region," Joseph reflected. "That was in 1541, during Cartier's last voyage in search of the fabulous kingdom of the Saguenay, where, it was said, gold grew everywhere."

Fascinated by the show the whales were putting on, Membertou was only half-listening. He exclaimed, "Look over there at the whale pods!"

Some ten white belugas performed, twirling and pirouetting like children as they swam closer to the schooner in a breathtaking display. Some expelled water from their lungs in a geyser, while others leapt out of the river and flopped onto their backs beside the ship, spraying the passengers with the cascade of water and foam their tails sent flying. The rose hue of dusk was reflected in the ballet of tapered bodies racing through and vaulting over the waves. The dolphins joined in as well, weaving backwards in a zigzag as they nonchalantly brushed against the hull starboard then dove and reappeared to portside. Farther on, a few marbled blue finback whales slept, drifting on the waves, snoring loudly, while the seagulls took great pleasure in scratching their sundried backs. For some it was mealtime; they gulped down huge quantities of krill and water. Membertou admired the show at length, then turned his attention to the Northern Gannet soaring overhead, on the lookout for herring and capelin.

That night, Membertou dreamt he arrived at Ile Caraquet on a beluga's back. Straddling the gentle animal and guiding it with braided ropes of seaweed, he made his appearance in a spray of foam to the general acclamation of the tribe.

Jean-Baptiste had a nightmare: his father had shut him up in a large chest of gold with nothing to live on but dry bread and water to punish him for his greed. He woke up bathed in sweat, trying to convince himself he just wanted to show the white man what good merchants his people could be.

As for Joseph, who manned the tiller, he sifted through memories of his childhood and the hours spent along the docks, where large foreign ships came to load up on furs, and barrels of sugar, molasses, and rum from the West Indies. Sometimes with his friends, he went to watch the shipbuilding by Rue Cul-de-Sac. The smell of tar there made him dream of the spice road followed by his hero, Sinbad. There were wood scents, too: oak, beech, elm, and the tall white pine used for ships' masts. And other more discreet perfumes: those of the clandestine rendez-vous. In fact, it was in among the cords of wood that he met Emilie, whose parents were building a new home, a large three-storey house close to Rue Sous-le-Fort by Cul-de-Sac. Joseph and Emilie went through a period of secret lovers' rendezvous, crossing over to Lévis on the ice as they invented another universe to the rhythm of the swaying carriage.

Joseph was abruptly awakened from his daydream by Jean-Baptiste, come to take over the watch. Tired from his sleepless night and his impossible daydreams, he fell asleep quickly, but his sleep was disturbed by a strange dream he had often had as a child. In a stone castle next to a river, a pack of hounds bayed, while people on horseback set off on a wild boar hunt. He was never able to make out the people's faces. When he awoke, he wondered whether the faces were those of his unknown parents.

The Saint-Jean-Port-Joli seigneurie came into view. Joseph headed for shore, delighted to think he'd be meeting the great oyster lover Seigneur Jean Aubert de Gaspé in person. Inside the manor, a long table was set in a large room with high wainscotting. Other than the treasure on Ile Caraquet, Membertou had never seen anything quite as beautiful: the silver cutlery laid out on a delicate starched tablecloth, the crystal chandeliers and the light from their thousands of candles, the servants in livery, the women parading their rich finery. But Joseph was in a hurry. He couldn't wait to see Quebec, his mother, and his friends again. Without admitting as much, he hoped for news of Emilie as well.

A few hours later, Quebec hove into sight. Joseph was overcome by emotion at the sight of Ile d'Orleans, then Cap

Diamant, topped by the Château St. Louis. His gaze lingered on the animated docks where, next to the Royal Battery, some thirty ships from France, Louisbourg, and the West Indies rocked; one was preparing to sail to France with its cargo of fur.

"I bet they have furs from our region," Membertou said.

"At ten times the price," Jean-Baptiste added.

Another ship was full to the brim with white pine to be used for masts for the royal navy. Jean-Baptiste was already busy imagining the trade he could do in Miramichi's great white pines. A ship from the West Indies attracted his attention. Men rolled barrels of rum onto carts; just the thought of the warm liquid coursing down his throat made Jean-Baptiste thirsty. For Joseph, it was the thought of Emilie that came to haunt him like a wound reopened. Memories were awakened by the seagulls playing overhead, just as they had when he and Emilie were young lovers. *Why can't I forget her?* he asked himself. *She was my first love, I know, but that's not reason enough. What is it about her that has burrowed so deeply into my heart?*

Chapter 8

I looked for a good location in which to set up residence,
but could find nothing more convenient or better than
the point of Quebec, called Pointe des Sauvages, and its
abundance of walnut trees.

— Champlain, in 1608

Even before the white man's arrival, Quebec[1] had been a
centre for loud festivities and music for the First Nations.
Joseph felt a wave of sheer happiness at the sound of the
thousand-pound bell ringing from the cape. Jean-Baptiste and
Membertou accompanied him as he walked past the Royal
Battery, eleven cannons set up along the river, and entered
Place Royale, the marketplace. There were gentlemen wearing
tricorn hats, chimneysweeps black with soot, natives wearing
gaudy costumes, and, close to Notre-Dame-Des-Victoires
Church (built on the foundations of Champlain's residence),
goldsmiths manufacturing religious objects. On a stage in the
centre of the square, a theatre troupe was enacting the exploits
of the coureurs de bois. The whole place was abustle with the
din of the market. Carts clattered down narrow lanes.
Drumrolls announced royal proclamations, edicts read out by
town criers, which prohibited pretty well everything. Peasants

---

1. Of which Cartier said, "…there is the city and the domicile of Seigneur
Donacona, which domicile is called Stadaconé."

were everywhere, some selling their chickens and vegetables, others carrying barrels of wine on poles slung across their shoulders. In the lanes dotted with yellow spittle, rubbish piled up, as did horse and cow pies, and the stench of fish and excrement floated in the air. But the scent of fresh bread, the fragrance of spices, and more pleasing odours such as the salt air from offshore overpowered the putrid smells. A town crier, wearing a feathered tricorn hat, a blue cloak embroidered with silver lys, and a lace ruffle, rang a bell. He announced the sale of indulgences, then declaimed, "Hear ye, hear ye. That all good people, seigneurs, gentlemen, spread the word, it is forbidden to sell drink to the Indians subject to a fine, imprisonment, or excommunication… Foreigners are prohibited from selling their products without a special permit…"

"Huh," Joseph observed, "I'll have to find a way to liquidate my goods."

They left the marketplace behind and headed in the direction of Le Chien d'Or[2] inn on Rue Buade. Joseph had been a regular there when he lived in Quebec. In the smoke-filled room, seated at tables groaning under large pitchers of beer, customers played hoca, cards, or dice. Joseph had trouble recognizing the place.

The decor had changed; the furs hanging on the walls were no longer the same. From behind the counter, the fat owner Philibert, explained, "My partner Gaboury moved to Boston after one too many run-ins with the religious authorities over sales of alcohol."

Joseph could not hide his disappointment. "Damn rules. Slowly but surely, New France is losing its best men."

"That's a fact," Philibert agreed. "Just last week, a family that refused to convert to Catholicism had to leave for New York."

Joseph sat off to the side with Jean-Baptiste and Membertou. Tired from the long trip and a bit overwhelmed

---

2. The Golden Dog, a carving dated 1661, decorated the front of the inn. A historical novel on the period covering the War of the Conquest, written by William Kirby, takes the name *The Golden Dog (Le Chien d'Or)* as its title. It is published by Stanké.

by all the commotion, he ordered a pitcher of rum for Jean-Baptiste and himself as well as a large glass of maple water for Membertou.

"Fire destroyed Widow Lamothe's house yesterday," someone said.

Fire was a constant danger because of poorly cleaned fire-places. Joseph knew all about it; he had seen many a fire during his childhood. At another table, people were complaining about how strict the ecclesiastical authorities were. "It's to the point where women have to conceal their bodies under blankets," one coureur de bois spat out. "Because of the damn edicts, they can't even have long hair or show their shoulders."

"Those priests see demons everywhere," his companion added. "Thank God for the forest and the Indian women. With all the rules meant to keep us from living, it's no wonder Gaboury gave up on the tavern."

Joseph wished he could have seen his friend, who had always welcomed him like a father when he stopped by for a drink with Emilie, sometimes even after closing hours. All of a sudden, the owner's son came over to their table and said to Jean-Baptiste, "You're an Injun, you can't drink here."

"The Indians lived here for thousands of years before the white man: I'm not moving."

Philibert ran over.

"His father comes from Normandy," Joseph intervened.

The owner burst out laughing. "He's as black as a crow… Get out before I call the guards… There's no way I'm losing my permit!"

Two hoca players stood up and tried to grab Jean-Baptiste. He made a fist and laid one of the men out on the table with a single blow. Jean-Baptiste was no longer merely angry: he was furious at being ordered around in his own country.

"My people preached equality when your ancestors were still living like barbarians," he shouted.

Membertou – on the warpath already – broke a pitcher of rum over one attacker's head. At that moment, soldiers burst into the tavern, just as the owner charged, armed with a broken bottle. It was time to leave behind the room full of broken chairs and unsheathed knives. Joseph, Jean-Baptiste, and Membertou took advantage of the confusion caused by the soldiers' arrival to slip out the back door, which gave onto a lane. Jean-Baptiste was purple with rage, incapable of understanding the white men's scorn. As for Joseph, he didn't dwell on his emotions. His sole thought was to lose the guards. Luckily, they were able to disappear into a crowd that had gathered nearby around a man, bareheaded, his hands tied, who was crawling on his knees.

"He's a Huguenot condemned to the whipping post," a bystander explained.

"Why?" Membertou exclaimed.

"He sold meat on a Friday so he has to pay for his sin at Notre-Dame-Des-Victoires Church."

"Such powerful clergy…"

"That's a fact!"

Joseph realized just how far removed he'd been from such practices since his departure for Caraquet's forests.

* * *

Joseph's mother worked as a volunteer for the Hôtel Dieu hospitallers, which was where he found her. Full of remorse, as though he had abandoned her, he held her in his arms for a long time. She had aged considerably, and he felt like he was seeing her for the last time. After telling her all about his new life and family, he offered her a coat and hat Angélique had made with her father's finest silver fox pelts.

"This will keep my old bones warm," she said as she thanked him.

As for the nuns, they bought all his oysters and pumpkin jam for what Joseph thought was a ridiculously low price: a few silver ecus[3] and a crate of apples. He did manage to barter for some silk fabric and ginseng, the plant with medicinal virtues that was being gathered in New France for sale at a good price in China, to take back to Angélique.

---

3. One ecu was the equivalent of five francs.

***

After a restless night spent torn between his life in Caraquet and Quebec, his memories and reality, his need to know more and the need to forget, Joseph decided to see Cristel, Emilie's younger sister. He hadn't spoken to her since his departure, back when he was desperately trying to find some clues to his fiancée's disappearance. He knocked on her door. She threw herself into his arms, as innocent and pure as the Emilie he had loved. They went for a walk on the ramparts by Château St. Louis overlooking the river, and talked at length. Cristel finally made up her mind. "I have something for you," she said.

She pulled a small package from her coat pocket and handed it to Joseph. He opened it and was rendered speechless by what he found inside: a letter and a portrait of Emilie. His whole body began to tremble.

From Nantes, Emilie had learned that Joseph was still alive, but just as she was getting ready to come home, she received other news from a ship that had stopped off at Ruisseau, news that Joseph had a wife and child. Silently, Joseph reread parts of the letter, "I don't want to spoil your happiness... A rich merchant from Jersey is looking after me... looking after me... after me... slowly I'm regaining the will to live." Emilie! Her name crashing in on him to the beat of the current beneath the cape: Emilie, a name whose power he could do nothing to neutralize. He fell into what felt like a drunken stupour, as though the air of Ile d'Orléans – or Ile de Bacchus as it was sometimes called because of its vineyards – had been fermented with all the wine on earth. Cristel tried to distract him, "Look at the fires over there on Ile aux Sorciers. That's the other name for Ile d'Orléans because of all the fires the inhabitants light at night."

Joseph felt like his brain itself was on fire. For the longest time, he stood on the ramparts contemplating Emilie's portrait by the light of the fires' flames. For the longest time, he stood transfixed, caught between the stranglehold of heaven and earth, the river and the cape, as though in a dream. When the distant fires went out, and the drunken stupor evaporated, and the current fell with the receding tide, he knew he had a choice to make.

"I'm dying to go after her," he confessed.

"You mustn't, my friend. You're happy at home with your new family. You will forget her. Emilie still loves you, but she has to follow her destiny now."

Deep down, he knew Cristel was right. Emilie's letter only confirmed that fact.

* * *

The *Phantom Ship* set sail the next day for Acadia and Ruisseau. Jean-Baptiste did not ask Joseph any questions since his culture taught that another's silence was to be respected. Jean-Baptiste's thoughts, too, were elsewhere; he was counting the profits from the sale of his cod. As for Membertou, he could feel Joseph's distress, and it saddened him because the boy had learned to love the man thanks to the strong bonds they had formed during their voyage.

Chapter 9

Vice reigns supreme within the colonies. The governors, district Intendants and ordnance officers sent to govern there are thoroughly convinced that their purpose is none other than to make their fortune and so they behave accordingly, thus ruining trade and serving as a huge obstacle to any progress in the colonies.
                                    – Michel Le Courtois de Surlaville,
                                         Vice-Governor of Isle Royale

Josette was born on March 23, 1744 in Ruisseau. A joyful Joseph danced passionately at Pointe-de-Roche, rediscovered the violin, and cared tenderly for Angélique, who had had another long and painful delivery. But, after a few months, he tired of playing nursemaid, and was bitten once more by the travel and adventure bug. His was the age-old story of a man who wants a large family but lacks the patience to look after it! Angélique knew there was no point trying to hold him back. She loved him too much to suffocate him, and the possibility of his earning a few ecus in Louisbourg, where there was a labour shortage, made it easier for her to accept his hasty departure. Membertou's reaction was another story. Not wanting to let his chagrin show, he took refuge in a world of fantasy, where he daydreamed of the treasure in the cave. As for Jean-Baptiste, his way of dealing with Joseph's departure was to focus on tending to the schooner, which offered the promise of profitable catches and an abundance of gold Louis. Saint-Jean did not approve of Joseph's going, but he did not feel he was in a position to teach Joseph right from wrong, for he was made from the same cloth as Joseph. So Joseph boarded the *Licorne*, a ship that arrived from Quebec loaded down with provisions for the Louisbourg fortress. On board, he met Nicolas Gauthier, one of Port Royal's wealthiest merchants, who made clandestine supply trips to Louisbourg. Gauthier operated stores, flour mills, sawmills, and schooners with which he plied his trade as far away as the West Indies.

"People on Isle Royale have nothing but oysters and seafood left to eat," he told Joseph.

"What happened?"

"The soil there is no good for agriculture. They're obliged to rely on assistance from Quebec, Port-Royal, or the mother country. Last year, the harvest was bad because of the heat waves, blight, and pests, which did extensive damage to the crops. Then almost all the cured and dried cod was sent to Paris and the West Indies. As for the New England colonies, they can't supply us with goods because they, too, were hit by the drought."

"So the English from Boston sell their goods to you?" Joseph exclaimed.

"That surprises you? There's no point beating about the bush: in peacetime there are more boats from the English colonies in Louisbourg than French ships. In wartime, it's more of the same," Gauthier said ironically. "The King of France prohibits trade with the English but, when the French ships don't bring us what we need, the authorities look the other way and we turn to those who have what we can't find elsewhere! They make a pretty profit while they're at it. And, just between you and me, the Boston market is a lot closer anyway," he explained.

Joseph felt as though he had a great deal to learn about Louisbourg. Gauthier continued, "France did send three supply ships, but one of the ships sank in the ice. What's more, a number of barrels of flour were underweight, and others were either too damp or contained an assortment of grains. It's the same thing every year, not that it matters as much when the harvest is good in Canada. When we're in a bad way, usually the Basques who fish for cod off Isle Royale sell us seabiscuits and pork fat, at outrageous prices, of course. But with a war looming, we don't know if they'll be back."

"If I understand correctly, Louisbourg's inhabitants are eager for the goods you bring them… What are you transporting?"

"Hundredweights of fine and whole wheat flour, hogsheads of buckwheat and wheat. I also bought livestock in Quebec as well as wine, cider, cognac… I forget how many barrels worth… and other luxuries for the well-to-do: almonds, soap, clothes, sheets, silk goods, shoes. Yet it's not nearly enough!"

"If Louisbourg is like Quebec, I imagine the authorities make sure their palms are greased in the process."

"Dear man, it's worse than that. Some officers are getting rich on the back of the king and the troops. The ordnance officer and the governor are involved, too. Not only are the soldiers' rations cut back, but tools and material that were supposed to be used to repair the fortress are being sold off in Boston."

"Can't you lodge a complaint?"

"What can a lowly soldier or merchant do when faced with an officer who has the government's protection? It's true they do sometimes go too far. De Saint-Ovide, the former governor, was accused of fraud and lost his position five years ago because of the rampant corruption and thievery. As for the current governor Du Quesnel, he's not much better. And the ordnance officer Bigot is worse than all the rest of them put together!"

"What crooks! New France's future doesn't look too promising with them at the helm!"

"Especially in view of the Austrian succession, which almost guarantees that France and England will go to war. If that happens, we'll be fighting in America. Imagine: Port-Royal and Grand'Pré are already under British rule, the Louisbourg fortress is about as solid as a sandcastle, and there are twenty times more English than French in the colonies."

Joseph had to agree. His thoughts turned to the family he had more or less abandoned in Ruisseau. What would happen to them if war broke out?

* * *

The sea was calm that day off Ile Saint-Jean, originally called "Abegweit" by the Mi'kmaq – "land rocked by waves."

Joseph found Nicolas Gauthier seated on the fore round-house. He looked worried.

"The livestock are dying. If we don't arrive soon, my trip will have been in vain."

"We can't be far from Louisbourg," Joseph said encouragingly.

"If the winds blow from the north, we'll be there in a few days… In any case, there's nothing we can do about it. What are your plans once we're in Louisbourg?"

"I was told they needed extra hands. So I'll try my luck."

"You should sign up as a privateer. If war's declared, there could be some interesting catches. As early as last summer, the British started trying to intercept supply ships from Acadia, and Le Kinsale, stationed in Canso, managed to capture a Louisbourg ship."

"I see! In any case, a soldier's life must be like a form of slavery."

"I don't want to discourage you, but they get pretty poor wages and, if they want to earn more, they're put to work on the fortifications. The officers are in charge of the canteens and liquor. So the soldiers are always in debt. On top of which, they're poorly fed, often on rotting pork fat rations. As for their clothes, the less said the better; their shirts are made of the cheapest fabric around. Corruption is rampant. The fishermen aren't any better off. The officers and authorities control the arrival of cargo and fishing gear. The same holds true for merchants, like the Dugas, who own a butcher's shop. They have to remit part of their profit to the very people who have them in a stranglehold. It's a sorry life!"

Joseph listened silently, with a sense of shock and concern. He hadn't come all this way just to turn back now. He had a hard time fathoming the stories of corruption that circulated about the Louisbourg leaders.

"An uprising is what's needed."

"A few years ago, the fishermen banded together to send a petition to the minister, to no avail. The soldiers are another matter. I'm afraid that eventually we're going to see mutiny. Especially since the Swiss soldiers in the Karrer regiment are not attached to France the way the other troops are. There have already been deserters to the English colonies. Following the example of the French Huguenots, the soldiers settle in Boston, Massachusetts, or Virginia.

"I know all about it," Joseph exclaimed thinking of Gaboury. "We're losing recruits to the enemy!"

"That's for sure! As though the enemy weren't strong enough already."

* * *

On April 30, 1744, a thick fog shrouded the ship, fog so thick it was impossible to see the fore roundhouse. The ice floes no longer represented a threat, however, and a flock of seagulls circled the ship, a sign that Louisbourg was near. Joseph gave a sigh of relief to think that he would soon be within reach of the fortress at the ends of the earth! On May 1st, when Louisbourg loomed out of the fog, he was dumbstruck. He had never imagined a fortress this big. From the lookout, he gazed at the star-shaped city built on Havre d'anglois and surrounded by ramparts within which more than seven thousand people lived. Soldiers, fishermen, and every other trade as well: carpenters, joiners, limemen, masons, stonecarvers, blacksmiths, locksmiths, bakers... just as in France's cities by the sea. Outside the ramparts was the fishing village: huts with sod roofs and, nearby, small boats, storehouses, and fish flakes on which the cod was dried. The smell of fish mingled in the air with smoke from the drydock where pitch was being boiled to repair the ships with. The bay, eight fathoms deep, was in the shape of a flattened bottle, and it harboured some sixty ships of various sizes. A forest of masts!

"Louisbourg is at the same time a fortress, a cod fishing post, and a huge trading post where France, Quebec, the West Indies, and New England exchange merchandise," Gauthier explained. "It's also a hideout for privateers and smugglers! Funny, I don't see any French or Basque fishing fleets. Boats from La Rochelle, Marennes, Saint-Malo, San Juan de Luz, and Sables d'Olonne are usually here earlier than this... I wonder if war has been declared in Europe."

The docks were crawling with a mottled group of people engaged in a frenzied exchange of merchandise – barrels of pork fat, sacks of grain, hundredweights of dried peas, baskets of cheese from Quebec.

"It's more animated than Quebec's harbour," Joseph observed.

Gauthier was busy pointing, explaining, and telling stories. "Look, another ship from Quebec. The barrels on the bridge must be full of cured salmon... The other French ship over there comes from the West Indies with a cargo of rum, sugar, and tobacco. Goodbye food shortages!"

"What about the ships flying a British flag?"

"They come from New England. Boston, New York. A potential market if we play our cards right."

Joseph looked at the fortress and the Château Saint-Louis, the governor's residence with its magnificent roof made of slate imported from Nantes. In the very centre of the castle, between the governor's suites and the barracks, stood the clock tower. As the clock chimed eleven o'clock that morning, costumed Mi'kmaq paddled their canoes alongside the *Licorne*. The commotion grew as the ship drew alongside the dock. Cannon shots boomed. The firepower was such that the whole fortress shook. A troop of soldiers waited on the docks. Joseph disembarked. The flagstones seemed to reel before him, just like the colourful, noisy, variegated crowd. The navy's drummers formed an honour guard, proudly wearing their red and blue uniforms – jackets, waistcoats, and breeches – and beating on their blue drums decorated with yellow fleurs-de-lys.

He also recognized the soldiers of the navy's Compagnies Franches with their grey-white uniform and blue trim, white jackets and socks, swords on their hip, Tulle musket with its bayonet attached and powder horn attached to the thirty-charge cartridge box.

"See the Swiss soldiers," Gauthier said pointing them out, "they're the ones wearing a red jacket with blue sleeves and white buttons. The authorities don't like them much because most of them aren't Catholic, and they only obey French sergeants grudgingly."

"What about the French soldiers?"

"The situation there isn't much better. Several of them are pretty sickly... They include habitual criminals and orphans recruited from Paris. If war breaks out, sign up as a privateer... It's more exciting."

Joseph was engrossed in the spectacle when a few Mi'kmaq and Abnaki joined the troops. On the square, all kinds of languages could be heard in a genuine tower of Babel! The Boston accent, the accent of the settlers come to trade farm products for rum and sugar, the strange speech of the Portuguese fishermen, the accents of tanned fishermen back from fishing off Martinique, or of fishermen used to the cold of the Baye des Chaleurs, or of Acadians from Port-Royal. There were Puritan merchants from Massachusetts, who covered their ears so as not to hear the French captains swearing. More exotic still: Brazilian parrots, African monkeys, and black slaves from the Caribbean. A carousel of colours and sounds, with cannons spewing fire, and a city abustle.

Chapter 10

Further to complaints that a few individuals are not locking up their pigs, which then do harm to the cod and hens and even endanger small children because of their voraciousness, it is hereby ordered that all those who own pigs enclose them in their yard or take them to the country. Failing that, any person who finds pigs eating cod or hens or running free is hereby entitled to kill such swine.

   – Le Norman de Mézy, ordnance officer at Louisbourg

Properly speaking, they have but two seasons, winter and autumn…

   – Thomas Pichon, *Genuine Letters and Memoirs* (1760)

On May 2, 1744, the day after Joseph's arrival in Louisbourg, a French sail appeared on the horizon, and a crowd gathered on the docks.

Peace or war? The question was on everyone's lips. The answer was quick in coming. Copies of the March 15, 1744 decree posted throughout the city announced that Louis XV had declared war on England. Excitement reigned. Officers dreamt of possible promotions, and merchants speculated about the profits to be had by arming privateers' ships. As for the inhabitants, they worried about food supplies. Joseph was very tempted to become a privateer; the prospect of capturing English ships and protecting the Acadian supply routes of

Grand'Pré and Port-Royal, which, alone, could feed Louisbourg, was increasingly attractive. Adventure! It would be easy enough to do since Maurepas, Minister of the Navy, had sent undesignated commissions to allow for the arming of ships and the privateers' war. But Gauthier, who said he had a choice position lined up for Joseph, advised him to wait.

Life in Louisbourg was far from easy. The barracks were dirty and infested with vermin. The straw mattresses, which were only changed once a year, were home to many an undesirable guest. Weather permitting, Joseph was not alone in choosing to sleep outside on the ramparts. The vile food took its toll on him: insipid seabiscuits, putrid-tasting raw pork fat or corned beef, and five pounds of molasses per month. Since the city was threatened with famine, there was no flour left with which to make six-pound loaves of bread, each soldier's ration for four days. A riot was brewing among the fishermen. Those from Louisbourg and the De la Baleine and De Lorembec posts spoke of raiding the king's stores. On Saturday, May 23rd, the pent-up frustration culminated in a public frenzy during the departure of the Dupont-Duvivier squadron, whose mission was to take the Canso post and thus protect the supply routes linking Louisbourg and Acadia.

But his day-to-day occupations brought home other realities to Joseph. Like all the other mercenaries, to supplement his pay he had to work on the fortifications repairing thirty-foot walls that were disintegrating from the effects of frost and humidity. It was hard work that led to many a hernia and fracture. Joseph was assigned to a group working on the batteries on Ile de l'Entrée, not far from the harbour. Fourteen hours a day of inhumane labour. From five o'clock in the morning until seven o'clock at night, in the cold and the fog, digging down to the rock (three cubic toises[1] worth by eight men in ten days), transporting from Port-Toulouse the earth used to make bricks, preparing stones to be carved to fit the bastion's angles, and cooking limestone in the ovens where the mercenaries' rage crackled with as much fire as the flames.

---

1. One toise is equal to approximately two metres.

In search of oblivion, Joseph gambled, playing hoc mostly, which was introduced to France in Mazarin's time. Gambling fever was everywhere; people vied to predict when the next ship would arrive or whether the newborn would be a boy or girl. In taverns, gambling incited people to drink tafia, and alcoholism ran rampant. When they weren't drinking, the men chased after native women. Alcohol and women were their only outlets. After their wages were distributed, soldiers disappeared into taverns to drown their sorrows and rake up gambling debts. In the public square, it was not uncommon to see a soldier collapsed over a wooden horse, his back red from the lashing he'd received for damage he'd caused while drunk. Joseph was drawn to all kinds of games: cards, dice, and games of chance. To him, risk-taking was one way of influencing fate and resisting the inescapable.

But Louisbourg did not have much to offer in the way of risks. So boredom began to gnaw at him. During his days on the ramparts, his eyes strayed to the bouquets of what looked like white umbrellas that carved up the fields – angelica, the lovely aromatic plant with medicinal properties that was also used in sweets. The flower's name reminded him of his Angélique, whose scent and taste were every bit as captivating. Nights on the ramparts, when he was alone under the stars, were worst of all. Surrounded by scaffolding and unfinished fortifications, lit by the diffuse light of the lantern in the tower that guided ships within the basin, he could not get warm under his heavy pea jacket and leather cape. He remembered Angélique's warmth, Membertou's affection, Geneviève and Josette's pink cheeks and fresh scent, and old Saint-Jean's good spirits. Sometimes he woke up perspiring and anxious, as though afraid he'd be forced to live forever parted from his loved ones, wondering what had gotten into him to leave all that for this godforsaken place. Other nights, memories of Emilie came to him, especially once the tall ships departed for Europe. At times like those, he was tormented by the desire to see her again. Even moreso when he read or reread her letter, remembered her features, and stroked her portrait, which he placed religiously in his little chest after each session.

Sometimes Angélique's features were superimposed on Emilie's portrait and the battle began again, one image chasing the other then fading away, leaving him with the first image.

May was not yet over when the Duvivier expedition returned to Louisbourg and announced the capture of Canso and several English ships, seven hundred head of livestock, and two thousand sheep. The city rejoiced; pride, excitement, and tales of adventure were in the air. Joseph's impatience grew as he watched the English prisoners file by. François Bauchet de Saint-Martin, captain of the *Signe*, was responsible for several captures as were Pierre Detcheverry and Jean Fougère, although the latter had a surprise in store for him since his captures didn't count because he didn't have a proper commission as a privateer. In a flagrant case of conflict of interest, knowing what side their bread was buttered on, Bigot, Duquesnel, and Duvivier had armed the *Cantabre* with cannons and swivel guns.

Gauthier finally found a choice spot for Joseph on the schooner *Le Succès*, with the famous Pierre Morpain, captain of the Louisbourg port. Morpain was a strapping fellow who had chalked up all kinds of exploits along the coasts of the American colonies. Before the fall of Acadia – Grand'Pré, Port-Royal, and the others – he had been part of a privateers' war some thirty years earlier, and the sea held no secrets for him.

Joseph went to fetch his privateer's sabre in the barracks located behind the king's bastion, the largest building in New France and probably in all of North America. It measured 375 feet long. Behind the Bourbons' coat of arms engraved in the stone, he heard voices raised and a heated discussion on the famine and English prisoners. Some fishermen were cursing the merchants, accusing them of depriving the locals of needed goods because of their traffic with the prisoners. It was true there had never been so many English prisoners in the city before – between those on the ships at anchor and those in individuals' homes – and their slightest actions fed the rumour mill. *The problem should be solved soon*, Joseph thought, *since they'll be exchanged for the French prisoners held in Boston.*

As the huge bell in the clocktower above the chapel rang out the angelus, Joseph joined Morpain's crew and entered the privateers' world. Much more of an adventure than mending his uniform, cleaning his musket, or cobbling his shoes. No more soldier's work! This was a different world. A people apart, whose code of solidarity was inspired by the law of the sea. With the help of the first mate Robichaud, Joseph learned to read the portolans, the charts that showed navigational routes as black dots on blue seas. They also showed drawings of blazons, frigates, and strange animals; monsters or winged mermaids for mysterious or mythical locations. He discovered how to wield a sabre, learned how to run across the deck, and climb the rigging. After some time spent scanning the horizon for sails or potential catches, aiming cannons at targets, and preparing to board, Joseph considered himself a match for the privateer Jean Bart – and Sinbad. His universe revolved around the space between the bow and the stern post, between port and starboard, a world bristling with masts – foresails, topmast, mizzens, bowsprits – and an empire dotted with guy ropes, yards, and sails, where the lug sail had to be furled, the jib brought in, and the topsails and mainsail brailed when the captain luffed in the wind.

In mid-August, *Le Succès* returned to Louisbourg with two catches: the *Nancy* and the *Kingsbury*. Other ships had also been captured, including the *William and Mary*, transporting Irishmen and coal. Morpain and his crew had a surprise waiting for them. Morpain was made commander of the *Caribou*, a king's ship armed with fifty-two cannons. There was also bad news. The *Cantabre* had been captured near Cape Cod, as had eight fishing boats off Newfoundland. That made Joseph think twice. He thought about his future, especially since the regularity with which they were capturing English ships made it clear that a blockade was to be expected. He took advantage of his few days off to find out the latest news.

A crowd had gathered by the docks – high society ladies, filles de joie, fishermen, gunners, soldiers as well as seamen from Portugal, Martinique, and Louisiana – in front of an auction tribune on which a black slave stood. *This city is more diversified and colourful than Quebec*, he thought. The harbour was congested with six ships from the Compagnie des Indes, the largest ships ever seen in Louisbourg, their holds full of exotic products (tea, coffee, spices, porcelain, silk) for the European market. Joseph admired the giants of the sea for a minute, then the heat convinced him to go inside for some refreshment. The taverns were packed because of all the sailors in town, and Joseph spent the afternoon playing cards and backgammon among pitchers of rum, raunchy stories, smoke, and a general hubbub, paying particular attention to tales from the strange worlds of the Orient mixed with more day-to-day concerns. Some people feared a blockade, "The Basque and French fleets haven't showed up, that means one hundred and fifty fewer ships for trade!" Others were worried about food shortages, "There isn't even enough food for us, and now we have to feed all the sailors from the Compagnie des Indes' ships… there'll be a famine this winter."

Still others discussed the privateers' war, which the English were winning. Joseph realized he had to be careful. So he decided not to return to *Le Succès*.

* * *

St. Louis Day. Because of the war and the famine, there was little rejoicing. No bonfire or fireworks, no military parade, no salvo of artillery, not even a religious procession. No one rang the hundred-pound bell captured from a British ship. But the lack of an official ceremony did little to change the drunken popular festivities where people celebrated to the point of forgetting their own names. It should be said that the public particularly loved the month of August because of its four holidays, including the feast of the Assumption on the 15th.

Joseph took advantage of the St. Louis holiday to rest in his barracks room not far from the Dauphine demi-bastion next to the gunpowder plant. He shared the room with sixteen soldiers who lived there, knocked about, cooked in the same pot, and slept two to a straw mat. But he forgot his surroundings as he savoured in a moment of idleness the wild raspberries he had gathered at the Cormorandière cove and lovingly polished the gold coin with Louis XIV's likeness on it that he had found lying on the beach. The coin came from the wreck of the *Chameau*, a royal ship that had gone down off Louisbourg in 1725 with its cargo of 700,000 gold livres – the Quebec garrison's pay. The storm had been so violent that all 310 passengers perished, including the Louisbourg engineer and Governor Ramesay's son from Montreal. The sea raged so wildly not a single pig that washed up on shore survived.

Joseph was just finishing his raspberries when two soldiers arrived. One was a young man named Jehan from Vendée, who had been involved in salt-smuggling operations and had the makings of a revolutionary. He had just barely escaped the galleys. Thierry was the other soldier: a poor orphan from Paris who thought his ticket out of poverty would be to sign up! *We're no freer than the black slaves here*, Joseph thought. But his gold coin gave him the illusion of wealth for a fleeting second, and he decided to invite his companions out.

"There's a new cabaret on Rue Dauphine Bastion. They've got good rum and leg of lamb at a reasonable price. It'll be a nice change from the slop we eat! The drinks are on me."

Jehan and Thierry eagerly accepted the invitation. They stepped out onto the narrow muddy street under a light drizzle. A pig wallowed in the filth.

"Let's catch it!" Thierry shouted.

Slightly stunned by the noise of all the festivities, the pig still managed to slip from between their hands several times. They finally cornered it in a dead end.

"I'll hide it in the barracks," Thierry offered.

An edict allowed inhabitants to appropriate roaming pigs since they had become such a nuisance in the city and a danger to small children.

"I'll meet you at the cabaret," he shouted as he walked off.

Joseph and Jehan entered the noisy, smoke-filled tavern. Unfortunately for Joseph and his companion, the tin porringers were empty; there was no lamb left. But there was still rum and wine, and they didn't deprive themselves! The gloom and the effects of the famine and blockade were more keenly felt on a holiday. Even the liberation of their friends who had been taken prisoner in Boston brought no joy because it increased the number of mouths to feed. Thierry arrived, but since the curfew was fast approaching, they had to head back to the barracks.

* * *

Joseph began eyeing another job. Gunners were better paid: they got six livres more per month and received bonuses for hitting their targets with the cannonballs. Theirs was an elite unit that had certain privileges, including being excused from working on the fortifications. Joseph's experience with the cannons on *Le Succès* helped him get hired on as an assistant gunner. He let his beard grow, polished his sabre, wore a blue coat with red trim and white buttons, and learned to lovingly polish the black cannons mounted on their red wooden frame. He threw himself into his tasks as a way of forgetting his troubles. It got to the point where his cannons became a fetish and every shot he fired sounded like music to his ears.

* * *

September passed, then October. On the 1st of November, the Day of the Dead, the weather was particularly foggy.

"Let's go to the fishing village to my friend DesRoches' house. Sometimes he serves meals," Thierry suggested.

"I can't," Joseph replied. "After sunset, the fortress is closed and the Dauphine gate is guarded by thirty soldiers. We risk a flogging or, worse, the dungeon."

"They'll never know. We'll come back at dawn with the merchants and fishermen coming into town."

Thierry's suggestion calmed Joseph's fears, for it was exactly what he'd hoped to hear.

The DesRoches home was a simple fishing hut with a thatched roof. Next to it was a big, sturdy rowboat equipped with a sail. DesRoches used it to fish for cod a few leagues off the coast. Inside on the hardpacked ground, the only furniture was a large table, benches, and a few small empty barrels for seats. Any cooking was done in a huge fireplace, and a big pot of boiled cod sat in the middle. On each side of the fireplace were bunk beds covered in straw. Above the entrance, a rifle hung on two wooden hooks. In an adjoining room were fishing gear and a few barrels of spruce beer made from spruce buds steeped in molasses and brandy. The DesRoches were in their sixties and were a simple, hospitable couple used to housing Basque and Norman seamen as well as evening "escapees" looking to get away from the monotony of the barracks. Jean Lelarge, a ship's captain at Louisbourg, and his brother-in-law Télesphore Samson were already there. Sitting next to the fire was Pierre Detcheverry, a Basque privateer paid by the French. He claimed the Basques showed Columbus the route to the New World. Detcheverry embodied the two great Basque virtues: through his physical strength and endurance he represented the first, indorra, and through his strength of character and stoicism in times of hardship, the second, sendorra, a moral counterpart to the first. DesRoches was busy giving the latest news. "Valérien Louis, the one they call 'the Bourguignon,' who used to be a soldier and stonecarver, refused to plead guilty to theft during his trial, even after they used a hot poker on him several times."

"It can't be easy to keep protesting your innocence under that kind of treatment," Joseph broke in.

"And his troubles are only beginning. The bailiwick's attorney ordered him flogged at the four corners of the city, then tied to the stake and branded with a hot iron: a fleur-de-lys on his shoulder. As if that weren't enough, he'll be sentenced for life to the king's galleys."

Joseph shivered at the thought of such barbaric treatment. There was no mercy when thieves were poor!

"Don't you have any better news for us than that?" asked Jehan, who hadn't lost his sense of humour.

"Not really," DesRoches continued. "Other than the fact that Abbot Leloutre's Mi'kmaq weren't able to recapture Port-Royal."

Captain Lelarge exploded, "How do you expect Indians to succeed with their tomahawks where Duvivier's troops failed with their rifles… We promised to send Louisbourg our warships *Caribou* and *L'Ardent*, but we never did… We missed our chance to take back Acadia."

The privateer Detcheverry was equally furious, "It's the governor who's at fault; he's too frightened by the English blockade. We could have won the battle with a few cannons. With my ship, if I'd been asked, I would have succeeded," he bragged.

"What about the Acadians from Grand'Pré and Port-Royal?" Joseph asked.

"I think they're going to wait to see which way the wind is blowing," said Lelarge. "René LeBlanc has a lot of influence over there and he's in favour of collaborating with the British."

"That's understandable. He has contracts with them," Samson said.

Mrs. DesRoches, a woman who never minced her words, put in her two bits' worth, "Patriotism is just another word for money and self-interest!"

Joseph disagreed. He thought, *Gauthier helped the French. It's true he has contracts in Louisbourg and that his daughter is married to a garrison officer, but he runs the risk of imprisonment and ruin if he's caught. He puts his honour before money.*

The discussion turned to the fortress.

"Louisbourg's walls will collapse at the first cannon shot," Thierry predicted. "Any fool knows you can't make mortar with sea sand."

Joseph let his thoughts on the art of war be known. "The engineers De Verville and De Verrier implemented principles of defence established by the French military engineer and marshal, the Marquis de Vauban, by building a fortress reputed to be a chef d'oeuvre where fortifications are concerned. But I don't see the logic in building a fortress that's surrounded by hills. If the British installed cannons on land, we couldn't defend ourselves since most of our cannons, the biggest ones, are placed so as to counter an attack coming from the sea."

"We're wasting money on the fortress instead of sending colonists. To think that rivers of blood are flowing in Europe when a few thousand French soldiers would be enough to ensure a victory," Samson said.

Detcheverry intervened, "The cost of Louisbourg is a carefully tended fiction. Don't forget the fortunes made in the cod trade, which has helped fill the Bourbons' coffers. There's also the need to protect New France and the fur trade. It never cost more to build the fortress, even in the free-spending years, than it costs every year to arm and send a large warship here. At little expense, France has a navy base and a trading port to enrich the mother country."

"Speaking of money," Thierry said, "you know the proverb 'No Switzerland without money.' Well, the Swiss in the Karrer regiment are unhappy. They're Lutherans and are only defending the fortress for the money. Now they're not being paid for their work on the fortifications. I'm afraid a mutiny is in the works."

A feeling of malaise blew through the hut. Hunger, war, mutiny, what next! Lelarge, who'd been planning to arm the *Brasdor*, a ship belonging to the entrepreneur Maillet, with cannons, muskets, sabres, axes, and a hundred-man crew, began wondering how sound his project was; it seemed he could well be up against forces stronger than he was. Like any good hostess, Mrs. DesRoches knew when a change was needed. She fetched a pitcher of rum that she set down on the table next to the steaming pot. "It's the best cod in all America," she explained. "My husband only kept the lingcod. He's been fishing here for fifty years and, when we lived in France, he made the crossing every spring."

"How long has there been fishing around Louisbourg?" Joseph asked.

"To give you an idea," Detcheverry answered, "when the writer Marc Lescarbot came to Canso in 1607 and met an old Basque fisherman, Captain Savalette from San Juan de Luz, the Basque was on his forty-second Atlantic crossing. And others had been coming long before that!"

Chapter 11

The port of Louisbourg could be called the key to the
French and British colonies in North America. Control
of the port would make the king of Great Britain ruler
of the entire northern continent as far south as the
French settlements along the Mississippi (Louisiana).
With an influx of British subjects, given this country's
healthy climate, within one or two centuries it could
become as populated as France and serve as a foundation
for the superiority of British power over the European
continent.

– Shirley, Governor of Massachusetts

Joseph was on watch duty on November 30th in the sentinel
box at the Dauphine demi-bastion. He stood guard for one
hour as prescribed by the winter schedule; that was quite long
enough for him to be chilled through and through despite a
few swigs of alcohol. It had been a particularly miserable day.
The sea fog had never lifted, a light drizzle drenched him to
the bone, and the wind whipped the coastline and cut off the
tops of scraggy spruce trees. Around noon, huge gusts of wind
blew and the sea pounded the capes. Late in the afternoon, the
gusts died down and wet snow blanketed the ramparts. The
snow fell in heavy flakes driven horizontally by a wind so
strong it cut one's breath off. It was hard to imagine a more
turbulent, melancholy landscape. All day long, the port was

busy gearing up for the departure for France of four thousand men and fifty-three ships, including four warships and six huge ships belonging to the Compagnie des Indes; the convoy would take advantage of the cover of darkness to sail unseen past the English cannons.

It was about time, Joseph thought. *The level of rationing was getting to be quite alarming.*

Joseph counted the ships as they left the port and wondered why he wasn't leaving on one of them. Off to see and touch Emilie, to come full circle, break the spell. The question lingered in his mind as he watched the unending procession of ships vanish into the night.

* * *

Joseph had matured over the long months spent rubbing shoulders with other soldiers and witnessing plots being hatched and unravelling on a daily basis. He was sick of seeing the officers and gentry getting rich on the backs of the soldiers and people; the injustice appalled him. "They're con artists getting rich at the colony's expense," he concluded. Troop morale was at its lowest point, and the horrid weather only made matters worse. What's more, the stench of rancid cod wafted constantly over the ramparts. Tension increased another notch when, a few days before Christmas, the soldiers received their bimonthly rations. The peas and dry beans for the soup had gone bad and caused illness and diarrhea. "Fresh vegetables are being hoarded for the people with money," was the word in the barracks. When the officers requisitioned the wood the soldiers had chopped to heat the barracks, it was as though they'd thrown a match into a woodpile. This was intolerable! Wood was as important as bread in the winter.

* * *

Joseph was on duty on the evening of December 26th at the mansion of the Governor Louis du Pont du Chambon. During the festivities, they needed enough wood to heat the fireplaces. Joseph was able to watch "high society" in action and see the distance that separated him from them. All kinds of beautiful people paraded through the mansion: members of the council and the bailiwick, the entire Admiralty, the king's scribe, the king's engineers and surveyors and, of course, the officers, who were all members of the aristocracy. Governor du Chambon was the successor to DuQuesnel, who had died in October. Du Chambon's wife was the beautiful Jeanne Mius d'Entremont. The new governor had lost his soldiers' respect because of his minimal expertise in the art of war and his underhanded money-making deals. The soldiers couldn't forgive him for having appointed his three sons and four nephews to command positions.

Between two trips to fetch wood, Joseph caught a glimpse of the infantry captain Joseph DuPont Duvivier, the richest man in Louisbourg, wiping his brow with an embroidered handkerchief. The gentleman – whose wealth came from his ownership of fertile lands in the county of Cognac – was not in a festive mood; he was worried about his defeat at Port-Royal when a victory would have bathed him in glory! He blamed Captain Michel de Gannes, who was busy playing pool right then, for his expedition's failure. As for De Gannes, his thoughts too were on his dispute with Duvivier, whom he hated passionately for his slandering tongue and the underhand dealings that had allowed him to monopolize fishing operations. But the most noteworthy guest was without doubt Commissaire-Ordonnateur François Bigot, responsible for the day-to-day administration of Louisbourg, economic policies, and issues of civil law, as well as guardian of the public treasury. Everyone knew that he used public funds to reproduce in Louisbourg the pomp of Versailles, and the soldiers suspected him of holding back from their pay the money he needed to fund repairs to the fortifications.

Candles lit a table groaning under succulent meats seasoned with rare spices, brandied fruit served on porcelain from China, wine, and fine liqueurs. Major Jean-François Eurry de La Perelle strutted about in his new uniform while savouring chocolates and talking to Bigot.

"A revolt is brewing among the soldiers," he confided to Bigot.

"Those wretches are never happy! We should hang the most insolent among them as an example to the others. That would calm them down."

"Or stir them up even more! No. In the fall, some soldiers paid the price, a noose around their necks, begging the crowd for forgiveness on the church steps. It only fanned the flames of revolt. I think we'd be wiser to give them better rations for Christmas, warmer clothes, and even a bit of brandy."

"They have the same privileges as the soldiers in the French empire and the Quebec garrison. Next you'll be wanting us to bring them iced drinks in the heat of August."

This was a reference to the picnic banquets during which the aristocracy and officers drank fresh drinks served on ice that came from a shed with a cone-shaped roof, which served as an icebox.

"Why not, when all's said and done?" insisted La Perelle, resigned to the fact there'd be nothing forthcoming from Bigot.

It must be said that La Perelle, who had more dealings with the men than Bigot did, was genuinely concerned. But even La Perelle was far from realizing that a mutiny was in the works.

La Perelle couldn't see outside because of the frost on the windows, and he tried not to think of the soldiers freezing in the pea-soup fog. He found it reassuring to think of how invincible the fortress was and to exaggerate in his own mind how long the perimeter of ramparts was, how deep the ditches, how many cannons and mortars there were, and the thickness of the bombardment-proof arches. Shortly before midnight, Joseph rejoined the soldiers who, for their part, had nothing to celebrate. They had received the usual gifts: a few pitchers of molasses brandy and salt pork. But nothing to dissipate the resentment and gloom, which was only made worse by the warm, inaccessible glow they could see coming from the mansion while a musical air was carried to them on the mist. Joseph began to regret his decision to seek a life of adventure; the thought of his family celebrating joyously at Ruisseau kept resurfacing. He had received news from Angélique from a coureur de bois. She told him about the emptiness she'd been left with after his departure. Angélique, his beloved, from whom he fled as though from himself. He imagined Saint-Jean, the tribe's patriarch, cradling his – Joseph's – daughters and telling them stories while Membertou lit his grandfather's pipe.

A fat lot of good my wandering has done me, he admitted to himself.

The night was far from calm. Swiss soldiers could be heard talking loudly and running back and forth.

"Some officers keep the names of dead soldiers on their lists so they can take their pay and rations," one of the Swiss soldiers said.

"They say they go so far as to sell the uniforms of dead soldiers," yet another exploded.

"It's beneath any soldier to clean the governor's latrine," a third one said in outrage.

An ominous silence descended on Louisbourg.

Joseph was awakened at daybreak by an infernal racket. The one hundred and fifty soldiers of the Karrer regiment were all yelling at once, swearing at the French soldiers, accusing them of cowardice for their reluctance to mutiny. The Swiss hated the French anyway because they felt the latter were usually spared while the Swiss were being sent to the front lines as cannon fodder. The leader of the group unfurled a long scroll and proclaimed, "We hereby make known our demands: compensation for our participation in the Canso expedition, payment of the amount owing us for work on the fortifications, warm clean clothes, enough wood for heating, and proper food."

"We'll end up on the gallows," one French soldier moaned.

"Would you rather die in poverty here?" his neighbour retorted.

The soldier René-Antoine LeMoine, known as Saint-Amant de Paris, announced, "The Swiss are right; I'm sick and tired of eating stinking stews and sleeping on vermin-infested straw mats while the officers fill their pockets with our pay and spend their time partying."

With that, he clutched his drum to him and began sounding the call to arms on his way out of the barracks. Joseph brandished his privateer's sword. Others took up arms and followed them out. They were joined by more soldiers, all responding to the drum roll. A few officers tried to oppose the revolt, but any influence they had was gone. Some of them, the most reviled, were lucky to escape with their lives. In battle ranks led by thirty fusiliers, the soldiers marched through the city banging their drums. Only the gunners and French sergeants refused to participate.

On the evening of December 27th, the garrison went into celebration mode. A celebration that turned into something more resembling an orgy. The mutineers pillaged the stores and distributed pitchers of alcohol left and right. Drunken soldiers stumbled through the streets of Louisbourg, and the debauchery lasted all night long. In the morning, seeing that Bigot and Du Chambon refused to give in to the garrison's demands, a group of soldiers decided to invade the mansion. Some threatened to massacre the population and flee with the contents of the colony's coffers; others threatened to hand the fortress over to the English. Finally, Du Chambon surrendered. The victory went to the heads of several soldiers, who thought they could dispense with leaders altogether, especially since they now controlled the king's storehouses. Already, some soldiers were starting to tell merchants what price they were willing to pay. Joseph agreed with the soldiers' demands, but the anarchy made him uneasy since it made the fortress vulnerable to the slightest attack. *After all*, he thought, *I came here to defend my country.* So Joseph refused to take part in the unrest.

The atmosphere remained tense all winter long. Joseph was determined to return to Ruisseau. But how? Ice blocked the bay, and the Mi'kmaq band that migrated every year to Miramichi, forty leagues from Caraquet, had already left. He didn't dare undertake the trip on his own through the woods and in the snow. Of course, there was no way to send a letter to Angélique, but he wrote one anyway, a beautiful letter written on birchbark that he stored in a small chest next to Emilie's portrait. His letter expressed all his love for her and assured her he would never leave again. His nights were dogged with homesickness, and he fell into a deep melancholic state. His friends Thierry and Jehan tried to distract him, but they themselves weren't doing much better. To Joseph, it felt like winter would never end. He withdrew into his torpor while the city succumbed to anarchy. Du Chambon and Bigot were in despair, especially since they feared a British attack on the fortress. They were obliged to grant impunity to the garrison. In exchange, the mutineers promised to return to the ranks and defend Louisbourg. Joseph was thrilled with the outcome; he, too, was ready to fight in order to join Angélique and his children as soon as possible.

* * *

In early May back on the old continent, the war of succession in Austria between France and England raged on. In America, the French from Louisbourg and New France and the English from the thirteen British colonies were still fighting through privateers, each one trying to destroy the other's fishing vessels. There was the omnipresent Abbot Leloutre, grand vicar of Acadia and sagamo of the Mi'kmaq, loathed by the English in the colonies as the devil himself. They blamed him for instigating the native raids that sowed terror throughout the English territories. The price paid for an Indian scalp in New England's markets was on the rise. Abbot Leloutre came to Louisbourg with the Beaubassin tribe to reinforce their alliances. The governor gave the Beaubassin tobacco, buttons, and polished copper decorations. Joseph was able to speak briefly to the abbot, "You wouldn't happen to have news of my family in Ruisseau?"

"No, unfortunately not. The Indians didn't travel far this winter…"

Joseph expected as much, but felt a twinge of sorrow all the same. On the evening of May 6, 1745, Joseph saw the phantom ship. A huge ball of fire seemed to be floating above the waves. Inside, a black three-master with white sails could be seen. Joseph clearly saw the black pirate flag with the skull and crossbones before the sails were consumed by flames and the hull turned to charred timber. Afterwards, he thought he heard a cannon shot in the distance. *A bad omen for Louisbourg*, he thought bitterly.

The next day the *Saint-Domingue*, a Basque fishing vessel, announced the imminent arrival of the enemy fleet. On May 9th, Joseph was freezing his toes off on sentinel duty at the demi-bastion when he spotted a supply ship approaching. It didn't take him long to recognize the ship belonging to a man he liked, a man who had had a price put on his head by the English, Nicolas Gauthier. Gauthier arrived at Port-Royal with fifty head of cattle on board. On May 10th, under cover of the night fog, *La Société* got under way carrying a message for Versailles advising of the garrison's situation and announcing the arrival of the first English sailships. On the morning of May 11th, the enemy fleet gathered in Gabarus Bay a few leagues from Louisbourg. The colonies of Maine, Connecticut, New York, Massachusetts, New Hampshire, and Rhode Island had supplied the ships and the armed combattants. The troops were under the command of William Pepperell. The English commodore Peter Warren, who was stationed in the West Indies with his warships, had joined him.

Luck was against the forces under siege. On one side, there were fifteen hundred men, half of whom had been recruited from the ranks of fishermen and locals and barely knew how to use their weapons. On the other side, there were more than eight thousand invaders, most of whom were trained soldiers. Du Chambon scuttled a certain number of low-tonnage sailships to obstruct the entrance to the port. Jean Lelarge sacrificed one of his schooners and lined up a series of floating masts in the bottleneck. The battery at Île d'Entree was fortified where it commanded the narrow passage to the sea. Those who built Louisbourg had carefully situated the bastions so as to cover all angles under crossfire between cannons and muskets; geometry's wisdom had been applied to the fortifications! The artillery on the lee side made the fortress almost impregnable. But their plan had neglected something quite unforgivable. Having dismissed the possibility of invaders arriving by land, they hadn't fortified the heights with batteries or isolated redoubts. Their feeble efforts to drive back the landing in Gabarus Bay were in vain.

"Why didn't Du Chambon listen to Morpain's advice?" Joseph asked Jehan. "With the soldiers who've been holed up in the fortress, Captain Marin's troops from Quebec, and the Acadian militia, we could have stopped the landing. But the Governor of Louisbourg is an incompetent coward. The Quebec powers-that-be don't see us as part of their strategic defence. The governor only wants to defend Quebec, just like Vaudreuil who let Acadia slip through his hands in 1713."

"A brave band of Mi'kmaq from the Mirliguiche post won't be enough to change anything either," Jehan added.

"Mirliguiche means 'milky bay' because of the way the water looks just before a storm. And that's what's brewing now, a storm," Joseph concluded.

* * *

After the landing, the English dragged their cannons through woods and swamps while Du Chambon ordered all dwellings and fishing storehouses outside Louisbourg's walls to be burned to the ground and all twenty cannons of the Royal Battery, one league outside the city, to be decommissioned since they served no purpose against an attack by land. To decommission the cannons, the soldiers filled them with powder after first blocking the muzzle. In their haste, they botched the job and the invaders were able to use the Royal Battery to fire on the city. The month of May dragged on for Joseph and the others, under siege and powerless in their fortress and bombarded by the cannonballs and projectiles raining down on them. Despair, amplified by the death cries of the dying, infiltrated the ruins.

There's still a faint hope, Joseph kept saying to himself, *as long as the battery on Ile d'Entrée stops the English fleet from penetrating into the basin.*

Joseph, Jehan, and Thierry volunteered to defend the Ile d'Entrée battery. In June, they were still hanging on to the island, but they had lost count of the number of cannonballs and days gone by. Each new attack was more difficult to repel than the last. Joseph remembered the old legends of the knights of King Arthur. But this time, there was no Merlin, no Excalibur sword, no Grail to their rescue. The smell of blood and powder was everywhere… as were the moans of the wounded who had faced the volley of shots bare-chested! Rumours of all kinds kept circulating.

"They say there are as many as fifteen hundred injured and ill among the English," Jehan said.

"Everything hinges on the reinforcements," pronounced Joseph, who, in between the cannonfire, scanned the horizon in hopes of seeing ships flying the French flag. The Minister of the Navy, Maurepas, had in fact sent a few ships to Louisbourg: the *Renommée*, which was forced to turn back because of the blockade, and the *Vigilant*, armed with sixty-four cannon. The *Vigilant* and several hundred soldiers under the command of the Marquis of Maisonfort were all captured.

At dusk one evening in mid-June, a fleet appeared in the distance. The soldiers defending Ile d'Entrée knew their fate was sealed…

"The British flag!"

With their reinforcements, the English launched a new cannon attack from the fleet and land artillery. Still, a handful of men resisted, glued to the last cannons glowing red from unending cannonfire. The large three-deckers drew nearer, and a multitude of fire-spewing cannons announced the apocalypse with the infernal organ music of rows of cannons firing in unison. An exhausted Joseph, his hands and face black with powder, his uniform in tatters, his beard singed by fire, knew the English were coming in for the kill. He aimed one last shot and hit the schooner full of red uniforms dead on. Eventually, the few Louisbourg survivors withdrew to a city surrounded by broken ramparts as the English fleet entered the basin. Joseph managed to carry his gravely wounded friend Thierry, but he could do nothing for Jehan, who was already dead.

Only one house was left intact. On June 26th, a population decimated by disease, sleeplessness, and hardship petitioned the governor to surrender. There was hardly any powder left, nothing but a few barrels. Just enough for a final salvo. What's more, a breach in the Dauphin bastion made an entry possible using fascines. The battle was over.

* * *

Gauthier confided in Joseph, "Unless there's a miracle, it's all over… but thanks to a clause in the surrender, I'll be able to escape."

"How's that?" asked Joseph, surprised.

"Certain people who don't want to be seen by the English are authorized to wear masks as they leave! Come with me… We'll hide in Beaubassin until my wife and sons join us."

"That's fine with me, but how? Surely not everyone can wear a mask."

"Listen closely… As stipulated in the conditions of surrender, two wagons will leave the camp under the conditions of surrender to allow deserters from the English armies to flee. I'll make arrangements with the commander to have you on one of the wagons."

"But what will we do in Beaubassin?"

"We'll hide out with the Mi'kmaq… Afterwards, Abbot Leloutre will help us escape to Miramichi. From there, you can rejoin your family."

Joseph's fears dissipated as he felt the rekindling of hope.

"There's no other solution," Gauthier continued. "The garrison will be repatriated to France. Those who stay behind will become slaves working for the English and will have to repair the fortress or extract coal from the mine!"

* * *

On June 28th, the officers acceded to every one of the inhabitants' demands without exception, and the fortress surrendered honorably. Louisbourg, the impregnable fortress, had
been taken! The surrender also decided the fate of Ile Saint-
Jean and the soldiers started looting in the Port-Lajoie[1]
region. The English were already talking about deporting the
Acadians from the island but had to abandon their plan
because there was no means of transportation. When the
French reinforcement ships the *Mars*, the *Saint-Michel*, the
Parfaite, the *Argonaute*, and the *Mercure* arrived within sight of
Louisbourg, the worst had happened.

Joseph left the ruins of the fortress in a covered wagon
just as Reverend Samuel Moody of Boston, a seventy-year-old
Puritan, was destroying the "idols of Satan's fortress!" with an
axe. Joseph had but one thought, to return to Angélique and
his family, vowing that, come what may, he would never leave
again. Nicolas Gauthier and Joseph were to rendezvous with
some patriots in the Beaubassin region, seventy-five leagues
away. Waiting for them there were Gauthier's sons, Joseph and
Pierre, as well as Joseph Broussard, known as Beausoleil, Louis
Hébert, Joseph Le Blanc, known as Le Maigre, Philippe
LeRoy and a few others, all guilty of grand treason. An
English proclamation identified them as Acadian rebels and
offered a reward of fifty pounds each for their capture.
Gauthier was particularly worried about his wife Marie Allain
and his youngest son, whom the British had put in irons in
Port-Royal. Although he could do nothing about the arrest, he
was able to bring good news to Joseph.

"Some Basque fishermen will be returning to their fishing fleet off Miscou. You can join them if you want."

"Of course I do!" Joseph exclaimed.

He all but hugged the man.

---

1. Today's Charlottetown.

Chapter 12

Leave, my cousin, and use the troops I've given you to take back Louisbourg. If that is impossible, take possession of an equivalent or at least settle in the land of Acadia in order to facilitate further conquests in my name. Go to the rescue of my colony Quebec in whatever way possible. Its subjects are loyal to me and I hold them dear; you will send them war munitions and the Ponthieu regiment will winter there. I entrust you, dear cousin, to God's care and my weapons to his blessing.
– Instructions written by King Louis XV
to the Duc d'Anville in 1746

A seaman who refused to pray "attentively and reverently" was under threat of punishment. On his first offence, he could be sentenced to a fine; on the second offence, to eight days of nothing but bread and water; on the third offence, to the ship's slipway. The latter punishment involved tying the condemned man by the wrists to a sail close, then having him hoisted by the close to the yard... and dropped abruptly into the sea.
– *Nos Racines – L'Histoire vivante des Québécois*

Joseph returned to the fold aboard a Basque fishing brigantine on its way to join its fishing fleet in the Baye des Chaleurs. After seventy-two hours at sea during which he never stopped counting the minutes, he finally set foot in Ruisseau. Angélique was waiting for him, more beautiful than in the dreams he'd had while standing guard shrouded in Louisbourg's fog. He hugged Geneviève and Josette close to him; they had trouble recognizing their father in this stranger who, to all intents and purposes, they were seeing for the first time. Membertou ran up to greet him next. He had grown considerably, was now tall and lanky. Traces of the man-to-be were already visible. The Mi'kmaq welcomed him with the simple hospitality of woods people. But there was a vestige of sadness in their expression, which seemed to prevent them from rejoicing fully. Joseph took Angélique in his arms.

"What's wrong?" he asked worriedly.

She dissolved into tears. "It's my father," she stammered.

She led him to the slate-roofed house. There, lying on a straw mattress surrounded by loyal friends, a sallow Saint-Jean was breathing his last.

"I wanted to see you one last time before I died," he articulated with great difficulty.

His thoughts could no longer be pinned down by words and, as death approached, his words turned to silence, the ultimate truth.

"I entrusted Membertou with a secret, a mission he'll explain to you... Continue the work already begun... Other white men will come one day... Do you remember when we saw from the island a large village along the coast..."

He could say no more, exhausted by the effort. For several hours, he hovered between consciousness and delirium – his childhood in Rouen, his time on the king's galleys – before sinking into a deep sleep.

Joseph felt the full weight of the new responsibility on his shoulders. How could he ensure the future of his family in this unsettled country? What was the mission entrusted to Membertou by his grandfather? It was impossible to talk to Membertou, who had shut himself off from the others in his grief. Membertou's thoughts were consumed by his grandfather's request, "When I die, you will place on my birchbark shroud the gold cross from the island treasure."

Saint-Jean wasn't the only person on death's doorstep. An epidemic, probably spread by infected material from a

European ship, decimated the tribe despite Angélique's potions and Fiery Elouèzes' incantations. The latter paced, wildly shaking his rattle carved in the shape of a bear and a man. The women painted the bodies green, red, blue, and yellow and wrapped them in the finest bark, and the men transported them to the camp to be installed on a platform a dozen feet above the ground in order to raise the deceased closer to the sky and keep wild animals at bay. Then the bodies were left to dry in the sun before being placed in a birchbark chest and buried with presents: bows, arrows, snowshoes, otter and beaver clothing, and urns full of corn. Everything the deceased would need for their final journey! Angélique was extremely agitated and aggressive.

"If you had stayed home, this wouldn't have happened," she finally accused Joseph.

Since his return to Ruisseau, he had reeled from one shock after another. Old Saint-Jean, who had represented the lasting nature of things to him and been like the birth father he'd never known, would be leaving him soon. *As if that isn't bad enough, Angélique blames me*, he thought sadly. *Saint-Jean's last moments have made us all edgy...*

Meanwhile, Saint-Jean, indifferent to the preoccupations of those around him, clung to life still.

* * *

Early May 1746. Although caught up in Austria's War of Succession, France was motivated by the energy of despair to make one last attempt to take back Louisbourg and Acadia from the English. Maurepas, the Minister of the Navy under Louis XV, sent a formidable armada of seventy-two ships... The line vessels, frigates, corvettes, store ships, hospital ships, and carriers of troops and provisions gathered off La Rochelle. One-third of the French fleet! Seven hundred cannons! Seven thousand men under the command of La Rochefoucauld, the Duc d'Anville. The most impressive array of naval strength ever sent to America by Versailles. Their mission was to take back Louisbourg, Port-Royal, and Grand'Pré, destroy Boston, and lay waste to the coast of New England.

The services of Théotime Chiasson, apothecary, were required by the *Northumberland*, an admiral ship in the fleet under the command of Pierre-Jacques de la Jonquière, who was slated to replace the Marquis de la Galissonnière, Governor of Canada. During their first week at sea, the opportunity arose for the apothecary to make the acquaintance of the Duc d'Anville, who had lost part of his gums along with the tooth a surgeon had extracted. It was not easy to do much better than that given the corkscrew-like instrument with its fitted metal hook on the end that the surgeon had to use for the delicate task. The apothecary was needed to prepare a powder to calm the duke's pain. The duke was a man of great courage, as Voltaire proclaimed, but moreso on the battlefield than where a toothache was concerned. Extroverted, fun-loving, and optimistic by nature, Théotime gained in rank thanks to the duke's gratitude and was regularly seen in the company of the officers. Wreathed in his newfound prestige, Théotime moved to the rear cabins where the officers stayed. His wife, Adélaïde, who usually served as his assistant in his Poitiers pharmacy, had been granted quite exceptional permission to accompany him. More exceptional still, their eleven-month-old daughter, Mathilde, was along for the journey. The family settled in among the flasks, fioles, herbs, and powders in what were rather confined quarters.

* * *

Meanwhile in New France, the governor dispatched Claude de Ramezay, son of a former governor of Montreal, and seven hundred men to link up in Acadia with the Leloutre tribe. The troops waited for the duke's fleet in the Beaubassin region. Ramezay put his nephew, Charles de Boishébert, in charge of the detachment responsible for running the English out of Port-Lajoie on Ile Saint-Jean. A mission that was carried out in record time!

* * *

The armada's departure did not augur well. Due to unfavourable winds, the ships were blocked for six weeks at Ile d'Aix. Disease was beginning to spread through the holds, and the English fleet patrolled offshore, ready to pounce on its prey. When the fleet finally left the island on June 22nd, rusty-black clouds the colour of coagulated blood seemed an ominous sign. However, the wind changed and allowed the fleet to elude the English squadrons. Neverthess, it still took the fleet almost a whole month to leave the Bay of Biscay, a month during which it suffered heavy damage: sails swept away by the wind, broken masts, and a few collisions. On July 23rd, south of the Azores at approximately 32 degrees latitude, the wind died down. The heat was so intense the deck was like a furnace, and the sun reflecting off the sea burned skin that had already been weathered by the salt spray. Stillness imprisoned the fleet like a noose. Three weeks later, the immobility and still-suffocating heat continued. Most navigators had never heard of such conditions before.

Typhoid fever, dysentery, and scurvy wreaked havoc, and entire sections of the ship were placed under quarantine. On board the *Northumberland*, Théotime spent morning to night trundling his kit, but the ipecac-based vomiting agents, the pharmaceuticals, and the cochlear spirit drops did nothing to combat scurvy. He was given permission to increase the rum rations, which were served with onions and beets, and the cooks spit-roasted a few sheep and oxen on deck, livestock that under normal conditions would have made it to Acadia alive. The meat did help somewhat, but so little...

Seeing the ships immobilized from morning to night was demoralizing for the crews. Time seemed to stop. The ship had become hell, and the only escape was into dreamland. A horrific stench rose from the dark holds where mildewed hammocks hung. An odour of excrement and vomit persisted in the air and, at times, it seemed to Théotime that the boat was nothing but one huge latrine. Not even the fumes rising from the pails of tar or the red-hot shot belowdeck managed to dissipate the putrid fumes. The holds were taken over by rats, fleas, and lice. Huge quantities of provisions rotting in poorly sealed barrels sold by unscrupulous merchants had to be thrown overboard.

Every day, in groups of seven, all using the same mess kit, the seamen received their ration and the inevitable dumpling stew and salt pork, sometimes accompanied by peas and dried cod. To drink there was nothing but vile water to which a bit of molasses had been added to make it more palatable. The rancid wine and bitter cider that still remained were kept for the officers! Drinking water reserves were getting dangerously low; only a few dozen barrels remained. One bright morning, Théotime found a dead frog in a barrel; its usefulness as a water quality gauge was ended! For some time now, Théotime hadn't needed to prescribe cornachine powder to patients needing a purgative: nature had taken over! But worse yet were the death rattle and delirium of the dying praying for deliverance. Some, shaken by violent fevers, threw themselves into the sea. Every morning, the chaplain perched on the round-house to sing the *Veni Creator*, then the crew knelt for the litanies to the Virgin Mary and saints before moving on to the ritual for the dead. One ship's boy carried a cross, another a torch. The remains, wrapped in an old cloth, were carried to the deck end and, after prayers and the sprinkling of holy water, thrown overboard, a cannonball carefully attached to the body. Théotime felt like screaming whenever Abbot Maillard recited the prayer for the dead. If the prayer wasn't being recited on the *Northumberland*, it could be heard coming from the vessels to starboard or port! Aside from a spell of vomiting, Théophile's health stood up well, but he couldn't say as much for his brave Adélaïde whose complexion grew more sickly and diaphonous by the day. She fell prey to the delirium that had invaded the holds. On August 9th, Adélaïde was the one they wrapped in an old guy-rope cloth. Poor Théotime! Reeling from shock, he was unable to shed a single tear. The desire to hang on, to survive burned deep inside him. He still had Mathilde, whose babbling translated her great serenity in the face of the hardship all around her.

On August 10th, the sky turned an ominous black. A tropical storm was brewing. Lightning struck, toppling foresail masts, exploding charge bag stores, and killing troops on the *Mars*. If he had to choose between the merciless heat and the storm, Théotime would choose the rain, especially since the men could finally replenish their supplies of fresh water.

Another month passed. The sickness had spread; no one had been spared. There were almost no able-bodied sailors left to man the ship. On September 15th, near the Acadian coast, not far from Ile aux Sables – known as "the seamen's cemetery" – a thick fog enveloped the fleet. A storm of unheard-of violence was unleashed and the temperature dropped. Seamen climbing down from the top mast tables to brail the sails dropped frozen to the deck, and only hot poultices to the chest gave them a modicum of relief. Jean Lelarge, the Louisbourg captain piloting the admiral ship, took refuge in prayer; at two o'clock that afternoon he prayed to an ink-black sky under which only shadows were visible on the ship! The powerful three-deckers were battered about like flimsy corks. At times, it was impossible to distinguish between sea and sky. Théotime felt as though his stomach had been left behind, clutching at clouds whenever the ship dived into the abyss and the masts grazed the crests of the waves. A transport ship collided with the *Amazone* and sank like a stone. Then a flame – Saint-Elmo's fire – shot out from the foresail mast, thunder shook the ship, and the sky sent jagged Dantean bolts of lightning streaking past the fleet. Lightning struck a ship starboard, sweeping away its topgallant and top mast and igniting the powder storeroom. The ship caught on fire like a small volcano spewing lava.

At daybreak, a thick fog still covered the sea, hiding the coast and its dangerous dunes. The ships shot their cannon or muskets and rang bells to signal their presence and avoid ramming each other.

"What good are navigational tools in weather like this?" Théotime worried. "Admittedly, the compass points to the north and the Jacob's staff gives our latitude, but where is land? The astrolabe determines longitude as long as the stars are visible, but under this jet-black sky and in this fog... We still have the sounding line to measure our depth but what else does fate, in its relentless pounding, have in store for us?" he sighed, fearing they would hit a shoal at any minute. The fog finally lifted. As far as the eye could see, there was nothing but desolation, a sea littered with masts, crates, and debris. The *Argonaute* was minus both mast and rudder; the *Caribou's* starboard cannons had been washed overboard. As for the *Mars*, its hold full of water, it set sail for Martinique with the *Alcide*. A trail of ships all the way to the West Indies. Some had run aground on Île aux Sables, a long, isolated stretch of land a hundred miles off the coast, as though reuniting with the ghosts of the fifty convict settlers the Marquis de la Roche, a Breton, abandoned there in 1598, only eleven of whom survived until rescue came five years later!

From the *Northumberland*, no matter how hard Théotime looked, he could not see a single sail on the horizon. Supplies were running low. The crew owed its survival to the capture of an English schooner en route for Boston loaded with supplies. A pilot was recruited as well from the English ship since Jean Lelarge had been laid low by fever; the Englishman was given the choice between piloting the ship or ending his days at the bottom of the ocean, with cannonballs for ballast. On September 20th, the *Northumberland* dropped anchor in Chibouctou Bay. But the other ships did not show up and, on land, there was no sign of life outside the colourful autumn leaves. The Duc d'Anville, suffering from scurvy, was desperate. Six days later, still nothing. That was when he lost all hope and died of apoplexy.

That same evening, Vice-Admiral d'Estourmel arrived on the *Trident* with what remained of the fleet: the *Gironde*, the *Mégère*, the *Diamant*, the *Léopard*, the *Tigre*, the *Castor*, the *Aurore* and a few troop carriers. It was high time. On board the *Trident*, the epidemic had reached such proportions that there were no healthy men left to pilot the ship. On land Bigot had asked the Acadians, Mi'kmaq, Maliseet, Abnaki, and Abbot Leloutre to find provisions and organize hospitals. Tents were raised along the coast for the invalids and a stubborn Joseph Le Blanc, known as Le Maigre, gathered together 230 head of cattle with the help of Nicolas Gauthier. The world was topsy-turvy: the former colony had come to the rescue of the homeland!

A stormy meeting took place among officers on September 28th. La Jonquière was against having the fleet return to France and wanted to take back all of Acadia. He eventually prevailed over Commander d'Estourmel, who left the meeting in an extreme state of agitation. The late Duc d'Anville's aide-de-camp Isaac de la Tournaye, who could sense trouble brewing, called on Théotime to watch over the commander, who was becoming delirious. Théotime was not doing that well himself, but he took up a position not far from D'Estourmel's cabin. When the moon was at its zenith, he heard a loud cry, "It's my fault the men are dying; this is punishment from God!" Precious time was wasted trying to knock down the bolted door. The commander lay in a pool of his own blood. He had killed himself with his sword. For Théotime, this was the last straw. He retired to his cubbyhole and let his head fall into his apothecary's mortar, as though he wanted to crush it with the pestle. He was incapable of moving, immobilized as if in a vulture's talons.

La Jonquière took command of the fleet, or more precisely, what was left of the fleet. "It's too late, alas, to launch an attack on Port-Royal," he despaired. "The autumn storms, illness… our only choice is to return to France."

The return was carried out under the same cloud of illness, famine, and storms. There was still no news of the *Mercure*, the hospital ship, or of twenty-one of the troop carriers. Close to three thousand men were either dead, missing at sea, or buried on Acadian soil. The natives gave the seamen's cemetery a wide berth when illness began to spread among them. That fall, isolated ships made it back to France, as though acting out the last scene in a Greek tragedy, which, had it played out differently, would have changed the course of history. Crushed by so much hardship, Théotime let the sickness run its course, and Abbot Leloutre accompanied him in his final moments.

"I entrust my daughter to you, Father."

"My son, go in peace to the heavenly kingdom. A Grand'Pré family will adopt her and raise her as their own."

Théotime breathed his last among Grand'Pré's orchards, carrying with him the last image he saw, a mauve sun rising behind Cap Blomidon, hoping against hope that his little Mathilde, now fourteen months old, would some day take her revenge on history.

Chapter 13

Old Caton always ended his speeches with "*Delenda Carthago*" (Carthage must be destroyed), a quote that has stood for obsession ever since. On June 24, 1746, after speaking to the Massachusetts Legislature of the need to deport the Acadians, Governor Shirley proclaimed, "*Canada delenda est.*"

Peace had been restored to Ruisseau. Almost miraculously, old Saint-Jean had survived and suffered no sequels from his illness other than a slight slurring of his speech. He did have to be careful what he ate, however. But he often gave in to temptation, despite his daughter's scolding. Angélique had been unable to find where he kept his small chest full of sweets; he had concealed it in a cavity behind a framed picture of the La Rochelle harbour. Who would ever think of looking there? Angélique and Joseph were reconciled thanks to the birth of their son on November 17, 1746. They baptized him René, like his mother's great-grandfather.

"A son to carry on the bloodline," Joseph said proudly.

His trials had definitely matured him and, this time, he didn't just dance and play the violin to celebrate their son's birth; he looked after the child's day-to-day needs: changing him, bathing him, feeding him, singing lullabies to him, and rocking him to sleep.

"He wasn't like this with the girls," Angélique remarked.

In her heart of hearts she forgave him, however, and told herself he had grown to accept family life. Saint-Jean was terribly proud of his grandson, another reason for feasting on pastries. Joseph had even more cause for rejoicing. Emilie haunted his dreams less frequently, and his memories of the times they had spent together faded as he opened up to Angélique's love and wove stronger ties with his children. Having been entrusted with the secret to the island grotto revealed by his father-in-law, he felt as though he were the guardian of several civilizations. It was a secret shared with Angélique since, during his illness, Saint-Jean had let slip some rather enigmatic words. *Now I can look on the future with serenity,* Joseph said to himself, *with a treasure to draw on should the survival of the Mi'kmaq or the Acadians be threatened.*

It never crossed his mind to take so much as a single coin for himself; the same held true for Angélique. Saint-Jean had thought it prudent, however, to keep Jean-Baptiste in the dark since he had his doubts about the latter's trustworthiness where riches were concerned.

The battles of Louisbourg that had been fought so much farther south had not affected life in the Baye des Chaleurs, however, around the hearth people in Ruisseau commented on the tragic tale of the Duc d'Anville's fleet. Certain episodes had acquired almost legendary status. It was said that during the return voyage to France, the crew of *La Palme* had a rather unique experience. Since there were no provisions left on board, a rat hunt was organized and the rats were sold for a king's ransom; even cockroach soup became a favourite dish. But some of the crew were reduced to gnawing on ropes for nourishment. That was when a seaman remembered the five English prisoners in the hold. In defiance of the officers, the crew decided to hand over one of the prisoners to the butcher: the lucky prisoner was to be the one who drew a short straw. Luckily, a Portuguese ship loaded with sheep happened by and saved the poor wretch; the crew devoured the barely cooked sheep.

"For once, white men appreciated raw food," remarked Membertou.

During the long evenings, the story was often told for years to come of the only victory of the war: a victory for the locals, namely the small three-hundred-man troop that decided to take back Grand'Pré after the defeat of D'Anville's fleet. Under the orders of Coulon de Villiers, the troop of natives, Canadiens, and Acadians set out from Beaubassin and arrived in Grand'Pré after a seventeen-day trek under falling snow through woods, marshes, fifteen-foot snowbanks, and over frozen lakes, during which they broke sleds and snow-shoes on stumps and dead trees. Abbot Maillard accompanied the brave men and gave them general absolution before the battle. With morale at its highest despite earlier disasters, they attacked the doors of the fortified homes, swinging their axes, and dispatched almost half of the six hundred enemy soldiers.

"To think that a handful of our combatants just about managed to take back Acadia, while a third of the French fleet was powerless to do a thing," Membertou said ironically.

"That shouldn't surprise you. They come here to wage war the European way, saying 'you shoot first, dear Englishmen,'" Saint-Jean added. "They know nothing about the country and look down on our way of fighting."

Joseph kept silent; he agreed with his father-in-law's comments but found Membertou's remark about the French fleet unfair. "After all," he reasoned, "neither we nor the French have any control over disease or storms."

* * *

In October 1748, fresh from its victory on the battlefields of Europe, France signed the Aix-la-Chapelle treaty. France decided to take back Louisbourg in exchange for the city of Madras in India and territories won in the Netherlands. It had been a long time since Ruisseau had received any good news, but Joseph saw no cause for rejoicing because Acadia, including Grand'Pré and Port-Royal, was left under English jurisdiction. "All it would have taken was one single warship from D'Anville's fleet for France to take back Acadia," he fumed.

But something more pernicious had been eating away at Joseph's patriotism ever since he learned that, further to the insurrection he'd been part of in Louisbourg, eight soldiers had been sentenced to death despite the promises of impunity, while obviously corrupt officers had been promoted! The something in question was hatred, and it was directed at all representatives of French authority. His hatred was such that he wondered whether he shouldn't adopt a new language and religion.

* * *

Unwelcome news circulated in the fall of 1749 in Acadia, that of the founding of Halifax on Chibouctou Bay, not far from the small island on which the Duc d'Anville had been buried. He must have rolled over in his grave at the sight of three thousand Irish, German, English, and French Calvinist emigrants landing there.

"This is what France's Catholic fanaticism leads to," grumbled Saint-Jean. "It leads to our enemies welcoming French Protestants with open arms!"

Joseph pointed out that the bell had tolled for Acadia with the founding of Halifax, and that, in future, the English would be in a position to rid themselves of the Acadians!

"To think that England has sent in one fell swoop almost as many settlers as France did over a whole century!" Saint-Jean commented.

Since bad news comes in threes, an earthquake shook the Baye des Chaleurs, unleashing a tidal wave that destroyed the camp as well as the fishing installations. They were able to rescue both Joseph's *Phantom Ship* and Jean-Baptiste's schooner, christened *Sikitoumeg* or "where the bay flows into the sea," by letting the waves carry them inland. Lightning started fires in Miscou, Ruisseau, and Poquemouche. The Mi'kmaq were terrified, convinced this was a display of evil Gougou's anger for listening to the missionaries. Fiery Elouèzes and Foaming Bear made the most of the situation, inciting the tribe to revolt against the white men and their missionaries.

"They're the ones who've brought sickness down on us," Foaming Bear yelled.

"They call us savages, then try to convince us that our beliefs in the immortality of the soul and the Spirit that lives in all of nature are wrong," roared Fiery Elouèzes.

But the evil Gougou left them no time to sow the seeds of revolt. A violent northwester blew in, sweeping burning treetops screaming through the air like raging devils. Their only escape route lay out at sea on board frail boats that were thrown about like wood chips.

Angélique and Joseph were desperately worried because Saint-Jean was on Ile Caraquet with Geneviève and Josette. The island had become one blazing inferno, and there was no getting near it. Sick at heart, they had to resign themselves to seeking refuge in the Grande-Anse grottos with René and Membertou. Like the warrior he soon would be, Membertou showed the requisite stoicism, but not so René, who huddled fearfully in his mother's arms. Of course, he wasn't even three yet. When calm descended once more, they stepped out of the grotto. As far as the eye could see, there was nothing but desolation.

"Look," Joseph exclaimed, "the grotto side of the island was spared by the flames."

Their joy was nothing if not intense when they were finally reunited with Geneviève, Josette, and old Saint-Jean, alive and trembling, but well. Back on shore, Jean-Baptiste was in despair; his charred schooner lay surrounded by blackened trees. Angélique's garden was in ruins, but that small annoyance was soon forgotten when she caught sight of her cow that had sought shelter by the three rocks of Pointe-de-Roche. Seeing themselves as tenants only on the land and being more attached to their freedom than to their possessions, the Mi'kmaq did not suffer overly from the devastation. They knew everything would grow back quickly, that the clean air would stay the same, and that next season, the blueberries they gathered in their birch baskets would be even bigger. Old Saint-Jean had earned Fiery Elouèzes' respect by surviving an encounter with the Gougou, whose den he had used to shelter himself from the storm. That side of the island was known henceforth as the "Enchanted Grove."[1]

Everyone had to start rebuilding. Membertou began manufacturing a canoe: a frame made of pine ribs steamed to make them bulge and strips of birchbark sewn together with fine spruce roots. Along the seams he applied a glue made of boiled moosehide and a layer of resin and, on the hull, an ochre mixed with pine oil. He pictured himself, his torso bronzed and muscled, proudly paddling his canoe at sea or down the St. Lawrence or other rivers and lakes, and over the Outaouais rapids, just like his Uncle Jean-Baptiste.

Angélique was happy that Joseph had put Emilie out of his mind and taken a more active role in the family; moments worth savouring that she wouldn't have traded for all the treasure on the island, especially not the evenings spent singing together to the violin. Joseph was there for his daughters; he showed them how to find the mother of pearl in clams used for wampum necklaces, the tube-like strands the Mi'kmaq traded with the Iroquois for corn. As soon as he was old enough to walk, René started to follow his father everywhere; Joseph tried to spark his curiousity rather than force him to learn. He had adopted the native outlook that banned spankings; a reprimand was enough, and if that didn't work the whole tribe ignored the culprit until he fell into step. Which was what happened to René when he refused to eat; faced with ostracism from the tribe, it didn't take him long to say he was sorry. As a reward, Joseph gave him several small beads carved in red stone that the Cree brought back from Minnesota to make pipes with. They had cost him more than twenty beaver skins. He carved twenty-four beads, engraving runes – the symbols the Vikings used in a divinatory game – on each one. René started learning how to play with them with Geneviève and Josette.

When he's grown, Joseph thought, *he can consult them for answers to important questions.*

There was a small celebration when Membertou finished building his canoe. Saint-Jean told a story suited to the occa-

---

1. Because the wood grove had not burned.

sion about a fleet of canoes, a well-known legend in the Saint-Jean River[2] valley and the whole Grand Sault[3] Falls region; "After they'd massacred a whole Maliseet village, a band of Iroquois captured young princess Malobiannah and made her serve as their guide..." old Saint-Jean began.

"What are the Grand Sault Falls?" Geneviève interrupted her grandfather's tale.

"A waterfall over a huge rock, that is particularly dangerous because of the mist it creates," Saint-Jean explained briefly before continuing. "Malobiannah sat in the lead canoe and, so as to hide the noise of the falls, she sang a warsong... The Iroquois only realized what she'd done when it was too late and they were already headed straight for the abyss."

"Did the princess die?" René asked sadly.

"Yes... but her spirit still watches over canoeists in the region."

The celebration ended with a feast accompanied by dancing and singing to drums and Joseph's violin.

---

2. Named by Champlain on June 24th, St. John the Baptist Day.
3. "Kapskouk" in the native language.

Chapter 14

The plan is to launch four operations to begin with: an attack on Fort Duquesne, the key to the Ohio valley; another on Niagara, the key post for the Great Lakes region; a third on Fort Saint-Frédéric on Lake Champlain; and a fourth on forts Beauséjour, Gaspareaux, and Saint-Jean in French Acadia. Afterwards, the Army will invade the thus-dismantled Canada.

– Robert Rumilly, in *L'Acadie anglaise*

This Day Finished the Picquetting & began the owen to Clear our Selves of one of the Egyptian Plagues.

– Winslow speaking of the deportation in his journal on August 28, 1755

While peace reigned in Ruisseau, in the Grand'Pré region a hundred leagues to the south the English were getting ready to begin the deportations. The region had been colonized in 1680 when the Lapierre, Melançon, Pinet, Terriot[1], and other families came from Port-Royal and settled in an area called the Mines Basin because of the traces of copper that had been discovered there. They founded two neighbouring parishes: Saint-Charles des Mines in Grand'Pré, and Rivière-aux-Canards, each with its own church and graceful steeple rising above a carved oak nave. In 1755, close to four hundred

---

1. Thériault.

families lived in the Grand'Pré region, which was a huge prairie criss-crossed by a multitude of rivers (Gasparot, Aux Canards, Habitant, Sainte-Croix…) flowing into a rich delta where centuries-worth of silt deposits had accumulated, washed in by huge tides that crashed all the way to the back of the Baie Française[2].

Late August 1755. Bells rang the angelus while smoke from the huts danced in the blue-tinged air. In the fields between the green of the sea and the forest, the farmers and others repairing the tide gates known as "aboiteaux" stood in their wooden clogs next to carts of salt marsh hay, lost in thought for a moment. They stood at attention like the white crests of the waves bobbing along Cap Blomidon. The moment was marred by the worry that had first surfaced with the capture of Fort Beauséjour in June and had been growing over the past two weeks, ever since four hundred Acadians from the surrounding area had been imprisoned inside the fort. Some thought of husbands, fathers or brothers imprisoned in Halifax for having refused, as village delegates[3], to swear allegiance. The oath would have meant having to take up arms against the French. Others worried about their church, which had become the general headquarters for Lieutenant-Colonel John Winslow's troops, a sanctuary emptied of its holy objects and defiled by heretics.

A few women, their heads covered with white shawls, brought out the evening meal and flasks of cider. Among them was Angéline Clairefontaine, her hair blowing in the wind. A striking figure with her shawl flung around her neck and her indigo blue sweater tied at the waist, she looked like a statue of the Virgin Mary. She was worried because the priest, Father Chauvreulx, had been imprisoned, which meant her marriage to Tristan might have to be postponed.

Meanwhile, little Mathilde Chiasson was walking through the Belliveau's orchards accompanied by her big black

---

2. Bay of Fundy.
3. Appointed by the Acadians to act as their representatives in speaking to the English regarding issues of importance such as the oath of allegiance…

dog Quenouille. After her parents died during their ocean crossing with the Duc d'Anville's fleet, she had been adopted by Angéline's parents, the Clairefontaines. Nine years had passed since then, nine carefree years, far from all the scheming and war. Papa Clairefontaine had been hard hit by his wife's death, but Mathilde, who was only three at the time, had only a vague memory of the loss. In any case, with the many neighbouring families and the spirit of mutual cooperation and assistance, there was always, in a neighbour's, an aunt's, or a cousin's house, someone to give her a mother's love.

From a clearing in the orchard, Mathilde caught sight of old Nazaire's smithy. He was the only inhabitant in the region who had a smithy, which he'd gradually equipped between trips to Boston, where he sold flour from his mill. The mill was operated with water from the Gasparot River and an ingenious system of valves, hatches, dykes, aboiteaux, and Archimedean screws. Nazaire, his arms bare and his face blackened with smoke, was busy hammering an oxshoe by the fire. He was always delighted to see Mathilde, a mischievous child who loved to play tricks on him and whom he saw, to a certain degree, as the daughter he'd never had. He put away his tools. "Come into the house, I have a snack for you," he said.

Nazaire lived alone with his son Tristan in a solid oak house with high gables and many windows, situated in a shady elm grove. He offered Mathilde a cup of spruce water to begin with, then a small mug of fresh milk with a beaten yolk inside, something like eggnog, and bread and honey. Mathilde ate in silence. She seemed preoccupied.

"What's wrong, little one?" he finally asked.

"I wish I were tall and beautiful like Angéline," she confided.

Nazaire had noticed she was wearing Angéline's earrings. "You know," he answered gently, "you're the prettiest."

He knew what plagued her. She was grown up for her age and felt a bit jealous of Angéline, whom Tristan loved, while he treated Mathilde like a little girl. To distract her, Nazaire said, "I have a present for you."

He held out an ivory comb from the Indies. Mathilde was thrilled. She put the comb in her long black hair and looked at herself appraisingly in the mirror.

"Tristan will notice me now," she sighed.

* * *

Under the rays of the setting sun, the ocean took on a red hue, and a warm wind blew through the pine trees and willows. As he walked along the hill bordered by beehives, Nazaire felt a flush of pride at the sight of the fertile plains and their patchwork of wheat, rye, oats, and flax. Every tool had been made by him: the carts and the harrows all bore his mark. From dawn to dusk, year in, year out, he had helped build this country just as his ancestors had done when they arrived a century ago. The meadows where the herds grazed had been taken back from the sea thanks to an ingenious system of aboiteaux, a type of dyke built of tree trunks and clay that stopped the tide from invading the land and incorporated built-in hatches to evacuate the water from the meadows. To the left stood the church where all of life's important occasions were celebrated: births, engagements, weddings, harvests, deaths… In the shade of the cemetery's crosses, the people's forbears watched over the grandchildren, happy to see them multiply so rapidly. *No, I could never leave here*, he thought.

Lately, the Acadians' freedom had been circumscribed by all sorts of regulations and restrictions. First they were obliged to provide the forts with firewood, under penalty of having the very frames of their houses requisitioned. Then all their arms were confiscated by the English soldiers, who left nothing but a hammer to the smith, a scythe to the harvester, and an axe to the logger. The English had proceeded by way of subterfuge: pretending to be a hunting party, two soldiers visited each home and asked for shelter and food. They were welcomed, for hospitality was sacred to the Acadians. But then the soldiers turned around and made off with their hosts' weapons in the night! Next, the English requisitioned all the canoes to stop the Acadians from fleeing to Louisbourg or to Ile Saint-Jean or, worse yet, joining the French troops. The Acadians who presented petitions to Governor Lawrence – either vowing their loyalty or protesting the theft of the weapons they needed to defend themselves against the wildlife and certain natives who might now see them as enemies – were categorically rejected. The governor made it known that he found their claims highly arrogant and insulting, that these petitions were a sign of contempt for the authority and government of His Majesty, and that the petitioners should be made an example of by being punished. During his long walk, Nazaire thought about these events of the past few months, and shuddered at the underhanded dealings, which boded ill for the future.

Nazaire had drawn level with the Clairefontaines' house. He stopped to rest by an old moss-covered well and used the iron-rimmed pail to scoop up cool water, which he drank under the shade of a pear tree imported from France. Feeling refreshed, he stood up and headed for the house. Once on the threshold, he didn't have to lift the heavy bronze doorknocker since the door had been left ajar because of the heat.

"Come in, old friend," Clairefontaine called out distractedly, engrossed in his game of checkers with Tristan. "Come, have a seat. Grab the plaster pipe and tin of tobacco on your way in."

Angéline sat spinning flax by the large fireplace, next to the pots and utensils that hung from the squared beams. She went to fetch the cider in its pewter jar; the jar felt quite light. She could have sworn it had been full last night, but it never occurred to her that Mathilde, wanting to be like the grown-ups, drank the cider on the sly. She was even further from imagining that instead of getting ready for bed, her sister spied on the "grown-ups" from the top of the stairs leading to her bedroom.

Nazaire drank his cider, then said, "There's a strange rumour making the rounds about the Boston ships anchored offshore; they have barbaric names such as *Endeavour*, *Industry*, *Elizabeth*... I don't like the thought of their cannons being trained on Grand'Pré."

"You worry too much lately," said Clairefontaine between two moves. "We're used to having the English around. Since

1713, we've been under their jurisdiction, and outside that damned oath of allegiance we never took, they haven't bothered us too much. They get worked up every once in a while; that's only normal since we're not far from Boston and, with Louisbourg, we control entry into the gulf. Anyhow, it's not the first time the soldiers have wintered in the village."

"That's true, but this time it's serious. Our delegates are in prison," Nazaire retorted. "Since the founding of Halifax, the English have fixated on one thing: having us deported. There are three thousand English, Irish, and German Protestants who are only waiting for the opportunity to take over our lands, our crops, and our herds. Not to mention the thousand French Huguenots from Montbéliard; what a disgrace to be betrayed by our own people! Why do you think they seized our archives containing all the land titles and information on our families? There's a reason why they refuse to have land surveys challenged in court; that would mean they recognized our property rights. There's that surveyor Morris and his skullduggery to worry about, too. He's taken down every detail pertaining to the location of houses and buildings, the amount of cultivated land, the number of cattle as well as the access to communications routes."

Out of breath, Nazaire stopped his accusations there. He wasn't far from the truth, but he would have been stunned to learn the title, not to mention the contents, of the report drafted by Morris in January 1755: "Some reflections on the situation of the inhabitants, commonly called neutrals, and some methods proposed to prevent them from escaping out of the colony, in case upon being acquainted with the design of removing them, they should attempt to desert and go over to French neighbouring settlements." Another scoundrel to be added to the Lawrence, Shirley, Belcher, Boscawen, and Winslow quintet!

"They can't deport us," Clairefontaine replied. "France and the soldiers from the Louisbourg fortress will defend us. Moreover, London will never countenance deportation. After all, George II is no barbarian."

"My father is right," Tristan said suddenly. "I don't trust Governor Lawrence and Belcher, the chief justice. Belcher only wants to give a semblance of legality to their sinister project. Worse yet, with the soldiers in our churches and Winslow in the presbytery, things are not looking good. I've heard rumours of a deportation, too. We've been neutral for too long. I always said it would be our downfall. We should take up arms!"

With those words, he stood up and began prodding the logs in the fireplace with a long poker. The flames shot up again and reflected off the pewter plates on the buffet. Tristan had in mind to repeat the exploit of Coulon de Villiers, who, with only a handful of men, ran the English out of Grand'Pré in 1747 in the middle of a snowstorm. Angéline kept quiet, but she, too, was troubled. In her innocence, however, she was incapable of imagining either evil or war.

At this juncture, the notary Octave LeBlanc arrived. He had come to prepare the marriage contract.

"Any news?" Tristan asked.

"I think the English want to see us swear allegiance because a war is in the offing in Europe... It's already started here. But I trust to Providence," said the notary, as though reassuring himself.

Nazaire couldn't help but think that the notary's attitude must stem from the contracts he had with the English. In fact, Nazaire saw LeBlanc as a traitor, especially given the bulge under his sweater – his chamois purse that looked to be bursting with silver ecus. But war was not what LeBlanc was here for. Angéline lit the alabaster lamp, and the notary brought out his goosefeather quill. He carefully wrote down the name and age of the parties as well as the amount of the dowry belonging to Angéline, whose trousseau consisted of beautiful woven and hand-embroidered pieces. Mathilde had tears in her eyes as she contemplated her prince and the spell he was under. He made her think of the description she'd been given of her father, to which her childish imagination had added height, facial features, and the timbre of a voice!

A clock struck nine, the hour of the curfew.

"Aren't you sick and tired of living like slaves?" Tristan roared. "I feel like joining the rebels in their camp in the forest."

116

"A rebellion would only provoke the English," LeBlanc warned him. "You mustn't give them the slightest pretext. Honest citizens such as ourselves have nothing to fear!"

"Lawrence is a little tyrant, who thinks of himself before anyone else," Tristan retorted. "He's never gotten over his defeat at Fort Beauséjour five years ago. Even his fellow countrymen hold him in contempt… You've blinded yourself to the fact they intend to boot us out of our own country. Both the Beauséjour and Gaspereau forts have fallen into English hands, and several hundred Acadians are being kept prisoner there. Monckton is pillaging by fire and sword the whole region around Tintamarre[4], Aulac, and Jolicoeur as far as Memramcouk. Boishébert had to burn down the fort and storehouses by the Saint-Jean River before Monckton's army rabble got to them, and now all he has left is a handful of soldiers and Abnaki with Father Germain upriver. And our delegates from Pigiguit[5], Rivière-aux-Canards, and Grand'Pré are imprisoned in Halifax for having refused to take the oath of allegiance. Our priests have been left to rot in jail cells as well. There are only Abbot Manach and Abbot Le Guerne left, and they took to the woods with a few Acadians and Indians."

"Don't forget Abbot Desenclaves in Pobomcoup, in D'Entremont's seigneuries," LeBlanc said.

"Don't even mention his name to me," Tristan retorted. "He's such a Loyalist the English will be wanting to adopt him!"

"But there is good news," LeBlanc insisted. "A French fleet and troop reinforcements have arrived in Quebec with Governor Vaudreuil. And the Anglo-Americans were defeated not far from Fort Duquesne in Ohio."

Nazaire cut in. "That will only serve to postpone the fate that awaits us. The victory there will incite them to exile us."

As he began to see the danger, Clairefontaine couldn't refrain from saying, "We should have listened to Abbot Leloutre and taken refuge in French territory."

---

4. The present-day Sackville.
5. Today's Windsor.

"If we had leaders of his calibre, the English would have had a hard time telling us what to do," Tristan added.

"Don't forget Beausoleil," Angéline chimed in. "When he does his war dance with the Indians, the English start to worry."

Seeing the tide turn against him, the notary LeBlanc insisted, "We must collaborate with the English. They'll ensure peace reigns over the colony, which will help us make more money."

"That would mean swearing the oath of allegiance and taking up arms against the French," Clairefontaine said. "Like many others, I would rather leave my country and my belongings behind than betray my faith, my language, and my race."

"But how can we?" Angéline asked. "The English have always prevented us from leaving, just like the Jews were prevented from leaving during the time of the pharaohs. They needed us to hold the Indians in check, cultivate the land, and supply the forts with food. They don't want to see us swell the ranks of the populations of Louisbourg or Quebec either."

Nazaire continued, "That's true. Since the signing of the Treaty of Utrecht[6] in 1713, the English have dreamed up all kinds of excuses. They started by saying, 'You can't leave until such and such a point has been clarified by Queen Anne, but she was already dead by then! Then they stopped us from leaving on English or French ships or even in our own rowboats. After that, they forbade us from leaving on the pretext we had to sow our fields first. They prevented us from building a road for fear we would flee with our belongings. Finally, they told us we needed a passport. When all's said and done, for more than forty years now, they've been making all the rules… and we meekly obey."

"And you think they'll let us go now?" Tristan asked incredulously. "I suspect it will be something much more treacherous. They'll banish us to hostile territory. Ever since Halifax was founded and Lawrence arrived, they've been in a position of strength and have no more use for us."

---

6. In which France gave Newfoundland and Acadia to the English.

The notary tried to make an appropriate retort but never got a chance because Tristan exploded, "It sounds like you're being paid to preach for them! Have you converted to Protestantism?"

Tristan was alluding to the privileges granted to Acadians who turned their backs on their faith. LeBlanc stood up indignantly. How dare this young man speak to him, a person of note, in such a way! He stomped out, slamming the door behind him.

"The devil take him!" Tristan concluded.

Under normal circumstances, a young person was not expected to address his elders so disrespectfully, but in this instance, Angéline and Nazaire admired Tristan's ardour and understood his exasperation. Clairefontaine was lost in thought and said nothing. He was thinking of the Acadian delegate in Halifax, who had insisted to Lawrence that he would continue to refuse to take the oath of allegiance and who, when the governor drew his sword, bared his breast and proclaimed, "Go ahead, Sir, and strike me! You will slay my body, but you will not come near my soul." Deep down, he regretted not having the same courage. He walked over to the fire and as he stirred the embers he thought, *Man proposes and God disposes*, while Mathilde tried to sneak back to bed unnoticed.

* * *

To celebrate Tristan and Angéline's betrothal, farmers wearing their Sunday best arrived from neighbouring villages in heavy carts pulled by oxen. Most came from the Grand'Pré townships: people from the Habitant River, the town where the Melançons and the Gautherots lived. Others came from the town close by, Rivière-aux-Canards, and from the small village of Pointe-aux-Boudrots, adjoining the town. A few came from farther afield – Pigiguit, Cobeguit[7], and even Port-Royal. Clairefontaine and Nazaire were clearly well-known and

---

7. Today's Truro.

respected in the surrounding area. The esteem they were held in was shown by the many gifts of household items, livestock, and poultry that were brought and the many hands that set to work clearing a plot of land for the young couple and building a house for them.

In the Clairefontaine's orchard, a platform was set up to be used as a dance floor for the guests. Fiddlers perched on the coping of the well kept time to the music with their hobnailed wooden clogs, making sparks fly. The women wore bright, gay colours and looked as lovely as ripe autumn apples. Angéline had bought fabric from the store that belonged to the Huguenot Josué Masuger and was run by his agent in Mines, the Swiss Joseph Deschamps; both of them undesirables who were not on the guest list. She used the white fabric to make her dress and the red for fringed decorations, keeping only one red ribbon for her hair.

For a wedding, the custom was that the bride-to-be had to weave a pair of sheets and the man build a pair of wheels: this was so much child's play for the two sweethearts who were accustomed to farm work. They held each other close and whispered softly to one another.

Mathilde spent all day getting ready. At long last, her beloved Tristan danced a cotillion with her. Not without some urging on her part. She was in seventh heaven dancing in her prince's arms.

"You're a good dancer, young lady," Tristan murmured.

The compliment made her blush. He thought, *Soon she'll be setting many a young man's heart to pounding.*

All night long, the stubborn, independent-minded, nearly ungovernable settlers sang old songs from France, told of their hunting and buccaneering exploits, and in keeping with the old Gallic tradition, gossiped and criticized everyone else's doings. On long tables covered in linen tablecloths, bread, mild cheese, scented honey, cider, and legs of beef and lamb were served to the delighted guests.

Suddenly the banquet was interrupted by a commotion coming from the other side of the orchard. Joseph Deschamps, Winslow's interpreter, came bearing bad news: an order stipulating that all the men and male children ten years of age and over must go to the Grand'Pré church the next day at three o'clock or have all their possessions confiscated. Naturally people were worried and unsure how to react. Brave peasants that they were, they had learned to adapt, willingly or reluctantly, to a sort of neutrality, and since the danger threatening them was too vague, it was impossible for them to become warriors overnight, especially since they had lived in peace for half a century. Nevertheless, Tristan did try to incite the men to resist.

"If you don't want to fight, at least go into hiding tomorrow with your weapons; I have a few muskets..."

Some supported him, but the notary LeBlanc and other eminent people gave long-winded speeches on Providence, the protection it afforded, and the need to obey orders. They managed to convince almost everyone that the purpose of the assembly the next day was to announce good news! Both the debate and the celebration ended there.

Chapter 15

The first European settlers found the Indian belief in "absolute freedom for all beings" deeply troubling to their Jansenist spirit, so much so that they condemned it for being an "uncivilized" belief and blamed it on the "primitivism of these savage peoples" …sexual relations were considered as normal physically and mentally, similar to the philosophy of the Nordic peoples of the 20th century… women were considered an integral part of family life and were entitled to the same satisfaction as men. Therefore, it was not frowned upon for unattached girls to spend the night in the home of unattached boys and the culpabilization of this act only occurred after a Christian view was introduced to our continent… It is also true that once married, women became extremely faithful spouses, although sexual virtue or faithfulness was not considered to be essential for a marriage to succeed.

– Bernard Assiniwi, in *Histoires des Indiens du Haut et du Bas-Canada*

While the people of Grand'Pré lived in fear and dread, a relative calm reigned over Ruisseau during the spring of 1755. Ten years had passed since Joseph's return from Louisbourg. The children had grown, and René was now almost nine years old. He was a lot like Joseph and was his father's favourite, which created a certain amount of tension in the boy's relationship with Membertou and his sisters, who held his special status against him. The mysterious air he had about him was also a source of irritation. However, people eventually grew attached to him both because of that enigmatic side and his great generosity. Like his father, he loved to dance and took part in all the tribe's celebrations. René had a surprising fascination for the jars and bottles he collected. He had also found a use for them; he threw bottles into the sea bearing messages written on birchbark, hoping the frail craft would reach the wondrous countries of the Orient that had been described to him by mariners on stopovers in Ruisseau. He was extremely inquisitive and was just as likely to ask, for instance, what the moon did up in the sky as whether there was life on the stars. If the answer was yes, a second question invariably followed, namely Did Christ die and rise again for the inhabitants of all the exotic planets as well? With Angélique in particular he gave free rein to his imagination. Sometimes, he talked to her about paranormal powers, like thought transmission, or tried to find out how Fiery Elouèzes went about making his predictions.

Twenty-one years old and as strong as a bear, Membertou was already considered to be a tribal chief. Women tried, with limited success, to attract his attention and distract him from his passion for firearms, which had been nurtured over the years by following his grandfather's example. He had built up quite an impressive armoury by procuring arms from the ships that put into port at Ruisseau. He could spend hours dismantling, reassembling, and polishing his arquebuses, muskets, rifles, shotguns, and pistols. He was particularly interested in the muskets, from the *Brown Bess* and *Queen Anne* – English arms of varying calibres – to the French muskets that bore the name of their place of manufacture: Charleville, Mauberge, Saint-Etienne, Tulle, etc. The Mi'kmaq had a soft spot for the lightweight Charleville. Membertou's dream was to invent a rifle that fired more rapidly than existing rifles, which one had to fill with powder, insert a lead bullet in the cannon with a rod, and add more powder in the firing compartment connected to a wick, an operation that involved no less than twenty-three steps!

Membertou's dexterity had encouraged Joseph to entrust him with the task of building stagesets for the plays put on at Ile Caraquet: satires and comedies that Angélique and other members of the Mi'kmaq created based on daily events over the seasons, depending on how much time they had at their disposal. The entertainment was welcome during slow times, just like the Order of Good Cheer[1] when Champlain was in Port-Royal. Joseph could put his talents as a choreographer and dancer to the test with René's help.

As for Saint-Jean, by now his hair was white and thinning and his face as wrinkled as an old apple, but his eyes still held the spark and spirit of his youth. He continued to exercise unparalleled authority within the tribe, and had added to his prestige through the proceeds from the sale of his furs. His brush with death ten years earlier had slowed him down, but he was still a mischievous gourmand. He spent a good deal of time with his grandchildren, which gave him another reason to replenish his supply of sweets from the ships that stopped over in Ruisseau.

* * *

In July 1755, Ruisseau had the honour of welcoming a French squadron. Having sailed from Brest en route to Quebec, the squadron stopped over in Ruisseau for a few hours to replenish its supply of fresh water. Fourteen warships, four frigates, and three thousand men! Under cover of fog off Newfoundland, the squadron had managed to elude the English. Only the *Lys* and the *Alcide*, two rear ships, had been captured by Admiral Boscawen. A third, the *Dauphin Royal*, the best sailing ship in the French navy, had barely escaped thanks to its speed. The brief stopover meant the inhabitants of Ruisseau were able to meet the new governor of New France, Marquis Pierre de Vaudreuil, the son of a former governor of Canada. He was said to be a proud and dedicated man who was interested in

1. The Order was founded in Port-Royal by Champlain and his companions to brighten up the long winters with performances and feasts.

Canada because it was his birthplace. Moreover, having been governor of Louisiana, he knew the continent. The marquis' words showed he was aware of what was at stake: "The struggle to hold on to New France will be a difficult one given the disproportionate forces present and the corruption that reigns in both New France and France. It may be made even more difficult by certain intellectuals, philosophers, and others who are in favour of abandoning Canada." He added, "Voltaire's writing has done more to hurt France's efforts to help its colonies than a whole English squadron."

* * *

Early September 1755. One fine morning, Joseph went out clam digging with Geneviève and Josette. Just by scraping the seabottom with a mattock they filled their bags. Manna from heaven. At fourteen, Geneviève was the spitting image of her mother: a blonde goddess who turned heads and made hearts beat faster. She was quite impulsive and somewhat prone to jealousy; she was jealous of her brother René, her father's favourite, in the same way Angélique was jealous of Emilie. She spent hours in front of the mirror, and since clothing was one way of partially satisfying her need to be noticed, for the island plays she made the costumes, which she happily wore at other times. She always had a young man on her heels. The young Mi'kmaq were very liberated sexually, at least until marriage; the custom did not sit well with the missionaries, but they were powerless to do anything about it. Geneviève did not understand why her father tried to avoid her. In fact, Joseph had been keeping his distance for quite some time to shield himself, without admitting as much, from a vague attraction he'd felt for her ever since he accidentally glimpsed her making love to Ardent Caribou on a small Pointe-de-Roche inlet. When she bent over bare-breasted to gather clams, he was reminded of that day. The more he tried to banish the image from his mind, the more insistent it became. To rid the image of its obsessive power, he decided to treat it as he would any other image of daily life, in other words accept it as his without trying to either refrain from thinking about it or dwell on it. The strategy reassured him somewhat and allowed him to turn his attention to Josette, who didn't stir up the same emotions.

His youngest daughter was an enigma to him. To begin with, physically she bore no resemblance to either him or Angélique, nor to anyone on her mother's side according to Saint-Jean. Pretty, slim, and dark-complexioned, she could have passed for a Spaniard or a Portuguese woman. That day it suddenly occurred to him she might resemble someone from his family. *Can't children be a living portrait, palpable witnesses to an unknown past?*

Standing in water halfway up his thigh in the rising tide, he asked himself other questions, *Was it my father or mother who had the dancer's gift, which has been passed down to my daughter in such abundance?* The graceful way she walked and gestured as though each sound, each rhythm gave rise to a dance step. Josette was also an enigma in his eyes because of certain character traits she had. In everything but dance she was incredibly slow, contrary to all the other members of the family. Even digging for clams. She would rather rest, passive and day-dreaming; an attitude that would be called laziness on other continents. Once again, none of these traits seemed to come from Angélique's side. Joseph was increasingly convinced that he had the privilege of gazing on the living portrait of one of his ancestors.

* * *

Joseph had settled down since his return from Louisbourg. His taste for adventure had diminished, and Angélique's love and devotion as well as his children's affection did the rest. He carried his forty years well; only his greying beard and a few wrinkles around the corners of his eyes marked the passage of time. During those years, he continued to travel between Ruisseau and Quebec on his schooner and serve, in a manner of speaking, as the Baye des Chaleurs' lookout and spy, reporting his sightings to the Restigouche post or to Quebec. Joseph took advantage of each trip to visit his mother and spoil her in new ways every time. His latest plan was to bring her back to Ruisseau to live, but she felt incapable of undertaking such a long voyage. Other than his business, the connection tying Joseph to Quebec was no longer Emilie but his mother. He had relegated to the back of his mind the desire to find his birth parents; his family was his adoptive mother, his wife, and his children.

Soon, though, upon his mother's death, he was again confronted by his demons. Joseph arrived in Quebec too late to see or speak to her, but he drew some comfort from the knowledge that she had gone peacefully in her sleep. He spent that day rehashing his memories as he walked through Quebec like a lost soul. In his state of shock, the desire to know the woman who had given him life resurfaced, stronger than ever.

Meanwhile, back in Ruisseau, families were preparing for winter – putting aside provisions, clothing, and firewood, and rehearsing the traditional play based on the Mi'kmaq legend about the evil Gougou[2], who snapped her enemies in two like sticks of barley sugar. According to the script, the chief's daughter was to be handed over to Gougou. The girl's desperate lover consulted witches, magicians, elves, gnomes, sprites, mutants, in short, any and all who had special powers. One such being could levitate objects, another could go into a trance at will, another could read people's minds. Each one had his or her own idea on how to go about conquering Gougou.

As the days passed and the bay grew rough, Angélique became increasingly anxious about the length of Joseph's stay in Quebec. He had already been gone for forty days, and soon the bay would be imprisoned in ice. Angélique missed him more each day, his quirks, his scent, his sensuality. For the past fifteen years, she had devoted her life to her husband and children – without neglecting the plays, her garden, and her work as a midwife of course. She didn't look her thirty-seven years. Her features had not aged but grown more beautiful; her face was completely serene. Her worry showed only in her eyes.

---

2. Mentioned by Champlain in his journal.

Not only was Joseph late returning to Ruisseau, but Jean-Baptiste had been acting strangely. He had lost all interest in fishing and being called captain no longer made him smile. All summer long, the schooner he had rebuilt stayed on shore, and he was plagued by strange periods of melancholy. The people whispered that the woman he loved was behind it all: Jeannette-Anne, a young Mi'kmaq of the tribe, who had not reciprocated his feelings for her. What's more, he had had trouble earning enough silver ecus to fill his chest. And he had come home empty-handed from the moose hunt. The game had been plentiful, but he had been too preoccupied to focus properly; humiliated at being the only one of his companions not to bag a moose, he withdrew to his tent. His friends found him sitting there, his muscles tense, his eyes blank; some thought he had been possessed by Windigo. He presented all the symptoms: depression, loss of appetite, nauseau, insomnia. Fiery Elouèzes confirmed that Jean-Baptiste had dreamt of Windigo, the monster with the heart of ice. He was being invaded by Windigo's cold breath and becoming the monster himself.

Gradually, he saw Jeannette-Anne transformed; she was no longer the woman he loved but a deer. He started salivating and the saliva ran from the corners of his mouth. A raging hunger gnawed at his insides; he felt an irresistible need to eat raw flesh. His eyes turned the colour of fire; he grabbed a knife and killed his prey. But the tribe had been keeping watch. Their ever-present vigilance had allowed them to substitute a deer for Jeannette-Anne. Jean-Baptiste devoured large quantities of raw fat, which gave strength to bodies suffering from his type of illness. Then he was made to drink a large jug of caribou blood, a remarkable tonic. At last, Jean-Baptiste grew calm and fell asleep, while Fiery Elouèzes and the whole tribe danced and chanted incantations to the great Manitou to exorcise the demon. Jean-Baptiste's suffering had touched Jeannette-Anne's heart, and she went to him. When he awoke, he had forgotten everything, and he found the warm, passionate woman he loved lying by his side.

Chapter 16

We are now upon a great and noble Scheme of sending the neutral French out of this Province, who have always been secret Enemies, and have encouraged our Savages to cut our Throats. If we effect their Expulsion, it will be one of the greatest Things that ever the English did in America; for by all the Accounts, that Part of the Country they possess, is as good Land as any in the World: In Case therefore we could get some good English Farmers in their Room, this Province would abound with all Kinds of Provisions.

> – Letter from Governor Lawrence, published
> in the *New York Gazette* on August 25, 1755

That your Lands & Tennements, Cattle of all kinds and Live Stock of all Sortes are Forfitted to the Crown... and you your Selves to be removed from this his province... I am Throh his Majesty's Goodness Directed to allow you Liberty to Carry of your money and Household Goods as Many as you Can without Discomemoading the Vessels you go in... hope that in what Ever part of the world you may Fall you may be Faithfull Subjects, a Peasable & happy People

> – Edict from Governor Lawrence
> pertaining to the deportation

Anno Domini 1755, September 4, three o'clock in the afternoon. A drum roll then the pealing of two churches' bells in Mines Basin. This was the signal. The men were to gather in the holy sanctuaries as ordered by the English authorities. Some Acadians talked of an ambush, without actually believing it. How could one believe in one's own death? Especially since the glorious weather of the preceding days had meant the harvest could be brought in, the wheat stored, and dreams nourished of the lavish meals that a land as rich and fertile as this offered for the winter months. Some believed their petition to the King of France six years earlier was finally being answered. In their petition, the Acadians had asked that the English and French sovereigns come to an agreement whereby they would either be allowed to stay or leave, but under reasonable conditions. They did not know that the request made by France's ambassador to London that the Acadians be allowed to leave with their belongings had been dismissed in the spring, supposedly because doing so would have deprived the King of Great Britain of too many "useful" subjects! Some did wonder why boys of ten had been called up as well. Their concern grew at the sight of soldiers searching each building without exception.

Armed with a musket, Tristan hid in the Clairefontaines' barn to observe the goings-on. The Redcoats carried muskets with bayonets stuck in the barrel and surrounded the church once they'd ushered all the men and young boys inside. By the time the doors closed on the last one, Tristan had counted 416 men and boys.

I'm not the only one in hiding then! he thought, relieved.

All of a sudden, he heard a noise that seemed to be coming from the hayloft. He advanced cautiously and found Mathilde among the stacks of hay and flax.

"What are you doing?" he said reproachfully, albeit glad for her presence.

She held her hand out for him to help her up. Tears ran down her cheeks, and she sought comfort in Tristan's arms.

"I… I…" she began, but her thoughts were so confused she couldn't articulate them.

"Don't cry, little one, everything will be all right."

But he didn't believe it himself. She cried a bit longer than she really needed to, happy to be comforted by her idol.

A distressing silence had descended on the village, and at one point Tristan felt his heart beating so loudly he thought it could be heard as far away as Cap Blomidon. Suddenly, the silence was broken – by shouting, the sound of metal, musket fire! Tristan raced back to his observation post. Soldiers opened the church doors and rushed inside. The doors closed behind them.

"I have to go see," Tristan exclaimed.

"No, don't. They'll kill you," Mathilde said as she clung to him.

The agitation died down almost immediately. The revolt had been suppressed. Tristan was still hesitating when he saw a score of men leave the church. He recognized Pierre Terriot, Jacques Roy, and Jean Bourg,[1] friends he hadn't been able to convince to take up arms.

"Would you go and find out what's happening, Mathilde?"

"Of course," she said enthusiastically.

Mathile could ask for no more: a mission from her prince!

* * *

She learned that twenty delegates had been ordered to tell the women of the village the contents of Governor Lawrence's edict sanctioning the deportation abroad and the confiscation of their land, belongings, and livestock. Until it was time to embark, they were to bring supplies to the men, who would be guarded in an enclosure next to the church. This was the news Mathilde heard. Her arms loaded down with loaves of bread from the Clairefontaines' house, she headed toward the church. Inside, a sorry sight awaited her. Several wounded farmers lay on the floor, and the plaster statues and stations of the cross had been broken, victims of the soldiers' rage. The Redcoats, their rifles at the ready, paced the chancel in front of the bare altar. The pulpit had been covered with a black sheet, and a crucifix lay on top. Mathilde spotted old Nazaire lying on a bench. She drew near. At first, she thought he was asleep,

---
1. Bourque.

but when she touched him she realized he was no longer breathing. Mathilde began to sob, while the resigned men sang *Vive Jésus* to give themselves courage. In her grief, she only caught snatches of the hymn:

"Let us bear the cross
Without choosing or complaining..."

It was as though she could hear Nazaire telling her the Poitou legends at bedtime...

"Let us bear the cross,
When we are in distress..."

She remembered the wonderful harp he gave her at Christmas...

"... Although bitter and hard,
Despite fate and nature,
Let us bear the cross..."

Mathilde cried for a long time, crouched next to her old friend, wondering how to break all the awful news to Tristan.

During this time, the soldiers were searching the Clairefontaines' barn. Tristan rolled into a tight ball under the haystacks and held his breath as the bayonets slid along his body. But he was unharmed. Mathilde returned to the barn at twilight. She did not let her disappointment show at finding Angéline there. Misfortune seemed to have brought them closer together and, that night, she let herself be rocked by her big sister. Tristan bore the news stoically when Mathilde told him about his father's death, his grief giving way to rage and the desire to take revenge for his father. He listened carefully to Angéline's news of what was happening with the resistants.

"Vincent LeBlanc and Théophile Arsenault took refuge in the forest, up the Gasparot, with an Indian band," she announced.

The news gave Tristan some small measure of comfort.

"Listen," he said, "I have an idea. Beside my father's mill, there's an old well that hasn't been used for a very long time. I've hidden muskets and powder inside. Bring them to me. I'll tell you my plan."

Under the cover of nightfall, Angéline and Mathilde unsealed a stone from the old well and found, as promised, six

132

muskets, gunpowder, and a few sabres that they carried back to the barn.

"Here's my plan," Tristan said. "Vincent, Théophile, and I will infiltrate the enclosure with the arms and, from there…"

"That doesn't make any sense," Angéline objected. "You could be killed. There's a militia group from New England there now too – Shirley's troops, who've just arrived."

"We have no choice."

"Yes, we do. Let's flee to the north, to the Saint-Jean River valley, or toward Louisbourg," said Angéline.

"Ah, no! Never! No one will ever say that Tristan Pinet was a coward. If my plan works, the revolt could spread as far as Port-Royal and Cobeguit. We have to give it a try. What do you think, Mathilde?"

"Come on, Tristan, she's only a child…" Angéline objected.

"I know, but she's brave. Let her answer."

Bursting with pride, Mathilde tried to look as grown up as possible and stated, "We have to fight!"

"Woe be to us!" Angéline murmured.

* * *

The plan backfired; it was as though Winslow had caught wind of the plot; he had doubled the number of sentries. It was a fact that an increasing number of young people were becoming agitated. Tristan, Vincent, and Théophile managed to penetrate inside the enclosure, but before they had time to hand out the muskets, they were surrounded by soldiers. Angéline cried when she learned that the man she loved had been captured, but she never blamed Mathilde. In fact, the ordeal drew them even closer together as she looked after her little sister as a big sister should.

"Someone will come to our rescue," Mathilde kept saying over and over again.

"But who?" her sister asked. "The English are masters of the house from Port-Royal to Petcoudiac[2]. Most Acadians did

---

2. Petitcodiac.

what we did. They shut their eyes. They didn't want to face reality; now it's too late. There's a kernel of resistance in Port-Royal, Cobeguit, and Memramcouk, but that won't help our situation. Boishébert may have given the English a good thrashing in the Le Coude[3] region, but that's a long way from here. So we can't expect anyone to come to our rescue."

"What about my godfather, Abbot Leloutre, and the Indians?"

"He had to flee to Quebec after Fort Beauséjour fell. There's a price on his head."

Angéline managed to convince them to let her father return home because of his age and health. That was at least one small consolation in the middle of their ordeal! But when she asked him what he thought of the tragedy, he retreated into silence for fear the rage stemming from his feeling of powerlessness would explode.

The day after Tristan's raid, everything happened all at once. First, soldiers set fire to Nazaire's house, mill, and smithy and to Vincent and Théophile's homes. Then Winslow decided that the most unruly prisoners would be boarded immediately, namely more than two hundred able-bodied men, including Tristan and his companions. The men refused to budge, and the only way the soldiers could get them to cover the distance between the enclosure and the shoreline was by constantly prodding them with their bayonets. Every now and then, a gesture of revolt and despair was quickly quelled at the tip of a bayonet. Women and children hung onto their poor loved ones' arms and hands. The air rang with sobs, cries, and shouts. Tristan tried to escape when he saw Angéline, but he crumpled to the ground when a soldier hit him with the butt end of his rifle. Several soldiers began dragging him toward the ship, despite the insults and blows Angéline rained down on them. When Tristan lost consciousness, Mathilde had to close her eyes to try to drive back the visions of horror. In her state of shock, she heard the crowd begin to sing a song on the futility of earthly existence,

---

3. Named for the angle of the river. Today's Moncton.

a song that preached submission and withdrawal into the bosom of the church:

"False pleasures, vain honours, frivolous goods,

Today we bid thee farewell…"

For Angéline, the song was associated with wonderful memories of one particular day she spent with her lover after mass. *Our first kiss, in a field of hay…*

"…Since God has destined us for glory,

Here below let us scorn all pleasure…"

Tristan stroking my hair, speaking of the beautiful children we would have…

"…Heaven the only prize for victory,

For the chosen crowns all desires."

Mathilde wanted none of it, but the effect the song had was to soothe tempers, and the soldiers were not quite so rough as they prodded the poor villagers toward the embarcation point where the Gasparot flowed into the sea, not far from the windmill, its arms stretched wide as if in blessing.

* * *

More for financial than humanitarian reasons, Winslow asked that each family feed its members who had been taken prisoner. This allowed Tristan to see his loved ones almost every day and alternate between moments of joy, tenderness, and rage. He had recovered from the blow to his head by now and was busy trying to come up with escape plans. But how? No matter how hard he racked his brain, he couldn't find an answer to that burning question. Especially now, for surveillance had been increased after October 8th, when twenty-four men had fled the schooner *Léopard* and the sloop *Endeavor*, at François Hébert's instigation. Their escapade was shortlived: their homes were set on fire, two of the escapees were killed, and the others surrendered when threatened with reprisals against their families.

In the village, all the talk was of those who were absent. Mines Basin had become a land of widows and orphans. Old Clairefontaine had only broken his silence once, when the

English confiscated for Winslow the black horses he loved so much.

"What blackguards! Those heretics are bent on appropriating every single one of the hundred thousand plus animals in Acadia!" he shouted, beside himself with rage.

On October 19th, boarding began at Pointe-aux-Boudrots. There was a line of carts loaded haphazardly with trunks and objects that had been carried off in haste. There were pregnant women, others carrying newborns, fearful little girls hugging their rag dolls close to them, the infirm being dragged along on their pallets, old people being transported on carts; a veritable funeral procession during which the deportees could be heard crying and the soldiers could be heard snickering and swearing. Families were split up and sent to different, already overloaded, ships. Angéline, Mathilde, and Papa Clairefontaine were heartbroken because the ship on which Tristan had been boarded was full, and they had to wait for the next transport carriers chartered by the Apthorp and Hancock agency of Boston. The travel agency had little regard for its passengers' well-being. Especially since, to cut costs, it had chosen ships that were already transporting cargo to specific destinations in the American colonies. The deportees' departure had been postponed several times because of supply delays, but the reprieve ended in the final days of October. Escorted by three warships, fourteen ships from Mines joined up with ten others from Beaubassin, carrying close to four thousand poor souls to their places of exile. Those waiting for the next ships, which were scheduled to leave from Grand'Pré and the parishes of Assomption and Sainte-Famille in Pigiguit, or from the parishes of Saint-Pierre and Saint-Paul in Bodguit, were in despair. They prayed for a miracle. But the first departures brought home to them the reality of their plight: their loved ones were gone! By high tide or low tide, night or day, under cloudy or sunny skies, the sails had disappeared over the horizon.

At the Clairefontaines', Mathilde, Angéline, and their father experienced spells of sorrow, despair, anger, and resignation. Old Clairefontaine finally emerged from his silence to announce what should have been good news. "I heard that Tristan is en route for South Carolina on board the *Prosperous*."

Upon hearing this, Angéline and Mathilde's eyes lit up. It was some consolation to be able to give a name to a place, a climate, describe a location, imagine cotton plantations, in short, have something to cling to.

"Let's hope he'll be better treated than the black slaves on the plantations," Angéline sobbed.

"Now that we know where he is, let's join him," Mathilde suggested, making her father and sister smile.

"That's impossible without a boat," Clairefontaine said. "It would take months to cross the forests and mountains. We wouldn't get far anyway, with winter fast approaching. But who knows, maybe we'll visit that part of the world at the British crown's expense," he added.

Shivering in the autumn air, Angéline drew closer to the fire. "Poor Tristan. I shiver just thinking of him on the frigid seas. And I'm not there to keep him warm or comfort him. All I can hope is that time will pass quickly and my loved one will come back to me." She began to softly sing *Tout passe*,

> "Under the firmament
> Change is everywhere
> All that is shall pass
> No matter what man does
> His days escape him
> Faster than the river runs
> All that is shall pass…"

Mathilde picked up her harp and began to pick out a few chords to accompany Angéline.

> "The beauty of youth
> Pleasure, strength, and good health
> All that is shall pass
> All that is shall wilt, disappear
> Nothing shall stand the test of time
> Like a flower in the fields
> All that is shall pass…"

The song had a calming effect on the family, so much so that Papa Clairefontaine fell asleep in his armchair.

Mathilde had put away her harp and was about to go to bed when there was a knock at the door. Wondering who it could be this late at night, a worried Angéline went to open the door. She hoped she wouldn't find herself face to face with an English soldier bringing bad news! She couldn't believe her eyes when she recognized Tristan, alive and shivering. Wild with joy, she threw her arms around him, ushered him inside, and sat him down by the fire. They kept making him repeat his story over and over, even Papa Clairefontaine who was no longer the least bit tired. Tristan told them about his adventure.

"After sunset, once the ship was at sea, I managed to go abovedeck. Given the cold and the size of the waves, the English never dreamt I would jump overboard. I swam as far as Cap Blomidon. The water was so freezing it felt like I was about to go under twenty different times, but the thought of you waiting for me and the warmth I'd find here gave me the courage I needed to keep on going."

Papa Clairefontaine handed him some hot rum. "There's no better remedy for the shakes," he said.

"I'll give you a backrub. Come close to the fire," Angéline said lovingly.

Not wanting to go unnoticed, Mathilde put in a word, too, "Would you like me to play a lullaby on my harp?"

"That would be nice…"

A few moments later, Tristan was sound asleep, given new life through Angéline's tender ministrations, the fire's warmth, and the music of the harp. But the damage had already been done, and all the loving in the world could do nothing to stop Tristan from being racked with fever. By morning, his body on fire, he was delirious; he spoke of plans to destroy the dykes and aboiteaux, just as a group of Acadians from Port-Royal did in 1704 as the invaders arrived. The Acadians flooded their fields as the Dutch had done when Louis XIV's troops came. Then he talked about digging a tunnel as far as the Gasparot. Angéline realized he was reliving his attempt to escape from the Grand'Pré enclosure when he and others tried to dig a way out before boarding time. The idea came to him from what he'd heard about a successful attempt by a group of Acadians in late September in Fort Beauséjour.

The Clairefontaines' joy turned to concern. There was a light snowfall that November 1st and Tristan, in his delirium, described the manna in the desert that would save the chosen people. That evening, in the shadows cast by the glimmering flames on the walls, he saw the face of the devil. He saw Redcoats roasting in the fires of hell. In actual fact, there were fires burning in the neighbouring village, Rivière-aux-Canards. Houses had ignited like burning bushes. This was Winslow's sign to the Acadians that there was no way they would be coming back. Dense smoke rose above the sod roofs. The dogs, abandoned yet ever-faithful guardians, howled beside the homes and, in many places, thinking the sun had risen, roosters crowed. Tristan heard the church steeple collapse with a thundrous roar, causing a burst of fire and a ringing din. The same scene of fire and plunder was being repeated elsewhere: at Memramcouk, Tintamarre, Port-Royal; thousands of homes, more than a century's worth of labour, reduced to ashes.

Since the soldiers lived in their village, it had been spared for the time being. It wasn't long before the soldiers learned of Tristan's presence, but Clairefontaine managed to negotiate a deal whereby Tristan could stay in his home under guard. The negotiations weren't that difficult since the village had become a prison and the only place Tristan would be escaping to was into delirium. The deal was clinched with all the savings Clairefontaine had accumulated over fifty years, hidden away in a chest buried underground by a cherry tree. The money dispelled any lingering resistance. In early December, Tristan was well on the road to recovery, and he began planning his escape once more. But winter was just around the corner, and the sentries were on high alert. Another "crossing" was announced for December 11th, in old tubs come from Halifax, Boston, and New York to take their quota of the destitute. At high tide one night, boarding began. Families were split up. Men, women, and children were piled into the boats any old way for the joyless trip to unknown lands. Families were scattered in a calculated twist to sap the morale of able-bodied men and render them incapable of waging war! Angéline and her father were forced to board the *Cornwallis*, headed for Virginia. Tristan's protests did nothing to change the fate reserved for him, and he had to be bound hand and foot to be dragged on to the *Prince Frederick William*.

A sorrow-struck Mathilde watched from the shore. She saw people lying prostrate next to campfires and others wandering aimlessly, mothers calling for missing children, and children crying for absent mothers. She caught a glimpse of old Octavie, who scooped up a handful of soil to take with her into exile. When her turn came and it was announced there was no room left either on the *Cornwallis* or the *Prince Frederick William*, she decided to flee.

As she ran home, Mathilde could hear the lowing of the starving cattle in the barns, more specifically the cattle that had not already been requisitioned by the English. No smoke rose from the chimneys anymore; only the weather vanes swung wildly on rooftops, as though bidding a final farewell. She finally reached her house. Her father's checkerboard and bits and pieces of china had been swept onto the floor. She was famished. She found some bread and honey that she devoured, as she wondered what would become of her.

"At least they're still alive," she sighed, "and I know where their ship is headed…"

Just then she heard barking outside. Her trusty Quenouille had found her. She snuggled close to her faithful friend for a few seconds, then headed back toward the shore and the fires dying down one after the other as the ships raised anchor. That night, she hid in the tall grass along the coast and slept huddled next to Quenouille, whose coat served as her blanket. She woke up with the first light of dawn, shaking from the winter cold, to discover that the nightmare had not been a dream. Lying along the shore she saw furniture, trunks, the precious belongings the refugees – crammed like sardines into the ships – had had to leave behind. Unsure where to go, she finally converted old Nazaire's root cellar into a hiding place. She carried her harp, bread, and jars of brandied jam inside with her. Sometimes she could hear shots ringing out, and one evening soldiers searching the area to flush out fugitives just about stumbled on her.

The last ships set sail on December 20th. On that day, the villagers left a deserted Grand'Pré behind. A silence as strident as the noise of a drill settled over the village. Something broke inside Mathilde that day. She wandered among the charred ruins for hours, unmindful of the soldiers who occupied the houses that had been spared. She didn't dare make a fire; her only source of heat was Quenouille, who watched her with big sorrowful eyes. She felt more and more chilled until she was consumed by fever. Next her stomach revolted because for too long she'd been living on cold vegetables, frozen potatoes, and nightmares.

Snow fell all day on December 21st, and sheets of snow blanketed Cap Blomidon. At dusk, Mathilde thought she saw something glinting above the cape – an amethyst, the sacred stone the Mi'kmaq called "the eye of Glous'Gap"[4], named for a divinity and seen as a lucky omen from the gods. She was in great need of the gods' assistance, for the thick fur the foxes had grown announced a harsh winter. Late Christmas Day, curled up under her mildewed blanket, surrounded by turnips, carrots, and cabbage, Mathilde no longer had the strength to leave the cellar. Her fever tipped her into delirium, and she was visited by dreams of fairies and by monstruous visions.

There was no Angéline to cradle her, take care of her, serve her hot, honeyed herbal tea, or rub her body down with a mixture of alcohol and camphor. She imagined Tristan's laugh, the ringing of cowbells, the angelus, Nazaire hammering on his anvil, all the familiar, reassuring sounds of her daily routine before the deportations… and the echo of songs from Poitou, transported across an ocean to brighten up the evenings, ringing through orchards full of apples, plums, and pears, while, nearby, the tumultous Gasparot raced noisily down its red mud furrow. She imagined the fields of wheat, barley, buckwheat, and hemp, the ordered squares along the

---

4. For the Mi'kmaq, the master of humans and animals, also known as Gluskap.

slopes and the marshes carefully drained by aboiteaux. She was rocked by their golden harvests and the fertile earth of the red orchards, the orange autumn leaves, and the green pine trees. She abandoned herself to the high tides of the Mines Basin as they lapped against the world's tallest dykes, forty-five feet high, especially during the equinox and the full moon. She remembered Papa Clairefontaine fishing serenely for sardines on the Gasparot while an aboiteau nearby waited for rain to dilute the seasalt so the golden stalks could grow. In a patch of light, she caught a glimpse of Nazaire ascending Cap Fendu. She saw herself at the age of three listening to Maman Clairefontaine tell stories as she knit and rocked the cradle gently by means of a rope tied to her rocking chair. She remembered the smells as well: the smell of the orchards in flower, of fresh apples, and bread piping hot from the oven, the more pungent smell of smoke from Papa Clairefontaine's pipe as he rocked her and she ate her bread and quark.

But her anguish returned. She was assailed by visions… and the marks of Satan appeared to her as she watched villagers stripped of all hope follow the dusty roads that led to the ships anchored offshore. Surrounded by soldiers, a lugubrious procession of desperate men and women, worried children, and howling dogs made its way through the smoking ruins. Off in the distance, she glimpsed the Cobeguit mountains, their ridges disappearing into the blue sky while grey smoke billowed from the houses on fire. That night a nightmare worse than all the others woke her with a start – a ship going under, carrying Tristan, Angéline, and her father with it. She didn't yet know that an epidemic had spread on the *Cornwallis*, and that half of the poor souls on it, including Papa Clairefontaine, had perished, or that in Charleston, Virginia, those who hadn't died were denied entry and sent on to England. She knew nothing of all that, but one glance at the frozen bay gave her a glimpse (this was no longer a dream) of ships surrounded by balls of fire rolling over the ice like barrels. When she heard the rattling of chains, she lost her will to fight. She could feel death creeping toward the cellar door; life was slowly draining from her and, leaning against a whimpering Quenouille, in her misery she shed more tears than all the weeping willows of Grand'Pré, her sobs echoing loudly back to her off the blackened chimneys, the wells, and the dykes.

* * *

During this time, the English were getting ready for Christmas, as seen in an excerpt from a letter addressed to Winslow by Commander Murray from Fort Edward on October 12, 1755:

"Thanks be to God! At last the ships have arrived. As soon as I've expedited these troublemakers, I'll be down to see you and we'll have ourselves a jolly good time."

Chapter 17

The inhabitants of these woods have come to tell you that as long as the grass grows in Grand'Pré and as long as the water flows in the Gasparot, the Indians will be your friends.

– Anonymous

Prebble wrote to Winslow from Fort Cumberland on August 24, 1755:
We are pleased to hear you have reached Mines and delighted to learn that you have arranged for suitable quarters for yourself and your soldiers by taking possession of the religious buildings; we trust that you will serve as good priests.

News travelled fast among the natives! By mid-September, people from Ruisseau had already heard about the Great Expulsion. In fact, as soon as the "great hunt" began, native hunters were spreading the news. A band of Mi'kmaq left Mines Basin and crossed the Chignectou isthmus to travel up the Petcoudiac River as far as Le Coude. Then they continued on to the Baie de Chedaïque[1] several leagues from Le Coude and decided, in order to spread the news, to follow the coast toward the Miramichi post, then on to Ruisseau.

---

1. Grande-Digue.

Saint-Jean assumed the English ships wouldn't show up until spring since the Baye des Chaleurs was icebound from mid-November to late April. However, he did worry about isolated warships and privateers, looking to profit from the period of conflict. Even in times of peace, English, Spanish, and Dutch pirates had been known to plunder the coasts, leaving both the inhabitants of the Baye des Chaleurs and seasonal fishermen from the Old Continent on constant alert. To set his mind at rest, he posted lookouts on the island until the ice arrived. René, Membertou, Josette, Geneviève, and others relayed each other to ensure someone was always on watch.

"We should send messengers to the Restigouche post," Membertou suggested.

He was thinking of the Mi'kmaq at the far end of the Baye des Chaleurs, a strategic position occupied by a French garrison that controlled the Matapedia River at the mouth of one of the routes to Quebec.

"Don't worry," his grandfather replied. "They would have heard the news before we did. In any case, a handful of soldiers won't be able to stop the invaders. Alas, I think this time the bell has tolled for the French colony."

* * *

In Quebec, on September 20th, Joseph learned that the Great Expulsion had begun. Two Abnaki canoed up the Kennebec[2] to the Chaudière[3] River and, from there to Quebec, portaging and riding along the crests of waves as fast as they could; they came asking Governor Vaudreuil for assistance, which he was unable to provide since he only had a handful of regiments to protect a continent bigger than Europe.

It's thanks to the unfailing support of the Indians, the Abnaki, Algonquin, Gaspesians, Huron, Maliseet, Mi'kmaq, and Montagnais that this eventuality has been put off for so long, Joseph thought. His only concern was to return to Angélique and his

---

2. A river in Maine.
3. This river crosses the Beauce.

children as quickly as possible. His sorrow at his mother's death was overshadowed by the danger threatening his family.

Meanwhile in Ruisseau, Jean-Baptiste had undergone a strange transformation. As a result of his illness and Jeannette-Anne's loving care, riches had lost their appeal for him, and money began to give off an odour less pleasing. Family grew in importance for him, and he envisaged getting closer to his father, whom he had always tended to blame for trivial matters. To mark the change, he offered his father a panther-skin blanket he had bought from a seaman.

Early in October, a dispute broke out between Saint-Jean and Foaming Bear over the hunting territories. Usually Saint-Jean used all his knowledge and wiles, coupled with support from the Elders Council, to divide up the hunting territories to everyone's satisfaction; but this time Foaming Bear – whose secret desire was to lead the tribe – kept coming up with one pretext after another, making an agreement impossible.

"It's my turn for the territories along Poquemouche River," he shouted at all the hunters.

"But the last time you were there, you had a hard time feeding your family," retorted Membertou, implying that as a hunter Foaming Bear left something to be desired. The supreme insult!

At times like these, Saint-Jean envied King Solomon his wisdom. The hitch in plans affected his honeymoon with Honguedo. He would much rather have stayed at home, surrounded by the rare furs hanging on his walls, his beautiful wife from the Gaspé at his side. Their liaison had begun after Saint-Jean saved her life during a moose hunt. Honguedo had been unstinting in her devotion ever since and had grown to love him. She made him forget the bitterness of his months spent on the galleys, and he could finally be more tender, making him seem younger. Despite his affection for Honguedo, though, his greatest passion was still the trapping life.

"One day, our furs will be worn in the courts of Europe..."

"Why not by merchants and farmers, too?" Honguedo added. "As far as I know, noblemen aren't the only human beings on this planet."

146

"You're right."

But he continued to dream of one day showing off his finest furs in Versailles or in the court of the Czar of all the Russias. With the money he earned he'd be able to bring settlers, fishermen, and trappers back to Acadia.

"It's soldiers we need, if you don't want to see your dream turn into a nightmare," muttered Honguedo.

He was well aware of that fact, but for the time being the dispute over hunting territories threatened to poison the tribe's life. When Membertou and Foaming Bear finally came to blows, Saint-Jean decided to catch the stubborn Foaming Bear in his own trap. He convened the Grand Council and declared, in the presence of the two antagonists, "You are a great hunter, Foaming Bear, and you have the makings of a chief. This winter, you will be responsible for deciding on the hunting territories. The honour will be Membertou's next winter. I have spoken!"

So the hunter became the hunted. Saint-Jean stood and lit the peace pipe, which he held out to Membertou before launching into the ritual dance of the great pipe of peace. Membertou took the pipe, then handed it to Foaming Bear, who inhaled grudgingly. But if he wanted to be a good chief, he had to meet everyone's expectations, which meant he had to give up the territory he'd wanted for the winter.

* * *

When Joseph set foot in Ruisseau on October 7th, Angélique was overjoyed. Her empathy for her husband's sorrow at his mother's death made her all the more passionate and attentive. But her warmth was not enough to assuage Joseph's suffering.

As a distraction, he threw himself headlong into preparing a religious ceremony around Gougou: a ritual celebrated in the spring every twenty-five years and for which, under shaman Fiery Elouèzes' direction, a gigantic monster had to be built, one that, according to legend, was easily taller than the tallest masts. Membertou, René, and a few of their friends built a mannequin on stilts that measured close to three toises;

from the northeastern tip of Ile Caraquet they chose two tall pine trees to serve as their frame. Josette and Geneviève covered the frame with ship's canvas, rags, furs, pine branches, birchbark, and ropes. René laid his bottles and jugs down facing huge bellows he had made out of skins to reproduce the horrible sounds Gougou emitted when eating her victims, howls that would be heard as far away as the coast and that would strike terror into the devil himself.

Angélique took part in the preparations as well, drawing inspiration from the first theatre in America[4] in Port-Royal. She suggested they send canoes loaded down with presents to Ile Caraquet to mollify the monster. In the lead, Neptune, god of the sea, pulled by four mermaids, would beat time with his trident for the sounding of the trumpet, the drumbeats, the cannon shots, and the children's choirs. To convince Joseph, Angélique proposed, "We could finish up with a feast worthy of the Order of Good Cheer."

"Your father would make a splendid Neptune, with his long white beard," Joseph said. "But we need the shaman's approval," he added.

Fiery Elouèzes needed some coaxing – for form's sake – but eventually he gave in. Work intensified. René decided to build a small megalith in which the presents would be placed while the mermaids launched into the Celtic dance of the four elements (water, air, fire, earth). Then Joseph added to the ceremony four costumed actors, who would bring on winged dragons the fruits of the earth (corn), the sea (wampum), furs representing the forest, and an hourglass, symbolizing time. All that was left to do was to protect the fragile material and the Gougou structure from the rigours of winter.

* * *

They moved camp in late October. The Mi'kmaq travelled in entire groups; the toboggans loaded down with everyone's belongings were pulled by women wearing snowshoes.

---

4. The Neptune Theatre with Champlain, Poutrincourt, Lescarbot...

Angélique did not agree with the traditional sharing of the workload whereby men hunted and laid traps and snares and women put up the wigwams and played the role of beasts of burden. Her bad mood was only made worse by Joseph, who was still preoccupied with his origins. She started to sulk, then decided to leave for Poquemouche River with the hunters' families.

In mid-November, almost no one remained in Ruisseau. Joseph and René kept busy putting the finishing touches to the sets for May's Gougou ceremony. Joseph had carved a large number of wooden masks out of great pinewood. René dipped the masks in deer blood or ashes, according to whether he wanted them stained red or black. Following the Iroquois tradition, whenever the pinewood was resistant to the treatment, Joseph took it to mean that the mask was worthy of serving in the ceremony.

Jean-Baptiste had stayed behind as well; he continued to distance himself from the hunting traditions, preferring the fishing life instead. His reasons would have been frowned on, since the Mi'kmaq valued hunters more than fishers, so the excuse that Jean-Baptiste gave for staying behind was to look after the old people who would have slowed down the hunt. It hadn't been easy, but his father had supported him, for he didn't want to see the elderly who might have hindered the hunt abandoned deep in the forest. However, the tradition had ensured the tribe's survival over the years, since there was nothing more important than finding food. And so they reached an honourable compromise, one that benefited both Jean-Baptiste, and indirectly, the whole band. When ice imprisoned the bay, he fished for smelt, through holes he drilled in the ice, using hooks or fibre hoop nets that he placed in the water. Afterwards, with Jeannette-Anne's help, he prepared his gear to capture the sea lions in spring; their fat and hides brought in a good income.

Working side by side drew Joseph and René closer together. The latter had noticed his mother's sulkiness before her departure for Poquemouche and asked Joseph one fine morning, "What's wrong with Angélique?"

Joseph wasn't sure what to say. He finally replied, "People in love don't always agree on everything. But don't worry, I love your mother very much."

It was true. His love for Angélique was founded on more than fifteen years of shared life punctuated by its share of both wonderful and difficult moments. They had always managed to overcome the difficult times.

In mid-December, Joseph and René rejoined their family six leagues to the east. They were happy to see their grand-father, Honguedo, Angélique, Geneviève, Josette, and Membertou again. They were greeted warmly by all. Angélique slept well nestled against her man and his warmth, ignoring her frustration for one night. But Joseph did not sleep well; he couldn't stop thinking about the encroaching war. Happy to see his family together again and proud of the finished sets, René dreamt of the precious stones on the island. As for Saint-Jean, he tossed and turned for part of the night, worried about the hunt, which did not look promising. His sweet Honguedo couldn't calm him. In the morning, he confided in Joseph.

"I can't seem to make them understand we need to put by stores for the winter. Foaming Bear and his band live from day to day without a thought for tomorrow. They make merry when they should be curing meat for the times when food is in short supply."

Joseph knew the problem well. "Right, once again we'll have to share our food with them when they have nothing left to eat."

"This time, I'm imposing conditions: we'll share our food, but they'll have to change their ways."

"Where are they now?"

"About twenty leagues upriver on the Tabusintac, close to Miramichi. I had news of them a moon ago. The hunting isn't good. Boishébert's troops are nearby, and many refugees are said to be living there in utter destitution. People fleeing from the deportation have arrived from all over: Grand'Pré, Port-Royal, Pobomcoup, Cobeguit, Beauséjour, Ile Saint-Jean... Most of them are on their way to Miramichi or Louisbourg."

"Don't forget that in a year or two, they'll all be heading back toward Ruisseau," Joseph prophesized, "because the English have started sailing up the coast."

"That's why we need food reserves," Saint-Jean insisted. "Both for us and the refugees. We have to be careful not to eat all our supplies like gluttons. Last week, a messenger came asking for provisions on Boishébert's behalf, and I sent half our reserves to the poor souls there. I even threw in my last crate of cognac. I could never reconcile myself to drinking it while thinking of all those people ravaged by hunger and cold."

"Your cognac!" Joseph exclaimed, struck by the extent of his father-in-law's sacrifice. "You do know who's going to benefit from your crate of cognac, don't you?"

"I made Boishébert's messenger promise that it would be used to comfort the sick and the children; otherwise, there'd be no more assistance coming from us. A few drops of alcohol when needed for the little ones will make their death that much less painful."

"What are we going to do?" Joseph fretted. "We can't defend a continent without a real army."

Chapter 18

They beg you to observe that the only reason for their misfortune is their sole attachment to France and their status as subjects of that Crown, something the English were unable to make them renounce... The inhabitants of Mines, Beaubassin, and of the Rivers (Memramcouk, Petcoudiak, and Chepoudie), are either wandering through the bush or prisoners of the English. It is rare to find one family left intact, and those who are have only one desire: revenge.

– Petition from the Acadians to Governor Vaudreuil in July 1756

As she lay next to Quenouille, Mathilde called out to Papa Clairefontaine for help. She heard voices whispering in Mi'kmaq, then saw a man staring at her. She didn't realize she was saved, and that Abbot Leloutre had just kept the promise he'd made to her father to watch over her. Before his departure for France in search of assistance, he had asked several Mi'kmaq to return to Grand'Pré to rescue the fugitives and discover Mathilde's whereabouts. The Mi'kmaq carried her to their camp and managed to bring down her fever with their herbal remedies.

Once she regained her strength, Mathilde left for the Beauséjour region with her rescuers, following the shoreline of the Baie Française. The situation was far from rosy. The

Acadians – hunted from every direction – fled through the woods and marshes to avoid both soldiers and warships. The English flag flew over Fort Beauséjour; the whole surrounding Three Rivers region (including Chepoudie[1], Memramcouk, Petcoudiac) was nothing but desolation. Whether in Chepoudie, where the Thibodeaus hid out in the woods, in Memramcouk, where the Gaudets did likewise, or in the Bonappétit's village, in the small town of Ruisseau-des-Renards or in the hamlet of Fourche-à-Crapaud, there was nothing but fugitives and destitution. Sometimes charred ruins spotted the snow, like the blackened steeple of Petcoudiac. Colonel Robert Monckton had fulfilled his mission: laying waste to the whole region so that the inhabitants who refused to surrender would starve. To earn their bonuses, his Rangers didn't bother distinguishing between a white or Indian scalp.

Mathilde and her friends stopped off at Toussaint Blanchard's house close to Sylvabro[2]. They stayed just long enough to warm up, have some stew, and attend mass celebrated by the Jesuit priest Labrosse at the Terre Rouge chapel in Le Coude, a neighbouring village in which almost all the Terriot family's children were buried.

The Mi'kmaq had been instructed to place Mathilde under the protection of Abbot François Le Guerne, who officiated in the triangle formed by the villages of Cocagne, Batture[3], and Chedaïque. The missionary was unstinting in his devotion to the thousand-plus Acadians who had sought refuge in the region. At last Mathilde joined him, with her loyal Quenouille. The abbot lived on the north side of the Baie de Cocagne, close to a small stream that the unhappy inhabitants had baptized the Ruisseau-des-Malcontents (Stream of Discontent). Justifiably so, since they had lost their land and property, their status as citizens and, in many cases, members of their family, who were either dead or scattered to the four corners of America. Abbot Le Guerne reflected on how far

---

1. Chapeau de Dieu ("God's hat").
2. Sylvain Breault (Dieppe).
3. Shédiac.

removed was the time when the explorer Verrazano baptized the country "Arcadia" because its lush vegetation and summer heat reminded him of a heavenly region in Ancient Greece of the same name. And how far removed the time when Nicolas Denys fell in love with the region, giving it the somewhat Rabelaisian name of Cocagne – "the land of milk and honey." Acadia was no longer a land of Cocagne, but rather "a land of Cain" in Le Guerne's view. Some inhabitants had built schooners to set sail for Port-Lajoie on Ile Saint-Jean, which was still French. Others, having joined the militia captain Joseph Godin known as Bellefontaine and his group of Abnaki, waged war along the Saint-Jean River, near Sainte-Anne-des-Pays-Bas[4]. Officer Boishébert's soldiers were on alert some thirty leagues to the north of Le Coude as they patrolled the Miramichi region, a hub for the exodus and Boishébert's headquarters. This was most refugees' destination since rumour had it there were still some provisions left in the king's stores there. Le Guerne decided to head for the same spot with Mathilde following behind as he headed out into the cold and blowing snow.

* * *

For thousands of years, natives had been coming to Miramichi to stage their religious ceremonies and hunt and fish for salmon in one of the most densely populated rivers in the world. By the winter of 1756, some 3500 exiles had settled at Baie-des-Ouines, Anse-du-Fort-Français, Pointe-Acadienne and Pointe-de-Boishébert. But the majority lived on an island on the Miramichi that the Mi'kmaq knew as Kwoomenigork or Pine Island and was called Sainte-Croix, as a reminder of the attachment the natives in that region had for the cross, a symbol that often decorated the bow of their canoes and one that they had used before the arrival of the missionaries. On the island, which measured less than one league in length, were two hundred shabby huts, a church, and Boishébert's

---

4. Fredericton region.

quarters. The village's nickname was Cap de l'Espérance – Cape of Hope! Hope was a spring the exiles had to return to daily to find the strength to carry on in the same way they quenched their physical thirst from the small freshwater spring that irrigated the island.

Miramichi was a place of transit, an arrival and departure hub for the refugees – when possible – with Ile Saint-Jean, Louisbourg, the Restigouche post or Quebec. Some went looking for their families through the devastated land; others, the strongest, joined the guerrilla movement or went in search of livestock wandering through the Three Rivers region.

Across from the island on the north shore of the Miramichi were the ruins of Richard Denys de Fronsac's house and fort. His father Nicolas had had jurisdiction over a large part of Acadia in the seventeenth century. The fruit trees he'd brought back from France were a reminder of his passage. In the fall the trees' fruit was a welcome treat for the refugees installed either in the ruins of his stone house, in the old store-house, or in the surrounding cabins, vestiges of the fur merchants' and cod fishermen's efforts back when Nicolas Denys was still alive. Boishébert had restored the old fort – its vertical wooden posts and its four lookouts – and armed it with ten cannons. He had also installed a cannon battery on the island's eastern point for better protection, but he hadn't foreseen the constant influx of refugees, most of whom arrived without food or weapons and in a pitiful state. After fleeing the Fort Beauséjour region in the fall of 1755, most of the refugees had had to use hatchets and knives to hack their way through the brush along nearly impracticable trails to lose their pursuers through marshes and clearings of dead trees.

"How can we wage war and still look after the refugees?" Boishébert lamented. Sieur Charles de Boishébert, captain and now commander of Acadia, did indeed have a burdensome task. As sole defender of Acadia, the twenty-six-year-old officer had been granted permission to stay on by Vaudreuil. Enrolled in the army at the age of thirteen, he had lived in Acadia since the age of sixteen. He only left the country once for a brief trip to Versailles to deliver dispatches to the Minister of the Colonies, and another time to the Great Lakes region to command a detachment. Boishébert knew the country well. In 1746, he had accompanied his uncle Nicolas de Ramezay to the Port-Royal headquarters and, the following year, he participated in the Grand'Pré victory. Before the fall of Fort Beauséjour, he was in command of Fort Latour on the Saint-Jean, a fort he decided to destroy rather than see it taken over by the enemy. He did manage to get his revenge on August 26, 1755, however, when he and a group of Acadians and natives took Major Frye by surprise just as the latter was setting fire to Chepoudie. That time, he and his few hundred soldiers, Acadians, Mi'kmaq, Maliseet, and Abnaki had to resort to guerrilla tactics against Monckton's many and seasoned troops. (He had abandoned the European-style warfare long before that.)

With his hundred or so combattants, all exhausted, malnourished, and insufficiently clothed, Charles de Boishébert had reason for concern; he was at an extreme disadvantage compared to the thousands of soldiers from England and the American colonies, who had the fleet's cannons to back them up. On Isle Royale, the Louisbourg fortress was preparing for an out-and-out siege similar to the ones carried out along the St. Lawrence River against Quebec and Montreal in particular.

"They'll be going in for the kill," Boishébert told Abbot Le Guerne. "The foreign armies have decided to wipe the French empire in America off the map. Once they've put an end to Acadian resistance, Quebec will fall. I've asked Vaudreuil for several hundred soldiers with whom we can invade Fort Beauséjour and maybe even Halifax, where we'll have the advantage of a surprise attack. But the governor doesn't seem to realize how important these territories, his first line of defence, are…"

"When his father governed New France, his strategy was no better," the abbot remarked. "Frontenac and La Galissonnière did, however, understand that the key to Quebec's defence was the defence of Acadia… All this waste for nothing," he sighed.

Boishébert's thoughts were on all the suffering as well as on the failing troops. Already there'd been some thirty deaths due to hardship, starvation, illness. He thought of all his heroes, dead or in prison, the dearest of all to him being Joseph Broussard, known as Beausoleil.

"Did you know he saved my life during the Grand'Pré battle in the winter of 1747 by diverting a salvo of musketfire? The English put a price on his head, but he wasn't easy to capture because he hid out with the Indians; he lived like them and spoke their language. But after the fall of Fort Beauséjour, where he fought to the very last minutes of the battle, they finally got the better of him. He was taken prisoner and deported to Carolina."

"He's not the kind of man who will stay in prison long," Abbot Le Guerne said, to comfort Boishébert.

* * *

The situation was no better in Miramichi or Ruisseau-des-Malcontents. There, too, the triple threat of famine, illness, and war hung in the air. And the king's storehouses were empty. However, Mathilde was treated to a few drops of Saint-Jean's cognac, which was distributed as promised to the invalids and children, albeit in minute quantities under the watchful eye of Sieur de Niverville, Boishébert's second-in-command. Others were given chunks of cider that had frozen from the cold!

Father Le Guerne couldn't keep up with the demand, and as soon as Mathilde was well enough, she helped him bring comfort to others, going from one hut to another to read the Holy Scripture to the afflicted. She meditated on the passage, "Blessed are the poor in spirit, for they shall inherit the kingdom of heaven." She guessed she definitely must have a place waiting for her in heaven!

Living in the camp were a great number of Mi'kmaq, for whom the missionary celebrated daily mass in their language, which Mathilde particularly liked. She began to take an interest in the language. She learned the rudiments by reading the writings of Father Maillard, who had published a grammar book, a catechism, and an examination of conscience in that language. Then a young candidate for the priesthood, Joseph Gueguen, became her tutor. He was fluent in Mi'kmaq and English and served as an interpreter whenever the natives captured English soldiers. Gueguen was from Morlaix, Brittany, just like the abbots Leloutre and Manach. Abbot Manach's kind attention and devotion as well as Gueguen's encouragement helped Mathilde learn the difficult language. Within a few weeks' time, she knew the basic hieroglyphs quite well. During that time, she formed a friendship with a young Mi'kmaq, an orphan like her, whose name was Tjigog, meaning "superman" – a title many Mi'kmaq claimed for themselves!

* * *

Camp de l'Espérance was eager for news. Word spread that a certain Charles Belliveau and his companions – who had been dispatched to South Carolina on board the *Pembroke* – had rid themselves of their jailers en route by throwing them overboard. The "mutineers" had found refuge along the Saint-Jean, not far from Father Germain's mission. Mathilde hoped her family was among those on board, but her hopes were soon dashed. She was despondent.

"I should have let the English capture me in Grand'Pré," she murmured to Quenouille. "There's nothing left to eat in camp. People are dying daily. I can't stand it anymore."

Sensing Mathilde's sorrow, Quenouille rubbed his muzzle against her cheek. That was the best he could do to comfort his little mistress.

In neighbouring huts, children could be heard moaning. People were boiling birchbark to make soup; some were reduced to making soup from their moccasins. It was rumoured that some of the refugees were hungry enough to eat the dead.

One thing that wasn't in short supply was dishes. Plates from New England, teacups from Holland, jars from France, pots from Louisbourg, rum bottles from the West Indies. They all had one thing in common, however: they were empty! A group of Mi'kmaq made their way to Poquemouche and

Ruisseau hoping to find supplies to bring back with them. The others waited and waited, but they never returned. Mathilde thought of Richard Denys de Fronsac's coat of arms, bunches of grapes on golden vines supported by two stags, and dreamt of feasting on the fruit. She finally shook herself out of her torpor to check the snares set for hare along the riverbank. She found nothing; either the hares had starved to death or they'd been eaten by a fox. High up in a tall spruce tree, a crow cawed, shattering the silence. Mathilde took off her mittens, pulled out her slingshot, placed a small white stone inside, and fired… the bird fell. "This will be something to add to the children's stew," she rejoiced.

That same day, good news reached Camp de l'Espérance. A schooner had managed to evade the English ships and skirt all the ice floes. On board were some fifty exiles and a cargo of supplies and livestock. The cargo represented a glimmer of hope for the children suffering from rickets and bloated bellies and a moment's joy for Mathilde as she recognized among the new arrivals some friends of her adoptive family: Olivier Blanchard and Catherine Amirault, Charles Dugas, a militia major, and his wife Anne LeBlanc, as well as their son Joseph. Jacques Léger, his wife Anne Amireault, their son Olivier and his wife Marie-Josephte Hébert were on board as well. They had all been regular visitors at Papa Clairefontaine's. Mathilde forgot her troubles when Olivier Blanchard sat down next to the blazing fire with his fiddle and began playing a wild jig, accompanied by all the spoons in the camp. But the burning questions on everyone's lips couldn't wait long. Each and every person wanted news of his or her family. Olivier Léger, who had travelled to Virginia on the same ship as Angéline, had some news for Mathilde.

"Beausoleil escaped from Carolina and is on his way to Quebec."

"It won't take him long to reach us," Boishébert said gladly.

"What about Papa Clairefontaine?" Mathilde asked.

Léger stared at Mathilde's face, lit by the wavering flames. *Poor child*, he thought. *But what's the good in hiding the truth from her?*

159

"Old Clairefontaine died of a broken heart during the crossing," he answered. "Afterwards the ship stayed in the Galveston[5] harbour for six weeks because the authorities refused to let the deportees off. Many died from epidemics, but when the ship finally set sail for England, Angéline was still in good health and good spirits. As for Tristan, I have no news, alas!"

Mathilde started to sob, and Olivier tried to comfort her.

"We're all condemned to death here," she cried.

"Don't ever lose hope. Today, tragedy, tomorrow, joy. We have to keep living. Soon we'll leave the island and move to the Restigouche post or Quebec."

"We're always running. Won't it ever end?"

"I still harbour the hope the King of France will send help and we'll be able to return to our villages."

Nothing could change his mind, not even hard facts!

---

5. In Virginia.

Chapter 19

...fish are in great abundance here: cod, herring, salmon, and lobster...

– Champlain

April 1756. Ice floes floated down the channel between Ile Caraquet and Ruisseau. Jean-Baptiste was sick and tired of waiting. He headed out with his schooner at the first opportunity, but ice blocked him at the point of the island and damaged the ship's hull. He barely noticed, so wrapped up was he in dreaming about the wonderful fish just waiting to be caught – schools of cod and salmon and pods of whales. He began dreaming of a fabulous fishing empire: fishermen, navigators, seamen, shipbuilders, and the navy troops New France needed in order to rid itself of the English. He could already imagine the bustling shipyard and trunks of great white pines that would serve as ships' masts.

The Basques, Portuguese, Bostonians, and fishermen from French ports won't be the only ones taking advantage of our seas' abundance. There will be local people, too, Jean-Baptiste thought.

He could already hear Angélique waxing eloquent on the bounty of the earth, Saint-Jean swearing by the importance of the forest's resources alone, and Joseph expounding on the need to train soldiers. Shortly before Jean-Baptiste left on his fishing excursion, Joseph told him, "A beaver pelt, a pumpkin, a codfish are all well and good... But the colony won't go far without protection."

The need for protection got Jean-Baptiste thinking. He armed his ship with small cannons, although he knew full well they wouldn't do much to rout the English. "But they'll make a lone privateer think twice before launching an attack," he concluded, as though in consolation.

* * *

These days, the formerly impulsive, quick-tempered Membertou exuded an air of calm and serenity. The change in him was born of his recent fascination with the shaman's activities. He spent hours and hours with Fiery Elouèzes. His grand plan gradually came to light: he wanted to become a shaman himself.

He wanted to enter into a trance during the "shaking tent"[1] ritual and communicate with the spirit world. Although Fiery Elouèzes had the power to predict certain events, the capacity to cast spells, and the gift of tracking down game and the enemy, he was extremely wary when it came to sharing his knowledge. But when Membertou confided that he was often visited by dreams, the shaman told him, "That's a good sign; shamans can't help dreaming. But first, you must be chosen and learn to observe, see, learn, feel."

Membertou fervently wanted to learn the shaman's secrets. Not so much to become a healer, poet, or magician, but to become a great priest. His people's spiritual guide. He knew he'd have to learn about the white man's religion as well, either to fight it, or integrate the good from it. He could already imagine how his influence would extend beyond the Mi'kmaq and lure the coureurs de bois and other white men away from the missionaries and toward the attraction of the native lifestyle. He began to take an interest in the Bible and the

---

1. The shaman enters into a trance and the tent begins to shake, at which point the shaman may see, for instance, a vision of where the hunters will find game, how to cure an invalid, or the status of people who haven't been heard from.

Holy Scripture. *I don't want to see the black robes gathering the Indians together in an enclosure to indoctrinate them. Only a religion that values challenge and adventure is made for this country*, thought Membertou.

Oblivious of the changes going on around him, Saint-Jean radiated happiness thanks to Honguedo and the passion she brought into his life. Joseph was in fine form as well; his mourning for his mother was over. He was preparing the Gougou ceremony when influenza struck the camp, giving Angélique more reason to worry about her family. She watched for the slightest signs of discomfort, rash, a sneeze, or a fever. Neither the shaman's remedies and incantations nor Angélique's herbs and potions did any good. So funeral rituals became part of the daily routine, and those who were still able-bodied spent their time either caring for the sick and dying or depositing the remains of the deceased on a platform specially built for that purpose.

Salmon began swimming upstream, and Canada geese began losing their feathers; summer was upon them. But the epidemic raged all through the warmest season. The Mi'kmaq still had to worry about food, so some decided to accompany Jean-Baptiste cod fishing as his makeshift crew. He fished for six weeks until mid-July. A few Mi'kmaq took an interest in shore duties, turning the cod skin-out on flat stones to preserve them from the humidity and evening showers. During that tragic summer, at least the cool, dry winds from the north favoured the operation. The Mi'kmaq also had to cure and dry the meat and fish. A few elderly women took on the task of curing the hides.

A touch of balm was poured on the troubled times when Saint-Jean's adoptive daughter Françoise, administrator of the Gaspeg trading post, reconciled with her father. A conflict whose cause had never been clear ended for unknown reasons. It was thought the influence of her husband, Pierre LeVicaire, who held his father-in-law in high regard, was partly responsible. The family – Françoise, Pierre, and their two daughters, Anne and Marie – were welcomed in Ruisseau with great rejoicing. A joyful Saint-Jean wanted to celebrate. Having harboured the hope of a reconciliation with his daughter for as long as he could remember, he gave her a present he had carefully chosen with her in mind. The gift was extraordinary: a diamond brooch he had spirited away from the island treasure. To his granddaughters, he offered two dolls made by Jeannette-Anne. The gifts sealed their reunion.

Angélique had been too busy looking after the sick to tend to her garden. That job had fallen to Joseph, who planted some sorrel for soup. Françoise, Anne, and Marie helped him, while Pierre fished tirelessly for cod with Jean-Baptiste. The epidemic had run its course by late summer, when the game began its journey south.

René tried to find an explanation for the epidemic using Celtic astrology, knowledge that had been handed down to him by an old Breton who called himself a druid and who, a year before, had spent the summer in Ruisseau tending to a wound. At Pointe-de-Roche, René erected a line of dolmens with which he could study the constellations. The stars were represented by a series of upended rocks. Thus he was able to confirm that the illness that had descended on the tribe was inscribed in one of the thirty-six constellations of Celtic astrology. The system was particular in that it linked each constellation to a tree, which in turn symbolized each constellation's roots in Earth's order.

"You were born on June 20th and are part of the Ursa constellation," he told Josette. "Your tree is the birch tree, creative and refined, and the reason you've been tired lately is because the tree is ailing from all the insects eating its shoots."

Josette didn't need his far-fetched explanation. She knew the cause of her fatigue was nothing more than too many sleepless nights spent looking after the sick!

Membertou and René's arguments were entertaining to behold. Each one was convinced of the truth of his beliefs.

"The Celts believed in one single God and in archangels, so why don't you read their bible?" René said ironically.

His goal was to convince Membertou of the soundness of Celtic astrology. He continued, "The tree is a link to heaven through its leaves, and to earth through its roots. It draws life from the sun and the air; it represents the beauty and tranquility of the cosmos and shows a way other than that of violence and the bloody struggles characterized by the animal kingdom."

"You talk as though you founded the movement," Membertou retorted.

"Well, you act like you're the Mi'kmaq's Grand Shaman," retaliated René.

Membertou counterattacked, "You exalt the plant kingdom, but what about weeds! Forgotten them?" he jeered.

"No," his brother stated. "Each plant has its usefulness. When you were running a high fever last year, Angélique gave you a potion made of weeds!"

René had just scored a point or two.

* * *

In early October, a certain Gabriel Albert – who hailed from Quebec and worked as a fisherman at Papôg[2] – came to see Pierre, Françoise, and their daughters aboard his schooner. It was love at first sight for Geneviève when the good-looking Gabriel's eyes met hers. Geneviève was transformed from her usual flirtatious, seductive self into a shy, dreamy young girl whenever she was in the presence of the man she loved. She was only fifteen, but her body was a woman's body and her passionate energy and character had been moulded by the summer's travails. Gabriel had only planned to stay in Ruisseau for a few days, but he kept coming up with ingenious excuses to prolong his stay. However, he did have to return to Quebec before the ice set in.

Their engagement, celebrated in early November, was about the only joyous event of the year. Saint-Jean offered Geneviève a pearl necklace from the island treasure, Angélique gave her a fur coat, and René presented her with a description of her cosmic constellation that showed she was placed under the protection of the oak tree. Oak trees did well in Acadia.

---

2. In Mi'kmaq, Papôg meant "slow-moving expanse of water." Today's Pabos.

"The oak is synonymous with strength and is a symbol of hospitality," he explained. "It represents stability and tenacity. It inspires respect and trust." From Josette she received a clay platter, from Jeannette-Anne mocassins embroidered with porcupine quills, and from Membertou, who was more interested in getting to Gabriel through her, a rattle carved in the shape of a bear's head that was said to help hunters enter into contact with the bear's spirit during the hunt. Joseph made the future couple very happy; he offered them a bottle of Armagnac from the same year as Geneviève's birth!

* * *

The winter of 1756-1757. Since a large number of refugees were camped along the shore of the Miramichi, the Mi'kmaq and Joseph's family set up their hunting camp in the vicinity of the Poquemouche River. But an influx of refugees was already expected. There had been a revolt in Camp de l'Espérance; embittered by their despair, several inhabitants of the camp accused Boishébert of hiding provisions. Many starving refugees made their way to the Poquemouche. The strongest arrived on snowshoes, the others on sleds. They had travelled twenty leagues from the north, drawn by the river teeming with fish and by the reserves Saint-Jean's clan still had. The reserves didn't last long. The poor people arrived in a pitiful state, having used up their last drops of sea-lion oil and sucked on the very last of the cattle hides Boishébert meant for the soldiers. They were reduced to chewing on a few deerskin shoes. The refugees spent the rest of the winter ice-fishing, which Jean-Baptiste saw as vindication. He had always known how important fishing was.

* * *

Spring 1757. Jean-Baptiste and Jeannette-Anne experienced a joyous event: the birth of a son. They sailed over a calm sea to Mont Sainte-Anne in the Gaspé on the other side of the Baye des Chaleurs for the newborn ceremony. On the mountaintop,

Jeannette-Anne presented her son Pokamo[3] to the sun, holding him up high and shouting loudly to attract the attention of the kind star, conqueror of cold and storms. The sun gave little warmth, however, to the Acadians, frozen to the bone, adrift on floating coffins, exile-bound.

---

3. "Who is always babbling."

Chapter 20

Acadian mothers are forced to watch their children die at their breast because they have no milk left. Most of them cannot go out in public because they have no clothes to cover their nudity.

– Letter from Governor Vaudreuil
to the minister on April 19, 1757

Excerpt from Boishébert's reports to the king in 1763:
Travelling across immense expanses of land. Trying to be everywhere a leader is needed. Pretending victory consists of burning forts to the ground and seeking shelter in the woods. Trying to slow the rapid spread of despair Announcing and promising a rescue that never comes Disguising hunger from those experiencing it. Finding food and clothing for many people among the wretched ruins of destitution. Taking from Peter to give to Paul. Wrenching from England and keeping for France almost an entire nation, which had everything to fear from the former and nothing to gain from the latter. Doing so day in, day out while outnumbered by the enemy and far from orders and assistance, which only arrived from Quebec slowly, rarely or after many obstacles. Such were the measures and effort required to defend Acadia.

Camp de l'Espérance, May 1756. Spring announced both a rebirth for the earth and a time for digging graves. Close to five hundred bodies waited in eternal repose. Rivulets of water, formed from the thaw runoff and the tears shed at burials, flowed into the graves like Petcoudiac's tidal bore.

Since Tjigog and Mathilde's main concern was for the living, right after the ice breakup they helped fish for seacows and lobster that they flushed out with fish spears. Salmon still abounded, in fact the noise the fish made at night as they leapt up and fell back into the water made sleep difficult. The two young friends looked for turtle eggs as well along the sandy shores of the Miramichi, eggs that could be used to make delicious omelettes seasoned with wild mint and accompanied by spring salads of dandelion leaves, wild leeks, and artichoke roots cooked in embers. But they also needed to put up stores of the products of the earth and sea. Tjigog and Mathilde picked an impressive quantity of fiddleheads and cotton stalks, which were used with waterlily leaves to wrap around meat then cooked in the embers to make a succulent dish. Tjigog seemed to know everything: he boiled burdock roots (best with a partridge carcass), braised marsh bulrush roots or ground them up as flour, and collected birch sap for syrup. There was only one dish Mathilde could do without: prickly thorns boiled with wood garlic and red ants gathered along the Cinquante-Six-Bretons River.

Ships loaded with goods and delayed because of headwinds finally arrived from Quebec. The members of the colony were able to assuage their hunger for a while. Since the ships had to return to Quebec, Boishébert decided to send close to two hundred refugees for whom he hadn't enough food and who had tried to loot the stores. At the summer solstice on Saint John's day, a flock of pigeons from the south blanketed the sky. Tjigog and Mathilde built small traps made of a few slipknots of moose-tail hair tied to a plank with a few seeds inside. They caught a fair number of pigeons and made pigeon pies just like the Denys family had a century earlier. At last, a treat for the camp's inhabitants!

Other refugees arrived. There were Alexis Cormier from Cocagne and his fiancée Elizabeth Gauthier, then from Aulac, Alexis Landry and his wife, Marie Terriot, Jean Cormier's widow and their eleven children, including four from Marie's first marriage. They had all known Papa Clairefontaine well. Mathilde's uncle, Joseph-Jean Chiasson, arrived unexpectedly with his wife Anne Haché from Ile Saint-Jean. Mathilde had never met them before, but she felt at ease with them. Slowly a family of sorts began forming around her. She dreamt of flourishing villages along the coastlines populated with small, charming houses and multi-coloured fishing boats. A happy, prosperous people. A young man, too, who would send her love poems written on birchbark. But she could never catch a glimpse of his face. Her uncle interpreted her dream for her, "Your dream means we'll rebuild our land. And that you will have a sweetheart," he added with a wink.

From then on, Mathilde's belief in the future returned. Her Aunt Anne loved to paint; she drew landscapes on birchbark that she then coloured using clay kneaded with plant essences. Mathilde was drawn to the art and, with her aunt's help, she began painting portraits of her loved ones. Soon she graduated to pictures of the natives with their magnificent hunting or war costumes festooned with swan, goose, and duck feathers. Tjigog was a frequent model, seen from every possible angle. Soon Mathilde had a whole collection of paintings that she distributed among the surrounding huts. After that, she turned to animals and spent a long time portraying the red fox that ferreted about the cabins. Her aunt and uncle saw her blossom, and were proud of her talent at combining colours, lines, and shapes. She managed to master angles, perspective, and the play of light and shadow. Gradually, as her vitality resurfaced, light also began to shine into the sadder parts of her being.

Mathilde was tall and precocious for her eleven years. Her body, blossoming into womanhood, was slim and lithe, her hair long and jet-black, and her character matured by her trials. Her dog Quenouille was always at her side. She often spoke to him and he growled softly as he listened. "You understand everything," she said, patting this being that was the only tie she had left to the village of Grand'Pré.

A terrible drought struck during the summer of 1756. The few vegetables that managed to grow had a bitter taste, and Mathilde spent a great deal of time hoeing and weeding her aunt's small garden. Only the worms were fat and well-fed. To her disappointment, Mathilde could no longer indulge her weakness for fine food. It was impossible to come by fresh cucumber, juicy tomatoes, and even less so, pastry or white honey on bread. She spent the summer gathering roots and wild berries, choosing among the "weeds" those that were edible. She had better luck with what she found in nature than with what she grew in the garden.

One day in late August, Mathilde, Tjigog, Joseph-Jean, Anne, and a few friends decided to dip into the summer's reserves. Luckily, despite the shortages, they still had the products of the forest. For breakfast, Mathilde prepared oatmeal with wild purslane seeds and pigweed. Anne baked bread made with chickweed seeds. Tjigog ground wild chicory roots to use as a substitute for coffee. Joseph-Jean toasted water lily seeds to make a kind of popcorn that they handed out to the children, who washed everything down with a sorrel drink. The evening meal was more substantial. First, a salad made of watercress, wood sorrel, and braised water lily roots seasoned with black mustard and powdered coltsfoot leaves (as a substitute for salt). Braised salmon seasoned with mustard leaves was eaten on its own since the garden hadn't produced any vegetables. However, the dessert basket was impressive: strawberries, raspberries, blueberries, plums, elderberries, and hawthorn[1] berries. When night fell, Tjigog smeared animal fat on rushes to make torches, and their voices rose in song as they sat around the fire. Native songs and others from the homeland: *Sur le pont d'Avignon, Le chant de l'alouette, M'en revenant de la jolie Rochelle*. Uncle Joseph-Jean started to sing, "C'est dans le mois de mai," then Aunt Anne continued with *Le Petit Boeuf*, followed by Mathilde's singing, "Mon père n'avait fille que moi… Marie-Madeleine, ton p'tit jupon de laine, ta p'tite jupe carreautée, ton p'tit jupon piqué…"

---

1. Of which the needles were used as sewing needles and as arrow tips or bait hooks.

The celebration ended in the early hours when no one could eat any more and their whole repertoire of songs had been run through.

* * *

En route to Carolina via Quebec, Beausoleil was authorized by Governor Vaudreuil to arm a small privateer's ship. By the fall of 1756 he began plundering the coasts of the Mer Rouge[2] as well as the Baie Verte region. From time to time, word spread through the camp of Beausoleil's catches. He had the English fleet on alert since he always appeared where he was least expected, freeing prisoners he then escorted to Louisbourg or Miramichi or capturing a one-hundred-ton schooner here or, to supply the Halifax garrison, a ten-cannon English storeship there. It was impossible, however, for him to conquer the English fleet with his three measly cannons and six swivel guns!

For his part, Boishébert and his small troop of regular soldiers and Acadian militia members fanned out through the surrounding countryside. They were everywhere at once: Beaubassin, Memramcouk, the Saint-Jean River as far as Cap Maringouin, and the Baie Française, making a laughingstock out of Major Scott and his unsuccessful raids. The natives took part in the guerrilla operation, too. Several brought back English scalps. It was fitting revenge for the high premiums (some twenty-five pounds) offered by the English for the scalp of any native man, woman, or child. The practice didn't shock Puritans since the indigenous peoples were not seen as children of God but as children of the devil; the Puritan attitude only strengthened the natives' resolve to rid themselves of the invader. And to show who the experts were when it came to taking scalps.

In the evening, the fire's flames were fanned with hope and fed by rumours and exploits, images of victory, and visions of heroism and conquest that grew into legends and fables on

---

2. Northumberland Strait.

172

a par with the search for the Holy Grail. When Charles Belliveau captured the *Pembroke*, it was made to sound like he had accomplished one of the labours of Hercules. What was initially but an anecdote took on gigantic proportions, like the exploits of the hero fighting the Moors in *The Song of Roland*. In actual fact, shortly before the deportations, Charles Belliveau had replaced the *Pembroke*'s mast. Having been refused payment, he threatened to hack the mast to pieces and the English captain caved in. As fate would have it, that same ship was the one on which Belliveau was sent into exile. However, with the help of Boudreau, Dugas, Granger, and others he managed to take over the ship. He then faced the ship into the headwind, shouting at the terrified Englishmen, "It's safe. The mast will hold, I know because I'm the one who built it!"

Like father like son, for his son Pierre and Bounan Le Blanc and the three Gautreau brothers seized an English schooner in Tintamarre a few weeks later. By that time, rumour had it that he had taken over practically the entire English armada. When a schooner arrived at the camp armed with eight swivel guns, loaded with supplies for the Port-Royal garrison, and carrying a choice captive, the commander of the Fort Beauséjour artillery, it wouldn't have taken much for people to believe that George II himself had been captured. The epic gesture was exaggerated in direct proportion to the level of despair.

Other news circulating in Miramichi included a Canadien and French triumph – the capture of the fortified town Oswego by Lake Ontario. The battle took place under Governor Vaudreuil's orders, despite Montcalm's hesitation, and the victory was largely due to the inhabitants' and the natives' help. On his way back from a spying mission in Halifax, Pierre Gauthier announced other victories south of Montreal, including the capture of Fort William Henry. Another arrival in the Louisbourg harbour was Admiral DuBois de la Motte's fleet. His presence and that of Boishébert and his militia was enough to frighten the English, who decided to postpone their attack until the following year.

When Olivier Léger, the descendant of Port-Royal's drummer soldier, heard the news, he saw red. "De la Motte, that coward! That idiot should have razed Halifax and captured the English fleet instead of twiddling his thumbs!"

In France, the French and Spanish fleets had driven back the English at Minorca. Joseph-Jean, a philosopher of sorts, summarized public opinion. "It's as though the French are victors everywhere but here!"

The products of the fall harvest were accumulating. Uncle Joseph-Jean was especially concerned with replenishing his supply of tobacco. He helped out with the wild rice harvest, which involved canoeing through the marshes, bending the rice stalks that rose above the water into the canoe, and using the paddle to beat the grains of rice onto the canoe bottom. Tjigog and Mathilde found the long nuts of the walnut tree in squirrels' nests as well as hazelnuts and chestnuts in great quantities. Anne prepared wine by crushing wild cherries with their pits for better fermentation. And a better taste.

But everyone was worried about what had happened to the Acadians' livestock. The men who ventured into the Memramcouk and Beaubassin region always came home empty-handed. "What did Lawrence and his henchmen manage to do with 100,000 head of cattle!" Joseph-Jean fumed. There was only one answer he could see: they must have sold them to the American colonies, sufficient reason on its own for the deportations.

In October, they learned that the English had intercepted a few French supply ships. Then rumours questioning Boishébert's integrity began to make the rounds in the camp.

"He keeps the best provisions for himself and only distributes food that's gone bad," someone said.

"The furs he sends to Quebec take up space that could have been used for refugees," another said.

"He's just like all the other officers who only care about getting rich at the king's expense," most thought.

"That's nothing but jealousy talking – gossip-mongering," Joseph-Jean retorted.

"He's a hero fighting on our behalf and suffering the same hardships as we are," Olivier Léger said in Boishébert's defence.

The topic of conversation changed when a group of some of the most badly wounded Acadians set sail for Quebec in November. Abbot Le Guerne was on the same ship, following a directive from his bishop who had appointed him as a priest at Ile d'Orléans.

"I'll pray for you, my dear Mathilde."

She would rather have had his presence than his prayers!

To fill the new void, Mathilde took up her paintbrush again. Encouragement came from a strange quarter. One of the English prisoners on the island, John Witherspoon, a Puritan farmer, was very taken with her paintings. His interest pleased her, although she didn't want the Englishman to see her pleasure. *I'm sure our enemies are receiving much better treatment than the Acadian exiles on the American coasts*, she thought.

She showed her thanks by not revealing a secret he confided in her, the secret of the journal he wrote in using tobacco juice. Other prisoners weren't as lucky. Certain Acadian prisoners had no choice but to write in their own blood.

* * *

With the first snowfall, the camp was seized by the frenzy of the hunt once more, for there was little food left. To assuage any hostile forces, Tjigog took part in a sacred dance with the other Mi'kmaq, then prayed to the animal spirits to ask for their favour. Mathilde travelled along the shore of the Miramichi with her friend, who had discovered a trail the deer used to go down to the river to drink. Hidden behind a pine tree, Mathilde pulled back on her bow when she heard his signal, the cawing of a crow. But Tjigog beat her to it, and the deer, an arrow in its flank, crashed through the trees toward Mathilde. In her agitation, she let her arrow fly, and the animal fell. Tjigog ran over, impressed by Mathilde's skill and the deer's size. He drew his big hunting knife, slit the animal's throat, opened its belly, and pulled out its liver. Disgusted by the sight of so much blood, Mathilde went off on her own while Tjigog ate some of the raw liver. He could never understand why the white men cooked this succulent meat, turning it such an unappetizing colour.

Tjigog and Mathilde were thrilled to be able to take the meat back to camp. That evening, the refugees ate heartily, leaving nothing but the bones for soup. Some of the bones were hung above the kettles to let the marrow drip. Other bones were circulated from one hut to another. Not that there was much in the way of calories left – the bones played a symbolic function. The hunt continued, but game was scarce and hunger returned to the camp. Disease also put in an appearance. Mathilde confided in her uncle, "They should have killed us instead of leaving us to suffer from hunger and cold, separated from our families."

"They can't afford to massacre us too openly since there would be protests in Europe. Only because we're white, like the English. They would have exterminated us by now if we were a native people."

"Why doesn't France come to our aid?"

"I often wonder. France is at a disadvantage in times of war because it doesn't have any natural protection against the other European countries. Being an island, England can invest in a strong navy to protect it from invaders. Their navy keeps a close watch on France's ports. And yet, France has managed to send troops to Louisbourg and Quebec under Marquis Montcalm. Unfortunately, France has not sent any to Acadia since our region is seen as unimportant in this war."

"So we have only ourselves to rely on."

"Yes, and we can only hope for one of two things: either that Quebec and Louisbourg won't surrender or that France wins the war in Europe."

* * *

Winter 1757-1758. Of the roughly three thousand Acadians living in Miramichi the previous winter, only about half were left. Those who weren't in their final resting place under the shade of a great pine tree somewhere had fled in the four cardinal directions – to Quebec, the Restigouche post, Ile Saint-Jean, and Louisbourg. Since the reserves of herbs, salmon, and pigeons had melted away as quickly as the snow under the sun's rays, and the king's stores were empty, it was decided to sacrifice the last horses. Tjigog and Mathilde roamed through the forests looking for food. They gathered frozen berries off the gaultheria[3] bush; they chewed on its leaves to help keep their stamina up on their long walks. They could still pick the reddish berry of the wild rose bushes, strip off the inner layer of tree bark (bark from the poplar trees served as an antidote against fatigue and bark from the lobolly, red, and jack pine trees staved off hunger pangs) and gather teaberry and fir tree needles. Not much! On their return, Mathilde had to fight to save Quenouille from the kettle. From Joseph Gueguen, who had left for the Quebec Seminary, she borrowed books on the history and geography of Acadia written by Nicolas Denys in the last century in an attempt to spark Versailles' interest in its colony. Denys described the fabulous resources of the sea, earth, and forests. But in this era of calamity, the wealth he described seemed like nothing but a mirage.

In March 1758, smallpox spread through the camp. It had been introduced by a group of refugees from Ile Saint-Jean. The sick, more numerous by the day, were isolated in the king's stores. Few people agreed to nurse them since it meant putting their own lives at risk. Charity only went so far. Experience showed that few people would recover, especially since all the hardship they'd been through had weakened their resistance. The only thing left to them was faith, and even faith began to waver for Tjigog when Mathilde fell ill with a high fever, headaches, and aching armpits. There was no mistaking it. Tjigog had survived a bout of smallpox as a child – his face still bore the scars – so he had nothing to fear from the disease. He nursed Mathilde, something he would have done anyway. In the morning, a nauseating stench wafted through the air in the big room, and Tjigog saw that old

---

3. So named in 1839 by the botanist Gaulther.

Terriot had died in his own excrement. Tjigog bathed the old man's body, then hurried over to Mathilde's side. Her face was still swollen, her eyelids puffy. There were new pustules on her skin, others had dried out. Her body was burning up and she was trembling with fever. Tjigog bathed her face with cold water to bring the fever down, then cleansed out her mouth with a bit of eucalyptus oil. He tried to talk to her, give her hope, mobilize her strength, but she couldn't hear a word.

In her hands, Mathilde clutched the little medallion containing a lock of her mother's hair that her father had put around her neck during their ocean crossing in Duc d'Anville's fleet. She was visited by Abbot Manach, who had heard about the orphan from Abbot Leloutre. Father Charles Germain and the abbot spent countless hours tending to the sick and dying, impassive in the face of danger because to die under such circumstances was a guaranteed entry to paradise. The priest administered last rites, touching a bit of oil onto Mathilde's swollen, burning skin. Tjigog was engulfed in sadness. Powerless, he spent hours trying to think of a way to save the one he loved. Meanwhile, Olivier Léger held a wake for his parents and Joseph-Jean built a cross on which he wrote: "Jacques Léger, descendant of the soldier drummer, and his beloved wife, Anne Amireault, passed away this day in Camp de l'Espérance, having placed their trust in God."

Chapter 21

Acadians are dying in great numbers because of their
past and present hardships and the greed of the
Canadiens whose only desire is to wring all the money
they can out of the Acadians and then deny them the
care so dearly paid.
– Quebec, December 1757, Bougainville's journal

In 1606 in Port-Royal, Champlain founded the Order of
Good Cheer. The fifteen gentlemen of the Habitation
were each given the role of *maître d'* in turn and were
responsible for preparing a succulent feast for the group.
– Marc Lescarbot, Port-Royal scribe, in 1609,
Histoire de la Nouvelle-France

Fall 1757. Joseph was in Quebec trying to sell his merchandise for a profit. Negotiations had not gone well because of the corruption that reigned in the capital. Abusing his authority, Bigot requisitioned supplies in the king's name then turned around and sold them at astronomical prices. Joseph had let his father-in-law's furs go for pathetically low prices. He had better luck selling the cod and was able to buy salt from Brouage, said to be the best salt for curing fish. The transactions were facilitated by an Acadian refugee from Port-Royal, Michel Bourgeois, who knew a few exiles who had some gold Louis. Joseph was joined on his schooner by Bourgeois, a rail-thin man who never stopped coughing.

"There are close to two thousand of us Acadians in rags and destitute in Quebec, where three years ago, we were the most prosperous farmers in America," Bourgeois said. "One group of Acadians wintered in caves dug out along the Assomption… But we can't blame the locals, who are in no mood to share since they've been rationed to four ounces of bread a day themselves."

"I've been told that the locals have taken to hiding their provisions and rifles and showing up dressed in rags to defend their colony, knowing they'll be fitted out with new clothes and rifles," Joseph added.

"But you can't blame them. The public can't be fooled; they know the war isn't the only cause of the shortages. Bigot and his band of rogues have seen no change in their lifestyle. They organize one ball, sumptuous feast, and evening's frolic after another. He's a real Ali Baba and his forty thieves! Several Acadians who arrived with money orders were only able to get part of their money back; the clerks pocketed the rest. Fortunately, there's a bit of salt cod and horsemeat being handed out!"

"With the cod I sell, I won't be adding much variety to your menu," Joseph exclaimed.

"No, but at least it's of good quality and there's enough of it to double the rations," Boureois said encouragingly.

Joseph was anxious to return to Angélique, his children, and Ruisseau's calmer atmosphere. But he had to wait for his cargo of Brouage salt to be loaded. He had filled the holds of the *Phantom Ship* with sacks of grain and slabs of salt meat he had purchased with several gold coins from the island treasure. Although no-one noticed his comings and goings to the island, he would never have dreamt of dipping into the treasure too often. He deemed himself fortunate to have the means of relieving somewhat the poverty of the refugees in Camp de l'Espérance and at the Restigouche post. He was all the more anxious to leave now that a smallpox epidemic had been declared. It was decimating the weakest members of the population, especially among the refugees. Just that morning, there had been a funeral for a young boy, Michel Gaudet, and his mother, Marie-Josephte Girouar[1]. The Hôtel-Dieu, the Notre-Dame hospital, and the General Hospital were full, and some families wondered if there would be enough survivors left to carry on the family name; the Richard family was one of those.

I'm so lucky to be able to return to my family! he thought.

While his thoughts were turned to the war and its injustices, Joseph hadn't noticed his steps taking him to the tavern Le Chien d'Or, where he had known such good times in the past. It was as though he thought he could be magically transported back in time. But a surprise awaited him there: a letter from Emilie left for him by Cristel! Joseph had refrained from visiting Cristel and her family for years because he didn't want to stir up old memories. With this missive from Emilie, however, he had a feeling he was about to come face-to-face with his past.

He sat in a corner, holding a mug of rum in one hand and the letter he dared not read in the other. It was as though he was afraid of the ill winds that might be unleashed if he opened this Pandora's box. When the alchohol finally started to kick in, he made up his mind:

Dear Joseph, he read.

There's no mistaking Emilie's handwriting, he thought, his heart pounding like the hooves of a herd of caribou.

I had to write, after more than sixteen years, to tell you the truth at last about what came between us. I couldn't tell you before this because I was afraid of ruining your happiness with your new family. I can now, I think, because I'm sure you've forgotten me by this time...

Joseph stopped, too overcome with emotion to read any further. He drained his glass and continued:

After you left on your hunting trip, I found out I was expecting your child. I was so happy. I was counting the days. That winter when I learned you had disappeared in the snow deep in the forest close to the St-Maurice forge, I thought I would go mad. I knew my family would have a hard time accepting my pregnancy. So I decided to leave. Once in Europe, I met an older man, a Jersey

---

1. Girouard.

merchant, a Protestant, who took an interest in me. I was desper-
ate, helpless, with no one to support me, and I accepted his help. We
left for the Isle of Jersey to flee religious persecution. Our daughter
Héloïse grew up there. She looks like me and I think she will be
happy since she has a very optimistic nature. I wanted to tell you: I
couldn't keep the secret to myself any longer, a secret that is yours as
well as mine. Be happy.

> *Emilie*

Joseph spent all that evening drinking alone in his corner and thinking. *I have a daughter with Emilie, and she looks like her*, he kept saying over and over to himself. He could see her now, a hint of irony in her brown eyes, her freckles, her chestnut hair like Emilie's.

Emilie's letter had awakened old memories. Joseph didn't leave the tavern until he was good and drunk. He didn't even notice the soldiers from the Royal Roussillon regiment as they strolled by in their fine uniforms. His mind was racing, busy making one plan after another, each one crazier than the last. One such plan was to leave then and there for the Isle of Jersey on board his schooner! He spent all that afternoon walking through the lower town. The smell of tar from the shipyard by Rue Cul-de-Sac reminded him of his clandestine meetings with Emilie behind the woodpiles. At dusk, feeling slightly less drunk, he stopped to pray at Notre-Dame-des-Victoires Church. He spoke to the priest, but felt no peace. He slept little and poorly that night. By the first glimmer of dawn, an idea had taken hold in his mind. His strategy was simple – to forget. But how? He remembered someone telling him the Algonquin shaman in Cap-Rouge had potions to help make people forget.

"Why not! What else can I do!"

He found the shaman, who said, "You have to find milk from a wetnurse and drink it hot every night. For one cycle of the moon. Add a few drops of this potion to it," he added holding out a small, stoppered bottle.

As though a mother's breast could bring about oblivion!

The shaman continued, "Then you must go out hunting and when you have killed a male moose, you must prepare a meal to eat with your family."

Joseph was rather skeptical, but he decided to follow the sorcerer's prescription as though his life depended on it. He was so preoccupied he almost forgot to bring Angélique the ginseng powder and roots she had asked for to use in her remedies.

* * *

Angélique didn't let her relief show when, in mid-November, just before ice imprisoned the bay, Joseph's schooner returned to Ruisseau. Seeing the expression on his face, she suspected Emilie was involved somehow. This time, she was determined to burst the abcess that kept forming between them. Her passion smouldering beneath the embers soon burst into flames.

"You want to go back to Louisbourg, do you?" she shouted angrily.

"Not quite," Joseph answered. "I'm thinking of going to France instead."

Angélique's disappointment showed on her face. "Why not China while you're at it?"

"Listen, Angélique, in a few moons' time, the English will have run us out of here. We have to prepare for the worst. With the island treasure, we could bring over soldiers, weapons, and settlers to defend the country. There's enough money to pay for a war fleet."

"I'll go with you then. I've always dreamt of walking through the Palace of Versailles."

Joseph hadn't expected this. He did plan to find reinforcements, but his real reason for going was to see Emilie and their daughter. He pretended to ignore Angélique's offer, which only fuelled her jealousy further.

* * *

The epidemic racing through Quebec did not reach Ruisseau. Moreover, the hunting was good, which meant supplies could be sent to the Miramichi refugees and help extended to the exiles travelling through Poquemouche and Ruisseau. Seeing all the work she would have with the sick and orphaned, Angélique forgot to snub Joseph.

The day before New Year's, Joseph killed a huge moose and remembered the shaman's words: "You must prepare a meal to share with your family." He hadn't forgotten to drink milk from a wetnurse either, a young woman who had just given birth. That night on the shore of the Poquemouche, he slept poorly, worried because the sorcerer's potion didn't seem to be working and tormented by thoughts of Emilie missing him on the Isle of Jersey and of the daughter he'd never laid eyes on.

He was somewhat calmer the next morning. Joseph knew this was no time for celebration, but he also wondered whether a small feast might not be a way to start solving the problems that haunted him. Seemingly able to read his mind, Saint-Jean reassured him, "Don't worry, I've kept enough aside for the New Year's Day feast!"

Saint-Jean knew that Joseph was an excellent cook when he put his mind to the task as a way of calming himself down in moments of great tension.

"I'll let the barrel of wine from Nantes breathe a bit," continued Saint-Jean, "then see if the p'tit caribou[2] is ready."

"We've got some wild rice," René announced.

"There are still some fiddleheads and wood garlic left," Josette added.

"I've brought some smelt and smoked salmon," Geneviève said in turn.

Joseph set to work. In the reserves, he found some hares and partridges that he boned. He also found a slab from the moose he'd killed, two quarters of caribou, and three of deer as well as several beavers and porcupines. He decided to make a six-pâtes[3], a dish made of six layers of corn pastry separating various kinds of meat, each layer sprinkled with spices and wood garlic. He innovated as well: on the right side of the kettle he alternated layers of caribou, hare, and porcupine. In the

---

2. In Mi'kmaq, this blend of alcohol and port wine was known as "ashkote-nibiish."
3. "Pag wadjawessi" in Mi'kmaq.

middle, he did the same with the beaver, the partridge, and the moose and on the left, with the beaver, the hare, and the deer. He marked the different sections to help recognize them, dug a hole in the centre that he filled with water, then dropped a clove inside. Now the special dish just needed to cook.

The others were busy as well. Josette looked after the garlic soup. Geneviève and Honguedo made smoked salmon and smelt appetizers. René prepared the wild rice, adding mushrooms, onion, garlic, corn, lard, and a few coltsfoot leaves. Angélique decided to add some sweetness with sugared pumpkin. She put the pumpkin over the fire then removed its seeds and pulp, replacing them with a mixture of honey, cider, and melted butter, and returned the pumpkin to the fire. Membertou was in charge of stoking the fire and supervising the flames' intensity.

The evening was mild. A few snowflakes fluttered down, and the delicious smells of good food cooking wafted through the air. Membertou had opened the barrel of sprucebud beer. Saint-Jean had already started in on the p'tit caribou drink, which had such a kick to it that he did something unheard of for him – he took out his flute. Joseph brought out his Stradivarius – his present from the gods. The parts and varnish of Stradivarius violins were so perfect that the instruments were coveted in all the courts of Europe. While waiting for the fire to work its magic, the family sat down in the big tent open at the top to allow the smoke out. They began with a Palm Sunday hymn then sang one song after another from Normandy, Brittany, and Poitou as well as ancient Mi'kmaq ballads sung by the beautiful Honguedo.

Finally, it was time for everyone to sit down to the feast. The appetizers were succulent and the soup exquisite. The six-pâtes was a source of merriment with all the treasures hidden under its pastry shell!

"The choice is yours," Joseph announced, "caribou, moose, porcupine, deer, beaver, partridge, or hare."

Everyone wanted to try a bit of everything. Afterwards, a moment of serenity, euphoria, and oblivion settled over them: this was the moment Joseph had been waiting for. "I have something important to say. Within a year or two, we'll be fugitives in our own country. I've decided to travel to Versailles to make the French understand our urgent need for help."

"Do you really think you have a chance?" René interrupted him.

"Maybe. The fabulous treasure on Ile Caraquet is no longer a secret for our family. I'll use the treasure to pay for a fleet. What's more, Governor Vaudreuil has given me a letter to smooth the way for me."

"Did you speak to Grandfather?" asked Membertou, who wanted to be sure Saint-Jean authorized anything to do with the treasure.

"I've discussed this at length with Joseph," Saint-Jean answered. "It might work. But if you leave in the springtime," he said, turning to Joseph, "you probably won't be back with reinforcements until the following spring. That's if the ship you're on manages to slip through the English fleet surrounding France's ports! By that time, we may well be on a cotton plantation somewhere in Carolina!"

Joseph didn't let himself be fazed. "Anyone for more treasure pie?" he asked. He didn't have to ask twice. He continued, "I see no other solution, unless we move to Quebec until it surrenders, too!"

Joseph's eyes had never left Angélique, who sat as though cast in stone. Finally, she exploded, "You want to go back to France to see Emilie!"

"I won't deny that's part of it," he confessed, preferring the truth be told. "I can't forget her until I've seen her again… I've just learned that I'm the father of her daughter, Héloïse, who lives with her on the Isle of Jersey."

He told them about the letter he'd received while in Quebec. Saint-Jean interceded on Joseph's behalf, "Angélique, I think Joseph is right. Let him go. You have no reason to be jealous."

"I'll take René and Membertou with me," Joseph offered.

The thought of spending such a long time separated from her husband and her two sons brought tears to Angélique's eyes. The girls were sad, too. Josette broke the silence by uncorking a bottle of maple syrup. The guests turned over the pewter plates that had served for the meat and salty part of the meal, and put the sweet nectar on the plate bottom. Joseph murmured to Angélique, "I love you."

"I'll wait for you," she answered.

Then he played a few notes on his violin while the distant lowing of a moose could be heard. Everyone was aware that terrible days lay ahead and many moons would pass before there could be another feast like this one. They even forgot to wish each other a Happy New Year.

Chapter 22

Destroy the vermin who are settled there…
> – A letter from Amherst to
> Wolfe and Boscawen in 1758

…Preparing to rob the fishermen of their nets and to burn their huts; when this great exploit is at end (which we reckon will be a month or five weeks).
> – Letter from Wolfe to his father, announcing
> the destruction of the Baye des Chaleurs
> settlements by the fall of 1758

Angélique did her best to hide how worried she was about seeing Joseph and her two sons leave for Europe. As for Joseph, he clung to the hope that his trip would be of some assistance to the colony and deliver him at last from the torment Emilie had become for him. He had decided to leave in May, after the breakup; any earlier was risky because of the large icebergs floating off Newfoundland.

Angélique decided to consult the oracles about Joseph's trip. She threw three egg whites into a bowl of cold water then started to read the configurations they formed. What she saw there frightened her no end: a boat sinking off an island, taking Membertou down with it! Eventually, she fell ill from all the worry.

"It's as though she's doing it on purpose," Joseph fumed.

He had no choice but to postpone his departure, which was a great disappointment to René, who'd dreamt of nothing but palaces for weeks, and to Membertou, who could imagine himself preaching the beauty of native beliefs. Joseph nursed Angélique lovingly night and day. He was extremely worried. The fever finally broke, but it took Angélique a long time to regain her strength. She wasn't better until mid-July. Once again the trip was possible, but news was circulating in Ruisseau that English ships were everywhere. This time, the trip was postponed until the following spring.

* * *

It was a sad day for both Acadia and New France on July 27, 1758 when Louisbourg fell. As though on her saint's day Saint Anne had been unable to protect her children! It was a repeat of the events of 1744; the English lined up their impressive fleet carrying soldiers from the regular armies and American colonies to fight against a band of courageous but disorganized people under siege and a few ships protecting access to the Baie de Gabarus; the ships did manage to hold off the English fleet for a few weeks, however. Finally, after bombarding the Acadians with cannonballs and fire, the English troops disembarked upstream from Louisbourg and laid siege to the fortress by land. A few weeks later, they made their triumphant entry into a city in ruins.

In Ruisseau, Saint-Jean was in his storehouse lustring his furs when the news reached him. "Quebec is still safe this year; the season is too far gone for them to dare launch an attack of any magnitude… But this is the end of the French empire in America," he predicted sadly.

"Perhaps we should leave the region and flee to Quebec," Angélique suggested.

She remembered how Joseph had laboured on the fortifications in 1744. This time the English had decided to raze the fortress and take the finest loot back to Halifax with them.

"No," her father answered, "our place is here. I don't want to leave the Mi'kmaq. In a year or two, Quebec will have fallen to the English too since France seems to have lost interest in New France."

Assailed by her own fears, Angélique didn't hear her father. "The English will come and deport us. I couldn't stand to be separated from you and my children! I've heard that Wolfe's fleet is already making its way up the coast destroying everything in its path."

"I'll post sentries night and day on Ile Miscou. If English ships approach, we'll strike camp and take refuge farther inland up the Poquemouche; we'll be safer with the Mi'kmaq in our forests not far from our bountiful seas than we will as refugees in Quebec."

Just then Joseph arrived. Since he had seen the fate reserved for refugees in Quebec the previous fall, he added, "Quebec is suffering from famine, epidemics, and corruption. Here, at least for the time being, we're left in peace."

Angélique was obliged to see the sense in what he said even though she had an awful feeling in the pit of her stomach.

* * *

After the fall of Louisbourg, a wave of refugees swept through Ruisseau, most of them from Ile Saint-Jean, the invaders' next target. They found shelter where they could in makeshift huts, just long enough to regain their strength. Some then placed themselves under the protection of the French troops in Restigouche, forty leagues to the southwest of Ruisseau, others headed for the fishing post of Papôg. Still others settled in Nipisiguit[1] among the ruins of Nicolas Denys' seigneurie. A few families from Camp de l'Espérance – Olivier Blanchard, Olivier Léger, Alexis Landry, and his brother-in-law Charles Poirier – decided to settle in Bocage, two leagues to the northwest of Ruisseau.

* * *

---

1. Meaning "boiling waters." Today's Bathurst.

Papôg and nearby Grande-Rivière, the Gaspé's civil and religious headquarters, were the most important fishing posts on the Baye des Chaleurs. Besides a general store, Papôg was the site of over thirty wooden fishermen's huts without stone foundations or cellars and with chimneys made of straw and clay. Solidity and simplicity were the order of the day. Next to a dozen huts, there was also a chapel by the sea where Recollet Alexis Duburon officiated. The newlyweds Geneviève and Gabriel Albert settled into one of the seaside huts. Angélique and Joseph's eldest daughter didn't want to leave her Gabriel's side for a second; she even insisted on going fishing with him. When she had to stay on land, she tended a small garden in which she planted cabbage, turnips, and sorrel as well as all the herbs needed to accompany meat and fish. At night when her husband returned, steaming soup awaited him – something to warm his body before he tumbled into a soft bed.

Sieurs François and Georges de Bellefeuille were responsible for the fishing posts from Papôg to Gaspeg. For income, they took the equivalent of one-eleventh of the fish caught and leased shore plots to seasonal fishermen. In the Baie de Papôg, which was almost completely closed off by a baymouth bar[2], was their seigneurie on Ile Beau Séjour. Saint-Jean knew the place well, because the De Bellefeuille family hailed from Rouen originally. His somewhat exclusive relationship with sieurs François and Georges meant he was always guaranteed space for his furs on ships returning to Europe.

Fifteen leagues to the northeast of Papôg was the Gaspeg post, which was managed by Pierre Révol, the son of a procurator from the Grenoble Parliament, who had been exiled to Canada for salt-smuggling. Révol Jr. coordinated the activities of the seasonal fishermen and the three hundred permanent inhabitants of Gaspeg. Appointed sentinel of the gulf by Vaudreuil, he was in charge of monitoring the movement of enemy ships and organizing the gulf's defence. There had even been talk of fortifying Gaspeg by burying two flat-bottomed anchors on either side of the Penouille basin and connecting

---

2. Small harbour located behind a sandbar, where boats can be landed.

them with two twenty-inch cables that would be submerged at low tide and serve to block any passage. But the wheel of history turned too quickly, and Brigadier Wolfe's fleet arrived within sight of Gaspeg in early September: seven ships and seventeen hundred men. Confronted with such a force, the flotilla of Basque, Breton, Rochelais, and Norman fishermen had no choice but to flee. The soldiers set out on a looting mission. Révol died just before the plundering began, no doubt thankful not to have to witness his whole life's work destroyed. Nor did he have to hear Captain Bell, an officer in Wolfe's fleet, exclaim in jubilation: "What a magnificent fire it all made!"

Françoise and Pierre Le Vicaire and their daughters did witness the horrendous spectacle. They saw the fur storehouse go up in flames. The soldiers went off to gather raspberries and cranberries once they were done pillaging the village.

On September 13th, Captain Irving played out the same scenario in Papôg, Grande-Rivière, and Paspecbiac[3]. Nothing was spared: houses, schooners, fishing gear and stores, twenty thousand hundredweight of cod, as well as the stores of clothing and food for winter. In Papôg, the looters carried away De Bellefeuille's reserves of liquors and cognac. Most inhabitants were able to flee upriver by canoe and hide out in the forests.

Meanwhile, Joseph, Jean-Baptiste, René, and Membertou were ferrying supplies to the Restigouche post on the *Phantom Ship*. Not far from Nipisiguit, they passed a small boat rowed by two Basque fishermen, Roussy (Françoise's cousin) and a young ship's boy whose name was Aspirot.

"Apaizak obeto?[4]" Jean-Baptiste shouted.

"The whole bay from Papôg to Gaspeg has been razed by the English troops. We're fleeing to the Restigouche post… The others are in need of rescue; they're hiding out among the ruins or inland… They can't escape by sea because most of the boats were destroyed."

---

3. Today's Paspébiac.
4. In Basque, "How are you?"

Réné felt strongly that they should go to their rescue. But Joseph hesitated precisely because of René's presence since no one could say for sure whether the English ships had left or not.

"Our schooner could outrun a warship," René declared. "We could sail at night…"

His arguments plus the fact that Geneviève and her husband were in Papôg finally convinced Joseph. As dawn broke, they could see what was left of the fishing post: piles of ruins and cinders. They brought aboard the people who'd been hiding back of the lagoons, including Gabriel and Geneviève, Pierre Gallien, and Father Duburon, who had two young native girls with him; just as the schooner raised its anchor they were joined by another man, Morin, whose seigneurie in Cloridorme had been destroyed.

Concern mounted in Ruisseau at the sight of small columns of black smoke rising on the other side of the bay. Angélique had but one wish: that her husband, her brother, and her children were all safe and sound. Meanwhile, there was much that needed to be done. Everyone pitched in. The inhabitants of Ruisseau and those of Bocage farther north – the families Blanchard, Cormier, Landry, Léger, Poirier, and others – camouflaged their dwellings and hid their small boats behind Ile de Pokesudie. Now there was nothing left to do but wait. It didn't take long. Using a mirror, the sentries posted on Ile Miscou signalled the appearance of two English sails on the horizon. The sea was somewhat rough, and the night promised to be pitch-black without any stars. Saint-Jean implemented a strategy based on one used in certain parts of Brittany that involved lighting a lantern attached to the horns of a moving ox. Out at sea, it looked like the light was a fixed point and, more often than not, any ships using the light as a guide ran aground. Saint-Jean attached a lantern onto the back of Ruisseau's cow and walked it up and down the coast. Their prayers were answered: one of the ships ran aground on the reef and broke its hull. The crew managed to swim to the second ship, which left immediately, a fact that Wolfe, proud man that he was, omitted mentioning in his ship's log.

The next day was a day for rejoicing. Especially since Joseph, Jean-Baptiste, René, Membertou, Geneviève, and her husband had arrived in Ruisseau. Angélique was relieved to be reunited with her family. But Saint-Jean kept to himself, worried at having no news of his daughter Françoise. The missionary Duburon had managed to rescue a few trinkets, iron fitments, and material from the Papôg looting. Something to win more souls with! But to his surprise, his sermon thanking God for His blessings made the natives laugh. The Black Robe chalked it up to the general rejoicing, without realizing that Membertou's translation made more reference to fornication than paradise.

The ways of our Lord are indeed mysterious, for the greater glory of God, 'Ad majorem Dei Gloriam,' the missionary thought.

After the sermon they were able to feast on the supplies found on the wrecked English ship; barrels of wine accompanied a meal of venison roasted on the spit.

"A toast to our victory," Léger proposed.

"Or to Montcalm's victory in Carillon," Landry added.

Outside Montreal the Canadien and French troops did indeed manage to drive back the invader that summer.

"But we've lost men as well, and each victory just brings us closer to final defeat," Saint-Jean concluded.

Françoise arrived that evening with her newly orphaned daughters Anne and Marie, whose father had been killed during the English raid. The news saddened all those who had known Pierre. Saint-Jean and his family could no longer deny the reality of the war ravaging the Baye des Chaleurs. For the inhabitants of Bocage, accustomed to three years of horror, the most recent happenings confirmed for them the fact they had not found a haven of peace, that the noose was tightening, and that the cannons stolen from the English and well camouflaged by Joseph would not be enough to change their destiny.

* * *

There were, however, two people in Acadia who were happy: the lovestruck couple in Camp de l'Espérance, Tjigog and Mathilde. Aided by Tjigog's love and constant care, Mathilde had miraculously survived smallpox. The few scars left behind hadn't altered the beauty of her face. But their trials were not over yet: that fall the English ships and a detachment of soldiers under the orders of Colonel James Murray carried on the destruction where others had left off. So the stone church on the north shore of Miramichi's inner bay was destroyed as well as several houses and the stores of food. Then Commander Murray sent a frigate, a fire ship[5], and six carriers transporting three hundred men to destroy Camp de l'Espérance. But the Acadians, the natives, and a hundred soldiers (the pathetic rescue force sent by Vaudreuil to defend Acadia) anchored a few ships armed with cannons and swivel guns so as to bar access to the river, then waited in ambush on either side and so managed to drive back the invaders.

"This is nothing but a moment's respite that will lead nowhere," Joseph-Jean lamented.

"If they can't win by fire and sword, they'll win by starving us to death," Beausoleil grumbled.

"We have to leave," Tjigog said.

After the Louisbourg battle, Boishébert left Miramichi right away. Proudly bearing the cross of St. Louis he'd just won, he made his way to Quebec and launched the final assault with a few soldiers, natives, and Acadians.

"And go where?" Mathilde asked.

They couldn't go back since Scott's soldiers had just destroyed the villages of Beausoleil, Sylvabro, and Le Coude. Other detachments commanded by Monckton had razed the houses still standing along the Saint-Jean in the Ste-Anne-des-Pays-Bas region and in René and Mathieu d'Amours' seigneurie. Now Wolfe's fleet had annihilated the fishing installations along the north shore of the Baye des Chaleurs from Papôg to Mont-Louis.

---

5. A small ship loaded with combustible material and used to set fire to enemy ships.

"I'm not budging," insisted Beausoleil, who had just lost his privateer's ship. "But you should go to the Restigouche post and ask for their protection. You'll find food there." Everyone agreed with his suggestion.

Mathilde left Miramichi with a heavy heart, for she had to leave behind her beloved Quenouille, buried under the shade of the great birch trees.

Chapter 23

The sea touched the clouds, Our ship followed suit, Riding the torrent of suspended waves. Doing nothing save rise and fall…

…the sea has borrowed some of its beauty from the blue vault of the sky. The heavens are the reflection of the water below.

– Dièreville, *Voyage à l'Acadie 1699-1700*

Joseph planned on being underway right after breakup in late April 1759. Scarcely a week before his departure, he was greeted by bad news. As he was perched in the great pines of the island's headland with his father-in-law waiting for a ship scheduled to put in at Ruisseau, he saw other ships off in the distance. "Could I be dreaming?" he exclaimed. "The sea is blanketed in sails!"

"It's the English fleet on its way to Quebec to launch an assault; the city's time has come," Saint-Jean sighed.

The white sails filed by all day long off Miscou: two hundred ships of all kinds: fighting ships, store ships, frigates, troop carriers, galiots. Still more filed by the next day, the laggards in the interminable procession.

"I'll not be leaving this year; the English fleet is everywhere," Joseph fumed. "I have to postpone the trip again!"

Joseph announced his decision to his family; Membertou and René were disappointed, but Angélique could scarcely hide her joy. Her most fervent prayer was that the English fleet stand by off the coast for another quarter century. As for Saint-Jean, he couldn't rid his mind of the vision of a fortress in ruins. For good reason since news of Quebec's surrender spread that fall – unsurprising news that he took with a certain fatalism while never dropping his guard. Not everyone had the same reaction. Some people were paralyzed with fear and resignation, others were consumed with anger.

Joseph remained in a foul mood all summer, blaming himself for his lack of daring. "I can't even send a letter to Emilie anymore... But I swear, next spring, nothing will stop me; I'll cross the ocean in my schooner if I have to."

* * *

When the French ship *Bonté de Dieu* arrived in Ruisseau in early June 1760, it seemed like a miracle. Few trading ships were risking the trip to the Atlantic coast to buy furs.

"How did they elude the English ships?" Saint-Jean wondered.

"Money must certainly mean a lot to them," Jean-Baptiste said.

"That suits me just fine," concluded Joseph. "Without them I had nothing but my schooner to confront the raging seas with."

Faced with the imminent departure of Joseph and her sons, Angélique concealed her sadness behind a mask of indifference; she didn't want to suffer any more. Although she understood Joseph's reasons, the loss she anticipated feeling was so intense it submerged almost everything else. "Why does he have to go? Haven't we had wonderful moments together? Three births, a few resurrections! Why? Why?"

As though watching a play unfold, she could see before her eyes scenes of their first lovestruck moments together when the birch trees sang a symphony reserved for them alone beside the Poquemouche... Her jealousy of Emilie grew stronger still.

For his part, Joseph was overcome with anguish at the thought of his separation from Angélique. What would

Versailles hold for him? He knew a catastrophe might prevent him from returning home from Europe. He was, in fact, abandoning Angélique, not to mention his daughters. Geneviève was too wrapped up in her Gabriel to realize fully that her father would soon be leaving, but the same did not hold true for Josette. Ever since her father and brothers' departure had been announced, her step had lost some of its spring, as though she were weighed down by sorrow. To lessen his guilt, Joseph kept telling himself, "This is fate's doing. I can't escape my mission; I must go for help. I'll keep my eyes open too for any information on my origins."

He didn't admit the real reason he was going: his desire to see Emilie and his daughter. He refused to acknowledge his apprehension about the possibility of an encounter and the fear of how Emilie might react on seeing him. He forced himself to believe his motivation was based on purely noble grounds of duty and heroism.

Membertou couldn't wait to leave. He was like a fearless knight above reproach, bent on defending and promoting the Mi'kmaq religion and meeting great theologians in Paris with whom he could discuss his spiritual quest.

As for René, his mood constantly changed. Although the thought of seeing with his own eyes things he had only read about in books excited him, because of his strong attachment to his mother and Josette, he was also afraid of being forgotten. He felt insecure, too, for his mother wouldn't be nearby to try to answer his questions.

Although Jean-Baptiste didn't let his sadness show, Saint-Jean expressed his sorrow openly. He feared he would never see his loved ones again: Joseph, whom he looked on as a son and admired more than Jean-Baptiste; Membertou, who would no longer be there to play tricks on him or to preach the good word; and René, who made him feel young again with his questions and imaginings. Despite his worries, Saint-Jean remembered to put aside a few precious stones in the event they'd be needed.

Joseph, Membertou, and René found themselves a cabin on the quarterdeck, close to the captain's cabin, for which they paid a fortune. Thanks to favourable winds, the ship was able to sail past Miscou into the open water. Joseph stayed in his cabin all day, overcome by a sadness he couldn't shake. What's more, the humidity set his back to aching as much as it had when he'd worked on the Louisbourg fortifications. Joseph was in a foul mood until the next morning. On the second day, all the rolling and pitching accentuated by headwinds made René seasick. He stayed with Joseph, who gave him a concoction for upset stomachs. René didn't like to own up to feeling anxious, but he was remembering the legends of sea monsters that can only be appeased by throwing them barrels to play with and sea serpents that wind themselves around ships, only letting go if the right tunes are played on the trumpet. Sensing his son's distress, Joseph tried to distract him, "The English ships are more to be feared than two-headed monsters."

From the very first, Membertou acted like an experienced seaman. He helped rig the sails in the masts, climbing up the rigging and sliding down the yards.

Off the Iles de la Madeleine[1], the sea grew calm. Everyone was worried about the white icebergs floating past the ship like drifting ice castles, which represented a more immediate threat right then than the English ships in the area. As protection against the icebergs, from the stern they hung barrels that could be jettisoned should a rapid manoeuvre be required to avoid a collision. The ship took the northern route following the forty-sixth parallel as recommended a century earlier by Intendant Jean Talon and as shown on Nicolas Bellin's maps. To avoid the English warships, the captain had decided to pass through the Strait of Belle-Isle between Newfoundland and Labrador, despite the danger the icebergs represented. As the days passed, the winds and currents remained favourable.

"Eskimos[2] ahoy!" Membertou shouted one fine morning.

At a few cables' length distance, a man paddled a canoe with surprising agility. The canoe measured four toises in

---

1. Named in 1663 after François Doublet's wife Madeleine; Doublet was Honfleur's apothecary.
2. Inuit.

length and was made of sea-lion hides and tapered at both ends.

"They're fierce warriors, just like the Beothuks," Joseph said.

"What are *beotuks*?" René asked.

"Newfoundland's Indians. They stain their faces with red ochre[3] which is why the Europeans called the natives Redskins. They refuse to have any contact with the white man."

Off the Grand Banks – known for good cod-fishing – Joseph caught a number of halibut, delicious fare. The fishing and the birds' agitation helped him forget his worries for a while. René was over his seasickness by then and played with the liver snatchers, white-bellied grey birds that were bigger than pigeons and had a hooked beak like a parrot.; he caught them with a stick he'd fitted with a hoop and net, then released them right away. Membertou probed the sea bottom several times with a lead weight covered in suet to which the white saltlike sand stuck. Using a log, he calculated the ship's speed; he threw a small oak plank into the water attached to a line that was knotted every eighth toise. That way he could measure time's passing with an hourglass.

A comical ceremony called "the baptism of the Newfoundlander"[4] was held, as was customary, as they passed over the Newfoundland bank. Seamen wearing animal hides and others whose faces were blackened with smoke demanded that each passenger sit on a rather shaky plank above a bucket full of water. The only way to avoid falling in was to offer the men enough money. Joseph, René, and Memberou had to shell out several ecus to escape a forced baptism!

On the ninth day, the occasionally fiery-tempered Membertou threw a terrible fit. A peg-legged seaman known as Gueule-de-bois stole his hunting stick with its carved hare and eagle totems, said to confer a hare's speed and an eagle's

---

3. A natural mineral colouring agent.
4. He had a long fake beard and an old cape that looked like a bearskin and was festooned with codfish tails.

sharp eyesight on its owner. Membertou pulled out his toma-hawk; without the captain's intervention, Gueule-de-bois would not have been long for this world. In accordance with the laws that governed the seamen, his punishment was extreme. He was suspected of being a "sand eater," in other words of cheating during his shift at the helm by turning the hourglass over early. He was made to drop his pants then was tied to the pump that served as a rack. He was given twenty blows with a martinet, a whip made of several knotted lashes. Gueule-de-bois passed out from the blows for a few seconds, his back criss-crossed with red marks. Regretting his angry outburst, Membertou took the poor wretch back to his cabin and dressed his wounds with a special ointment that Angélique used to soothe pain and speed up healing. Thus, he made a friend of yesterday's foe, and his new friend taught him the seaman's craft and the art of knot-tying.

On the evening of the eleventh day, the creaking of the rudder kept René awake. He missed his mother. He lit a can-dle and began composing a poem to her. Joseph woke up, filled his pipe with Chevalier Bart tobacco, lit his pipe, and walked over to his son.

"Are you homesick?" he asked.

"Very," René began to cry. "But I want to see the castles of France."

There was a moment's silence, then he asked his father in a tone of reproach, "Why didn't you bring maman?"

Joseph didn't know what to say. "She would never agree to leave her father alone for such a long time."

He missed Angélique. He could imagine her curled up against him. Since his son couldn't sleep, the two played chess. René won the first game; he sacrificed a bishop to lead his father into a trap. Joseph didn't like to lose, but he didn't let it show. René lost the second game when Joseph confused him with a war of pawns. René didn't like to lose either. Joseph couldn't scold him since he knew exactly where his son's atti-tude came from.

The heat was such that Joseph took off his shirt as they played. A tattoo on his shoulder depicted two greyhounds and an ermine and, underneath, several inverted fleurs-de-lys against a grey background. René had seen the tattoo many times before in the sweat lodge, but he never tired of hearing his father's fabulous story of his origins.

"I left Nantes when I was still a babe in arms... Unfortunately, that's all I know because my nurse died during the crossing. The tattoo is the only clue to my origins. I wonder who my parents were and if they're still alive."

The question bothered him more than he ever let it show. Often, on Louisbourg's damp ramparts or in times of solitude in Ruisseau, he had puzzled over the enigma. His only clue was that the tattoo seemed to be the work of a skilled artist; that was the only trail he had to follow... that and the violin, the Stradivarius on which a name was engraved: "Le Bouthillier."

He was overcome with fatigue. He gave René a bit of maple syrup before he tucked him in to make sure he had sweet dreams.

The ship was advancing at a good clip. René spent more and more time with Gueule-de-bois, who taught him swordsmanship. The seaman was very agile despite his peg leg, or perhaps because of it. Membertou delved further into mystical meditation. He liked to imagine himself as the spiritual chief of the native peoples of America, leading religious celebrations to the beat of the tam-tam. In a moment of exhilaration, he even took himself for the new Messiah, the one who would give the natives the means of resisting the white man's religion. He remembered Fiery Elouèzes' stories about the great shamans and believed himself to be their heir. But he was influenced by the white men as well. His grandfather had often spoken to him of Father Gaulin, whom the Mi'kmaq nicknamed the second patriarch. He was a man of simple faith, who shared the Mi'kmaq's life with them and stood up to the cold and fatigue of long portages. Membertou saw himself as a worthy successor to the man, but according to native customs and traditions. "My name hints at my destiny: Membertou like the great Mi'kmaq chief who was baptized with great ceremony in 1610 in Port-Royal. A chief who ensured the safety of Champlain and De Poutrincourt for several winters. Yes! I'll show those Europeans what Indian honesty and probity are!" Membertou exclaimed. He knew the power a name could hold.

Joseph spent a great deal of time on the bridge thinking about his future and reflecting on the Acadians' fate. He had visions of his fleet arriving to drive the English off the land, deporting them… to the jungles of the Amazon! He thought of Emilie waiting for him. Now that he was on his way to her, however, his excitement over seeing her again had given way to relative calm. He spent hours dreaming of Angélique's perfume, as though they were lying together on their bed of furs surrounded by the aroma of maple fires. His daydreams were an antidote against the stench of the holds, a smell that neither vinegar nor burning coal could neutralize. An incredible stench wafted up as well from the bilge, a narrow space beneath the Sainte-Barbe[5], in the bowels of the ship. The stench meant the hold was dry. Good news for the captain! But on the twentieth day of the crossing, a metal plate came undone and the water began to rise in the hold. The pumps couldn't keep up. Since the leak couldn't be repaired from within, the crew made a scaffold to allow the carpenter to work, and the captain cut the ship's speed. But the sea was getting rough, and a wave swept the unfortunate man away. Having spent his childhood in his adoptive father's smithy, Joseph went down to the scaffold with a lead plate, tow, and suet. Fighting against an increasingly stormy sea, he managed to install the lead plate and plug the leak. When he returned, the crew gave him a hero's welcome, but René was angry with him for risking his life and was too upset to tell his father how proud he was.

On the twenty-ninth day, the *Bonté de Dieu* arrived within sight of the French coastline. The crossing hadn't taken long. The crew sang the *Te Deum* to thank Providence. The ship sailed up the Loire for some twenty leagues, as far as Nantes, the busiest French port on the Atlantic coast, situated

---

5. Where the gunpowder was stored.

as it was where the river divided into several branches and formed small islands covered by trees and houses. The travellers were surrounded by a sea of masts; Joseph recognized a Dutch galiot, a popular ship because of its low draft. But he was more interested in the big ships belonging to the Dutch West Indies Company that he'd first seen in Louisbourg. On the docks were huge warehouses where rich ship owners stored exotic products from their trade along the Nantes-Africa-Indies triangle. Gueule-de-bois showed Joseph the building that housed the Bourse, overshadowed by the imposing mass of the cathedral, which seemed to be standing watch over the wealthy mansions on Ile Feydeau. On the opposite shore, Membertou admired the windmills, fields of wheat, and pastures. As for René, he watched children playing on the shore next to hull carcasses, in a festival for the senses of sunlight, bright colours, harmonious notes, and the pleasant smell of tar.

Chapter 24

The situation of Acadia's inhabitants gives me great sorrow, and I have done what I could to have measures taken to alleviate their situation.
— Letter from the Marquis de la Galissonnière to Monsignor Pontbriand of Quebec, May 19, 1752

It was market day in Nantes. Villagers in clogs wearing their Sunday best flooded in from the surrounding area to buy foreign goods: sugar, taffia, cotton, tobacco, spices, coffee, rare wood, and a thousand other products. *This abundance makes it hard to believe France has been at war for all these years,* Joseph thought.

The streets were jammed with berlins[1], carriages, coaches, and horses, not to mention all the people arriving in horse-drawn barges. Membertou was struck by the number of religious brotherhoods whose members he passed, each one wearing a distinctive uniform, as though a synod was in town. He recognized the Recollets, the Capucins, and the Jesuits. As for Joseph, he was struck by the dirty muddy roads down which sewer water and rubbish swept. The whole place was a beehive of activity with its rag merchants, crockery menders, strolling singers, and life-scarred port harlots who hailed seamen as they came ashore. Plantation owners wearing white

---

1. A covered carriage with a hooded rear seat.

linen and blacks in multicoloured costumes gave the streets a tropical air. René had never seen a black man before, and he asked Joseph about them. Joseph didn't quite know how to explain to him that here, as in America, the trade in slaves existed. "Ships leave Nantes with baubles to buy blacks in Africa and trade them to the cotton and sugar cane plantation owners in America and the Indies."

"But that makes them slaves," René said, surprised.

"That's right! The city's wealth is largely based on the slave trade, just like the wealth of the colonies in Carolina in fact. There are even a few slaves in New France."

"How do Catholics dare?" René said indignantly.

Joseph was in no mood to make excuses for the choices Christians made. "Not all circles agree blacks have a soul. And the slave trade is a profitable one, that argument alone holds weight. Do you see the tall black man standing over there... He must be worth something like five hundred livres. They're considered as so much livestock. And their value increases when they're good-looking, strong, and healthy, with healthy teeth."

"And the Africans go along with this?"

"Of course not, but it should be mentioned that some African kinglets are worse than the slave-traders. They're ready to do anything and everything for a few baubles."

René had a hard time believing that a Christian nation could auction off human beings because of their skin colour. Membertou pretended he was only half-listening, but he could only conclude that white men and their religion were ridden with hypocrisy. Which made him think the responsibility of rebuilding the Ark of the Covenant and freeing the black brothers with whom he identified would fall on him. *It's the same for us Indians*, he thought. *The whites try to destroy our culture and customs to better dominate us.*

The three made their way through the crush of people then strolled at a more leisurely pace toward the districts of the nobility in St. Pierre and the wealthy mansions of Ile Feydeau. Joseph had had his fill of talk of the dark side of human nature. The trade in ebony wood – the expression used in salons to refer to slavery – was the least of his worries. Governor Vaudreuil had given him a letter to introduce him to the Court in Versailles. A letter that was almost three years old already! Back then, Joseph would never have imagined that Nantes would be his first stop. His thoughts turned to the Marquis de la Galissonnière, a former governor of Canada, who had had an arsenal and a shipyard built in Quebec as well as a line of fortifications along the Great Lakes and the Mississippi River as far as Louisiana, a line the English had not yet managed to demolish. Joseph was anxious to meet the great strategist. La Galissonnière was one of the few governors to have recognized the importance of Acadia as a lynchpin for the defence of New France; he had had Fort Beauséjour built there, not far from Grand'Pré. Thanks to the fort, two thousand Acadians had been able to place themselves under Abbot Leloutre's protection in the French zone of influence.

Unfortunately, La Galissonnière was replaced by La Jonquière in 1750 after just two years in Quebec. But he continued the fight in Europe as a member of the commission responsible for dividing Acadia up between France and England. *This is a problem that's been stagnating for close to fifty years and to which today's solution is the deportations*, Joseph thought sadly.

They skirted the Duguay quay and arrived at the Marquis de la Galissonnière's manor. They entered a magnificent park – an exotic botanical garden with harmonious shades of green, brown, yellow, and red and their concordant shapes, a reminder to Joseph that the marquis was a botanist of some renown who had ties to the great minds of the time. The smell of salt air mingled with the perfume of the plants and flowers and took Joseph back to the wide-open spaces of home. He remembered Angélique's theories on the life and soul of plants. Joseph and his sons did not have long to wait. Upon reading Vaudreuil's letter, the marquis' son Jacques agreed to see them. "Unfortunately, my father is no longer with us…"

"I'm sorry to hear that. I didn't know," Joseph said with feeling. "Your father remains in the memory of New France as a man of courage and honour. The greatest governor since Frontenac."

"My father did all he could for France. In 1756, he commanded the fleet that conquered the English in Minorca off the Balearic Islands...

If only we had just a part of that fleet now, Joseph thought.

"The king appointed him Marshal of France," the marquis continued, "but, unfortunately, he was unable to savour his triumph; he died in October of that same year. His passing left a great void."

Joseph was truly dismayed, especially since he no longer knew whom he should contact to request soldiers and arms, unless he confided in the present marquis and told him the secret of the treasure that lay safely among his furs.

"Please be my guests," the marquis offered.

The sun was setting and the smell of daffodils, roses, and lily of the valley mingled with that of hundreds of other flowers. The servants set a table next to a small spring of fresh water that wound its way through the maple and fir trees imported from Canada. The opulent table setting – an embroidered tablecloth, silverware, crystal glasses, and Limoges china – represented a totally different world. Membertou appeared indifferent to all the opulence, while René was speechless, too overawed to taste the local wine, a Muscadet brought in by a servant in livery.

Jacques de la Galissonnière had another guest: François Bonamay, Nantes' regent of the Faculty of Medicine. Bonamay, greying and pot-bellied, was a family friend and advisor on botanical matters. The discussion focused on the book he'd just published, entitled *De Florac mammetensis prodomis*. The conversation didn't touch on Joseph's concerns; he did manage to mention, however, a few plants from Acadia that were unknown in France. After a while, the marquis noticed his guests' embarrassment in the etiquette-ordered world. "What region do your ancestors come from?" he asked Joseph.

"Unfortunately, I don't know. I was adopted at a very young age by a Quebec family. The ship I was on came from

Nantes and my adoptive mother told me its passengers were fleeing from the religious persecution of the Huguenots."

"Henry IV actually proclaimed the Edict of Nantes here, giving freedom of religion to the Huguenots," Bonamay said. "But things soured later on under Cardinal Richelieu..."

"You have no clue?" the marquis insisted.

"Yes, a tattoo, but I've never known what it represents. And a violin with a name engraved on it."

Joseph showed them the tattoo on his shoulder.

"Good Lord!" the marquis exclaimed. "That's the coat of arms of the dukes of Brittany. Two greyhounds and an ermine... and a few inverted fleurs-de-lys."

The marquis was flabbergasted. "What year were you born?"

"1715 from what I've been told..."

"A strange rumour circulated in Nantes circles that year," Bonamay interrupted. "One of the dukes' nephews, Jean Le Bouthillier, was infatuated with a gypsy girl passing through Champtoceaux. He met her when she danced for the nobles, during the harvest feast..."

The name was the same as the one engraved on his violin, but the only word Joseph heard was "danced." *Maybe that explains why I love dancing so much*, he thought.

Bonamay continued, "There was a great deal of persecution at the time. Your mother may have had the tattoo done before she disappeared. And your father couldn't protect you since he died shortly after in his bed, a suspicious death..."

Joseph didn't know what to think. How could he shed light on the mystery? At any another time, the quest would have fascinated him, but now his mission was more important than anything else. After Bonamay's departure, Joseph decided to confide in his host; his warm welcome inspired confidence. He spoke to him of the treasure and of his plans to arm a fleet.

"I can arrange a meeting for you with the Minister of the Navy," the marquis explained, "but you'll have to go to Paris. Meanwhile, please stay here as my guests!"

* * *

René had to say goodbye to his companion Gueule-de-bois, who returned to his family on Ile d'Yeu. He decided to satisfy his curiosity and explore Nantes. On the pillory square, a poor wretch was serving his sentence while being jeered at by "honest folk." René didn't like what he saw and quickly turned down a street filled with activity – Rue de la Juiverie. He listened to musicians playing the bagpipes and the bombard and admired the bulbous balconies decorated with many carved symbols representing Nantes' trade: spheres, seamen, Indians, and black people. The balconies jutted out from half-timbered houses several storeys high, supported by carved wooden pillars and beams. In exchange for a few coins, a king's astrologer read his sky chart for him, but his American birthplace seemed to throw off the soothsayer, who had no data on that continent in his big book. So René didn't pay much attention to the misfortunes the fortuneteller predicted: the death of loved ones, his own exile, and other similar events. He paid even less attention because the minstrels were humming a tune Angélique sometimes sang:

"Depuis le mois de mai, les fleurs sont rouges…
mignonne… si mignonnement…"

He continued exploring. Where the two streets De la Juiverie and Des Petites Ecuries met, a public entertainer was telling the story of Merlin the Sorcerer. "He was born on an island nearby called Noirmoutier. The son of a priestess and a demon, at the age of ten he married a witch of great beauty who sought to change sand to gold. The vessel overheated and exploded, carrying away the sorceress. To amuse himself, Merlin took clay, a whalebone, and a phial of blood to create the giants Grandgousier and Gargamelle, who gave birth to Gargantua."

* * *

The next day, the marquis' coachman drove René and Membertou through the surrounding countryside. They stopped across from the old Oudun cemetery where several Acadian ancestors from the families Richard, Dupuis,

Blanchard, LeBlanc, and Samson were buried, and others still whose names were engraved on the tombstones. Membertou's thoughts were elsewhere. For once, he wasn't off in some mystical dreamland. The nearby forest reminded him of the excitement of a hunter's life, and he was daydreaming about a bear hunt. "My grandfather hunted bears in these forests," the coachman told him. "Unfortunately, there are no bears left now."

As for René, he wasn't interested in either bears or cemeteries. Captivated by the ancient Celtic civilization – which was why he'd erected dolmens in Caraquet – he had got it into his head to go to Corsept to see the White Stone menhir, which sterile women visited at night reciting magic incantations as they circled around it. That made him think of his mother, the midwife. Angélique. He was hit by homesickness as sharp as a wound reopening. He went to find Membertou, but his brother had disappeared into the forest looking for birds from America, and René had to postpone his expedition. He sulked, angry at Membertou for having upset his plans.

On the return trip, they saw the Nantes cathedral, which towered a few steps away from the castle of the dukes of Brittany. René prayed for his mother in front of the statues of the Nantes martyrs Rogatien and Donatien, who had proclaimed their faith before the Roman Empire. He could only marvel at the splendour inside: the lit candles, the stained glass, the paintings, the delicately carved statues. Bach's *Magnificat* rose from the organ; the cathedral seemed to be drawn closer to heaven on the strength of the organ's notes. The smell of incense helped him forget the damp and mildew. Outside, a storm broke. Sound, water, light, and mystery. Membertou could not remain impassive before such magnificence; turning to the East, from whence comes light, the symbol of Christ, he saw in the storm a sign confirming his mission to spread the native religion.

* * *

The marquis sent a carrier pigeon to the Versailles court to announce Joseph's arrival. Everything seemed under control, so the marquis left on a hunting excursion, a falcon on his wrist. While waiting to leave for Paris, Joseph decided to visit the harbour. He met some Breton fishermen who often made the trip to the Grand Banks to fish for cod. *Many of the ships there leave from Nantes. It's not surprising they have a gold ship with ermine sails on the city's coat of arms*, he thought.

Rue Henri IV reminded him of the Nantes Edict. His thoughts turned again to his past and he started to track down information. He was told about Champtoceaux, a small village on the Loire, a dozen leagues from Nantes. Once there, however, no one could tell him anything, only that they'd heard tell of a gypsy dancer.

"My only other avenue is through the family of the dukes of Brittany…"

Discouraged by the huge task ahead, Joseph stretched out on the banks of the Loire and lay unmoving until the sun's rays dissolved in the water. The moon rose, then the evening star appeared above the river, and he felt as though he could see his birth parents making love under the moonbeams.

Chapter 25

The sighting of one single French ship would have
brought about the surrender of the city of Quebec.
— Governor Vaudreuil waiting for a fleet
to appear to take back Quebec in 1760

Restigouche, May 1760. According to an ancient legend, to
reach Restigouche the Mi'kmaq's ancestors walked in the
direction of the rising sun, only stopping every evening at sunset, and kept on walking for seventy-six days. They gave
Restigouche's bay the name "Gtan Nemetjoei"[1] and the surrounding area "Papisi genatjg"[2], because the region was their
rallying point in times of peace. From their capital Tchigouk[3],
the Mi'kmaq reigned over the Miscou, Poquemouche,
Nipisiquit, Miramichi, and Percé bands. This was what Tjigog
told Mathilde when they arrived in Restigouche, seventy
leagues to the west of Miramichi.

"What does 'Restigouche' mean?" Mathilde asked.

"A five-fingered hand: Restigouche[4] is the thumb because
it's fed by four rivers."

_____

1. "Sea teeming with fish."
2. "Place of celebration."
3. Atholville.
4. According to Father Pacifique, the name "Restigouche" was given to the whole
region by a Mi'kmaq chief as a reminder of the extermination of a group of Iroquois
that he signalled by shouting, "Listo gotj!" or "Disobey your father!"

214

Stationed in Restigouche was a regiment of soldiers under the orders of Jean-François Bourdon[5], Sieur Dombourg, commander and lieutenant of the navy troops for the Restigouche post and the rest of French Acadia. The post was nothing but a simple fort surrounded by a stockade, with a barracks, stores, a hospital, and several other buildings. Nearby, the native village was home to some sixty families with their chief Joseph Claude, whose father had been made responsible for the whole region by Governor Beauharnois in 1730. Mathilde, her friend Tjigog, her Aunt Anne and Uncle Joseph-Jean were not the only refugees in the Restigouche region. Close to two thousand exiles streamed in from all parts. The last to arrive, those from Ile Saint-Jean and the Miramichi, had to spend the winter in total destitution in makeshift camps either at Petite-Rochelle or Pain-de-Sucre, a mountain that towered over the post. Despite everything, they fostered the hope of better days when they would be reunited with their families, their land, and their former prosperity. But the news could not be worse. France was losing the war in Europe, and in America, the situation was steadily deteriorating.

Deploying the few able-bodied troops left in New France during the winter of 1760, the Duke of Lévis laid siege to Quebec, where the English had retreated after the victory over Montcalm on the Plains of Abraham. That spring, the French troops conquered the English in Ste-Foy, then Murray and the rest of his troops retreated once more to the fortress where they struggled with famine and epidemics. Each camp clung to the hope the fleet that sailed up the St. Lawrence River would be their own. There were only a few pockets of resistance left, of which Montreal and the Restigouche post were two.

* * *

Mathilde was growing fonder of Tjigog by the day and spent all her waking hours with him. On May 17th, they canoed as

---

5. Husband of Marguerite Gauthier, Joseph Gauthier's daughter.

far as the native cemetery on Ile aux Hérons in search of a small aspergillum that Father Ambroise, a Recollet, had forgotten during a burial ceremony. Across from them were the green mountains of the Gaspé, to their left the interior of the Baye des Chaleurs, the cul-de-sac where, in 1534, Jacques Cartier looked for his famous passage to India and, next to it, the Miguasha[6] Point and its hidden fossil treasure. On the island, the long-legged herons were able to watch Tjigog, perhaps inspired by the spirits of his ancestors, go about winning over Mathilde, who willingly gave in to the sensations he produced and gave herself over to him. In all purity, without holding back, without reservation, without any defences. "I want to know what love is. I want to feel love. Show me…"

And so, after nearly freezing to death in a Grand'Pré cellar, after burning with fever in Camp de l'Espérance, and suffering through poverty, hunger, thirst, and pain, Mathilde was introduced to a new realm of well-being in which her senses seemed to reach the ultimate state of perfection. After reliving the thousand worries and torments of the past few years, she finally found peace in Tjigog's arms. As Tjigog's warm breath caressed her skin, she felt the burn of a sharp, sudden pain that faded quickly, giving way to a sensation of sheer bliss.

"Your body… its fire… so good." The last two words said over and over again.

So good that Tjigog and Mathilde felt as though they could hear among the rustling leaves the song of Mi'kmaq souls on their final voyage. Mathilde had no way of fully expressing the pleasure she felt in her body, her heart, and her mind. It didn't matter. She loved Tjigog. Why? It was a mystery. She loved Tjigog as one loves at the age of sixteen, wholly, generously, idealistically, and, above all, blissfully.

* * *

Aside from Tjigog and Mathilde, there were very few happy people at that time at the Restigouche post. Commander

---

6. Native term meaning "long time red."

Bourdon was worried about the future because of all the refugees and the empty storehouses. After the fall of Louisbourg in the summer of 1758, he had made his way to the Restigouche post by way of Ile Saint-Jean.

Bourdon was well liked by the Mi'kmaq because he spoke their language; the Acadians, too, held him in a great deal of esteem. He used his influence to encourage the Acadians to come to Restigouche rather than be taken prisoner at Fort Beauséjour. In fact, that winter he sent a letter to the inhabitants of the Baie des Ouines and Richibouctou.

I am very surprised to hear you have come to an agreement with the English without first advising me... Where is your zeal for the mother country, your firm commitment to your religion? Which, after all the years of fasting and fleeing through the woods, exposed to a thousand dangers, have been lost today in an instant.

His exhortations bore fruit. In Richibouctou, he had the support of another patriot, Joseph Dugas, militia captain, and Joseph Le Blanc's son-in-law, known as Le Maigre. Now Bourdon had to feed all these people and he was sick with worry, but Dupont-Duvivier, a former Louisbourg officer, arrived just then with even worse news: "According to an Algonquin who just arrived from the Matapedia, the English fleet is sailing up the river."

"So Lévis won't be able to take back Quebec," Bourdon said sadly.

Other officers came for news. The Canadian-born captain Saint-Simon, who had fought with Boishébert in Louisbourg, arrived, full of energy. Marot, the troops' surgeon and major, came too, as did Bazagier, the king's commissioner and navy scribe, recently arrived from Ile aux Noix on the Richelieu.

"There's nothing left for us to do but pack up and go," sighed Marot.

"Why would we give up now, with the French fleet on its way?" Saint-Simon said indignantly

"Quit dreaming," Marot retorted. "France has lost the war in Europe. At best, it will send us a few rowboats! With the English armada coming up the river, what else can we do?

They've already destroyed everything as far as Quebec. In the fall, there'll be nothing but fire and ashes all the way to Montreal. New France is dying. We can't stop cannonballs with our bare hands; we have to surrender."

Saint-Simon, who had no desire to lay down his arms without a fight, proposed, "Our ground defence is in good shape. All we need to do is consolidate our batteries at Pointe-à-la-Garde and Pointe-à-la-Batterie; the English won't dare land."

Duvivier agreed with him, but Bazagier, who was used to recounting events rather than creating them, was more neutral. "In any case, we have to wait for instructions from Vaudreuil."

"We don't have to wait for anything," Marot corrected him. "When you're dying, you don't need authorization to kick the bucket. We have to evacuate the post."

"Now I understand!" Saint-Simon exploded. "Monsieur Marot is only interested in saving his own fine skin… Tell me where exactly will the two thousand Acadians go? Do you plan to put them up in your scented cabin during the ocean crossing?" he jeered.

The quarrel could have seriously poisoned the climate among the staff. Which was why Commander Bourdon, who had kept his own counsel thus far, thought it best to intervene, "Gentlemen, we'll have lots of time to quarrel and create bad blood later. I think it would be wise to wait, reinforce the post's defences, and send an emissary to Montreal to find out what Vaudreuil's intentions are. After all, the English haven't yet taken Montreal. Don't forget that in 1711, Admiral Walker's fleet broke up on the reefs around Ile aux Oeufs. We should wait for news from François Le Mercier, who left for France on the *Machault* to petition the king for help. Don't forget Vaudreuil asked for four thousand troops and ten thousand tons of supplies and munitions, which would amount to a convoy of several dozen merchant ships escorted by warships."

But he didn't believe it himself. It didn't help that his service record had not been acknowledged by Versailles. *I was part of the Duc d'Anville's fleet and I fought at Port-Royal and*

Louisbourg, where I'm the oldest lieutenant, yet I never received a captain's commission, he thought bitterly.

* * *

After the English troops' raid on the north coast of the Baye des Chaleurs, Alexis Landry, Olivier Léger, Olivier Blanchard, Charles Poirier, and Alexis Cormier left Bocage for the relative safety of the Restigouche post. That spring they could be found repairing a schooner, an old carcass they would have left to rot on shore under any other circumstances. They were given a hand by Joseph Dugas, who was a gifted carpenter. He was proud to have as his ancestor Abraham, the armourer who acted as lieutenant-governor to Governor D'Aulnay.

"Even Governor Lamothe-Cadillac was impressed by his judgment," he said to all and sundry.

"If you free us from the English," Olivier Blanchard teased, "I'm willing to appoint you Viscount of Restigouche!"

Dugas was not the only one boasting of illustrious ancestors. Joseph Boudreau was another. It seemed like every Acadian of the time was named Joseph! A native of Beaubassin, he had just arrived in Restigouche with his fiancée Jeanne-Marie Haché. Boudreau's ancestor was Michel, a former lieutenant-general of Port-Royal. He was neither a seaman nor a carpenter, but he knew the land well since he had had a large farm in Beaubassin and was blessed with strong arms and a fierce desire to find a peaceful country. So he put his shoulder to the wheel. Olivier Léger, who was Blanchard's cousin and another joker, nicknamed Dugas the Sultan of Acadia, which made Boudreau his Grand Vizier.

Since he came from a family of soldiers, Léger armed the schooner with swivel guns, a kind of small mobile cannon. He installed four in all and camouflaged the last one on the mast platform. He knew full well that the schooner wouldn't hold its own for very long against a real warship, but he hoped Alexis Landry could rig the sails to maximize the wind's effect. Landry had no equal when it came to sensing which way the wind blew, in both the figurative and true sense. So it was a pleasure for him to assemble the sails and the rigging. Alexis saw it as his mission to ensure the future of the Acadian people in America and had made a solemn vow to that effect to his sons buried in Camp de l'Espérance. Seeing the way his daughter Agathe looked at Joseph Dugas, he could tell their relationship would lead to more progeny for him. Joseph Dugas tried to warn Alexis Landry that outfitting the schooners was all well and good but what they really needed was a safe haven. He told him a true story, "After the fall of Quebec, the Acadians who sought refuge there obtained written permission from Brigadier General Monckton to return to Acadia along the shores of the Saint-Jean. Do you know what they were told when they arrived in November? That the authorization had been obtained under false pretenses and that their permit was for another Saint-Jean River. Guess where they are now. Halifax. And from there they'll be sent to England's dungeons."

* * *

Tjigog struck up a friendship with Louis de Lentaigne[7], a Norman who, after the destruction of Papôg's fishing installations, had decided to enrol in the Dupont-Duvivier company. On May 19, 1760, Tjigog was invited with Mathilde to the baptism of Louis's son Eustache. The baby's godmother Marie Chenard carried him proudly through the church. Recollet Ambroise celebrated the ceremony, watched over closely by Bourdon, who stood in for the godfather and saw this as an opportunity to honour his soldiers and raise the refugees' morale. Little Eustache suffered loudly from the heat that day. To cool him off, his mother Marguerite Chapados decided to take off his diaper. Next to the baptismal fonts – a small mountain spring – Eustache peed on Tjigog as he stood nearby...

"That's a real warrior's spray," Tjigog said laughing.

"You should give him a gift," Mathilde pointed out, for she had been told that gift-giving was a native custom under the circumstances.

---

7. Today's Lanteigne. A descendant of Sieur de la Championnière.

Uncle Joseph-Jean and his wife brought fiddleheads gathered on the Pain-de-Sucre mountain. They'd shown a certain coolness toward Mathilde ever since she'd fallen in love with Tjigog. Aunt Anne didn't approve of the match, without really knowing why. *Maybe I feel responsible to her parents, who wouldn't want her living like a coureur de bois,* she thought. Olivier Blanchard's wife Catherine Amirault was there with her son Thaddée-Maxime. She'd brought as refreshment a jug full of ginger water.

"So much has happened since Father Le Guerne baptized my son in the spring of 1756 in Petcoudiac. But what does the future hold?" she asked Anne, thinking of her children's future.

Father Ambroise had more than one string to his bow. He had unearthed flour God knew where and prepared small heart-shaped cookies to hand out. When he declared, "Tahoé nka méramon ignemoulu; nkameramon achkou ouigitesg..." (Friends, I give you my heart of which you will always be part...), the natives fell to their knees and gave thanks to heaven. He chose that moment to read out a letter he had sent to the Archbishop of Quebec, Monsignor Pontbriand:

We wish God continued Grandeur and ask for His benediction and gifts for myself and for that part of his flock entrusted to me, for which I am eternally and respectfully grateful...

Denys de Saint-Simon listened to the celebration with a heavy heart. "When I hear the word 'flock' I think of sheep, and that's not the way to win wars."

He couldn't accept the coming defeat. Nor the consequences it would have for his future, namely the obligation to leave the country he'd been born in.

While the luckiest savoured their cookies, a Mi'kmaq standing next to a salmon totem entertained them. He swallowed a flintstone after grinding it down with his teeth, then lit a pipe, chanting all the while, and stuck a small stick measuring a foot in length down his throat. Although Tjigog had seen the magic trick before, Mathilde had not, and she got very upset when the man turned bright red and began to choke. But he pulled the stick back out, an intact stone on its tip. The celebration ended with high mass and a young native choir. During mass Father Ambroise raised heavenward a gold chalice that Jérémie Godin, known as Bellefontaine, had rescued from the Grand'Pré church.

* * *

In 1685, Richard Denys transferred to the Quebec Seminary a plot of land located by a small creek that fed the Restigouche River, for the purpose of setting up a permanent mission. Tjigog built a stockade of pilings at the mouth of the creek. At high tide, alewife and plaice swam over the obstacle to fill up on marsh silt. At low tide it was an easy task to gather up the fish imprisoned behind the stockade. On that May 20th evening, the catch was good for Tjigog and Mathilde, but Mathilde was not feeling too well because of a quarrel fed by old superstitions. Her period had started that morning and during the day, she had put Tjigog's rifle away. According to certain Mi'kmaq beliefs, her action destroyed its power as a firearm. She thought the superstition was as ridiculous as the one that said the eyes of fish should be torn out when the fish are caught so as not to be seen by their kind. Tjigog's reply was that his beliefs were no more ridiculous than Mathilde's. "Look at you wearing your cross above your heart so you'll be placed under Jesus' protection!"

The sun was setting over the bay, and the sky was ablaze.

"Look," she exclaimed. "There's a ship in flames on the horizon."

"Corte Real has returned," a trembling Tjigog mumbled.

"Calm down, that's a lot of nonsense."

Tjigog was paralyzed with fear as the ball of fire approached. Mathilde had heard of the legend and tried to calm her friend. "Look, there's another one," Mathilde pointed out. "So there's not just one phantom ship, there's a whole fleet!"

"And it's French, I can see the fleur-de-lys," said Tjigog, relieved.

They raced back to camp to spread the good news. There was much rejoicing since it had been years since the Acadians had seen so many French ships and soldiers, especially not the Acadians who had lain low in the woods for years wondering, in times of despair, if France were actually a country or just an illusion. But some were quite disappointed to learn there were only three ships: the *Marquis de Malauze*, a twenty-eight-cannon frigate, the *Bienfaisant*, and the *Machault*, two merchant ships armed with a few cannons and only two hundred soldiers. They also had six small English schooners they'd seized en route, which compensated for the French ships lost and brought back for some the hope that the wind could turn in their favour. What the optimists saw were supplies, munitions, and soldiers.

The fleet commander François Chenard de la Giraudais, told of their adventure, "Last fall, France lost nearly its whole fleet fighting against England in the Cardinals battle. So it's almost a miracle France was able to send any help. Many people want nothing to do with Canada and agree with Voltaire, who said, 'You know the two nations are at war over a few arpents of snow in Canada, and much more has been spent than what Canada is worth.' Due to the pressure to cancel the expedition, its departure had to be delayed, especially since the seamen refused to leave before receiving their pay for the previous year. Finally, on April 10th, six ships left Bordeaux carrying two thousand tons of merchandise and four hundred troops. It was already late and we had to reach Quebec before the English, who were blocking the coasts with the Royal Navy. Unfortunately, two days later the English sank the *Soleil*, and on April 17, it was *L'Aurore*'s turn. You would have thought that with such promising names as Aurora and Sun..." he said, with a lump in his throat. "Afterwards, everything went well until April 30th, when the *Fidélité* sank off the Azores. Near Anticosti Island, we interrogated the crew of a small English boat, who told us the English had preceded us by a few days. We had no choice; we had to turn back, either to put in at Louisiana or the Baye des Chaleurs. We opted for the latter and set sail for Restigouche. We need to replenish our supply of water and biscuits and send the instructions from Versailles to Governor Vaudreuil."

"I'll go up the Matapedia to Montreal," Saint-Simon proposed. "And come back with the governor's instructions."

"What about the English schooners?" Du Calvet asked. He was a recent arrival in Miramichi, who looked after the stores' inventory.

"We captured them in the Baye des Chaleurs, not far from the ruins of Papôg. They were on their way to Quebec via Boston and Louisbourg with a good supply of food."

"That's good. You'll have your work cut out for you distributing it to the unfortunate people here," Bourdon added.

The comment brought a smile of satisfaction to the face of Du Calvet, who was always trying to increase the rations and whose goodness was well known.

Bourdon stayed up late reflecting on New France's fate, which couldn't be bleaker, and on his own. He had had to yield to the authority of Gabriel François Dangeac, who commanded the king's troops, but he had no bad feelings toward his successor because he knew a man of experience when he saw one, and he was relieved not to have to sign the coming surrender. He did wonder, however, what good a fleet was that left late and arrived after the English fleet.

"However, Vaudreuil stressed the fact in his dispatch to the court that it was better to lose ships to the ice rather than arrive too late... Four thousand men requested, four hundred granted, and only two hundred who made it safe and sound. What now?"

He leafed somewhat dejectedly through La Giraudais' ship's log and read,

We left the Bordeaux River on April 10, 1760. Cool winds from the N.-E. at 10 in the morning. We were out of danger's way where the river was concerned...

"Out of danger's way!"

Chapter 26

We pity the poor human race bleeding itself white on our continent for a few arpents of ice in Canada.

– Voltaire's correspondence

Nantes to Paris, almost one hundred and twenty leagues. With the relays it would take six days, even at a gruelling pace. Joseph, Membertou, René, and a servant of the marquis settled into a berlin pulled by four black horses. During the long trip, Joseph quit thinking about his origins, his mission, Angélique, and Emilie, and dreamt of the good times he'd had with his children. He found it hard to believe that twenty years had gone by since his arrival in Ruisseau. He'd had just enough time to win over Membertou before Geneviève was born. Unlike Membertou, Geneviève was gentle and loved to play quietly with the dolls her mother made for her, dolls that looked like Geneviève with long blonde curls. She was conscious of her looks at an early age; she loved to spend hours in front of the mirror playing with her mother's combs, powders, and perfumes. While Geneviève worshipped beauty, Membertou valued strength; whenever he walked in front of a mirror, he stopped to admire his muscles. Joseph approved of his son's attitude more, and whenever Geneviève's vanity got on his nerves too much, he made her angry by asking, "Who's the fairest one of all?" then providing the answer himself, "Membertou!"

This had the desired effect. However, it didn't take long for her to learn to say, "No, it's not Membertou because boys aren't *fair*."

As for Josette, she had always been different, rather secretive and solitary, adept at eluding Membertou's provocations. When she was with Geneviève, she entered into her sister's world of fairytales and sleeping beauties awakened by prince charmings. Membertou, an adolescent by then, grew apart from his sisters and started showing an interest in other girls. To the missionaries' despair, among natives the game of love was considered to be both healthy and natural. Membertou had had his share of experience, and his popularity was high among the girls of the tribe. Around eighteen, though, he grew increasingly taciturn, irritable, and quick-tempered. Joseph was surprised by the transformation that began when a descendant of the Baron de Saint-Castin passed through Ruisseau with his wife from the D'Amour family, and their daughter nicknamed Perle-de-Rosée. The daughter rebuffed every advance Membertou made, yet went with other young men from the camp. Joseph suspected Membertou's heart had been broken, and that he now harboured deep resentment against women for their capacity to humiliate men. That was the explanation Joseph found for Membertou's religious zeal. He didn't deny Membertou's spiritual desire, but his religious craze after Perle-de-Rosée's departure led Joseph to believe Membertou's attitude was more impulsive than deep-rooted; a quest for eternity born of bitterness. That day saw the beginning of Membertou's interest in the shaman's activities.

The sun was already high overhead when the travellers stopped by a creek on a small bridge of moss-covered stones. Accustomed to the country's eating habits by then, Joseph used his knife to carve a leg of lamb, summer sausage from Lyon, then ham from Bayonne, and of course cheese and crusty bread that he shared with his sons. Joseph washed down his meal with copious quantities of Muscadet, the local white wine. René had adapted well to the food, but not so Membertou, who dreamt of pemmican[1], smoked salmon, and wild raspberries.

---

1. Dried, concentrated meat.

They resumed their travels. Joseph's thoughts turned to his son René, who looked like him – tall, fair, and slim, with grey eyes. The generous boy was interested in everything out of the ordinary – magic and the occult. As the youngest in the family, he was quite spoiled and, consequently, undisciplined. *He's almost a young man now. Soon he'll be interested in women.*

Disturbed only by the occasional grunt from the coachman, whinnying of horses, or jolt of the berlin, Joseph spent the afternoon rehashing his memories of René climbing trees to find birds' eggs to make omelettes with. He could see him again hidden in the tall grass savouring tiny wild strawberries or playing tricks, like the time he put an eelskin in Josette's bed, making her cry out in terror at the sight of a snake! He felt a moment's sadness remembering his son's bout of red measles and his mother rocking him in a red blanket. "Red has healing power in cases like this," she swore.

Joseph felt guilty about his children, and his neglect of them due to his obsession with his own quest; his not being present enough, physically or otherwise, especially vis-à-vis Membertou, whom he'd adopted as a son, but over whom he felt he had lost all influence.

Joseph came back to the present for a moment. The berlin was following the Loire, which had returned to a more modest level after the spring's floods. From time to time, a barge passed on its way to the Atlantic, but there was nothing like the traffic in Nantes. René had eyes only for the castles, an uninterrupted procession of dungeons, iron bars, crenellated stone walls, and slate roofs. At times, it felt like the fortresses were within hand's reach, that all he had to do was reach out to touch the drawbridges, which connected hyphen-like the ordinary world to the princely abodes beyond the circle of water. He marvelled at the sight of the palaces belonging to France's nobility, who accumulated droits de seigneur, privileges, and wealth while the villagers cultivated the noblemen's lands.

"How does one become a nobleman?" he asked his father.

"You're either born noble, or the king gives you a title of nobility in recognition of an act of bravery or importance of yours that benefited the kingdom."

"Are you given a castle then?"

"Not necessarily; some nobles are quite poor and have neither land nor personal fortune."

René couldn't hold still, so enchanted was he with the palaces he glimpsed. He remembered his grandfather's stories about the Hôtel des Invalides, built to house soldiers who'd been wounded fighting for Louis XIV, one of whom was his grandfather's uncle. René imagined an immense golden dome reflecting sunlight into the courtyards with arcades several floors high emitting spirals of light that seemed to settle at times on his grandfather's uncle's head like an emperor's crown. His grandfather had also talked to him about Versailles, a palace bigger than Ile Caraquet and taller than the giant spruce trees of Pokesudie, with white marble walls, diamonds in the windows, and fountains in the gardens that sprinkled the clouds like the autumn tides above the capes of Grand-Anse.

Membertou, who had recently begun to take an interest in the Bible, meditated on a phrase from Ecclesiastes: "Vanity of vanities! All is vanity... all is vanity and a striving after wind." It was true that the episode with Perle-de-Rosée had affected him, but Joseph didn't know that Membertou had been affected by something else, too – the island treasure. Most people who discovered a fabulous treasure would see their passion and desire for power, glory, and consumption exacerbated. Not so Membertou, who was true to his native culture in which the land, like the sea, was not for sale. All things belonged to all people, and it was unthinkable to eat venison without offering some to one's neighbour. On the contrary, the sight of all the jewels had made him see the fragility of all things and the injustice brought about by wealth. Gradually, he began taking an interest in his people's religious values rather than in those of the missionaries. He hadn't forgotten his other passion, however – hunting in the forest and great open spaces.

"Look," shouted René as their diligence[2] passed in front of a superb manor.

---

2. A large closed public horse-drawn carriage.

Membertou didn't pay much attention. He would rather savour the memory of the first game he'd hunted at the age of five. The whole tribe had celebrated the kill, and the hare he'd snared was boiled and shared out in minuscule portions to everyone except the hunter and his parents as was customary. The memory was as alive as his first moose had been… although, that time, the tribe was able to celebrate for much longer!

After seven days of delays, stopovers, and departures, their posteriors aching from the bumps in the road, Joseph and his sons arrived within sight of Paris and the towers of Notre Dame cathedral looming ahead. The bells rang as though sending out a prayer above the noise of the city. It had rained that afternoon, and the cathedral's great rose window looked to be pierced by a rainbow falling into the Seine. Membertou thought of Noah on his ark – Noah, who saw a rainbow after a dove brought him a freshly plucked olive leaf. For Membertou, the rainbow was a sign drawn in the heavens by the Great Creator to show him his decision to become a shaman was the right one. He stopped to look at the sculpted scenes on the Portal of the Last Judgment. The weighing of souls; the chosen being transported to heaven by angels; the others being led to hell by demons. He didn't agree with the white man's religious view because he failed to understand how a loving god could punish his creatures in such a way.

René thought of his grandfather, who, as a young boy, had seen on Notre Dame Square a performance of *Theophilus's Miracle*, a play by the trouvère[3] Rutebeuf. After selling his soul to the devil, Theophilus is finally saved by the Virgin, who cancels his contract with the devil. Then, before the portal to St. Anne, René's attention turned to the dragon slain by St. Marcellus, Bishop of Paris in the Fifth Century. The bishop could be seen thrusting his crosier down the dragon's throat as rainwater trickled from the gargoyles' mouths.

Joseph was disappointed with the turn events had taken. Nothing had gone as planned. First, he had had to make do

---

3. A troubadour of the spoken word.

with De la Galissonière's son, who albeit a nice man, was not his father. "His father would have helped me more because he knew Canada and the importance of that country for France's future. He would have accompanied me to Paris instead of letting me travel alone." The young marquis had provided him with letters and passes, but Joseph felt uncomfortable confronting unassisted a milieu governed by rigid etiquette and hierarchy.

Inside the cathedral above the organ, the setting sun sent beams of light through the rose window. In the upper part of the stained glass, the twelve virtues were represented by female warriors wearing a crown and bearing a lance with which to fight the twelve vices. But Joseph was not in a very Christian mood. The suffering caused by the deportations had dampened his former enthusiasm. And yet, he felt the need to reflect, meditate, and even to pray. *While I'm here*, he decided, *I might as well pray in front of that which is most holy*. He headed for the treasure room to meditate on the precious manuscript, the *Livre des Serments*, where he swore to himself he would fulfil his mission. He had gold, and didn't gold open all doors?

René was bewitched by the magic he could feel. He felt as though he were walking through a huge upside-down ship down which the cathedral's builders had passed: workers, stonecarvers, sculptors, glassworkers… His head was buzzing with questions about the architectural techniques, the symbols engraved on stone, the books of psalms with ornate illuminations in their green vellum bindings stamped with St. Louis' coat of arms. He imagined the sound of trumpets, the coronation of kings, and, on Place de Grève, feast days with their fireworks and cannon shots. Impressed by all the beauty and knowledge housed in the cathedral, he thought of the books he'd read on alchemy and told himself that one day he would find a way to transform the stones of Ile Caraquet into gold.

As he went from one stained glass window to another following the history of the creation of the world, from Adam and Eve's temptation through the redemption of the sins of the world, even though he didn't believe the stories, Membertou was impressed. The idea came to him to build for his people a temple that would rival this cathedral. *There will be paintings of unicorns*, he promised himself. He did a quick tour of the treasure room to see the crown of thorns, the holy nail, and a gold-coated, jewel-encrusted fragment of the True Cross that St. Louis had brought back from the Crusades. In the sanctuary with its chalices, ciboriums, and patens engraved with golden angels, he felt for a moment as though he were in the island cave. But when he saw the collection of bishops' rings meant to be kissed by serfs living in poverty, a wave of disgust washed over him. Looking at St. Louis' tunic and the small chain with which he practised self-flagellation, Membertou thought how he himself would remain stoic in the face of torture. "As an Indian, I would be able to suffer pain better than a European!"

Then he decided to pay homage to the Great Creator. He lit almost every candle in the cathedral, and the light rose heavenward, its golden hue as nothing, in Membertou's view, next to the light of the Great Creator.

Joseph and René joined him then, ready to leave. They took the Notre Dame Bridge off Ile de la Cité and made their way to the right bank of the Seine and the Louvre, the palace in which the monarchy used to live before the move to Versailles, which was now home to a group of artists. Joseph glimpsed stovepipes sticking out of the palace; the crumbling, neglected buildings were clearly suffering in their stones and soul. Innkeepers' shacks were like a blight of pustules along the Louvre's walls. Its days of splendour when kings lived within its walls were long gone. Since a building was under demolition, the diligence had to turn into the Marais, down narrow streets whose gutters were strewn with rubbish between dilapidated buildings with gaping facades and boarded-up windows – buildings often seven stories high that leaned dangerously and didn't let in the light of day. At the sight of the tottering buildings, Joseph was reminded of the earthquake that had shaken Lisbon five years earlier and its twenty-five thousand victims. *An earthquake here would be catastrophic*, he thought.

To the left and right, blind men, beggars, the lame, the maimed, and amputees displayed their misery for all to see.

Membertou was incredulous. "They call this *civilization!* How can they let people live in poverty surrounded by so much wealth?"

Joseph too wondered why in this so-called age of enlightenment there was so much darkness.

Without great conviction, he told his sons that a number of the wretched souls before them were only disguised as poor or ill and returned every evening to their normal appearance back in their unsavoury districts, their "cour de miracles." They feasted on the fruit and products they wheedled out of naive bourgeois. But he had to acknowledge that what he saw was not just an act. Joseph explained to his sons how the king and nobles had great wealth and privileges, the bourgeois had a bit less, the peasants had very little, and finally the beggars had nothing at all. "Like in heaven," René interrupted him. "In the missionaries' pictures, God is up high on his throne and the angels a bit lower down. Next come the saints, then the souls in purgatory and finally the damned, who suffer and have nothing."

For once, Membertou agreed with René. The human order had used the divine order to justify its legitimacy!

All the injustice he saw made Joseph think of his peaceful life back in Ruisseau. He started to miss the great forests, the salt air, the breeze in the sails of his schooner, Angélique's warmth, and his daughters' smiles. He sorely missed the hospitality of the tribe and the freedom he enjoyed in New France!

Finally, the diligence came out on Place de Grève, the square for public celebrations and executions, a square that led gently down a slope to the banks of the Seine. A gallows stood in the centre of the square, and the coachman explained, "This is where prisoners are executed. Before you arrived, the king's servant Damien was quartered. He had nicked his master with a knife."

"Why?" Joseph asked, surprised.

"I'm not sure... I think he wasn't quite right in the head and he blamed the king for not fulfilling his duties. Our king, known as the Beloved, is not all that well loved these days because of his spending habits and the scandalous life he leads. What's more, people are fed up with the war and taxes."

René shuddered at the thought of a man being quartered. "How excruciating!"

A warrior must be able to withstand pain and resist all temptations of the flesh, Membertou said to himself.

The landscape changed when they reached Rue St-Antoine, which was said to be the most beautiful street in Paris. The street was surprisingly wide, which made it a perfect place for strolls and public celebrations. It passed through the Marais, the former marsh that monks and Templars cultivated in the XIII century and which had become a posh, fashionable district with its prestigious hotels and discreet classical buildings, its courtyards and gardens. This was the district in which the Affected Young Ladies, libertines, and philosophers held their salons and where the great seigneurs had their palaces decorated by the best artists of the XVII century.

At 62, rue Saint Antoine, the diligence drove through a carriage entrance supported by Doric columns and came to a stop in the courtyard of the Hôtel de Bethune-Sully, a large, magnificent building. The mansion was made of freestone with a sculpted façade: the lintels with curved pediments displayed sculptures of which the most striking illustrated the four elements and the four seasons with naked goddesses and figures representing the signs of the zodiac.

The travellers were welcomed by the Viscount Turgot de Saint-Clair, who lived in the pavilion on the right during his stays in Paris. The viscount read the letter from his friend the Marquis de la Galissonnière asking him to offer his guests hospitality. His wasn't the warmest of welcomes, but at least he provided them with rooms.

Chapter 27

The descendants of the French who acclimatize to the country (Canada) and the Savages who are brought to knowledge of the Faith and profess as best they can will be deemed to be French naturals. Should they come to France, will they be entitled to the same privileges as those born there?

– Cardinal Richelieu, in the charter
of the Compagnie des Cent-Associés

You have no right to prevent people from doing what they see as right since that is their culture. I gladly carry your banner during the procession of the Blessed Sacrament. Why will you not allow me to carry my people's peace pipe?

– Chief Orambeche in 1719

The Viscount Turgot de Saint-Clair had a niece named Aglaë. She was a beauty. With her long black hair and dark skin, she looked a great deal like Perle-de-Rosée. Membertou was not indifferent to her charms, and the sight of her set his skin to tingling despite himself. The friendly young woman asked all kinds of questions about New France and native customs and let her attraction to Membertou show. "Could you teach me archery?" she asked, seeing a quiver of arrows in his luggage.

Glad to have the opportunity to show off his hunting skills, he agreed to teach her the next day.

That evening in bed, before Membertou went to sleep, he felt the sudden warmth of temptation in his loins. It was as though the Pompeiian-style friezework on the walls with its vestals – holy virgins – were taunting him. Eventually Membertou fell asleep, but his dreams were peopled with angels who looked like Aglaë while Gougous armed with tomahawks prevented him from approaching her!

The next day, Aglaë led Membertou into the Bois de Vincennes. It didn't take them long to travel the few leagues on horseback. Wearing an Amazon outfit – a dark skirt, a bright red overblouse fringed with marten fur, and highly polished leather boots, her hair caressed by the wind – the beautiful young woman led her chestnut mare. She reminded Membertou of a painting he had noticed in the palace, of a half-naked woman who represented daylight. For the ride, he had exchanged his forest garb for the pearl grey frock coat of a horseman. No one would have recognized him back in Ruisseau. At Aglaë's request, he brought along bows, quivers, and arrows, all the hunting gear he'd transported from Ruisseau. His heart started pounding when she took his hand and led him down a less-travelled trail.

She stepped lightly, like a deer in springtime. A gentle breeze carried her perfume, a blend of iris, lily, and camomile. They stepped out into a small clearing in which tall oak trees towered, and the first archery lesson began. Aglaë proved herself to be very skilful, even though she was continually asking Membertou for advice. He had to guide where she looked, her shoulder, her arm, her hand. His desire grew at the touch of her satin skin. Around noon, after much practice, Aglaë spread a small polkadot tablecloth in a shady corner of the clearing and brought out of her basket a herb omelette prepared that morning by the cook. Membertou gathered some wildflowers and made a bouquet that he laid in the center of the tablecloth.

"Have you ever had an omelette made from swans' eggs?" Membertou asked.

Aglaë was forced to admit she hadn't. She asked him to describe how immense the forests were. She had trouble imagining the infinite spaces and bucolic rhythm described by Membertou.

"Is it cold in the wintertime?"

Membertou explained that in Canada, winter could last as long as five months and that the cold was extreme with a great deal of snow; he told her about snowbanks that could measure several toises deep and how the branches of large conifers sagged under the accumulated weight of all the snow, and about the inhabitants who wore furs to keep warm.

"What about the bears? How do they make it through the winter?"

"In the fall, they put fir tree branches in a cavity in the ground to make a kind of den covered with a roof of branches. They settle in for the winter, sleeping and occasionally licking their paws. At spring thaw, you have to keep at a safe distance because they're famished by then…"

Membertou interrupted his description, stood up, and pantomimed a bear looking for food, breaking off the branches of beech trees to extract the beechnuts[1]. Aglaë joined in. Membertou caught her playfully but didn't dare embrace her the way he wanted to because he was afraid of being hurt as he had been with Perle-de-Rosée. To help him return to his senses, he launched into a hunting tale.

"There's a huge animal called a moose. To hunt it, you have to track it in the woods through the snow on snowshoes, night and day for several days. Until it's exhausted. We have many uses for moose: its meat is delicious, especially moose tongue; its hide is used to make clothes and blankets; its intestines and stomach are used as recipients; its nerves and tendons as thread; its bones for tools; and its teeth decorate our costumes. Then, most important of all to us, we pray to the animal's spirit for forgiveness…"

Out of breath and agitated, he didn't really know what he was saying anymore. *Has she noticed the effect she has on me?* he asked himself. He couldn't guess Aglaë's thoughts; she let nothing show.

---

1. Anecdote told by Father Clarence d'Entremont in *Nicolas Denys*.

"Come eat," she said.

She took pleasure in her meal, her gestures slow and refined. He watched her furtively. From time to time, she wiped her lips with a small handkerchief. Then Aglaë brought out some crystallized fruit and blackcurrant wine. Membertou ate and drank his fill, then she asked, "And your houses?"

"They're called 'wigwams.' They're made of birchbark or animal hides. We can fold them up and carry them with us when we go hunting. They're much smaller than your castles! But there's no space lost. Even the French recognize what optimal use the wigwam makes of such limited space."

Aglaë had read Montaigne's *The Good Savage*, which gave her a rather romanticized view of native people. She asked, "What about hospitality?"

"Hospitality is sacred and must be offered, even to the enemy. Property accumulated is to be shared. Honour and joy come from having another person accept your gift. That is its meaning. But, unfortunately, since the white man's arrival with his brandy, medals, and cheap trinkets, customs have been changing."

He didn't dare tell her about his dream of becoming a shaman to breathe new life into the traditions... if he managed to resist temptation!

It was time to go back to the hotel. Out of gallantry and a desire for an excuse to touch Aglaë, Membertou locked his hands together to help her step up into the saddle. Near Rue Saint-Antoine, Membertou caught sight of a poor man carrying a portable toilet and rags crying, "Relieve yourselves, Mesdames!" Courtesans could "relieve themselves discreetly" in the middle of the street: sheltered from all eyes under their veils and many skirts. Membertou was shocked. He was even more shocked when, just as he was about to turn down a narrow street, someone offered to rent him a sort of leather umbrella to shelter himself from the turds and urine being emptied from chamber pots by the inhabitants of the upper floors of the buildings.

Back home, he thought, *we don't have such bad manners. Cleanliness is maintained through the sweat lodges and dips in cold water. It smells much more pleasant and is better for one's health!*

* * *

René accompanied his father on a tour of Paris. They passed through the manor's garden and orange grove, which gave directly onto Place Royale[2], a huge square surrounded by pavilions and manors, the ground floors of which had arcades two storeys high topped by a slate roof pierced with skylights. The square was a hub of activity, with its carousels and amusements, as well as being the place where duels were fought in defiance of the royal edicts. In front of the home where Richelieu was born – the cardinal who drove France's Protestants to ruin – Joseph meditated on his mysterious origins. He was still lost in thought as they arrived in front of the Hotel Bouthillier-de-Chavigny, in Rue des Francs-Bourgeois. René was intrigued by the congestion on the streets – handcarts and tipcarts with squeaking axles, porters, water boys, and merchants selling scrap iron and rabbit skins, and a herd of pigs wearing bells. He lingered, fascinated by the district's animation: the washerwomen's cries, the strolling musicians playing their hurdy-gurdy, the drinking songs of the drunks in nearby dives. Fishmongers called out their wares: "Mackerel here, still alive and thrashing!"

"It's here! It's here!"

"Chilled herring, fresh herring!"

"Baked apples! Piping hot!"

"All for your pleasure, Mesdames, all for your pleasure!"

The district also had its share of beggars and cripples and of shining palaces and wealthy inhabitants wearing lace jabots and riding in golden carriages – such a contrast between stark poverty and opulence. On their return, Joseph was given a message bearing the wax seal of Versailles. He carefully opened the missive, which announced he was to have an audience with the minister in two days' time. Joseph was awed by

---

2. Place des Vosges.

his invitation to court. A bit nervous too, because the conversations he'd had with the viscount had shown him that the court knew nothing about his faraway continent and cared even less; in fact criticism was being levelled at the king for spending his ecus on its snowbound forests and feather-wearing Indians since the war had increased the cost of living in France. But ever since France began retreating from the battlefields in Europe and its colonies, rumours of peace abounded.

* * *

After the angelus, Joseph, René, and Membertou found themselves in the viscount's dining room. The Greek myth of Dionysus – the god of wine, good food, and ecstatic delirium – was depicted on the ceiling. On the wall hung Abraham Bosse's painting on the theme of taste and another painting by Chaudin on food. A popular cookbook had the place of honour on the buffet, next to Erasmus's book on etiquette and table manners. But Joseph was too worried about his audience in Versailles to take in the decor. He couldn't even talk to the viscount about his concerns since the viscount was away. The meal was eaten in silence. René was busy with the Epinal riddles he had bought on Place Royale. Membertou barely touched his eel in tartar sauce (eel was a highly prized delicacy among the Mi'kmaq) or the sauté of turbot à la crème. The reason he had lost his appetite was quite simple: Aglaë had taken over his senses! He was the first to excuse himself and go to bed, where he could remember Aglaë's warm skin against his. As he walked through the library, he didn't even notice the smell of leather from the thousands of bindings, nor the soft Gobelins carpet he walked on, nor the Regency sofa in golden wood covered with a tapestry illustrating La Fontaine's fable, "The Dog and the Wolf."

Maybe I'm just a curiosity to her, like a traveller from afar for a nobleman, he worried.

Membertou didn't know what to think. Temptation was definitely present, however, no denying that with the huge erection raising his quilt. He did fall asleep eventually, without bothering to put on his nightcap or the gown lined with rabbit fur laid out for him since he had a hard time imagining himself in such a get-up.

René's dreams were of the winged angels decorating his bedroom. Meanwhile, Joseph leaned on his dormer window. He stayed up almost until daybreak, his gaze fixed on Joseph Vernet's paintings illustrating the ports of France. As the big clock on the square marked the passage of time, he kept trying to come up with a plan to ensure he led one of those fleets back to Acadia.

* * *

At Membertou's urging, Joseph scheduled a meeting with Father Minelli, a Jesuit theologian who had walked the halls of the Sorbonne and the College Louis-le-Grand – the preserve of the nobility in the Latin Quarter – for close to fifty years. Now retired, he officiated in the Saint-Paul-Saint-Louis church on Rue Saint-Antoine, a baroque church inspired by the Gésu church in Rome. The sun was radiant that morning. On barges carrying wood for the winter down the Seine, seamen and their families bustled about their floating homes. Not far from the homes of Rabelais and Villon, Joseph and Membertou rested for a few minutes under a huge elm tree, eating the chestnuts they'd bought from a street vendor and watching an emaciated bear on a leash put on a show.

"What a bunch of barbarians!" Membertou exclaimed indignantly. "How can they subject animals to such abuse?"

At the entrance to the church a man sold blessed scapulars, which were said to "chase away the red-tailed devil." Father Minelli was celebrating mass, his arms raised to the dome, his eyes turned to the cupola shaped like an ogive[3] on which a golden sun was painted against a blue background, making it seem as though the worshippers were contemplating the sky. Membertou was reminded of his sister Geneviève,

---

3. A pointed or Gothic arch.

whose name was that of the patron saint of Paris, whose statue stood before him. As the faithful prayed for one hundred days of indulgences for the souls in purgatory, Joseph waited impatiently for the ceremony to end as he stood in front of the reliquaries containing the hearts of Louis XIII and Louis XIV.

His sons joined him after mass, and they followed the illustrious Jesuit down long, dark hallways covered in paintings telling of Christian evangelization. Several torture scenes showed missionaries from the Société de Jésus, including Saint François Xavier, being flayed alive. At the entrance to the Jesuit's office, there stood a statue of St. Louis de Gonzague, the angelic patron of youth, pointing at the earthly pleasures with the following phrase, "*Quid hoc ad aeternitatem?*" (What is this compared to eternity?)

Father Minelli repeated the phrase for their benefit. Thinking he was welcoming them according to the customs of a civilized nation, Membertou responded with a small speech in Mi'kmaq praising the king and wishing the missionary good hunting and a paradise peopled with salmon and deer. His words did not seem to please his venerable eminence, who found the switch from Latin, a religious language, to a decidedly profane language quite unseemly.

An Indian from Canada! he thought. "Welcome to Christ's large family," he finally said aloud.

He had reservations about the welcome extended to the natives, even though Pope Alexander VI clearly stated in the bull "InterCaetera" proclaimed in 1493 that natives were human and could be evangelized. Delighted to hear the word "welcome," Membertou wasted no time handing the Jesuit a copy of Father Biard's Mi'kmaq catechism as well as a few amulets entrusted to him by Fiery Elouèzes. The priest ignored the presents and launched into a sermon on impurity, secretly hoping to outdo the great preacher Bossuet in his sermon at Saint-Paul-Saint-Louis. "The captives whom the Iroquois slowly burned to death and the stench of their flesh burnt by the red-hot tomahawks, all of that is as nothing compared to hell," he proclaimed. "The sin of the flesh is the scourge of Christ and the cause of Virgin Mary's tears, it is the perpetuation of Adam's

and Eve's pride, the original stain that must be atoned for..."
His allusion to Iroquois torture served to antagonize
Membertou, but he didn't let it show.

Finally, the priest got down to business, "The founder of
the Quebec Seminary, Monseigneur de Laval, had a great deal
of affection for the Indians, whom he called his good savages.
But I must show caution before referring you, since the Jesuits
have many enemies, including the king's mistress, the
Marquise de Pompadour... I also need to know your views on
the role of Indian missionaries."

"I have no desire to become a missionary," Membertou
explained. "I just want to promote my people's religion by
becoming a shaman, but I do hope to reconcile the Indian and
Catholic beliefs, which are very similar. We believe in the
soul's migration after death and in just rewards for both the
good and the evil. For a certain number of years, the evil atone
for their mistakes by eating nothing but birchbark. The good
eat their fill of moose and beaver, the product of extraordinary
hunts. But we don't believe in hell or eternal punishment, nor
do we understand why an infinitely good god would let some
of his creatures burn in hell with no hope of recourse."

"Man is evil because of original sin, and only exemplary
conduct can redeem him, if God so wishes... Your habits are
contrary to God's plan; you continue to eat meat on Friday,
you encourage nudity in your sweat lodges, which is a vice...
You authorize the carnal act before marriage..." at this, his
words stuck in his throat.

"Why do you let us eat beaver? Not everything that lives
in the water is a fish! One hundred and fifty days of fasting
every year is too much. Our harsh climate and the effort
needed to hunt require hardy meals. As for sweat lodges, we
use them for their healing properties. Your own missionaries
recognize that none of our people suffer from gout or excessive
weight. Do they not say the body is sacred because it is the
Creator's temple?... So we must take good care of it. Why this
insistence on the sins of the flesh? Isn't evil in the eyes of the
beholder? There is no rape, no prostitution among our
people."

The eminent prelate's temper began to flare. "Our priests have great difficulty understanding your superstitions. Some were tortured by the Iroquois. That's the price that has to be paid sometimes to enter the kingdom of heaven," he added with a show of humility.

Joseph couldn't help interjecting, "The Indians resort to torture less often than the religious inquisitors. And they don't mistreat women. You call that loving your neighbour?"

"Torture isn't gratuitous; it is meant to extract a confession from the heretic."

"Is that so?" Membertou retorted. "Well, the Iroquois resorted to torture with certain missionaries because those priests were trying to destroy Iroquois beliefs. Don't forget the French give arms to the Iroquois' enemies. So, as representatives of France, the priests are also seen as the Iroquois' enemies. Certain missionaries have said that all Indians are liars, heathens, and thieves. Other priests were told to quit caressing young Agnier children if they valued their life…"

With his bright red face, Father Minelli seemed to be on the verge of an apoplectic fit. Never in fifty years of theology – other than during the witches' trials – had he heard such heresy. "Get out, heathens, Satan's crew!" he erupted, throwing the amulets as though they had burned his fingers.

Membertou had thought he would be welcomed like a foreign ambassador imbued with his people's mission. To calm his son's anger and bitterness, Joseph tried to make Membertou see that not all priests were like the one they'd just met.

* * *

The next day, Membertou and Aglaë set out for the Bois de Vincennes. Comfortably ensconced in a poste chaise – a two-wheeled horse-drawn vehicle – they passed through the Hôtel Bethune-Sully gate. They rode down the narrow Rue de la Bastille, where the walls of the prison by the same name rose fifteen toises high, a sinister place bristling with battlements and surrounded by ditches filled with water from the Seine.

Increasingly under Aglaë's spell, however, Membertou only spared a cursory and contemptuous glance for this product of white civilization.

"Without the Indians, France would never have lasted ten years in America because of the climate, disease, and the English, whose numbers are twenty times greater," Membertou explained to Aglaë. "The Mi'kmaq consider your king as a father, a protector. We have always been loyal to him, and he has always insisted the Indians not be bothered, that they should be entitled to hunt and fish where they please. Cardinal Richelieu even stated that a baptized Indian must be considered as a French citizen. But I see no respect in Paris; we're treated worse than dirt."

"Not by me!" cried Aglaë.

He could tell she was sincere. It was true that Aglaë's attraction to Membertou owed something to her interest in the exotic and the charm of a foreigner. But there was another reason as well, which was linked to the customs of the day: milky complexions were in fashion, and tanned skin was thought to be ugly. Consequently, many stunning young women like Aglaë suffered silently and inflicted one sacrifice after another on themselves, hiding from the sun under parasols, veils, and large hats, and rubbing their skin with powders and bleaching agents. Membertou's fascination and passion had acted like a boomerang on her. Their love was inexplicable, like all love. A gift from the gods!

In a heady moment back in their small clearing in the Bois de Vincennes, Membertou composed an ode-like poem inspired by Solomon's Song of Songs, but a native version.

"Behold, you are beautiful, my love; behold, you are beautiful. Your eyes hold the mystery and light of a polished shell, and your gaze speaks of the gentle seafoam on warm sand. Your voice is like the caress of a breeze on the pebbles at dawn."

Aglaë decided to play along, although they both took their game quite seriously.

"Behold, you are handsome, my love; behold, you are handsome," she said in turn.

244

Membertou let himself be carried away by the tide of his own poetic enthusiasm, "Your scent is more delicate than that of the wild rose under the full moon when the loon sings, fresher than the scent of a newborn sleeping on his otter fur. Your breasts are more golden than the warmth of the sun, the curve of your belly is like the sky cradling the earth at dusk, and your hips are like a hammock swaying under the stars.

"Behold, you are beautiful, my beloved; behold, you are beautiful, like the dew on the water lily in the pond. Come with me, the snow is melting, the earth is singing, and lushness caresses the ground. Let us celebrate. Let the corolla of the daisy open to the tern's song."

Aglaë, her voice as sweet as a reed flute, answered, "Behold, you are handsome, my beloved; behold, you are handsome!"

At the foot of the great oak tree, Membertou kissed Aglaë, shyly at first, then with increasing passion. Finally, under instinct's rule, he almost tore away the many skirts and lace blouses that prevented him from merging with her bronzed flesh. Aglaë's desire grew ever more intense under her beloved's caress. Memberto felt a rumbling intensifying like a herd of caribou charging; it came from the wilderness and found its echo in the Bois de Vincennes. Aglaë had never known such ecstasy. The watered-down attentions of the Parisian nobility lost their lustre next to this force that seemed to come from the depths of the forest. She tipped outside of time and space and drew blood from Membertou with her nails. He felt as though the warm breath of the Great Spirit brushed his shoulder when his loved one, sated, dropped back on the fresh grass. And the Italian motto in Aglaë's bedroom (written above the fresco of a winged child carrying a quiver symbolizing love) came to be *Puri-nulla-nuociam* – "Pure, we never cause harm." In the purest native tradition of giving and sharing.

Chapter 28

Seigneur De La Giraudais must understand that it is
only in the event of absolute and proven impossibility
that His Majesty would authorize his travel to Louisiana
and on to Saint-Domingue. What is important is that
his efforts be deployed in order to reach Canada.
– Postscriptum to instructions for the rescue fleet,
written in the hand of King Louis XV

Restigouche, June 1760. The commander of the
Restigouche post, Gabriel Dangeac, knew the country
well since he was born in Plaisance, Newfoundland. In 1713,
when France handed Newfoundland and Acadia to the
English under the Treaty of Utrecht, Dangeac passed through
Louisbourg, where he wed Geneviève Lefebvre de Bellefeuille
and was promoted to the rank of captain of the troops. He
earned the Saint-Louis Cross there, for bravery shown
defending the fortress.

In Restigouche, Dangeac was faced with several pressing
needs. First, he felt it imperative to reinforce the batteries con-
trolling the channel. He entrusted the task to his assistant
Donat de la Garde, who had four twelve-pound cannons and
one six-pound cannon carried off the *Machault* as well as mortar bombs, fleur-de-lys cannonballs, and specially shaped
(studded, gridded, starred) cannonballs designed to destroy
sails and rigging. Noël Labauve was eager to help; he could

already hear the whistling of the barbell- or chain-shaped cannonballs wreaking devastation on the masts, a whistle of revenge that sounded sweet to his ears. While caressing the munitions, he recited the Latin prayer engraved on his powder horn. He took immense pleasure in polishing the artillery, carefully storing the twelve-pound cannonballs, and calculating the angle of the cannon. For a while, it seemed to take his mind off the tragedy of 1755 when war and disease carried away his mother and his wife, Catherine Richard, and dotted his exile with eight small crosses: those of his children. He entrusted his last two children to his sister-in-law Marguerite d'Entremont – who had lost every one of her children – and took to the maquis with his rifle. He carved a notch into the rifle butt for every English man he killed. By the time he reached Restigouche in the spring of 1760, there was no room left on his rifle, showing just how dear the English were to him! But he wasn't the only one seeking revenge. Pierre Frigault[1], who fought in Louisbourg in 1758, knew quite a bit about artillery. De la Garde had made him responsible for properly storing the hand grenades and the barrels of black powder that had to be kept away from humidity and flames. Pierre Gallien, Louis de Lentaigne, Jacques Morais,[2] and a group of soldiers paid in blood, sweat, and tears to haul the *Machault*'s twelve-foot-long cannons weighing three thousand pounds each and capable of firing twelve-pound cannonballs. Captain Dupont-Duvivier did likewise; he consolidated the battery located on the other side of the channel with the help of the Mi'kmaq and a group of Acadians.

Second, the soldiers needed to be fed. Not far from the village La Petite Rochelle, on a former concession belonging to Pierre Le Moyne d'Iberville, Dangeac had ovens built to bake bread and biscuits in. It had been a long time since Mathilde had last smelled bread baking and even longer since

---

1. Nicknamed "Frigolé," meaning "the man who does the frying," most likely due to an ancestor who was a cook.
2. A man from the Ouelle River region who fished in the Baye des Chaleurs between the sowing and harvesting seasons.

she had tasted freshly baked bread. Surrounded by wild raspberry and blackberry bushes, accompanied by the songs of robins, chickadees, and jays, she was happy; she didn't hear the cannons firing nearby, for she was too caught up in her work while dreaming of warm bread and honey.

Lastly and as always, the destitute refugees needed assistance. Which was what led Dangeac to write in his journal on May 25, 1760:

During this time of destitution, I was faced with over one thousand five hundred starving, exhausted souls obliged to eat beaver hides all winter long. I had them given a half-pound of flour every day and a bit of beef while waiting for orders from the Marquis de Vaudreuil. The little I could do for them brought them back from death's door, and I continue to this day.

Dangeac, who had his doubts about the supplies' value, was nevertheless comforted to think that he was able to help the poor refugees somewhat. *In any case*, he thought, *I don't have much choice if I don't want them looting the stores and ships.* It was true that the barrels of red wine and containers of brandy were meant solely for the staff, as were the salt pork and ham. An impressive cargo of shoes had been brought from France for the soldiers in Quebec, but Dangeac had a feeling the soldiers would never have a chance to wear them. So he traded a certain number of the shoes for furs from the destitute, who, only a few years earlier, had lived in opulence on their fertile lands. What a sight the refugees made in their buckle shoes! Distribution was entrusted to Pierre du Calvet, who was to keep careful records on what each person received. He was delighted to be able to help the refugees. News of the new supplies travelled fast, and many Acadians made their way to Restigouche in boats of every kind. That was why the privateer Le Blanc, known as Le Maigre, arrived from Richibouctou. Not only had the English put a price on his head, now he had shoes on his feet!

On that 10th day of June, the weather was unbearably hot and humid. Tjigog, who'd helped unload the munitions, slipped away with Mathilde, who couldn't stand the heat from the ovens any longer. They canoed as far as a small inlet on Ile aux Herons where Tjigog had secretly built a hut well hidden in the forest. First, they had to light a small fire of grass and twigs to chase away the mosquitoes, of which there were an abundance at that time of year. The smoke created a screen behind which they swam. The water was warm in the back of the bay and they gazed at the surrounding mountains while floating on their backs and letting themselves be rocked by the waves.

"This is a sacred region for the Mi'kmaq," Tjigog explained. "According to legend, God created man at the mouth of the Restigouche, then gave the Gaspé Peninsula to the newborn as a gift."

"Do you believe the legend?" Mathilde asked.

"Well, not really. Especially not since I was baptized. When I have doubts, I look at my tattoo."

On his arm was a tattoo of a cross made of black and vermilion gunpowder. The name of Jesus appeared above the cross with the motto: "The one and only truth," underneath.

"There's a boat," Mathilde pointed.

A small boat was approaching the island so they hurried back to the inlet to avoid prying eyes. There were two passengers in the boat. At the point of the island, one of them made a false move and the canoe tipped over. Tjigog dove to their rescue. As he swam closer, he recognized Frigault and Gallien, who had fled the battery to avoid the day's chores. Frigault was trying as best he could to keep afloat, but after resurfacing three times, Gallien sank underwater. Tjigog dove and saw the man caught in thick seaweed. With great difficulty, he managed to drag him back to shore.

"Quick!" Mathilde shouted.

She hadn't wasted any time. She had put smoke inside a moose belly used for storing sea-lion oil. Tjigog stuck a length of tube in the end to use as a cannula. He introduced the small tube into Gallien's posterior and placed both hands on the moose paunch to push the smoke out. It might be too late already since Gallien had been underwater for quite some time. Then Frigault, who had recovered quickly, helped Tjigog hang Gallien by his feet from the first solid branch they found.

Now all they could do was wait. Slowly, very slowly, the smoke enema made Gallien cough up the water he'd swallowed, and he regained consciousness.

No one in camp ever heard about the incident since the witnesses swore a vow of silence, each one having his or her own reasons for not letting word of the escapade get out. However, Gallien felt undying gratitude to the man who had saved him from a certain death.

* * *

On June 12th, the rescue fleet commander Chenard de la Giraudais ordered his soldiers to unload the recently captured schooner *Augustus* and placed it under the orders of Sieur Lavary Le Roy, whose mission was to explore the surrounding area and warn De la Giraudais of approaching enemy fleets. De la Giraudais was no longer sure he should have listened to the soldiers who had served in Louisbourg and had urged him to come to this bay. He had nevertheless given in to their arguments, which were presented so convincingly because of their attachment to the region. Most of his men had either fought in Louisbourg or had family in the region. The only other alternative De la Giraudais had was to return to France or set sail for Louisiana with all the risks that entailed. Olivier Blanchard, a natural navigator, was appointed to pilot the *Augustus*. Tjigog asked to be part of the crew. His request didn't sit well with Mathilde, who accused him of abandoning her. She had a premonition that, after losing first her birth parents then her adoptive parents, now she was about to experience another loss. She knew they had to fight, but the thought she might be left alone yet again distressed her greatly.

On June 22nd at four o'clock in the afternoon, Commander Dangeac hosted tea, an English custom practised by high society both in Acadia and New France. He was a naturally passionate and impulsive leader who looked the part of a grand seigneur with his waxed moustache. Bourdon, who was still "at odds" with France for failing to recognize his services, was among the guests as was De la Giraudais, who left his ships for a few hours; he had asked Dupont-Duvivier to supervise the supplies being unloaded then hidden in caches in the forest in case the stores were looted by the enemy. Dangeac had invited the officer Donat de la Garde to inquire about the state of ground defences. Another guest was Du Calvet, invited to talk about merchandise and the refugees' morale. Bazagier, the king's scribe, had also responded to the invitation in order to describe the event first-hand. As for Marot the surgeon, Dangeac didn't remember inviting him, but he knew Marot never passed up an opportunity for some fun.

All these fine folk took their places around a spruce table set up next to a small inlet with a view of the channel and the ships. No dirty soldiers, no refugees, no natives, no people in rags. Guests had to be hand-picked; after all, the porcelain that had just been taken out of the *Machault*'s holds could only serve eight people – genuine Chinese porcelain from the Ch'ien Lung period. The entire set included a teapot decorated with a blue dragon, a creamer with a red dragon, a sugar bowl adorned with two pheasants as well as tea bowls on which flowery landscapes were painted, not to mention a waste dish and eggshell-coloured saucers in porcelain. Traditionally, a bit of fantasy (porcelain, perfume, jewels, clothing) was transported with the supplies and munitions to sell to the merchants. In this way, certain officers were able to line their pockets and certain ship owners to cover their expenses.

That afternoon, Dangeac had a great deal he wanted to get off his chest. "How can we make those idiots in Versailles understand that the country is not just empty expanses of ice and snow? One day France will be overpopulated; it will need ore, fish, space, challenges, new ideals… and all it will be able to do is mark time and feel nostalgic for the grandeur of the good old days. The court doesn't realize how abandoning its empire in America means losing ground to the other world powers."

"Yet the Ministry of the Navy approved a rescue effort by February 15th at the latest," De la Giraudais said.

De la Garde interrupted him, "You have to realize the financiers from Bordeaux were fairly hesitant about financing a fleet that risked coming under attack by the British navy; they've had a number of losses since the war began. We can't blame the crew either for refusing to leave until they received what was owed them for the previous year's expedition. I would have done the same!"

"The court should just have paid them instead of squandering the people's money on fancy balls. When it comes down to it though, they're not interested in Canada outside its furs and cod," Bourdon concluded.

Du Calvet hadn't said a word. He was still preoccupied with the merchandise inventory and unhappy about all the boxes of fancy trinkets and porcelain cluttering up his holds, which were of no use in Restigouche at a time when the refugees' rations were so meagre. *We could have traded them in Quebec,* he thought, already calculating what the profit would have been.

"Instead of fancy trinkets, we could have brought over more supplies and munitions," he said reproachfully.

Despite his own rancour, Dangeac couldn't agree. "The fancy trinkets pay back the ship owner and help pay for the crew and cargo."

But Du Calvet wouldn't back down. "The ship owners abuse the system by jacking up the cost of supplies. Take Joseph Cadet, for instance, Bigot's right-hand man who looks after the colony's provisions: he sells at exorbitant prices products that he obtained for next to nothing in peacetime."

"But look what good it did him," Bourdon cut in. "Wolfe's ships didn't spare his fishing installations in the Gaspé. Thirty-six thousand hundredweight of cod destroyed. That hurts!"

Marot took a sip of tea. He was only half-listening, busy thinking about the injection he had to prepare for a former Louisbourg officer, an injection into the bladder for an infection that looked like venereal disease. He couldn't wait to return to France. He hated this country of savages, where his wig didn't keep its curls the way it should for more than a day.

Bazagier didn't like tea. He poured himself a glass of red wine instead (his great weakness), which he drank from a crystal glass from Bohemia. Nothing escaped his attention; he had to produce an adequate report of events after all.

Since Donat de la Garde had had enough tea, he turned his cup over in his saucer and balanced his spoon on top to show he had finished. He daydreamed of sailing off Minorca and lobbing cannonballs at the English fleet.

In an attempt to pay homage to De la Giraudais, Dangeac said, "When the English spotted us leaving Bordeaux, it was thanks to your manoeuvres to attract most of the enemy fleet that we were able to save a few ships."

"The chase lasted for ten hours. Thankfully, the *Machault* is swift and night had fallen," De la Giraudais said modestly.

He thrust out his chest and took his pipe out of his pocket. The pipe was made by the company R. Tippet of Bristol; his brass and copper snuffbox came from the Netherlands; on one side was engraved a passage from the Gospel, on the other, the motto, "I promise to quit eating sweets beginning tomorrow!" He filled his pipe, lit it, and puffed away, his thoughts on sweets. His gourmandise was well known, as was his tendency to postpone till tomorrow his diet, so that his girth, which kept growing every year, was never reduced and his gout never cured.

"I hope Saint-Simon made it to Montreal all right with the instructions for Vaudreuil," said Marot, who had never forgiven Saint-Simon their last confrontation.

"Don't worry," Bourdon replied. "He knows the country like the back of his hand. But he won't be back before mid-July."

"Just to be sure, I'm going to send another emissary tomorrow with the court duplicate," Dangeac proposed.

"I'd rather not be in Vaudreuil's shoes. The responsibility for all of New France is riding on his back…" Bazagier said.

"Meanwhile, we're stuck here in the back of this bay," Marot sighed.

Chapter 29

Listuguj: Ula wegewas'g'p tan Hiatew ugjet Pilei Wenjuagina tujiw 1760. eg (in Mi'kmaq)

Restigouche: where New France's fate was sealed in 1760.

"The English fleet has arrived! I had to abandon my schooner... didn't even have time to set it on fire..." Sieur Le Roy finally managed to stammer out upon his arrival at Miguasha Point.

Rounding Ile aux Herons, Le Roy had come face to face with the *Fame*, a seventy-four-cannon ship commanded by Admiral Byron, whose nickname was "Jack the Storm," the same Byron who had had Louisbourg razed that spring, and had sent to Halifax all the seized furniture and equipment to decorate and consolidate public buildings there! The *Fame* was followed by the *Dorsetshire* and the *Achilles*, as well as by two frigates, the *Repulse* and the *Scarborough*, each respectively armed with seventy, sixty, thirty-two, and twenty cannons.

Dangeac did a rapid calculation. Two hundred and fifty-six cannons! He didn't even have fifty on his three ships to fight back with; worse yet, a certain number of the ones he did have were now part of the land battery. He also had six small schooners captured from the English that were being used as prisons, and some thirty Acadian sloops and brigs from

Miramichi and elsewhere, which had come to Restigouche since the arrival of the French fleet. "In any case, our small boats would be no match," he concluded. On land, all he had was the regular troops from the navy – two hundred soldiers. almost all of whom had fought in Louisbourg, three hundred Acadians capable of bearing arms, and approximately two hundred and fifty Mi'kmaq – to confront over a thousand English soldiers. Dangeac confided in De la Giraudais and Bourdon, "I think ours is a lost cause, but I have no intention of surrendering without a fight."

"The disadvantage isn't as great if we provoke a land battle instead of a naval combat. Let's take the cannons from the *Marquis de Malauze* and the *Bienfaisant* to consolidate our land batteries," Bourdon proposed.

"Of course," De la Giraudais said enthusiastically. "After all, with no instructions from Vaudreuil, after God we are masters here. Listen, the channel is quite shallow downstream from the De la Garde battery; we could sink five or six schooners within demi-range of the battery."

"Excellent idea," Dangeac said. "What are you waiting for? Go give your orders."

* * *

On June 25th, the flagship *Fame* ran aground within a league of the batteries. However, the good news managed to sow discord among the leaders. Dangeac and De la Giraudais wanted to attack the ship, but the other officers tried to dissuade them. "Their cannons will pulverize us. They have two fully armed bridges," De la Garde thundered.

"We'll sow terror if we board them with a group of Mi'kmaq," Dangeac proposed.

"It's craziness," Dupont-Duvivier retorted. "There are four hundred men on board."

"Let's board from the prow under cover of night," De la Giraudais suggested.

"With a full moon, we'll have a tough time going unnoticed," Dupont-Duvivier objected.

The experience of the past years – a long series of retreats and defeats – had knocked the stuffing out of the men and officers and paralyzed their will to strike, so much so that Dangeac hesitated to give the order to attack. By the time he finally made up his mind, it was too late – the *Fame* had been towed off the sandbank by the *Achilles* and the *Dorsetshire*, after having unballasted a few anchors and some cargo of little importance.

The English and French navies played a game of cat and mouse over the next few days. English ships approached the battery, probed the channel to find a passage, failed, ran aground, had themselves towed... and started all over again, all the while under fire from the French batteries, soldiers, Acadians, and Mi'kmaq. On July 2nd, Admiral Byron managed to sail the *Fame* and its seventy-four cannons right past the battery commanded by De la Garde. The sun was already at its zenith, and the battle had raged since dawn. Noël Labauve was black with powder, and Frigault, his assistant, was as red as a rooster and drenched in sweat from all the exertion. On a raft, Tjigog kept busy with Lentaigne's help ferrying barrels of powder to keep the battery supplied, despite Mathilde's furious objections. Gallien and Morais had been slightly wounded by metal shards from their twelve-pound cannon, which exploded at the far eastern end of the battery.

"Retreat!" De la Garde ordered.

The situation was getting worse by the minute, and the English cannonballs were falling ever faster. De la Garde had already started to disable the cannons – sticking a special nail in the cannons' sights so they could be exploded and not fall into enemy hands. Already gravely wounded, Noël Labauve swore he would not back down, that Restigouche would be his last refuge... When the Redcoats were close enough, he lit the fuse to two hand grenades, a kind of hollow cannonball full of cannon powder. He didn't throw them, though; when they exploded he died, taking several attackers with him.

Dangeac watched the operation, his eye glued to the sight, and said a prayer for Labauve, then fumed to see the other attackers carry off the – albeit useless – battery. Then the

English set fire to the houses in the Acadian camp. Almost two hundred homes in La Petite Rochelle were destroyed. They weren't palaces, of course, but they did offer their occupants the safety of a roof over their heads and symbolized an anchoring point. The log chapel went up in smoke as well. Fortunately, the villagers had foreseen such a disaster and had withdrawn farther down the bay.

Dangeac took his ships toward the back of the bay, transporting the cargo on smaller boats because of the shallow water. But once there, it was impossible to go any farther. He had two new batteries installed at Pointe-aux-Sauvages and Pointe-à-la-Mission on either side of the narrow bay and sank five other schooners to block the way.

"If this keeps up," the privateer Le Blanc said to himself, "soon we won't have any schooners left."

At daybreak on July 8th, the *Repulse*, *Scarborough*, and *Augustus* (the latter was a schooner armed with four small cannons captured from Sieur Le Roy at Miguasha Point) managed to get past the sunken ships; the other enemy ships, however, could go no farther because of their draft. The French had only ten starboard cannons on the *Machault* (twelve-pound cannons), the three four-pound cannons from the Pointe-aux-Sauvages' battery and the five cannons from Pointe-à-la-Mission to fight the fifty-six cannons the English had. The *Marquis de Malauze* – where the English prisoners were being held for their own good (on land the Mi'kmaq would have scalped them) – couldn't take part in the battle even though it was directly in the line of fire. As for the *Bienveillant*, most of its cannons had been taken on land to arm the batteries.

The battles began to lessen in intensity after a few hours. The commander of the *Machault* called on Olivier Léger's services to seal the leaks caused by cannonballs. During this time, Olivier Blanchard, Charles Poirier, and Alexis Landry transported barrels of powder to the cannon batteries on the coast. De la Garde, Gallien, Frigault, and Morais fired at the English ships from the Pointe-à-la-Mission battery. Lentaigne probed the bottom of the bay with Tjigog's help to pilot the ships to the back of the dead end if necessary. Dupont-Duvivier, Joseph-Jean, and Joseph Boudreau raced to hide the merchandise unloaded from the *Bienveillant* and the small schooners. Since the risk of looting was high, Du Calvet, paper and goose feather pen in hand, took note of all that was transported from one spot to another. He was so caught up in his task that he seemed unaware of the battle raging in the bay.

Ever since the ovens had been destroyed, Mathilde, her Aunt Anne, and a few other women had been in charge of preparing the combatants' meals, which was no small task under the circumstances. Others nursed the wounded under the supervision of Marot, who, despite his cowardice, was going about his work conscientiously.

The English managed to blow up the south battery, the Pointe-Aux-Sauvages battery, while the combined fire from the *Machault* and the Pointe-à-la-Mission battery on the north shore did serious damage to the *Repulse*.

It's too bad the channel isn't deeper! thought De la Giraudais. The *Repulse* would be underwater by now.

The ship had been damaged beneath its waterline, one of its masts was broken, and a large section of sail lay on the bridge.

"Concentrate on putting their cannons out of service," Dangeac ordered.

And so they did. But fifteen minutes later, Lentaigne, a sombre expression on his face, told Dangeac, "We have almost no powder left because a number of barrels were transported onto Dupont-Duvivier's schooner."

"Take a few rowboats and go fetch the powder," Dangeac decided.

It was a dangerous enterprise to be out in a rowboat under enemy fire, especially a rowboat full of kegs of powder. But Lentaigne volunteered for the mission and Tjigog offered to accompany him, praying to heaven that Mathilde wouldn't see him during the desperate operation. They each took an oar and, after a quarter of an hour spent rowing, they reached Dupont-Duvivier's crew. Joseph-Jean and Joseph hurried to load some twenty kegs into the rowboat. Not enough to allow them to hold out for much longer – but there was no time to waste. Loaded to the hilt, they pushed off. At the back of the bay, nothing could be heard but clamouring, echoes, rumbling, explosions, and cries. At times, the smoke was so thick the ships could no longer be seen, which made Lentaigne's and Tjigog's job easier. They reached the *Machault* without too much difficulty. But the situation was getting worse.

"I can't stop the leaks anymore," Léger shouted. He and his men were in water up to their neck.

At the pumps, the men couldn't keep up. At eleven o'clock, there was more than a fathom's worth of water in the hold. De la Giraudais and Dangeac decided the time had come to abandon ship and, at noon, as it should be, they were the last to leave it. They headed for the Pointe-à-la-Mission battery to serve as reinforcements.

"To have come so far and see it end like this," Dangeac said sorrowfully.

"At least they won't have our ships," De la Giraudais said, his face contorted.

In fact, the *Machault* had just exploded; next it was the *Bienveillant*'s turn, a burst of iron and flames, one last salvo for honour's sake, a painful inferno that engulfed the cargo they hadn't had time to unload. In the middle of the channel still stood the *Marquis de Malauze*, which had played its role by staying in the line of fire and making it more difficult for the enemy to take proper aim. The English didn't want to touch the ship since several of their fellow soldiers were prisoners on board. But time was short because the English rowboats were about to board the *Marquis de Malauze*. The captain shut the prisoners in the hold – they didn't want to disembark for fear of the Mi'kmaq – then cleared out with his men. The English decided to sink the ship; however, six of their own who had stayed on board to drink wine and brandy went under with it.

On shore, Dangeac and his men were preparing to repel the second enemy assault. The Acadians were together in several groups under the orders of the militia major Joseph Dugas, his assistants, Joseph and Pierre Gauthier, and the militia captains Joseph Vigneau, Armand Bujeau, Abraham

Hébert, and Benjamin Allain. Halfway through the afternoon, Byron sent an armed schooner and seventeen barges transporting 425 soldiers to land at the back of the bay. But hidden behind the trees along the shore, determined French soldiers, Acadians, and Mi'kmaq were lying in wait. Eventually, the English had to beat a retreat from the Pointe-à-la-Mission battery that just kept on firing.

Since the English had no desire to fall into a land battle, the fleet raised its anchors in mid-July near the end of the second quarter of the moon, the season when birds lose their feathers. The *Repulse* hobbled along behind the fleet.

Dangeac took stock of the situation, "For seventeen days, we stood up to five warships and 256 cannon with nothing more than a frigate and two merchant ships. And we prevented them from landing."

"We have no ships left, but the garrison is still in fighting shape, and we still have two batteries with twenty or so cannons," Bourdon said.

"Plus several months' worth of munitions and supplies," De la Giraudais added.

The refugees weren't fooled by the surface optimism, which was primarily geared at keeping up the troops' morale. An exhausted Saint-Simon returned from Montreal with Vaudreuil's instructions. He had been counting the hours, hoping against hope he'd arrive in time for the battle. He was terribly disappointed and reacted very badly to Tjigog's attempt at humour when he said, "Do the cycles of the moon last longer in Montreal than in Restigouche?"

Chapter 30

It used to be the Court of Versailles
Would send good taste our way
Now we've got the riffraff instead
in power and there to stay
The fact the Court so lowers itself
Should come as no surprise:
Isn't that what a market is for
A place to find fish and lowlives?
  – Anonymous letter mocking the king's mistress, the
  Marquise de Pompadour, née Poisson (meaning fish)

Versailles, summer 1760. The Viscount Turgot de Saint-Clair, who had been busy avoiding Joseph every way he knew how, now suddenly decided to accompany him on his trip to Versailles. The viscount did have business there, but the "peasant" had begun to impress him with his ability to obtain an audience at court more easily than he himself could have. He took advantage of their hours-long drive by poste chaise[1] to hold forth on the merits of French civilization.

"Versailles endeavours to show the harmony of the universe, to recapitulate the world's history. Europe's best craftsmen have built a poem in marble, gold, and light…"

---

1. A carriage, usually closed, for two to four people.

Joseph was only half-listening. His awareness of the extreme importance of the upcoming meeting had filled him with doubt and fear.

"How can I, a simple inhabitant of the French colony, convince Berryer, the Minister of the Navy?"

He knew little about the man. He had read in the *Gazette de France* that the former policeman was more interested in the surveillance of his subordinates and cracking down on abuses than in organizing the navy and defining general policies. There was no information to be gleaned from the viscount, either. He was still talking, "The creators of Versailles took inspiration from the myth of Apollo, the sun god, who is omnipresent in statues and frescoes representing mythology, the four elements, the four continents, the four cardinal points."

His words only heightened Joseph's dread. Accustomed as he was to the huge expanses of forest and sea and to the effervescence of small towns such as Quebec and Louisbourg, he had trouble imagining what role he could play at Versailles. He tried to get hold of himself by concentrating on what the viscount had to say.

"Is it true that almost all France's nobles live in the palace?" he asked

"Yes," Saint-Clair said, "there are close to two thousand people, some of whom left their castles in other regions to move into a garret room at court."

"Do you live there as well?"

"Not yet," the viscount answered, ashamed at not being among the chosen ones.

Before them the Château de Versailles appeared, stretching as far as the eye could see, surrounded by flowers, gardens, palm trees, and orange groves – a harmonious blend of greenery and colours down which the Grand Canal wound its way for close to two leagues.

"There are fourteen hundred fountains, some of which are only in operation when the king passes by," the viscount told Joseph.

Joseph's feeling of dread was forgotten as he stared in amazement at the fusion of water and light, a festival of liquid crystals gushing against a backdrop of sculpted vases.

"To think all this began with a simple hunting lodge for Louis XIII!" he exclaimed.

He could never imagine feeling at home here, however; the geometry was foreign to him. With its two thousand windows and its thousand chimneys, Versailles bore no resemblance whatsoever to the Louisbourg and Quebec châteaux, which paled next to Versailles' height, length, and beauty. Confronted with these buildings that had no match in Canada, his thoughts turned to the forests back home and the many species of tree that changed with the seasons. Even the sea, with its many faces, bore no resemblance to the water symphony rising above these fountains. In his mind, two worlds collided, two types of beauty; on the one hand, the beauty of the wilderness and of nature, familiar and reassuring, a reflection of the human heart and instincts and, on the other hand, the beauty of human civilization, a product of the mind and reason. The gardens seemed cold and calculated to him, elements of a nature tamed and bearing the Versailles stamp. His discomfiture in the hierarchical universe made him sure he would say something wrong the minute he opened his mouth. He felt very alone, without allies or reference points, without Angélique's warmth and Saint-Jean's wisdom.

A guard examined their passes, then the poste chaise was directed to the large Place d'Armes stable, which housed two hundred carriages and over two thousand horses. The viscount took leave of his travelling companion at that point, wishing him good luck in a rather ironic tone. Under the impassive gaze of a row of busts of famous people from antiquity, Joseph made his way to the Marble Court. To enter the Council Chamber, he had to pass in front of the Queen's suites and the Oeil-de-boeuf antechamber on his left, and the King's Chamber, the Clock room, and the King's interior room on his right. There he wondered for the first time whether his father had once lived in a similar decor. He imagined him standing by the fountains clothed in silk and satin, surrounded by liveried servants, in conversation with the king.

Joseph's daydream was interrupted by the captain of the guard, who asked to see his pass before ushering him into an antechamber. To the obvious surprise of two ladies decked out in powdered wigs who were awaiting an audience, he was immediately led into the Council Chamber, which was to a certain degree the very heart of French life, the room in which the king and his ministers came to important decisions affecting France and its citizens. There the king also received his courtiers, come to pay tribute to him, or to request a favour or his blessing, or to offer their services. Sometimes commoners came to submit their complaints to him as well.

Minister Berryer was inside, dipping his quill pen into a gold inkwell in the shape of a fleur-de-lys, the Bourbons' emblem. The decor was lavish with white and gold wainscotting, long curtains framing tall paned windows and, in the middle of the room, the Council table, covered with a blue satin and gold brocade tablecloth. A huge crystal chandelier hung above the minister's head. *What should I say? What should I do?* Joseph wondered.

He'd thought he was ready, but right then his heart was pounding so hard he could feel a tightness in his chest, while his hands shook slightly and an unpleasant flush engulfed his body. He felt another flush when he realized the minister was continuing to write as though he didn't exist. He tried to concentrate on examining the man before him. A big man, slightly obese, with a red nose, and big sail-like ears that gave him a comical air. Joseph didn't know what to do; it seemed to him the minister could be nothing but sympathetic to his cause, but his instincts told him to be cautious. Joseph wondered again whether Berryer had any true power. He had heard the minister's position was precarious and that he wasn't in the Marquise de Pompadour's good books; several people said he was incompetent but, with the amount of jealousy in the air, it was hard to separate truth from fiction. The minister finally looked up and stared at Joseph for a few seconds before stating, "The king was just here. He has gone to play a game of billiards in the Diane salon..."

He's trying to impress me with his importance, Joseph thought.

"The Marquis de la Galissonnière asked me to receive you; he claims you have an interesting plan to win the war in New France."

His tone was cold, distant, ironic. Joseph was indignant that Berryer hadn't asked who he was, if he had family, how the crossing and the trip from Nantes had gone... He tried anyway, telling the minister about daily life in Canada in order to bring him onto a more human terrain and see if he was sympathetic to ensuring the survival of Acadia and New France. But the minister showed signs of irritation, "The Marquis de la Galisssonnière said something about a treasure," he said brusquely.

Joseph had no intention of getting onto the subject of the treasure yet. He tried flattery, telling the minister he had heard about his skill in reorganizing the navy and his interest in New France. But the latter was accustomed to similar manoeuvres and wouldn't be put off track. So, deciding to take the plunge, Joseph stared the eminent man in the eye. "Since 1755, the British troops and the troops from the English colonies in America have been chasing us out of Acadia. It's been two years already since Louisbourg surrendered..."

"Yet I heard the fortress was impregnable..."

"I fought there in 1745. It's no better than a sandcastle. All the English needed to do was unload their cannons on land!"

France's past mistakes were of no interest to the minister, who changed the subject. "A fleet of six ships left Bordeaux to take back Quebec. We should have good news soon."

Joseph couldn't ignore such unenlightened optimism, "Six ships! Given the number of English ships, that fleet won't get far. Meanwhile, His Majesty's loyal subjects are being pursued in Acadia and deported as far as England's prisons. Families are being scattered and living in the worst possible deprivation..."

The debate over the Acadians' fate seemed to irritate the minister, "It's not easy looking after an entire Empire. What's more, when the house is on fire, why bother with the stable?" (As though to say, "Quite witty, aren't I?")

He tried to make up for his remark, "What has happened to you is tragic."

Joseph felt like blurting out that the stables were in Paris. But he held his tongue.

"Don't forget," Berryer continued, "we have to wage war in both America and Europe. We have neither enough ships nor enough seamen. We also have to defend the French coasts and our colonies in the Indies at Pondichéry."

The Indies were of little concern to Joseph, and he went back on the offensive. "With its huge expanse, its vast wealth, and its seas teeming with fish, New France guarantees the prosperity and commercial might of the French empire. You should make a more serious effort if you don't want the continent to go to England."

The king's representative did not appreciate having a man from the colonies dictate what his policies should be. "I think the English will sign a peace treaty soon," he said in his own defence. "If not, and especially if we lose the war in New France, we won't have the people on our side... Public opinion is slightly more favourable to the Indies since it's a tropical country that produces molasses and rum."

As long as they have their sweets, Joseph thought, and continued, "But it's no bigger than the palm of my hand. When France loses its colonies in America, the English will be even stronger in Europe, and France will regret having lost the American continent."

Finally, the minister asked, "So what you do propose?"

For Joseph, the long-awaited moment had arrived, but he didn't trust this man.

"The Marquis de la Galissonnière spoke to you of a treasure unearthed on Ile Caraquet. It could finance a fleet and an army to attack Boston and Halifax and chase the English out of Acadia. That would open up a second front in New France and help relieve the pressure on the Great Lakes region."

"That's an excellent idea. Moreover, the possibility has already been proposed and abandoned for lack of money. But this changes everything. You know the proverb 'as fake as diamonds from Canada' that's been in use since Cartier brought us a cargo of worthless stones from Cap Diamant. We'd have to see for ourselves the treasure's worth. Where have you hidden it?" he asked in a honeyed voice.

Joseph could already imagine long, greedy fingers eager to seize his gold coins, and he answered in vague terms, "Well-guarded in an abbey."

His reticence did not go unnoticed.

"Next week I'll be able to tell you more. Come to the costume ball in the Hall of Mirrors…"

Joseph knew that a decision this important couldn't be made on the spot, but he was nevertheless disappointed. *After all, I have the money,* he thought.

He wasn't used to this kind of delay. When it came down to it, he was leery because he sensed the minister's lack of interest in Canada. He thought of the Acadians, scattered to the winds and suffering while the mother country took its sweet time making up its mind to do something. But he couldn't say anything more; the minister had signalled their audience was over.

* * *

For Membertou, fabulous hunting trips, spruce tree forests, fierce caribou, and especially, the omnipresence of the spiritual realm were all behind him now. In tribute to the beauty of Paris, he proudly recited Ronsard's verse off by heart:

"Paris, place of kings, whose ample brow
Is without equal under the heavens."

Although he actually meant it as an ode to Aglaë, not Paris!

He decided to buy some pistols for his grandfather from a gunsmith in the Latin Quarter while Aglaë waited for him in the Procope café reading Manon Lescault. After what seemed like a very long time, Membertou finally returned to Aglaë.

"This is where the great thinkers D'Alembert, Diderot, Voltaire, Rousseau, and others prepared the new order," she said.

"You're certainly in need of a revolution," Membertou grumbled. "First, I was insulted by your priests, which shows a serious lack of fraternity. Then my money pouch was stolen while I watched a puppet show. If men were free and equal, there would be no thieves and we would obtain a fair price for our furs instead of being exploited by the noblemen and merchants."

"Don't things like that happen in your country?"

"No, what belongs to one belongs to all."

"So you think you're superior to the French," she said ironically.

Membertou didn't notice her mocking tone. "We're nicknamed EL'NU ('true men') or Mi'kmaq, which means 'allies.' We can withstand the rigours of hunger and cold such as the French have never seen. How many white men fast for eight days? They all have gout and big bellies and can't keep up with us in the forest."

"You shouldn't judge us too harshly. I'm from this civilization and you seem to think I have a virtue or two."

It wasn't in Membertou's make-up to ask her to forgive him for hurting her, but his eyes expressed his confusion.

* * *

To René, the viscount's library seemed much better than his mother's. There were volumes on the legend of Nicolas Flamel, who discovered the secret to making gold in the Middle Ages. René came up with plans for the laboratory he'd build; it would be full of tubes, stills, sulphur fumes, flasks of quicksilver, toad venom, and magic cure-all powders. He promised himself he would find the renowned philosopher's stone whose wonderful properties included that of changing metal into gold and even, it was said, conferring immortality. When he wasn't working on his alchemy plans, he kept busy devising a game he called *The Island of Slaves*, based on the book by Marivaux, who narrowly escaped being sent to the Bastille because of his story set on an island in which the masters become servants and the servants masters.

The further Joseph got with his mission, the more difficulties he encountered along the way. He cursed Voltaire and his friends for the influence they had on the policies regarding New France. However, he did agree with one of Voltaire's pronouncements:

"Paris is a huge barnyard full of
Strutting roosters and
Parrots repeating meaningless words."

Joseph had a week's wait ahead of him. By his own calculations, if he slept five hours every night, that still left him with about 130 hours minus the time spent eating. Like anyone who arrives in Paris without any relatives or knowledge of the milieu, Joseph was at a disadvantage. Although he had money, he had no idea how to find his way through the jungle.

There's no way I'll go back to see Father Minelli. Turgot de Saint-Clair won't help me; in any case, he doesn't seem to have any influence at court. I absolutely have to talk to the king in person, which is unlikely to happen at a masked ball.

Joseph came up with one crazy scheme after another, including scaling the walls to the king's balconies to reach his suites!

Who has power at court? That's it, representatives of the church.

He thought of Abbot Leloutre and an idea came to him. Didn't the chaplain general of New France and Acadia, Abbot de l'Isle-Dieu reside in Paris? He asked around and, after two days spent paving the way and being made to wait in antechambers and parlours, he was received by the abbot. The man at least had the merit of being interested in Acadia, which he had defended in writing and with the money he sent. But neither the priest's warm welcome nor his kind words could allay Joseph's concerns. What's more, the abbot's response was disappointing, "I'll try, but I don't have much influence at court since I'm not in the king's good graces."

Joseph realized he would have to do it alone. He spent the next few days asking around to see if he could find someone willing to arm a fleet and recruit soldiers. He gleaned information in both luxurious palaces and sordid dives, dirty smoke-filled places where the dregs of the port were found. He obtained names, meetings, but there followed nothing but delays, shilly-shallying, and fraud. The ship owners he met didn't fit the bill; either they demanded an authorization from the Court, or they tried to extort money from him. Joseph persevered and continued to roam the streets of Paris, his stomach in a knot, with no appetite. He had no time to look after René and Membertou, who seemed to be doing just fine without him in any case. He slept little and poorly, his dreams haunted by emaciated faces. When sleep wouldn't come, he read the local papers, the *Mercure Gallant* and the *Gazette de France*, to find out more about the nobility's habits and their influence at court as well as about the daily concerns of ordinary people, both in the hope that a brilliant idea would come to him and to better prepare himself for the meeting in the Hall of Mirrors. He leafed through several volumes in the viscount's library and spared a brief glance for the work of the great thinkers of the day, who were drafting the *Encyclopedia*, "the general work of efforts by the human mind in all domains." He read in one of the newspapers that work on the encyclopedia had ruffled some feathers and people were trying to prevent its publication.

Since his arrival in France, Joseph had been able to think calmly about Emilie, perhaps because of her proximity, but he missed Angélique. On his travels through Paris, he bought for Angélique texts of a few plays by Racine and Molière. With the time for the costume ball fast approaching, however, it didn't take long for him to return to his worries.

Chapter 31

That is the old spirit! If the skies fall upon our heads we must
like true Gauls hold them up on the points of our lances.
— William Kirby in *The Golden Dog*

When Joseph arrived in the Hall of Mirrors, its beauty made
him forget his troubles momentarily. Golden rays of sun-
shine streamed through the windows and arcades and reflected
off the bevelled mirrors inside, while outside under the setting
sun, the shadows lengthened over the gardens and basins. A
blaze of glory played on the parquet floor, the mirrors, and the
crystal chandeliers and made it seem almost as though he'd
entered an unreal, magical world peopled by a strange, loud, costumed crowd. But the sight of all of high society sauntering at
ease in their role brought him back with a jolt to his own
anguish. Under an arcade supported by red marble pilasters and
topped by a bronze marquee on which the fleur-de-lys and the
royal sun were framed by two French roosters, he saw the man
who had been on his mind all week long: King Louis XV, the
Beloved in person, disguised as a bat! His get-up looked ridiculous to Joseph. He drew nearer, but courtesans crowded around
the king like so many bloodsuckers. Queen Marie Lesczynska
was at his side, dressed as a nymph. The Regent[1] sparkled in her

1. A famous diamond.

hair. She seemed tired, and the small domino[2] she carried couldn't hide the sadness etched on her face.

The queen's loyalty to her husband is one of resignation, Joseph thought.

He saw the king's mistress, the Marquise de Pompadour, not far from the king. Her face was perfectly oval and her silver brocade robe highlighted her beauty. Joseph noted her chestnut hair styled the Egyptian way, like Queen Nefertiti.

It's true she has the bearing of a queen, Joseph observed.

During his travels through Paris, Joseph had learned of the influence and hold she had over the king and his policies, which was why many people sought to find favour with her. For that same reason or because they had never forgiven her for her common roots, others hated her. *Maybe I should be trying to meet Madame de Pompadour instead,* he thought. But he felt awkward in his privateer's costume. The idea for the costume came out of his constant fretting about arms, soldiers, and the war, and because he remembered well his time in Louisbourg. No one either saw or noticed him, and he realized he wouldn't be able to approach the king. He started looking for Berryer.

Drawing inspiration from his game, René wore beggar's rags. He went from one group to the next listening to the gossip. He wasn't the least bit embarrassed about playing the beggar in the Hall of Mirrors; on the contrary, it was his way of protesting against the parade of riches. Two women disguised as Muses were talking about Madame de Pompadour.

"The king has her stay above his apartment," the youngest one said. "There's even talk of him having an elevator installed."

"She keeps him entertained," her companion added. "You have to admit she's clever; she's careful never to humiliate the queen. And she has the backing of the artists and the literati."

Nearby, a few other women disguised as witches were discussing the trial of a soothsayer who had gone too far with her love potions, poisons, and abortive concoctions. Other guests dressed as theologians analyzed the trouble the king

---

2. A half mask worn with a masquerade costume.

was having with the religious authorities, commenting on the debate around Jansenism being used by Parliament to prevent the State from functioning by postponing the task of registering royal edicts. Some guests were outspoken about a certain Fontenelle, who had died at the venerable age of one hundred years. In the quarrel between the Ancients and the Moderns, it was said he had taken the latter's side.

None of this meant much to René, who headed toward the south end of the Hall of Mirrors to find the Peace Salon, the most pleasant room in the castle, where the sun shone all day long. The room was also used as a games room by the queen, who gave concerts of secular and religious music there on Sundays. Above the huge chimney was a portrait in a large oval frame of Louis XV granting peace to Europe. *I hope he'll bring us peace as well*, René thought, before turning his attention back to the people in the room.

A few guests were playing cards with a Henri IV deck illustrated with figures from Antiquity, but most lounged in chairs called "mortal sins." The position of a person reclining in one of the chairs was such that it gave rise to certain fantasies and caresses. On seeing René, an old woman wearing a brooch bearing the coat of arms of the dukes of Brittany exclaimed, "How are you, my dear godson. How tall you've grown!"

At his look of stupefaction, she added, "Come now, you were more quick-witted the last time I saw you. Don't you recognize your old aunt?"

Too stunned to inquire further, he stammered out, "You're wrong, Madame, I'm not your godson."

He moved on, intrigued, promising himself to mention the incident to his father. *Do I look like a godson of the dukes of Brittany?* he wondered.

At the other end of the Hall of Mirrors, in the War Salon, Joseph recognized the minister disguised as a crocodile. Berryer was stuffing his face by the long tables that groaned under Europe's finest dishes. He plunged both hands into a huge platter of beef garnished with marrow-filled vol-au-vents, sweetbreads in puff pastry, and ham mousse tarts.

Joseph's stomach knotted. Such abundance killed his appetite since it reminded him of all the good people dying of starvation back in Acadia.

"Do you have food as fine as this in your country?" Berryer asked, his mouth full.

Joseph was disgusted; he would gladly have smashed in the viscount's clown nose.

"Sturgeon with a chicken fricassee and wild blackberries in maple syrup are delicacies back home. But tell me, where are you at in your dealings?"

"I've spoken of your project. The ministers are in favour, as is Madame de Pompadour…"

"Did you speak to the king?" Joseph interrupted him.

Berryer was digging into the ring loaves of squab conserve covered in chocolate jam. Food trickled out of his mouth as he replied, "Not yet. His Majesty is busy with his gardens. Tulip bulbs have just arrived from Holland. But the king will approve the project, you can be sure of that, as long as there is enough treasure. We will have to appraise its value before authorizing the operation."

None of this appealed to Joseph. Not in the least. *Once I've handed over the treasure, what guarantees do I have? How can I arrange a meeting with the king?* he worried. He thought for a minute and remembered a conversation he'd had with the viscount about influential people at court. The viscount had mentioned the Duc de Choiseul and his interest in New France, and had spoken highly of him in his role as Secretary of State for Foreign Affairs. An idea began to blossom.

"Yes, you're right," he told his gluttonous companion, "the treasure needs to be appraised. Give me a few days to make the necessary arrangements."

The minister smiled, revealing his big yellow shark's teeth. His fetid breath was characteristic of many Versailles noblemen.

The sun set in the Hall of Mirrors. The forty-one chandeliers shone on the white damask curtains adorned with the king's emblems in gold brocade. Instead of the gardens being reflected in the mirrors, now it was the beautiful women parading down the Savonnerie carpets who were reflected, each more beautiful than the next. The Affected Young Ladies wore three skirts one on top of the other: the secrète[3], the friponne, and the modeste. Each young lady had a beauty spot according to a code: next to the eye for passionate, in the corner of the mouth for lover, on the forehead for majestic. They wore powder from Cyprus, essence from Nice, cream from Florence. A few ladies danced the minuet in a show of grace and elegance – slow, swaying movements, the swishing of silk and satin dresses, and a rainbow of colours, pale green, bay green, cinnabar red, against which the white chiffon and lace stood out. Joseph took special note of the satin corsages binding their chests so tightly that their breasts seemed about to leap out of their nests and rival the gleaming stones that decorated their costumes.

But nothing produced a greater impact than the entrance of Aglaë on Membertou's arm. They created a sensation in their native costumes. Membertou hadn't forgotten his bow, his quiver of arrows, and his tomahawk. He strode in with a proud, haughty warrior's gait. Several young nobles were already jealous of Membertou, who had become the darling of the ladies of Paris, but Membertou could not have cared less. Only his beloved counted for him.

"The day after tomorrow," Aglaë suggested, "You can come with me for the king's rising. He'll be surprised to see an Indian there, and you'll have an opportunity to speak to him about your father's project."

Drunk on the perfume of orange blossoms wafting from the wreath of flowers Aglaë wore on her head and on her breath perfumed with Trésor-de-la-Bouche, a spirit water by Sieur Pierre Bocquillon, and charmed by the beauty spot on her forehead as well as by the flush on the curve of her breasts, he simply replied, "Yes," as he would have to any demand Aglaë might make of him.

Then he shook himself, "I'm not the first ambassador from my people. Some came with Jacques Cartier, including

3. The one next to the body.

275

Chief Donnacona's son, who died of homesickness. Another killed himself, hitting his head again and again on the walls. Some were exhibited from one city to the next like circus animals. The French even tried to impress them by parading France's troops past them for inspection. Another so-called discoverer, Champlain, came to court as well to show off his curiosities. Then a few Agnier, considered as enemies by the French, ended up on the king's galleys. He asked for even more since it was said they were strong and inured to pain."

"You're too harsh. Our king had a young Iroquois as his companion during childhood. I've been told that an Abnaki chief named Nescambouit[4] was received by Louis XIV during a special audience. The king presented him with a sabre and showed him the highest regard..."

She stopped talking as a group of young nobles wearing Greek warrior costumes approached. She recognized Godefroy, Berryer's son, who had been wooing her for some months.

"Our friend is feasting his eyes on the beauties of this empire... Do you have anything as beautiful in your country?"

Membertou's first desire was to scalp the man, but he took the fight on to another terrain instead.

"I come from huge forests, but the harmony of nature, passion, and beauty extolled here in verse also exist where we come from."

Pleased at the effect his words were having, he continued, "Ever since I first set eyes on Aglaë, I've forgotten all the other splendours here thought to be supreme!" That made Godefroy's companion laugh. To avoid losing face, Godefroy retorted, "Although Aglaë is splendid, I'm surprised to see her include you in her retinue."

No native man would ever let the woman he loved be insulted. And the bear part of Membertou was let out of hibernation when Godefroy suggested, "I'd like to see your skill at the art of war. Let's retire to the garden..."

---

4. "He who is so important and whose merit is so great that not even the mind can grasp his greatness."

"The war hatchet has been buried for too long," Membertou said ironically. "It's beginning to rust!"

Aglaë shuddered and tried to intervene. In vain. The small group headed for the Apollo basin, where the storm burst before the god of light sitting in his sun chariot pulled by four horses, surrounded by fountains and light, enveloped by the Lulli refrain coming from the Hall of Mirrors.

* * *

By asking Berryer for more time, Joseph harboured the hope he would be able to meet the Duc de Choiseul and obtain an audience with the king. He managed to approach the duke between two dances. Small in stature, with a dimpled round chin, a high, balding forehead, and a haughty air, the duke had firm ideas about what should be done to see troops land in England and reform the French army and navy.

"Our fleet is in a pitiful state. It has to be our priority. I might be able to help you next year."

That was too far in the future. Joseph retorted, "France doesn't care much about its colony. At best, it sees the colony as a bargaining chip. However ridiculous it may seem, there is more honour here in attending the king's rising and handing him his breeches than in defending the territories of the Empire. You know, France has done next to nothing for Acadia, and it makes me ashamed. New France was colonized thanks to the seigneurs' efforts: Poutrincourt, Razilly, D'Aulnay and a few others. All the king gave them was a concession that he then revoked, at times for no reason, and he left it up to them to get the settlers established. The seigneurs bankrupted themselves for an ungrateful mother country."

Now that he had the duke's attention, he continued without stopping to take a breath, "The Baron de Saint-Castin, who commanded the Abnaki in Maine, spent thirty years putting up a rampart between the colonies of New England and Acadia. Do you know what his compensation was? His land was stolen from him, and he was never able to recover it after his return to France. There are poor people in my country who have been scattered in all four directions, not to mention being sent to England's prisons. I beg you, do what you can to ensure the king hears me out!"

Joseph explained his plan and means, and told Choiseul about his interview with Berryer.

"I'll speak to the king tonight," Choiseul promised.

Joseph knew that promises could be either broken or kept, but he did feel reassured. He began to daydream about his meeting with the king, a dream that was interrupted by Aglaë who ran in out of breath, her eyes red.

"Godefroy provoked Membertou at sword point and the duel went badly... for Godefroy. He's lying in a pool of his own blood... a blow with the tomahawk... Membertou had no choice, but no one will side with an Indian from Canada..."

Joseph was dismayed. "Membertou hasn't been hurt?" he asked. "Where is he now?"

"He's safe and sound, hiding in the stables. You have to flee," Aglaë insisted.

"But I'm to meet the king soon... The Duc de Choiseul is going to secure an audience for me..."

"You can't, you could end up having an audience with the gallows instead. You have no one here to protect you."

Joseph had to admit that Aglaë was right. Their lives were in danger, but he didn't want to abandon his mission. "Membertou could hide outside Paris until I meet with the king..."

"I doubt very much your meeting will take place now. You're more likely to be placed under arrest."

"Unfortunately, I'm afraid you're right," Joseph concluded. "But I'll be back."

They finally left Paris. Without Aglaë – something Membertou couldn't understand. In his country, when you loved a man, you followed him. The rage, anger, and hurt that assailed him contorted his features.

"Why won't she come with me when she swore she loved me? Is she just like all the others – does her word, her honour not mean a thing?"

For the time being, Joseph was more worried about the need to find refuge than about Membertou's feelings. Remembering the ship shown on Paris's coat of arms and the motto written there, *Fluctuat nec mergitur*,[5] Joseph decided to flee from Paris down the Seine to Rouen on a horse-drawn barge. "I hope they'll be looking for us on the roads to Nantes."

He recalled a poem by Joachim du Bellay:

> Happy he who, like Ulysses, has travelled safely...
> ...when will I see again, alas, in my small village
> smoke rise from the chimney, and in what season
> will I see once more the walls of my humble home
> My province and much more!

---

5. She is tossed about by the waves, but she does not sink.

Chapter 32

The inhabitants of the three Miramichi posts, the Chipegan post, and the three Caraquet posts were much to be pitied that July: they complained that it had been thus for years now.

– Bazagier's notebook, Paris,
last day of December, 1760

The Restigouche post was bustling with activity that summer of 1760. First, a ship had to be chartered to send Vaudreuil's dispatches to court. He was busy organizing the last kernel of resistance in Montreal. Since all warships had been sunk, the choice fell on the largest ship that was still seaworthy: Nicolas Gauthier's schooner hidden in the Bonaventure harbour. Sieur de la Giraudais had the schooner armed then rebaptized it the *Petit Machault*. The ship was going to transport a cargo of the finest furs from the region as well as a painting to be offered to the king. The painting, which Mathilde had sketched by the full moon, depicted the Restigouche battle. The scene had been inspired by Tjigog, who had told her that three stars not far from the North Star represented three Mi'kmaq who left by canoe one day for the Ursa Major, but never reached their destination. In the same way help from France never arrived!

The distribution of supplies and assistance had to be organized not only for the 160 Acadian families and 250

Mi'kmaq families living in Restigouche, but also for the families of the Acadian refugees living in dire poverty in the surrounding villages: thirty-six in Caraquet, thirty-five in Miramichi, sixteen in Papôg, and Gaspeg, five in Chipagan, not to mention the Mi'kmaq living there. To make matters worse, the Chipagan fishing post had been methodically fired on by the cannons in Byron's fleet on its way back to Louisbourg, and the wretches hadn't forgotten to finish in Miramichi the destruction begun by Murray in 1758.

Dangeac mobilized all available forces to execute Vaudreuil's orders, namely organize the resistance and arm privateers' boats. He grumbled, "The governor gives us instructions, but he doesn't know yet that the war fleet no longer exists."

There were still, however, fourteen small boats of between thirty-five and ninety tons, most of which needed some major repairs. Restigouche became a huge shipyard in which anything that could float was repaired, including schooners and rowboats. Although the Acadians had yet to learn a seaman's trade, they were generally excellent carpenters. So Landry's hammers, Dugas' saws, and Poirier's planes were enlisted for the cause. Olivier Blanchard helped with the calculations, his strong point; Joseph Boudreau contributed his specialty, oakum and tar, and Olivier Léger checked the angles with his level. Thus, Sieur Gramond armed the boat *La Fortune*, whose twenty-five men, including Joseph-Jean, captured a few English ships off Gaspeg that were carrying supplies from Boston to Quebec. Another crew led by Sieur Juny manned the refloated *Les Bons Enfants*, captured several boats off Ile Saint-Jean, and saved the life of two Acadian families as their skiff sank off Ile d'Anticosti.

* * *

War or peace, defeat or victory, nothing affected Mathilde as much as Tjigog's moods. She was so happy in his arms that nothing could bother her, not even the collapse of the four pillars of heaven. Not on that moonlit July evening in any case.

"The moon is the sun's wife and the mother of the human species," Tjigog told her. "The moon protects pregnant women and dispenses nursing milk."

Tjigog's reflections came from his desire to start a family. But that happy thought was dampened by his concern for his friend Tough Lynx. Tough Lynx had arrived from the Saint-Jean River where he'd been gravely wounded after a skirmish with the English. Mathilde would never forget his stoicism as both his legs were amputated. The barbaric operation was practised with saws and knives under horrendous hygienic conditions by a surgeon who was more like a barber than a disciple of Hippocrates, the only anesthetic being a bottle of rum. That was the first time she saw tears in Tjigog's eyes.

July 27, 1760, the feast day of St. Anne, the venerated patron saint of the natives, was a sad day for Tjigog, for that day Tough Lynx was buried in the cemetery at Bourdon Point. Father Ambroise reminded the refugees gathered there of the ephemeral nature of life. As though they needed to be told! As recently as the previous day, Father Etienne, with the four Godet brothers[1] as servers and bearers, had led another funeral service, this one for Germain Savoie, who died from wounds received during the same naval battle.

But everyday concerns returned to the fore and, on August 10th, the *Petit Machault*, whose launch had had to be postponed due to leaks, left for France. Everyone had tried to finagle their way on board, and De la Giraudais was far from happy with the frail, overloaded skiff, which had to cross an ocean. The next day, the militia majors Joseph and Charles Dugas as well as captains Pierre Gauthier, Armand Bujeau, and Abraham Dugas set sail in an old tub in the direction of Caraquet. A few days later, Dangeac decided it would be prudent to send a second ship to be sure the news from Canada reached the Court, especially since he'd just received instructions from Vaudreuil advocating the evacuation of the post and repatriation to France. A few ships would have been nice!

---

1. Gaudet.

* * *

At twenty-six, Antoine-Charles Denys de Saint-Simon was already an experienced armsman. Born in Quebec, by the age of twelve he was a cadet in the navy. In 1755, he was there for General Braddock's defeat in Ohio. Afterwards, he was transferred to Acadia, and in the spring of 1760, Governor Vaudreuil appointed him as Dangeac's assistant at the Restigouche post. To say he loved to fight was an understatement. A man of action, the fiery officer had taken a leaf out of his ancestors' book. His great-uncle Simon was Nicolas Denys' brother, he who, a century earlier, governed the coasts of Acadia for fifty years.

Saint-Simon Jr. had decided to arm with ten swivel guns and three cannons the thirty-five-ton schooner belonging to the Bujeau[2] family. It was nicknamed the *Corsaire Acadien* because its crew was comprised of a group of forty-seven Acadians, including Acadians of Poitevin origin[3], others from Port-Royal, Grand'Pré, and Memramcouk, and fishermen or soldiers of Norman descent[4] from Papôg and Gaspeg, who came to Ruisseau to trade goods and kisses. Since Mathilde categorically refused to leave Tjigog's side, she was authorized to join the crew. She even carved a spot out for herself among the men thanks to her skill at aiming the swivel guns.

During the whole month of August and into September, the privateer boat Tjigog affectionately called *Mean Gougou* captured several ships off Gaspeg. From their catch, they were able to supply the surrounding posts. On September 19th, the day of the half-moon "when the buck pursues the doe," another captured ship brought with it the makings of a celebration; its hold was full of barrels of rum. In early October, the "moose loving" moon had barely begun when a frigate gave chase to the *Corsaire Acadien*. Nightfall was still a long way off, and the schooner had to flee the enemy fleet, which was armed

---

2. Bujold.
3. Boudreau, Blanchard, Cormier, Dugas, Landry, Léger, Poirier...
4. Albert, Brideau, Frigault, Gallien, Gionet, Lanteigne, Morais...

with twenty-two cannons. Saint-Simon took advantage of the light southwester blowing toward Caraquet to head in that direction. Several crew members knew the region, some because they had overwintered in Bocage two years earlier. Gabriel Albert suggested, "We could round Ile de Pokesudie and go upriver to the Baie de Chipagan. Our draft is lower than their bloody frigate's."

"It won't work," Frigault replied. "The tide is too low and we'll run aground before we reach the river…"

"Well then, we'll fight on land," said Sieur Parisé, the Restigouche officer assisting Saint-Simon.

Little by little, the *Corsaire Acadien* was able to outdistance the English frigate thanks to its lighter weight. The men seemed hypnotized by the distant shore, as though the ship's speed could be increased by blowing on the sails. But the best they could do was run aground and abandon ship, which they did a few cables' length distance from shore. Cannonballs were already whistling through the rigging and sails. The foremast hit Lentaigne, who was knocked out and over into the ice-cold water. Tjigog saw where he fell and jumped in to rescue him. Despite the paralyzing effect of October's freezing currents, he managed to bring him to shore. The crew was already loading the muskets. Mathilde was running toward Tjigog as he stood up and misfortune struck: a shot struck the man she loved full in the chest. Mathilde collapsed next to a bleeding Tjigog. His eyes glassy, he had only enough strength to caress her hair and tell her in a faltering voice that he would have wonderful memories to carry in his heart during the greatest voyage of all. His life's blood spilled out onto the sand and into the river water to be joined by Mathilde's tears. Her universe had come undone one more time.

* * *

Life in Ruisseau was nothing but an interminable wait for those who were absent in the fall of 1760. The departure of Joseph, René, and Membertou had left a gaping hole behind for everyone, and Angélique didn't know anymore who she missed the most. So she kept herself busy with a thousand daily tasks. Jean-Baptiste shuttled back and forth on supply runs between Caraquet and Restigouche; that was how he learned all about the naval battle so quickly. As a precaution, the inhabitants of Ruisseau concealed all signs of life so they wouldn't be the next victims of Byron's fleet.

Saint-Jean scanned the horizon, hoping to see a familiar sail appear. But the sea remained silent. The old man could feel death approaching, and he caught himself wondering whether there was such a thing as life after death. He surprised himself, since the religious persecution of his youth had made him cynical and indifferent to the matter. He thought it highly unlikely that a God who creates man in his image and likeness would tolerate wars, suffering, famine. Of course, he'd been reminded of free will, that he as a man had the capacity to choose between good and evil, but he still wondered, *Is man truly free? Or just doing what is possible?* He had other questions, too. *What explains the way things and beings change if there is no cause, no logic? What explains the natural order? Since for every effect there is a cause, how is it possible not to go back to the first cause of all?*

During his lifetime, he had seen certain things and beings reach varying levels of perfection, as though according to a hierarchy, and this led him to believe there must be an optimal state of perfection, an absolute. He had also seen how everything had a function: the fruit of the earth served as nourishment, the caterpillar turned into a butterfly, the sun provided heat and light, the clouds announced storms. He asked himself, like Pascal the philosopher, *Can there be a clock without a clockmaker?* But his heart, suffering from past resentment, resisted. Doubt continued to haunt him.

There were some small consolations, however: the touch of his wife Honguedo; a visit from his daughter Françoise; and fur from the animals he'd hunted, which was thick and soft this year. To while away the time, he polished his firearms: first his favourite musket, a 42-inch, .70-calibre English Brown Bess, then his Charleville musket from the French armies. Without saying a word aloud, for fear of alarming Angélique, he worried about Joseph, René, and Membertou.

* * *

Angélique experienced Indian summer in all its colourful glory as she gathered her supply of medicinal herbs for the winter: sarsaparilla, aniseed, yarrow, plantain, tansy as well as rye-ergot, with which she made a potion for heart problems that she gave to her father daily. She stocked up on raspberry bush roots, which she decocted and mixed with milk to cure infantile diarrhea, and on larch resin, which, with a bit of molasses and castor oil, served as a remedy for intestinal worms.

In her daydreams, she relived her long walks with Joseph through the autumn leaves, a symphony to delight all the senses: the crackling of leaves under their feet, the smell of pine and spruce trees, the tango of colours in the gentle shafts of light alternating with shade, and their caresses while the squirrels put up reserves in the old oak trees, the bees buzzed around their honey pyramid, and the birds beat a farewell with their wings before heading south. She felt a first twinge of sorrow – for everything she missed – then another twinge – of jealousy – when she thought of Emilie.

Her daughters caught up with her. They gathered herbs, bark, and fruit to make dye with: lily of the valley for golden-green, citronella flowers for pink, blackberries for purple, horse chestnut bark for red, and others to cover the whole range of colours. Finding herself alone with Geneviève at one point, Angélique talked to her about her concerns.

"Listen," she said, "I know what passion is like… If you want to wait before having a family, I have herb teas that will prevent pregnancy… for the time being."

Geneviève felt lucky to have such an understanding mother.

Angélique loved her children dearly, more than the island treasure, more than Joseph even. She couldn't bear having her two sons so far away. A ship that stopped over in Ruisseau brought her letters from Joseph, René, and Membertou. News from Nantes, as her men were preparing to leave for Paris. But since then, nothing! Nothing but worry!

286

Winter preparations were well underway. Angélique made medicinal oils from cod liver oil and ointments from pine gum. Then she gathered scurvy-fighting white cedar bark and wild rose berries. Josette and Geneviève made all the clay and birchbark containers in which the peas, beans, cornmeal, and oils would be stored. Other tribe members repaired canoes, cut strips of hide for snowshoes, and made long, straight fledged arrows. The primary concern was always food: salmon, trout, and river eel, to be smoked or salted, smoked meat that had to be hung from trees to protect it from animals and the damp ground, not to mention a load of supplies for Restigouche and Camp de l'Espérance. Saint-Jean had been told about the extreme poverty in Miramichi, which reminded him of his early years in Canada when he worked in the Miramichi post trading furs, a time of abundance compared to the galleys. The memories saddened him. But his good mood returned when he took part in the torch hunt along the Pokesudie lagoon; they camouflaged themselves inside a canoe set adrift, then lit the torches as soon as they were surrounded by ducks and teals. The birds swirled around in great confusion. A few blows with a stick were all that was needed to fill the canoes.

Jeannette-Anne kept busy sewing fur coats until it was time for her to deliver her baby. In accordance with the Mi'kmaq tradition, she gave birth in silence, then returned to work. Jean-Baptiste made a backboard in which little Thérèse-Anne could be carried. Whenever Jeannette-Anne worked outdoors, she leaned the board up against a tree so her daughter could look around and know the world she would be discovering.

Chapter 33

The islands in the English Channel are bits of France
that fell into the sea and were picked up by the English
— Victor Hugo

The wind from the Ocean gives Jersey exquisite honey,
extraordinarily sweet cream, and dark yellow butter
smelling of violets.

— Chateaubriand

On the Seine, August 1760. The precious stone Joseph
showed the ship's captain would have been enough to
convince him to take them all the way to hell if they had
wanted. Which was why Joseph and his sons found themselves
shortly after midnight on a horse-drawn barge making its slow
way out of Paris via the Seine. Too slow for Joseph's taste, who
was afraid they'd be discovered before they reached the Isle of
Jersey. *Life is strange*, Joseph thought. *Our freedom will be
granted by England, which has jurisdiction over the island.* Since
arriving in France, Joseph hadn't been able to picture Emilie
clearly anymore; the picture faded even more as he drew nearer
to Jersey, giving way to images of deportees waiting to be liberated from England's prisons. He was worried about the others, too, who, to avoid deportation, had to play hide-and-seek
in America's huge forests. On the fateful day of August 23,
1760, at the very end of the blackberry month, Joseph admit-

ted to himself, *I tempted fate. One man alone cannot change fate. I was too proud.*

In a gesture similar to monks renouncing the ways of the world, he decided to shave off his beard, something Rene was not the least bit happy about. He was afraid he wouldn't recognize his father afterwards. But Joseph had decided he needed a change, it was as though he wanted a break with the past. In response to René's vehement protests, he did compromise and agree to keep his moustache. René told his father about the strange episode with the old woman, the one who had taken him for her godson.

"That's hard to believe!" Joseph exclaimed. "But not impossible."

The incident further fuelled his belief that his father belonged to the family of the dukes of Brittany; heredity had just confirmed it through his son. But he relegated the information to the back of his mind because he was in no mood to dwell on his origins. *Some day I'll go back to Brittany.*

René missed his mother terribly. He hadn't thought much about her in Paris because of the novelty each day held. Plus, his alchemy plans and his game on the new social order had kept him busy. But he'd had to leave the viscount's house in haste leaving everything behind. Fortunately, Aglaë had found him in time in the Versailles gardens to tell him Joseph was looking for him and that Membertou was hiding out in the stables.

As for Membertou, his universe was dreary and grey without Aglaë. He didn't look for explanations or justification. He just felt a huge void and a gnawing pain in the pit of his stomach. He immured himself in silence and Joseph and René respected his wishes. Paris was far behind them by the time the sun rose and they decided to disembark. Joseph's "magic stones" had the desired effect, and they set off on the road for Rennes and Saint-Malo ensconced in a berlin.

René forgot his homesickness at the sight of the fortified city of Saint-Malo. He remembered the stories his grandfather told about the privateers' capital. Several captured English ships in the harbour were proof of the city's dynamism. The imposing abbey of Mont-Saint-Michel could be seen in the distance. Near the château belonging to Duchesse Anne, Joseph rented a privateer's boat to take them to Jersey. No questions were asked; the glittering stones were enough. He felt there was no safer ship to take them to the island.

"After all, privateers are specialists in the art of eluding the enemy."

To tease his brother, still one of his favorite pastimes, René said, "Saint-Malo is the city Jacques Cartier set out from to discover Canada."

Membertou gave a start. "The Indians had been living in America for thousands of years before Cartier arrived. The white men *discovered* nothing. They spread disease and vice."

It wouldn't have taken much for Membertou to throw his brother overboard that day, but at least René made him break his silence. Several inhabitants of Jersey were on board, including Le Gresley, a teacher who summarized in his local dialect[1] the history of the Anglo-Norman islands.

"The Duc de Normandy, William the Conqueror, conquered England in 1066. Ever since, the isles of Jersey, Guernesey, Alderney and a few other bits and pieces have been under its rule. The inhabitants, the Normans, have kept the French language and culture, traditions reinforced by the French who still live nearby on the coasts of Brittany and Normandy. In short, the territory belongs to England, but has its own laws and parliament, and beautiful islands blessed with a fairly mild climate because of the warm ocean currents.[2]"

"I've heard Catholics aren't welcome there," Joseph said.

"Of course not! Many French Huguenots moved to Jersey to flee persecution. The island is no place for papists. By 1560, the churches were cleaned out by the Calvinists and transformed into Protestant temples."

To avoid awakening suspicion, Joseph said he was fleeing from religious persecution in Canada and that he hadn't found the hoped-for freedom in France. Aware that all the island's

---

1. Jersey is old twelfth-century French.
2. Gulf Stream.

inhabitants knew each other, he decided not to betray his and Emilie's secret, although he was dying to ask about her.

To avoid warships, the captain waited for nightfall. His plan was to take a detour to make it seem as though the ship was coming from England. Not far from Jersey was Sark Island, an untamed rock of majestic beauty – nature in the raw, almost treeless. Le Gresley declaimed the words with which Rabelais immortalized the island,

"Islands full of braggarts, thieves, murderers,
and assassins. They are worse than cannibals."

"Don't worry," he said, reading the anxious look on Joseph's face. "Jersey is a very quiet place. In 1483, Pope Sixte 14 proclaimed in a bull that the islands and their surroundings as far as the eye could see would remain neutral in times of war. That pirates would be excommunicated. The tradition of peace dates back almost two centuries."

A dark mass loomed ahead in the first glimmer of dawn, and Jersey appeared: seven leagues by three in size. On one side were tall granite cliffs pocked with caves, on the other long beaches of white sand dotted with small inlets. Then the ship dropped anchor in a huge bay across from St. Hélier, the capital.

How will Emilie greet me after all this time? And my daughter Héloïse?

It wouldn't be long before he had an answer to his questions.

* * *

Emilie was waiting for Joseph. She had never stopped waiting in fact. After all these years, she couldn't believe it. She reread the letter Joseph had sent from Nantes. She put it back in the bronze chest that held all the letters she had written to him: one per month since she left Quebec twenty years ago, except once when she was very ill. Over two hundred letters she had never sent, with two exceptions.

Her husband, Alexandre Le Breton, died when he was well on in years. He had been good to her and she had given him friendship and affection if not love and passion. Alexandre made his fortune trading with the Newfoundland fisheries, and they lived in a grand house known as a "terreneuve" (Newfoundlander), with a large front door in a sculpted porch and windows, all of which were topped by a slate roof. Although her husband's estate meant she didn't have to work after his death, Emilie accepted a position as a governess for the children of Seigneur de Carteret, the island's bailiff, to help compensate for the large family she would love to have had.

Her days were full; they started with her knitting Jersey sweaters, then puttering around in her pottery corner. She cultivated flowers as well: carnations, chrysanthemums, tulips, and a small field of lavender. She was older, but age only enhanced her beauty and, like Penelope, she had kept her suitors waiting for four years since she'd been widowed. The long hours she spent at the château gave her opportunities to read, play music, decipher legal documents, and learn English, Dutch, and Spanish since visitors from several European countries stayed there.

The thoroughly exhausted travellers hailed a coachman. The man knew where Emilie lived: on the other side of the island, close to the Baie de Bonne-Nuit. Down narrow small roads bordered by poplar, oak, and chestnut trees, they passed by farms with walls made of granite. The farms had massive chimneys and windows showing the date of construction and the family coat of arms carved into the stone. The outer wall and gates were built from stone as well. The trip was made in silence. In Membertou's case, it was as though he had shut himself up in a fortress; in René's case, curiosity silenced him.

I refuse to like her, René said to himself about the woman who competed with his mother in his father's heart, but he was curious to meet her.

Joseph was busy trying to remember their last time together before he left for the Trois-Rivières region. It was so long ago and his memories so vague, but he hadn't forgotten their last embrace, when Emilie had promised with tears in her eyes, "We'll be married next spring. Hurry back!"

Did she know she was pregnant then? he agonized. *Why didn't she wait until summer to leave?*

The questions racing through his mind were all the more troubling because the answer was drawing ever closer. At last, he caught a glimpse of the house and a small field of lavender that fused with the purple and rose of the setting sun over the sea. Joseph asked René and Membertou to wait in the coach while he went to see if Emilie was in. Really, it was a pretext so he could see her again for the first time in private. He stepped down from the coach and, his heart pounding as if it were about to explode, he walked around the house and saw before him Emilie, distilling lavender perfume. There, where the scent of lavender mingled with the sea breeze, he took her into his arms. She trembled like a swallow, numb with cold, which had found warmth and shelter after a long, drawn-out voyage. She stammered, "You haven't changed, you look even more handsome than you did in my dreams. I know what it means to have waited."

She hugged him even closer as she sobbed, her tears sliding down Joseph's face so he couldn't tell whether he too was crying or not.

He was too moved to speak; there was so much to say he didn't know where to start. So Joseph and Emilie communicated without words, gazing greedily on each other like delighted children.

They walked inside. Emilie set the table. The refinement of her every gesture, her easy walk, her radiant expression captivated Joseph. She had outdone herself preparing island dishes that she left to cook slowly in the embers of wood and seaweed. They were joined by Joseph's sons. As though to lighten the solemnity of the moment, René broke the silence with questions about Emilie's life and comments on the local food and the various succulent dishes that graced the long table. There was a certain complicity between René and Emilie. She asked him about the ocean crossing, seasickness, Paris, and Versailles. René answered with a hint of pride that he had good sea legs and was busy working on important alchemy projects… Joseph watched in silence, pleased to see them get along. But Membertou was another story; he only grunted when Emilie tried to make him talk about life in Ruisseau. Joseph decided to ask whether Héloïse was there.

"She left for the Isle of Guernsey," her mother replied. "She's become infatuated with a French Huguenot refugee there. Her excuse to me was that she was going to visit my late husband's brother. I don't know when she'll be back. I worry about her; she's very bohemian and rebellious. I think she has your adventurous spirit," she teased Joseph.

"I hope it won't complicate her life too much. My desire for adventure in the Laurentian forests caused us a great deal of trouble."

Joseph remembered the day he left, leaving Emilie alone in Quebec to worry about the child she was carrying. *If I had only known*, he thought.

René stopped talking all of a sudden. His expression became guarded, and he felt a pang of jealousy. Not only did he have to share Joseph with Emilie but now with Héloïse as well. As the youngest, he was used to having a special place in Joseph's heart, and now suddenly he felt threatened by the unknown Héloïse. He didn't like to see his father's marked interest in her. He decided to join Membertou, who had gone to bed.

Despite his fatigue, Joseph stayed behind a bit longer. Especially since he could speak more freely about Héloïse with René and Membertou gone.

"I can't wait to see her. Does she know I'm her father? That I'm here? What will she do when she sees me? Maybe she hates me because of all the suffering you both went through because of me."

"Joseph, please, don't blame yourself. You couldn't know I was pregnant, and I had no way of knowing you were still alive. I explained everything to her and I've talked to her about you at length. Héloïse understands that fate played a trick on us. She's looking forward to meeting you."

That was how the evening ended. A gradual winding down like grains of sand sifting through the hourglass above the chimney. Then on to the land of dreams in this house by the Baie de Bonne-Nuit, also known as the Baie du Bon-Repos.

René woke with the first light of dawn.

"Come with me to visit Lillie," Emilie proposed.

"Who's that?"

"She's the one who gives me warm milk. Ten times her weight in milk in just one year. The Jerseys are a pure breed."

But René didn't seem all that excited about Lillie, a small, light beige cow with dark eyes that was grazing in the pasture.

"What interests you?" Emilie asked.

"Anything to do with magical powers."

"Not far from here is the Fontaine des Mittes, which gives the power of speech to the mute as long as they drink from it before sundown."

René was more interested in dolmens. He asked whether there were any in the region.

"It's said that at Hougue Bie, a brave knight slayed a dragon that was terrorizing the island. The knight's squire wanted to pass the exploit off as his own so he killed the knight. The knight's mistress had a dolmen erected in his memory. You might want to visit it. But first, you need a hearty breakfast of eggs, lard, mèrvelles[3], and black butter, not to mention Lillie's warm milk."

After breakfast, René set off to explore the island with Alphonse Mourant, Emilie's servant. Iberians, Celts, and Gallois had all passed through. The Romans had conquered the island, naming it Caesareal. Membertou stayed in his room back in the "terreneuve" all day.

* * *

Surrounded by the scent of pines and ferns, Joseph and Emilie took a path bordered with heather, gorse bushes, and brooms to the Bonne-Nuit inlet. On the shores of a turquoise sea, they lay down on the hot sand at the foot of a pink granite cliff. It was the moment they'd both been waiting for since the dream began.

---

3. Type of doughnut.

"I cried for so long after leaving for France. I thought you had died, leaving part of you behind in my womb. Paradoxically, that was also what gave me the courage to persevere. I often wanted to return to my family. I don't know why I ended up staying. Héloïse grew up and..."

Emilie didn't feel like dwelling on all the missed opportunities.

"What is Rue Cul-de-Sac like now?"

"There are new houses everywhere. But I'm afraid the landscape will change because of the war and the English cannons."

Then Joseph told her about her sister Cristel.

"The worst part," she confessed, "is not being able to see my loved ones, hear their voices, hug them, and be with my parents in their final moments. The sorrow is greater with every year that passes. Oh, Joseph! Don't ever leave me again; this time I would die. Angélique has had you for long enough. Your children are almost grown. It's my turn. No, don't listen to me; you have to go back."

Joseph could see how heartbroken she was. He rocked her as she cried tears of sorrow and joy. For him, each tear was like a drop of gold watering his soul. Her tears gradually subsided while Joseph remained undecided: should he or should he not give in? He had thought that seeing her again would serve to close that part of his life, that he could put it behind him. But the magic between them was still there, even stronger and more firmly rooted. He felt plagued by his duty to his family, the love he felt for Angélique, and the vague guilt that kept him from giving in to his passion for Emilie. Through her sobs, she said, "Come, I'll give you a massage; it will help you relax. I learned the technique from some travellers who stayed at the castle and had been to the Orient."

Joseph took off his clothes and stretched out on the cool sand at the waves' edge. The warm sea spume rolled in to die at his feet. As Emilie began massaging him, a kind of telepathy grew between them. As she caressed Joseph's feet, she relived all the trips he had made between Quebec, Caraquet, and Louisbourg. She felt the fatigue in his feet and made it disappear. She massaged his wiry legs that had walked the bridges of ships and the coasts of the Baye des Chaleurs. Meanwhile, Joseph could feel the strength and gentleness of arms that had rocked their daughter and hands that had kneaded bread and spun wool. He felt vaguely anxious at the thought those same hands had also caressed Alexandre. Emilie massaged his shoulders, then caressed his neck. She could feel the weight of Joseph's troubles. She gently touched his hair that had blown in the wind on Ile Caraquet, and when she reached his eyes, she was overcome with jealousy at the thought that those eyes had looked on Angélique with love. She touched his lips, as though to hear him say he loved her. Her gentle, all-enveloping touch had breathed life back into Joseph, and when she reached his chest, it was as though his heart was lit up by a diamond of light. Trembling, he opened his arms wide to embrace her. They tumbled in the warm waves, in the limpid blues, greens, turquoises, and in the golden light, as though returning to Creation's origins, before Good and Evil, when life took form in the water. They immersed themselves in the sea, so reminiscent of mothers and birthing, the sea washing all dirt away. To the sound of waves crashing like a joyous pealing of bells, they made love to each other for a long time in the shade of the great cathedral rock.

Once their desire and senses were sated, Joseph turned to an account of his misadventures in Versailles.

"Abbot Leloutre is a prisoner in Elizabeth Castle," Emilie said. "But he still has influence at court. Perhaps he can help."

"It would be a great relief if he could."

He remembered talking to Abbot Leloutre in Louisbourg. Leloutre, the grand vicar of Acadia and friend to the Marquis de la Galissonnière, was a thorn in the side of the English, who accused him of fanaticizing the natives and inciting the Acadians to revolt.

"Isn't it difficult to see him?"

"Not at all. He can't leave the fortress, but he's quite free to move around inside his prison. And I know the governor of the castle."

Elizabeth Castle was located on a small island across from Saint-Hélier. It was an impregnable fortress from which escape was impossible. With the support of Seigneur Dumaresq, who had a great deal of influence on the island, Emilie and Joseph were able to meet George Collingwood, the commander of the rock- and seaweed-strewn island, who authorized a meeting with the abbot. So at low tide, Joseph set out toward the dark, sinister stone mass blocking the horizon not far from the black reefs; a distance of one league. Shaking, he passed under the great Tudor rose and the queen's coat of arms engraved on the entrance archway: the lion of England and the dragon of Wales. More than a hundred large-calibre cannons on wheels formed a barbed battery and covered all shooting angles to defend the granite fortress. On the ground in front of the soldiers' barracks, he noticed a crater, a vestige of the previous century's civil war, when the fortress was bombarded with 450-pound projectiles containing forty pounds of powder. Trying to rid his mind of memories of Louisbourg, he followed the soldier escorting him. They went up and down stone staircases, crossed dark, humid, vaulted caves and finally arrived at the abbot's cell.

The moment when he found the former general vicar of Acadia was an intense one. An emotional Abbot Leloutre fell to his knees, thanking God for having made the encounter possible. Joseph followed suit. *At long last, for the first time since I set foot in Europe, I've found comfort in this difficult mission*, Joseph said to himself. And not from just anyone, but from a passionate devoted man who'd been called Acadia's Moses, and who could perhaps provide him with the means to attain his goal at the Court of Versailles. As for the abbot, he was particularly thrilled because it was the first time since his imprisonment that he'd been able to speak to an Acadian, touch him, and hear the news in person of his adopted country. He looked like an ascetic in his long black cassock. His square jaw showed his determination as did a trace of arrogance in his gaze. With his bushy beard and thick black eyebrows, his face was the kind one didn't forget, but most striking of all were his eyes, lively and piercing, and illuminated by an inner flame that was all the brighter right then because of the tears welling up.

Abbot Leloutre ushered Joseph into his clean, soberly furnished cell: there was a crucifix on the wall, a bed, a desk, a few chairs, and a table with a sweater on it. "Yes, I knit. It helps me forget. Knitting has become so popular on the island that a law had to be passed forbidding men from knitting during harvest and kelp-gathering time. And then they try to say that men have all the rights!" he said with a touch of humour.

"It must help you forget that the English have finally managed to cage you," Joseph said sympathetically.

"It's the second time I've been put in prison. This time I'd taken my father's second name, Sieur Desprez, but my ruse didn't work. I asked the English authorities for a trial, but they're careful not to grant me one. So my only recourse is to wait for the war to end... But tell me about the Acadians."

Joseph told him about the poverty, hunger, disease, scattered families, the situation in Camp de l'Espérance, and the resistance in Acadia.

"To think I was called a fanatic!" the abbot sighed. "It's true I did everything in my power to alert the Acadians to the coming deportations, but I did so with honour and dignity and encouraged those who tried to take back Grand'Pré and Port-Royal. Duvivier, Ramesay, De Villiers, Boishébert, Beausoleil..."

It was almost as though he was mounting his own defence.

"The people spreading tales are trying to discredit you," Joseph pointed out, "but the Acadians and the French recognize your dedication."

"Not everyone. Rumours are often harder to shake than the truth. I spent fifty thousand livres, money from Versailles and personal funds, to dry out the Beauséjour marshes so aboiteaux could be built as an incentive to the Acadians in Beaubassin, Port-Royal, and Grand'Pré to come cultivate what was fertile land. Admittedly, I lobbied for the Acadians to emigrate to Beauséjour or Isle Royale because I knew how determined the English of Halifax were to be rid of them. You know some people believe I set fire to the Beaubassin village to force the Acadians to come under French jurisdiction. Others blame me for emissary Howe's death in Fort Lawrence, when the truth is I warned him not to contact the Indians. I tried to sway people, but I never used the sacraments to blackmail them; I couldn't have lived with my conscience if I had. It's also true that I encouraged the Indians to fight the English, but it must be said in our favour that the English stole their land and offered fifty English pounds in Halifax for Indian scalps. It should surprise no-one, therefore, that I paid for English scalps but, whenever possible, I paid a ransom to the Indians to free their English prisoners; I even have documentation from the Halifax authorities attesting to that fact."

Leloutre had forgotten Joseph's presence by then; he was too busy rehearsing his defence in preparation for his trial. "I tried every way I could to humanize the Savages, but they have their customs and there is no such thing as a gentle war. My biggest regret is not being able to make the Acadians understand that their neutrality was their greatest enemy, and that the deportation had been in the works for years. If the Acadians had used guerrilla tactics, the English would never have succeeded in their sinister schemes. My motto, from my birthplace Morlaix, is, 'If an Englishman bites you, bite him back.' I'm sorry I didn't follow my motto enough."

Seeing that Abbot Leloutre could easily go on pouring his heart out for hours, Joseph tried to explain the purpose of his trip, the difficulties encountered, and the avenues the treasure opened up.

"I have a chest full of gold and precious stones and enough money to finance a war fleet. It's a gift from heaven that I was unable to use because of our misadventures in Versailles."

The priest stared angrily at the coast of France through the window of his prison cell. "The colonies are the least of their worries. Although France's population is twice that of England, there are twenty times fewer French than English in America. At Court, all they think about is indulging in lustful debauchery. It's a frivolous world: with the Affected Young

Ladies holding forth in the salons, the encyclopaedists disparaging faith, and the courtesans whose only interest is in earning the king's favour. They use reason and science to ridicule beliefs and separate morality from religion. This whole business will finish badly! Too much questioning of the truth and the established order leads to chaos."

Joseph felt the abbot was straying too far from the subject at hand. "I'd like to tell you the secret of the treasure so if I die, you can use it to help the Acadians. The treasure is at the Melleray abbey close to Nantes, guarded by the head abbot. The password is *phantom ship*."

"What good news! I'll write to Abbot L'Isle-Dieu; perhaps he'll be able to convince the king. It's my turn to tell you a secret. I'm having talks with Huguenot merchants, the Jersey inhabitants of French origin. As British subjects, they have a certain amount of influence on English policies; the merchants hope to make their fortune with the cod trade, and they see Acadia, with its teeming seas, as a potential base for a world empire. But, for that to happen, they need workers adapted to the country. So Charles Robin and his brothers are planning to write to the governor of Halifax asking him to stop the deportations so they can set up fishing posts. The English might accept since economic interests are at stake."

"But the Acadians will be quasi-slaves in the pay of the Robin brothers," Joseph argued.

"Better to choose the lesser of two evils, my son; slavery is better than annihilation. At least the Acadians will stay at home and keep their language and faith. They can fight for their rights once the storm has blown over,."

Joseph, well aware there was no easy solution, acknowledged that Abbot Leloutre's plan made sense. The missionary continued, "You know, I can't leave this prison, but I do receive many visitors and letters. I know what's going on. I know, for instance, that Virginia refused to let the Acadian deportees in; close to fifteen hundred of them were sent on to England in appalling conditions. The survivors have been detained in Liverpool, Bristol, Penryn, and Southampton," he said with consternation.

"How are they being treated?"

"Not like kings! They weren't expected in Bristol, so they were left for three days and nights on the quays. Smallpox caused terrible losses among those who hadn't already succumbed to fatigue and despair. I've been corresponding with the Duc de Nivernais, France's ambassador to London, to arrange for their return to France. The money from the treasure comes just in time."

"Why are you doing all this?"

"Because the Acadians are my family now, and they're suffering. I'm not looking for gratitude. The Acadians are a generous people, certainly, but their growth has been suffocated; a people in full flight, whose wings have been clipped; a young oak felled by harsh weather. You have terrible times ahead of you. Acadia has been a land of compromise since its foundation; to guarantee its survival, it created alliances with the Indians; for its economy, it tolerated trade with the English from New England; in short, your neutrality has been your undoing."

Joseph thought there was no use trying to make sense out of the suffering of a people, but he didn't feel like arguing the point. Before he took his leave, he wanted to confide in the abbot about the two loves of his life. He spoke about his engagement to Emilie, his departure for Caraquet, his marriage to Angélique, his children.

"You know," said Abbot Leloutre, "It's impossible to see the Church's teachings in the same light after living with the Indians. The latter believe in offering visitors what they prize above all else: their spouse. I don't agree, but I can't deny there is beauty in such a gift. Over its history, the Church has been given to great surges of humanity: marriages were annulled, heretics were pardoned… Today, most of the greats of this world have mistresses and the practice is more or less tolerated. Recently, Acadians from Saint-Malo presented a petition to allow marriages between people who were almost brothers and sisters, and Abbot L'Isle-Dieu recommended that the dispensations be hurried along so the Acadian branch is not lost. It was accepted. The Bible could not have foreseen such situations."

He added, "The ways of the Lord are inscrutable."

Joseph was surprised to hear the abbot take a near-heretic stance, one that more or less justified every human acting according to his or her own conscience.

Before concluding their meeting, Abbot Leloutre spoke of Thomas Pichon, who had delivered military information to the English in 1755 that facilitated the capture of Fort Beauséjour. "Watch out for that man. He lives in Jersey now, and receives two hundred pounds a year from England. The man's a snake who would sell his own mother to satisfy his desire for power and money. It's better he not find out you're here."

Abbot Leloutre didn't want to say anything further. He gave Joseph his blessing, then said, "I have a strange question to ask you. After the tragedy that befell the Duc d'Anvilles' fleet, I promised a good soul I would watch over the little orphan Mathilde Chaisson. She was adopted in Grand'Pré by the Clairefontaine family. Would you happen to have news of her from the Camp de l'Espérance refugees?"

Joseph knew nothing of Mathilde and regretted not being able to tell the missionary she was safe and sound some-where. He left the abbey when the bell sounded, signalling the time for leavetaking due to the rising tide.

His meeting with Abbot Leloutre had brought him peace and, that evening, once René and Membertou were fast asleep, he sat in up his big lavender-scented bed after a soothing bath in seaweed. Small Chinese jade and porcelain bottles of snuff sat on his mahogany bedside table. Emilie joined him, saying, "Smoking is frowned on. But taking snuff is different, even for women. It's said to have medicinal properties."

Joseph was at peace, ready to try anything Emilie suggested. As he took the snuff, he told her about his visit with Abbot Leloutre and what the priest had said about their relationship. Then he suggested, "Why don't we visit Héloïse in Guernesey instead of waiting for her here?"

"Oh, yes! She'll be thrilled. Any time I ever talked to her about you, she always asked whether she'd see you one day. And I worry when she's far away."

Lying on pillows filled with both hopseed and the seeds of everlasting flowers, they fell asleep in each other's arms and dreamt of being together for eternity.

* * *

The next day, René visited the Royal Square at St. Hélier and was particularly struck by an unfortunate wretch in stocks. "It's so cruel. They've cut off his ear and put him in stocks. I met a friendly Acadian, an exile, who told me what the poor man's crime was," René said.

"We could invite the Acadian here," Joseph suggested. "Did he tell you his name?"

"Yes. Thomas Tyrell."

"Oh, no! Listen, you have to avoid that man at all costs because he could make trouble for us. His real name is Thomas Pichon, the traitor from Fort Beauséjour. Tyrell is his mother's maiden name. I hope you didn't mention me?"

"No, I had to leave just then with Monsieur Mourant."

Joseph was somewhat reassured. After a moment's hesitation, he decided to tell his son about his travel plans. "We're leaving for the Isle of Guernsey. To visit Héloïse, your sister."

René made a face. "Can I stay here?" he asked. "There are more dolmens I want to see."

Maybe he's jealous, Joseph thought anxiously. But he understood René's reaction. *He needs time to see that my love for him won't be any the less because of Héloïse.*

Membertou had barricaded himself in his room and didn't want to go with them either. Joseph didn't insist, especially since he preferred having Membertou stay with René. He took comfort in the thought that old Mourant and his wife, Dame Lecouteur, would watch over them. Joseph hugged his sons as though he were leaving a piece of his heart behind. Emilie only managed to get a grunt out of Membertou, but René shouted with joy when she gave him some Armorican[4] and Roman coins discovered not far from the dolmens on the island. Emilie

---

4. Armorica – the northwest part of France, especially Brittany.

and Joseph set sail for Guernsey on a three-master that navigated the coasts between the Anglo-Norman islands.

A few hours after their departure, a comet streaked through the sky. A bright, blood-red moon shone that night. At the same time, in the Baie de Bonne-Nuit René glimpsed a flaming ship that seemed to be rising out of a ball of fire. *I thought you could only see the phantom ship off our coasts*, he thought, surprised.

Around midnight, a storm blew in, and all night long, as Membertou slept soundly, René could hear the wind racing across the bay and howling through the attic. At daybreak, a sea littered with debris washed ashore pieces of wreckage, merchandise, trunks. René walked down to the shore to find out what had happened and learned that the small schooner carrying Joseph and Emilie had sunk at sea. Mad with grief, René threw himself into the water and started swimming out toward the wreckage to rescue his father, whom he imagined clinging to a mast. That image was soon replaced by another more terrifying one when he thought he glimpsed Joseph's lifeless body on the sea bottom, a captive of the seaweed. If it hadn't been for Membertou, who stopped him from drifting toward the currents offshore, he would have joined his father in the depths of the sea.

The news was a terrible shock to Membertou, although it did wipe all thought of Aglaë from his mind. He spent his time looking after René, who couldn't stop crying. The long wait began. There were said to be a few survivors. Hour after hour, family and friends waited for confirmation. A few bloated bodies, wrapped in seaweed and drifting on the waves, had been washed up on shore but not Joseph's or Emilie's. Membertou and René still clung to hope. Several bodies carried away by the currents had yet to be found. The minutes seemed like days, the hours like years, the days like centuries.

Every night, René had nightmares of monsters, skeletons, and witches looming up from the briny deep to swallow his father's ship. Sometimes the image of St. Hélier appeared carrying his head in his hands as in the legend after his decapitation by pirates. Next came images from books of magic spells, the devil's literature: the *Grand* and the *Petit Albert*. The menhirs, dolmens, megaliths – Faldouet's and Rocqueberg's – that picked up the energy of the cosmos and served as passages into the world of the invisible now seemed to him like cursed sites where witches flew on brooms to celebrate the witches' sabbath, evil sites that needed to be exorcised. "They cast an evil spell on my father that led him to perish along the coasts shrouded in fog; an evil curse in punishment for leaving my mother."

As the days passed, René became so tense he developed a sort of eczema, whose cause he saw as yet another curse. Then in his dreams he left on witch hunts using a book entitled *Malleus Maleficarum* to identify the witches. The book, written by a Dominican, instructed witch hunters to ask suspected witches if they were acting on the devil's orders or not. If their answer was no, they were thrown into the water: if they drowned, they were innocent; if they survived, they were guilty! Membertou tried to reason with him, but René retorted, "Magic exists, just think. Using egg whites in a glass of water, our mother predicted that a ship would sink off the coast of an island. Witches are everywhere, even in America; many of them come from Jersey and celebrate their sabbath in Salem, Massachusetts. Remember the story our grandfather told about the beautiful Acadian demoness Marie, who was burned at the stake at Port-Lajoie on Ile Saint-Jean?"

After listening to all the plausible arguments Membertou presented to assuage his fears, René could no longer believe that witches were behind the tragedy. Since he still didn't understand it, he blamed himself for his father's death. "If only I'd gone with him! If only I hadn't been jealous of Emilie and Héloïse!"

After a week's wait, there was only one thing left for them to do: return to Ruisseau. So Membertou contacted Abbot Leloutre, who organized their trip home on one of the Robin brothers' ships leaving for Boston.

Chapter 34

You have taken over our country now, and you are still
not satisfied; you want to force us to adopt your religion
…How can we ever believe you? Ever since we met, you
have robbed and abused us so often that you cannot
blame us for mistrusting you!

Brother, you say there is only one way to believe in
God! If you speak the truth, tell me why, among your
own people, there are so many different views on the
matter and so many different ways of understanding the
teachings of your book?

Since you can all read the same book, do you not all
read the same words?

– Chief Red Jacket in 1805,
quoted by Bernard Assiniwi
in *Histoire des Indiens du Haut et du Bas-Canada*

October 1760. Sieur Parisé recited Mi'kmaq prayers as
Abbot Maillard interpreted at Tjigog's gravesite. Gallien,
Gionet, Frigault, and Lentaigne lowered Tjigog's mortal
remains into the ground. Tjigog was laid out in his warrior's
costume with, at his side, his bow, his arrows, his tomahawk,
and the skin of a wolf, his totem animal. Saint-Simon gave the
signal, and a salvo of musket fire sounded, then nothing but
silence, a silence heavy with sadness, while the whole camp
bowed their heads. Lentaigne cried for the loss of a friend to
whom he owed his life. Gallien, too. Mathilde was at the

ceremony without really being there, as though she had left with Tjigog. Afterwards, she sought refuge in her tent and refused to see anyone. All night long, the wolves howled as though they wanted to signal Tjigog's passage into another world.

* * *

In Ruisseau, the *Corsaire Acadien*'s flight had been watched from a distance. Unfortunately, the English frigate stayed out of range of Ruisseau's cannons. So Saint-Jean, Jean-Baptiste, and a few Mi'kmaq gathered up supplies, furs, and tools and headed to the place where the ship had foundered, a three-hour walk from Ruisseau. The *Corsaire Acadien*'s crew was busy setting up makeshift shelters and recovering what was left of the ship. The new refugees needed assistance getting ready for the winter, which was no small task.

Most chose to stay not far from the ship, in a place baptized "Pointe-aux-Pins" for the occasion. Gabriel Albert returned to Ruisseau where Geneviève waited, crazy with worry ever since his departure for the Restigouche post. François Gionet preferred setting up on a site closer to old Saint-Jean, whom he knew from past trading. Pierre Gallien did likewise, while Blanchard, Landry, Léger, and Poirier decided to return to Bocage to take possession of the huts abandoned two years earlier during Wolfe's raid.

More news reached Ruisseau in November 1760, both bad and good. The bad news was the surrender of Montreal on September 8th and, to no one's surprise, the surrender of the Restigouche post on October 28th. The good news was that the person responsible for the deportations had died. "Ironically enough, Acadia has been the French empire's last holdout, the place where the fleur-de-lys was lowered for the last time, to be replaced by the Union Jack[1]," Saint-Jean muttered.

Dangeac refused to believe Montreal had fallen and kept the English commander Major Elliot under guard for a few

---

1. Great Britain's flag created in 1606 by James I.

more days before releasing him; he negotiated to have the supplies in the storehouses left behind for the Acadians.

"If France wins the war in Europe, New France may still be returned to the French," Saint-Jean told himself. But, in his heart of hearts, he didn't believe it.

The good news was that Governor Charles Lawrence, who had ordered the deportations, had died suddenly in Halifax as he was leaving a banquet marking the Montreal victory.

"He probably died of gluttony," Saint-Jean commented.

"Deportation doesn't sit well on the stomach," Angélique added.

Saint-Jean was increasingly worried about the prolonged absence of Joseph and his children. But there was no time to dwell on their absence or do any soul-searching because haste was needed to build shelters before the winter cold and snow blew in. Everyone pitched in to chop down the pine, spruce, and birch trees and square them off to make walls. Then all the cracks had to be filled with moss and clay, and the walls and roofs had to be covered with birchbark before the chimneys could be installed. The Acadians were as handy with an axe as the European nobles with a sword, and the work was done in a spirit of cooperation with no time wasted. Anyone not helping with the actual building was kept busy finding winter supplies, a major concern since Ruisseau's inhabitants' supplies of vegetables, fish, and game were insufficient for all the mouths that needed to be fed. More beechnuts were gathered – to replace wheat flour among other things – but it still wasn't enough. The best they could hope for now was a good hunting season.

* * *

The Robin brothers' ship bringing René and Membertou home managed to elude the enemy ships and approach Canada. It was flying the British flag, but the crew was ready to raise the French flag should they cross the path of French warships, a highly useful ruse often resorted to. The ship stopped off in Saint-Pierre-et-Miquelon to stock up on drinking water. The tiny islands no bigger than the palm of a hand that bordered Newfoundland had been ceded by France to England during the signing of the Treaty of Utrecht in 1713. Although a few deportees were being held prisoner on the island, René and Membertou had too much to deal with with their own grief to spare more than a passing thought for them. Finally, in mid-November, the ship dropped anchor in Ruisseau. The trees had lost their leaves, the ground was waterlogged, and the sky was grey. René and Membertou's mood matched the grey, sombre landscape.

The joy at the travellers' return soon turned to dismay when the news of Joseph's death spread. Angélique didn't seem to realize her husband would not be returning; in her denial she didn't shed a tear. At first, Geneviève, Josette, and Saint-Jean also rejected the idea that Joseph had perished on his ship. But their denial soon turned to anger at the injustice of such a tragedy, for which they blamed the heavens. Their anger gave way to sorrow and a certain peace. As for René, it hurt to see his indifference to his sisters, his grandfather, and even his beloved mother, buried as he was under images of drownings, shipwrecks, and bodies littering the shore. His distress was so painful to see that it shook everyone else out of his or her sorrow. The shaman Fiery Elouèzes held exorcism sessions and tried to communicate with René's totem animal, the loon, but in vain. Foaming Bear spun until he couldn't breathe anymore, Jean-Baptiste told native legends from the Great Lakes region, the tribe held palavers, dances, and energy circles to no avail; René was unreachable. Angélique was told to give him ice-water baths, but she couldn't see the use. Something had to be done, but what? René had lost a disturbing amount of weight and was no longer eating.

Saint-Jean hadn't been appointed sagamo for nothing. He had dug deep to help René on two other occasions in the past. First, when the boy was only seven and refused to go to sleep because of his fear of the dark and his frequent nightmares of hordes of white ghosts come to spirit him away.

Saint-Jean could never determine the exact cause of his grandson's fear, but knowing René identified strongly with the native hero known as Tukvikgug, he sat him on his lap one night when the boy couldn't sleep and told him a story.

"A young princess by the name of Maïka lived on the summits of the Chic-Choc mountains in the Gaspé and reigned over the tribe of white ghosts. The monster Abyss, who lives in the centre of earth, kidnapped her and held her prisoner in a black cave on Ile de Pokesudie. To free her, the winged ghosts called on Tukvikgug for help. After a terrible fight, he brought down the monster, but only a child has the power to rescue the princess, which is why winged ghosts come for you at night."

"It must be so dark inside that cave!"

"Don't worry. I have a talisman from Tukvikgug that will protect you. It's a small, engraved silver disk set with stones that shine in the dark. Once you're in the cave, Tukvikgug will sing of his exploits fighting Abyss; you just have to follow his voice."

Bolstered by the promised virtues of the talisman and his hero's song, René imagined himself entering the cave to rescue Maïka. In the story his grandfather had him act out, the fairy of Light appeared to him to explain that Darkness is nothing but a time to sleep and dream of the Light. She also assured him that because of his courage, from then on, darkness would no longer threaten him; on the contrary, in darkness his strength would be increased tenfold. In return for his services, she promised to grant him one wish. His wish had been to accompany Joseph to Quebec, and it was granted. From then on, his fears disappeared. The next year, he started wetting his bed. Saint-Jean discovered that the root of the problem was quite simple: a bear leaving hibernation had surprised René peeing behind a tree and René had had to run for his life to avoid being devoured. The shame he felt at not being able to control himself at night only served to aggravate the boy's shock and fear. Old Saint-Jean took René with him one morning, and they spent all day peeing everywhere in fun: on trees, leaves, flowers, rocks. They took great pleasure in turning on fountains, geysers, springs, and droplets. René never wet his bed again.

But this time was more serious, and Saint-Jean spent a long while mulling over what he should do. On a late November day when the sea was not too rough, he took René out to his observation post on Ile Caraquet. René loved the spot because of the feeling of total freedom it gave him, like that of the seagulls soaring over the Baye des Chaleurs.

"I know you miss your father terribly," his grandfather ventured, "but what's the point of letting yourself die?"

The dialogue had begun and by roundabout means old Saint-Jean managed to convince René to share the thoughts tormenting him. "If only I had gone to Guernsey with my father, nothing would have happened... I didn't want to meet Héloïse, and I was jealous of Emilie."

Saint-Jean knew there was no point trying to reason with René or show him how absurd his idea was, and how it fed his sense of guilt. To be certain he understood what was troubling his grandson, he tried to clarify what had happened. "Would the ship have left any later if you had gone with your father? Could you have stopped the storm from breaking by some magic spell?"

René shook his head sadly in response.

"Let's try something. First, close your eyes and imagine a pink loon swimming on a blue lake..."

René obeyed, outwardly unenthusiastic but intrigued nonetheless.

"Now, imagine your father dressed like a privateer and make him come to you. On a thunderbird, a beluga or in a pink bubble: you choose."

René quite liked their imaginary game. He chose the thunderbird, representing lightning, and tried to focus on the image. Following his grandfather's instructions, he asked his father's forgiveness for all the mischief he'd ever done.

"What did he say?"

"That he loves me and forgives me..."

"Now ask him if he wants you to let yourself waste away. Doesn't he have a mission to entrust you with?"

René concentrated. This took a bit longer and was a bit harder. Finally, René acknowledged his father wanted him to live a full life and look after his mother and sisters.

"You're gifted, my boy. Let's see if you can enter the pink bubble with the thunderbird and sit next to your father... That's it, he's sitting beside you, giving you love and strength. He's making you laugh. Taking you to unknown worlds. From now on, whenever you need him, just make the pink bubble come to you."

A feeling of peace washed over René.

"There's one more step. Imagine a black bubble now. Remember how darkness represents strength, a reprieve from the light. Put your sorrow, your badness, and your doubts inside that bubble. Then let it fly over Miscou and burst over evil Gougou's head. The fairy of Light will show herself and make the pink bubble appear at the tip of her wand."

René said nothing, fascinated by his grandfather's tale.

"For one week, three times a day, take yourself off to a quiet place and play this game," Saint-Jean ordered. "I just about forgot. I have a surprise for you." He took his grandson by the hand and led him to an enclosure where a young, quite tame-looking moose was gamboling. As they entered, the animal drew closer. "You can harness him up to ride along the paths in the summer or on the bay in the winter."

René could feel new life welling up inside him already. He baptized his new friend "Oregnac," the Basque word for "moose." Within a few days, René had undergone an amazing transformation and begun to smile again.

Membertou's many ordeals had matured him. The superficiality and hypocrisy of "the greats of this world," Aglaë's desertion of him, and Joseph's death had shattered his illusions. But he found comfort in turning to his native religious beliefs. "God gave us a different coloured skin and way of life. Since he made us to be different, it's only normal that we have our own view of him and celebrate him in our own way."

He began to take an interest in the girls of the tribe once again.

As for Angélique, she still refused to believe Joseph was dead. "I'll believe it when I see him in his coffin," she said.

Her husband had been away so often and for such long periods that this just seemed like one more time. Her only outward signs of distress were a slight weight gain from all the sweets she'd been eating and a certain feverishness during her long walks when she whipped the air with a piece of driftwood in time to her steps. However, she was thrilled to see the renewed zest for life René had... her son who so resembled Joseph. Her beloved child threw himself enthusiastically into helping gather together the provisions that old Saint-Jean sent to the refugees.

René began to feel tender and protective toward Mathilde. He developed an almost irresistible need to look after the orphan and comfort her for the loss of Tjigog. René knew that, without his grandfather's help, he too would have let himself die. One evening, when Mathilde's aunt and uncle were out, he visited her in her hut. She didn't say a word, just sat at the table in darkness, indifferent to the world around her. René lit a small lamp, a hollow turnip filled with codliver oil that had a lid with a hole pierced in it for the woollen wick. A flickering flame lit her sad, impenetrable face. Careful not to rush her, René only spoke about himself, his trip to Europe, the palace of Versailles, his father, his grief, whatever crossed his mind. He knew Mathilde needed a presence and a voice to bring her back to the life that frightened her so. At evening's end, he could see her eyes held an invitation for him to return. That night, he fell asleep with joy in his heart.

* * *

During the winter of 1761, the weather was mild and the hunt plentiful, which meant Ruisseau's inhabitants were able to feed the refugees, most of whom had nothing but the rags they wore on their backs. Saint-Simon took pleasure in the hunt, especially since old Saint-Jean gave him what was a priceless gift for a hunter: three fine dogs to help him track moose. Not wanting to lose any of his prestige, the shaman Fiery Elouèzes cooked a dog in Saint-Simon's honour, paying him the tribute of serving him this meat fit for the gods. The officer appreciated the mark of esteem, especially since the meat truly was succulent. In his free time, Saint-Simon tried to train franc-tireurs[2] and talked of strategies and ambushes. Pierre Gallien was interested in strategy as well, but for other purposes. He hoped to find the best way to catch Angélique's eye. René realized his intentions and didn't approve of the match since he knew that Gallien's constant attention meant the man would one day take Joseph's place.

At winter's end, Sieur de Niverville and his twelve soldiers in Miramichi finally learned the news of New France's surrender. They surrendered their arms and returned to France. Sieur de Saint-Simon decided to follow suit as soon as the ice melted since he refused to accept defeat. He left by boat for Halifax, knowing that under the agreements reached during the surrender of the Restigouche post, officers and soldiers were entitled to a safe-conduct for their return to the mother country. Several soldiers accompanied him. One officer, however, Sieur Parisé, decided to stay behind in Caraquet, and two soldiers were granted permission to settle there: Chapeau, who settled below Ruisseau, and Bertran[3], who built a hut at the head of a small creek two leagues west of Bocage. Before leaving, Saint-Simon gave a Spanish pistol from among his belongings to Saint-Jean as well as several books on the history of France to François Gionet, whom he greatly appreciated. The latter was touched; his memories of his homeland were still very much alive. He was forced to leave France at the age of fifteen, having been condemned to exile for poaching on a nobleman's land. He had signed up for thirty-six months on a merchant ship; however, he fled the ship when it landed in Gaspé.

May was a time of departures and new beginnings. Olivier Blanchard decided to settle a dozen leagues or more to the northwest of Ruisseau at the mouth of the Nipisiguit River, which he reached with his four boys and his daughter on board his fifteen-ton schooner. Pierre Gallien chose to live on Ile Caraquet, in the ruins of the former home of Seigneur Denis Riverin, who had headed up the fishing empire at the

---

2. Guerrilla fighters.
3. At a place known today as Bertrand village.

turn of the century in the Baye des Chaleurs. Gabriel Albert, François Gionet, Louis de Lentaigne, and Michel Galland settled in the surrounding area.

During moments of leisure, René took Mathilde to the island observation post to rest and admire the blue sky, the sea, and the mountains of the Gaspé in the distance. And to accustom Mathilde to the love he felt for her. His love made him see with new eyes the shades of blue that enveloped them on the island.

Cod fishing was in full swing for Jean-Baptiste, Gabriel Albert, and Pierre Gallien. In the space of two years, the price paid in Quebec for a hundredweight of cod had gone from 25 to 250 livres. But it was a tough life. They had to run a line down the length of the boat and bait it after each catch. The line burned their hands, and the sea water opened up old wounds. Their rough clothes were far from waterproof. It took a great deal of courage or passion to spend such long hours in wet clothes. Not everyone was cut out for the job! Pierre Frigault, for example, was more used to a soldier's tasks. As for Alexis Landry, his interests lay elsewhere, in working the land to reap its rewards.

"There are dykes on the Rivière Nord. We could repair them and set up aboiteaux," he suggested. "We can let water in from the river occasionally to deposit a layer of silt on the land."

"The land is fertile," Léger agreed. He could already imagine hay, wheat, and oats standing as tall as a man.

"We'll have misotte[4] for the livestock," Charles Poirier noted. "That way we'll be following the same cultivation practices as in Grand'Pré, Port-Royal, and Memramcouk."

Thanks to the aboiteaux, the Acadians didn't have to clear the forest to cultivate the land as had been done in New France. There was a spot with aboiteaux in Caraquet along the Rivière Nord that predated the arrival of the first settlers. Some thought the aboiteaux were the work of Vikings, who had come to these parts circa 1000 A.D. looking for land for

---

4. Wild hay.

vineyards. It was known with certainty that they had stayed for a while since the blood of Angélique's native ancestors had been joined with theirs. Then conflicts arose. It wasn't known exactly why, but the scarcity of women was suspected. The Vikings left after first cultivating the meadows. Those were the aboiteaux Landry referred to. All that was needed was to make them operational again, which Landry did with Léger and Poirier.

The summer of 1761 unfolded in a climate of uncertainty and anxiety about the fate the English had in store for them. Their choices were between exposing themselves to deportation, seeking exile in Quebec, hiding out in the woods, or living freely on their land while hoping against hope that the conqueror would leave them in peace. In the ruins of the former Esnault seigneurie on the shores of the Poquemouche, Saint-Jean had set up supply caches in which he stored cured meat and fish. Jean-Baptiste had travelled to Raymond Bourdages' grain mill in Bonaventure for flour that Bourdages had bought from the king's stores before the Restigouche post fell. The women put up preserves: blueberries, strawberries, raspberries, wild cherries, blackberries, and cranberries, including grisettes[5]. Angélique showed Mathilde how to preserve the grisettes, which made extraordinary pies. Since wax was hard to come by as a seal, a bit of alcohol was poured on top of the contents of each jar before the lids were closed. The alcohol both preserved the contents and gave them a delicious taste.

* * *

Pierre du Calvet, the former Restigouche quartermaster, arrived in late July on a sloop called the *Sainte-Anne*. The instructions for his mission came from Murray, the governor of Quebec – the same man who had laid waste to Miramichi – and were signed by him:

---

5. Smaller than cranberries, pink with grey spots.

In the service of His British Majesty,
to the principal inhabitants of the Baye des Chaleurs,
Restigouche, Miramichi

Quebec, July 7, 1761

Sieur Calvet has been sent to ascertain your numbers and the
quantity of ships needed to transport your people to Quebec. Your
ships in working condition will be used first for the purpose of the
expedition...

There is no need to describe the dismay of the 174 people who comprised the thirty-seven families in Caraquet. Some said it was better to place themselves under Governor Murray's protection than to wait for the arrival of Attila's hordes from Halifax. But for that, they needed to find ships to take them there! Others refused to leave the Baye des Chaleurs. Almost everyone was wary. Anyone who had captured ships with their privateers in the spring didn't want to give up their ships. Several either refused to have their names appear on the census or gave false information. Most didn't mention their boats for fear they'd be confiscated.

Saint-Jean trusted Du Calvet, so the problem didn't lie there. Two years earlier, he had sold him two oxen when Du Calvet was transporting English prisoners to Halifax. Du Calvet even wrote in his journal:

"I escorted them myself with sixty men in a boat as far as Ile de Quarraquet, where having had two oxen slaughtered, I gave them provisions and sent them to Halifax."

Yet Saint-Jean was worried. He did not want to leave, but he felt he should consult his loved ones. A family council was held and they all finally agreed to write to Governor Murray and tell him of their decision.

Chapter 35

This man, old Saint-Jean, is a native of old France. He
married an Indian and has lived here near fifty years.
— the merchant Smethurst during his trip
to Caraquet in October 1761

...Now is the time to evacuate that country entirely of the
neutral French and to make the Indians of it our own.
— Letter from Governor Murray
to Colonel Amherst, April 18, 1761

I s the territory of the Baye des Chaleurs under the jurisdiction of Halifax or Quebec? Acadia or Canada?

The question preoccupied the inhabitants of the Baye des
Chaleurs. Although it seemed innocent enough at first, the
answer would nevertheless determine whether or not they
would be among the deportees. If they were under Quebec's
jurisdiction, that meant their troubles were over because they
would be protected by the clauses of the general surrender of
Canada signed by Vaudreuil in Montreal in the fall of 1760. If
they were under Halifax's jurisdiction, the opposite was true.
During Governor Nicolas Denys' time, the former Acadia
included the territories[1] of the Atlantic regions as far as Cap

---

1. New Brunswick, Nova Scotia, Prince Edward Island, part of Maine and the
Gaspé.

Desrosiers past the Gaspé, and therefore all the Acadians of the Baye des Chaleurs could be subject to deportation. Whatever the case, as Pierre Du Calvet explained, they must travel to Quebec at Governor Murray's request to seek refuge there.

"Why don't they let us live in peace along our coasts?" Jean-Baptiste asked.

"Because while they wait for the war to end in Europe, the English who want to trade in the Baye des Chaleurs are afraid of harassment from Acadian privateers. It's a question of big money!"

"Can the governor's word be trusted?" Léger asked.

Saint-Jean proclaimed, "The word of an Englishman is never to be trusted!"

"I don't think the governor approves of the deportations," Du Calvet replied. "In any case, you'll be treated decently in Quebec, and you will have the same rights as the inhabitants of New France."

But Gabriel Giraud – Saint-Jean – had already made up his mind; no matter what jurisdiction he was under – Quebec's, Halifax's, or Rome's – he was going to stay put. Most of those who had taken part in the Restigouche battle were of the same mind. Saint-Jean retired to his study to write General Murray using his goose quill and parchment paper bearing the coat of arms of his family – originally from Normandy – that he kept religiously in his chests. He thought of basing his argument on the many years he'd lived in the Caraquet region. There were many who could corroborate his presence here, including the Louisbourg engineer Sieur l'Hermite, who had passed by in 1724 looking for trees to make masts for French warships; Saint-Jean's hospitality had so impressed him that he wrote of him in his journal. Saint-Jean could have written at length about his years trading in Miramichi, or described the thousand and one events of his life among the natives in Caraquet and Poquemouche starting as far back as 1730, his dealings with merchants from France, Quebec, England, and the American colonies or his efforts to attract settlers to the Baye des Chaleurs. Fearing, however, that too long a dissertation would not be read, he wrote a simple letter.

Karaquet, August 27, 1761

Monseigneur,
In humble submission, I perused the letter with which you were gracious enough to honour our inhabitants last July 7th. It is my honour to advise you, Monseigneur, that for more than thirty years now I have lived in Karaquet, while the Acadians have only been here for two or three years. Based on my long years of owner-ship, Monseigneur, I hereby take the liberty of asking that I be left here with my family...

He would rather have told the governor to go to hell. However, reminding himself that necessity knows no law, he overrode his principles and handed the letter to Joseph Landry and Jeanne Robichaud, who hoped to find asylum in Quebec. Angélique had reluctantly given in to her father's request that they all remain, despite her fear that one day she would see her children deported or scattered to the four winds.

Although the inhabitants of Bocage were afraid the Halifax executioners would again try to lay claim to the former Acadia, by force of habit, they continued to stall and leave as much room for latitude as possible. They adopted the age-old strategy of playing for time whereby they had originally extended their stay in Acadia until 1755. However, the strat-egy had also sealed their eyes and ears, and had kept them from seeing or hearing the coming calamities until it was too late. Now, after much agonizing, they finally sent the follow-ing letter to Governor Murray:

...We would have been delighted to be able to execute them (the orders) immediately... however, since we are unable to build craft (boats) at present and the season is too far advanced for us to reach our destination without seeing our families perish, we would beg that you allow us to spend the winter in Caraquet... having worked to put aside a few supplies of roots and dried fish to try to sit out the winter, we assure you that come spring we will do everything

possible to make our way to Quebec... Be assured of our ever-present desire to execute the orders you deem fit to send us...

And so on and so on, forever seeking a better alibi, for they were in no position to be sending abusive letters.

The interminable discussions and parley around whether to leave or dig in took on epic proportions. Saint-Jean proposed staying put. He saw himself as offering the wisest solution, like King Solomon, because he had spent close to half a century slaving away on this land. But not everyone agreed. Léger suggested, "We could join the French troops in Montreal; we could fight better there than here."

"But Vaudreuil has already signed Canada's surrender," Gabriel Albert retorted.

Alexis Landry harboured a secret hope that he would be confirmed as the one to lead his people to the Promised Land. "With all the resources it has in the sea, the wild hay from the meadows, and the abundance of our forests, Bocage is our biblical Jerusalem," he said. "While waiting for the storm to pass, why not move to Bonaventure and its protected harbour? Several refugees from the Restigouche post have settled upriver with supplies and schooners."

Membertou swore by the exploits of the great warrior Kao-Coke and did not agree. "We can hide out just as well here as in Bonaventure. Moreover, in Ruisseau we always know which way is north. All we have to do is look toward the sea to see the Ursa Major and the North Star. We've lived on this land for centuries, and no person, no god, no devil will make us leave. If we must, the men will fight."

His remark was an indirect barb at Landry and his clan. Alexis was beginning to feel the need to flex his muscles, he whose name of Celtic and Germanic origin[2] meant "rich or powerful land," or "sovereign of the land and lord of the manor," although malicious gossip claimed his name was nothing but a derivation of "lavandière" or "washerwoman," designating the women who washed laundry by hand, and which, worse yet, had been anglicized to "launder."

---

2. "Land rick."

"Easy to say when you've never known exile, which you obviously haven't. We've been chased across America for over five years, made to bury in foreign lands our children who died of hunger and privation. When our families are reduced to slavery in the marshes of Georgia, it will be too late for philosophizing. Yes, we must fight, but not while we're still looking after children who are two, five, ten years old. We must be cautious and ensure our people's survival."

He was beginning to sway the others. Unaccustomed to any challenges to his authority, Saint-Jean could feel his ears turning red. "Tordieu[3], Membertou is right," he swore. "The English would have retreated in 1755 if you had fought. Here, we know all the best places an ambush can be launched from in the forest. Moreover, we have cannons, let's use them! You Léger, you can apply the science you learned from your soldier ancestor to defend our coasts," he proposed ironically.

Frigault, Albert, Gallien, Gionet, De Lentaigne, Morais, and Parisé – the Acadians of Norman descent – supported him, moved by their desire for revenge. The conflict between the Acadian inhabitants from Nova Scotia and the new arrivals, the Normans from the Baye des Chaleurs' region of Acadia, was becoming increasingly acrimonious. Since they all saw themselves as saviours – a characteristic trait of Normans – the result was chaos like nothing the seagulls had ever seen before. No one knows who started it precisely, but the people from Bocage called the Ruisseau inhabitants mixed bloods and Creoles while the latter called the former jealous, whining gossips.

"Bunch of cowards!" the people from Ruisseau cried, proud to be descendants of the man who had brought England to heel, William the Conqueror.

"Gang of fornicators!" retorted the Bocage crowd, who scorned life with the Mi'kmaq in Ruisseau as being one long orgy. Although the native peoples were their allies, the Bocage bunch didn't always look favourably on the intermingling of blood. They saw themselves as the true descendants of the

---

3. A Norman-Viking swear word, the god Thor.

founders of Acadia. Being from Grand'Pré, Port-Royal, and Memramcouk, they believed a true Acadian had to be a farmer, not a fisherman. They hailed from Poitou originally and had lived in the country for generations, which was not the case, they pointed out, for the Norman soldiers, fishermen, and adventurers who, to top it all off, entered into intimate relations with the Indian women.

Angélique could not tolerate the insults being levelled at her people. It should be said in her defence that she also had a terrible toothache, which a clove had done nothing to eradicate. She grabbed a woman from Bocage by her chignon. The fray degenerated into fisticuffs and ripped bodices, a fight punctuated by shouts and jeers in accents from Poitou and Normandy.

But at least two people were untouched by the brouhaha, the lovestruck René and Mathilde. Their month of August played out deliciously as they picked from the blueberry and wild strawberry suckers the fruit they would put up for winter. Far from prying eyes, they came to know each other to the cicada's chant. Sometimes, they canoed to Ile Chipagan to gather raspberries near Nicolas Denys' former manor that had been built in 1645 and was now falling apart. The vineyard and a few pear trees cast some shade along its rough-hewn stone walls two feet thick; inside, the walls were made of clay mixed with a bit of wild hay. Broken bits of white and blue ceramic tile were strewn over the floor. Some fishing tackle lay in a corner of the main room, forgotten there by seasonal fishermen, along with empty bottles of rum. Once they'd filled their baskets to the brim, the lovebirds settled in to smoke a clay pipe, their gaze turned to Ile Miscou where four Jesuit missionaries were laid to rest. Without exchanging a word, their warm bodies spoke to each other. René told his lover about the island:

"It has a long history; Indians have been coming here for thousands of years. At low tide, you can see the wreckage of a Viking ship. Cartier came through here looking for the passage to the Indies. Early in the last century, the Jesuits founded the Saint-Charles mission here, and merchants set up a trading post for fur traders, whalers, and walrus hunters."

"So this part of Acadia is as old as Port-Royal?"

"Yes, Basques, Bretons, and Normans came here. The Normans had an easier time than those who came from Poitou since they were accustomed to the winter cold."

"Why isn't there anything here today?"

"In the last part of the last century, a gunner drying gunpowder accidentally set fire to it when he lit his pipe. The island was razed. Then Governor Denys died, and the fishing trade gradually began to decline. There are nothing but ruins to show this was once a fishing and trading hub — broken-down ovens and whale ribs bleached by the salt and the sea. Others say Gougou took revenge on the residents since it's rumoured she hides out somewhere on the island."

The sun had dropped closer to the waves. It was time to return to Ruisseau. They skirted Miscou with their little sailboat. A few fathoms from the coast, a bubble of fresh water no bigger than two fists emerged from the sea bottom; a mysterious spring that provided fresh water for a radius of twenty paces. They filled a barrel full. René was reminded of his grandfather who, when he first came to this country, had worked in Miscou for the Comte de Saint-Pierre, who organized the trade in seacow oil and ivory. As for Mathilde, she let her thoughts wander as her gaze swept past the narrows to the plain draped in mauve heather, seagrass, brush, marshes, lagoons, and secrets.

"I would love to live on this island with you," she confided. "We could make it into our kingdom and have children living on every small inlet."

On their return that evening, they radiated happiness. Angélique watched the pair in amusement, pleased to see her son's happiness and to know that Mathilde had been healed by the magic between them.

Chapter 36

... destroy on this coast the lair of the French vermin, who caused such damage over the past two to three years by intercepting our ships headed for Halifax, Louisbourg, and the shores of the St. Lawrence.
— *The Boston Newsletter*, December 10, 1761

The small havens of peace in Ruisseau and Bocage were nevertheless disturbed in the fall of 1761. Justice Belcher, Lawrence's successor, had entrusted the Beauséjour fort commander, Captain Roderick MacKenzie, with a mission: expel the Acadians settled in Miramichi, the Baye des Chaleurs, and the Gaspé.

The loutish captain arrived without warning in October with his regiment of Highlanders. His raid was especially effective because of Du Calvet's actions, which had calmed the inhabitants' suspicions. Uncle Chiasson, Aunt Anne, Joseph Boudreau, and his wife Jeanne-Marie had all gone to Chipagan for a funeral in the Brideau family. For some, by the time they saw the English soldiers landing in Chipagan it was already too late; they had no time to hide. Pierre Douaron[1] and his wife Anne Forest ended up in the filthy holds of English ships. Captain MacKenzie forged ahead until he was within view of Île Caraquet. Morais, Parisé, and several Mi'kmaq,

---

1. Doiron. He was born in Menoudy, which means "Hand of God."

including Membertou, were busy curing herring on the beach when the English ship loomed into sight. Membertou suggested they use the evil Gougou stratagem. "Let's put up the scarecrow we made for the religious ceremony facing into the wind. Her gigantic limbs will flap around while we yell and shout."

To deceive the English even further, Membertou and Sly Fox paddled toward the English ship looking suitably terrified and so incited the English to give the island a wide berth.

In Ruisseau, Pierre Frigault saw the enemy ship and had time to warn its inhabitants before fleeing farther up the Poquemouche. He was accompanied by Josette, the young woman he was courting, and they found shelter in the ruins of Sieur Hénault de Barbaucannes' residence, the physician from Tours who, a century earlier, had settled in the region with his native wife. Having hidden the cannons on the coast, Saint-Jean was able to sink an English ship with Foaming Bear's help, but given the enemy's strength in numbers, he decided to join Frigault, together with his family, and set up camp next to the caches of food and gunpowder.

The Cormier, Landry, Léger, and Poirier families left the maple, beech, and birch forests of Bocage under cover of night and crossed the Baye des Chaleurs on their way to Bonaventure. They settled farther up the Bonaventure River, next to Raymond Bourdages' grain mill, where several Restigouche refugees and soldiers had already arrived, their dwellings camouflaged so as not to be seen from the shore.

Some twenty leagues to the southwest of Ruisseau, the English captured Olivier Blanchard, his wife, his daughter, and his four sons, who had found refuge in the ruins of Nicolas Denys' last residence in Nipisiguit. He might have been able to withstand an attack by MacKenzie's roughneck soldiers if he had armed the small fort in time, since it had four bastions, a palisade of eighteen-foot posts, and six cannons. But he was only able to get off a few shots. Jean-Baptiste, Gabriel Albert, and Pierre Gallien, who'd come to trade their products in Nipisiguit, were still on board their schooner when they heard the cannon fire. They had to abandon ship and flee into the woods when an English ship bore down on them. They were not the only ones in hiding. They met a man by the name of Gamaliel Smethurst, a New England merchant, who had a permit from Governor Murray to begin trading in the region. Smethurst was afraid of Acadian reprisals and terrified by the idea he might serve as a scapegoat. Luckily for him, Jean-Baptiste knew him well, having seen him often in Ruisseau. Moreover, Smethurst was quick to swear by the gods that he wholly disapproved of the expulsion methods. *Right, because it's not good for trade*, Jean-Baptiste thought.

But there was no time for lengthy explanations. So Gabriel Albert unearthed a rowboat, which must have belonged to the Blanchard family, and on that dark and frigid fall night, they set sail for Poquemouche.

Seeing Smethurst, the Poquemouche natives' first desire was to scalp him. He had a very hard time convincing them – particularly the giant warrior Ferocious Caribou – of his good faith.

"You pretend to trade with the French in Nipisiguit so you can gather them together in one place for the English to take prisoner," Ferocious Caribou growled threateningly.

Moaning River was of the same opinion. He traced a circle on the ground, using a dot for the city of Quebec and a rectangle for Halifax.

"Say my little finger represents Quebec and my thumb Halifax, Poquemouche is in the middle; we'll be invaded in no time," he predicted. He then demonstrated by bringing his thumb and little finger together.

Jean-Baptiste and Saint-Jean were made to vouch for Smethurst's loyalty.

MacKenzie left nothing but desolation in his wake. The invaders had destroyed the watercraft and dwellings and carried off supplies, barrels of cured fish, hundredweights of dried fish, and even beds. Their plan was to force the refugees to turn themselves in. Jean-Baptiste was devastated to hear his fishing facilities had been destroyed. His cod empire had been reduced to a pile of ashes! But he had no time for self-pity because Membertou had just arrived with news of the Baye des Chaleurs' Acadians, who had been captured by the English.

"They piled close to eight hundred Acadians into their filthy holds. The season is too far gone for them to continue their raids; they're ready to lift anchor for Halifax. We have to do something," he moaned.

Saint-Jean felt a crushing weight on his shoulders. "How can we free those poor men, women, and children locked up in the holds?" he wondered aloud in despair.

To try to redeem himself, Smethurst suggested, "Why not negotiate with MacKenzie?

"That might not be a bad idea," Jean-Baptiste said. "In the spring, MacKenzie sent all the Indian chiefs a letter saying they wouldn't be disturbed if they wanted to trade with Fort Beauséjour. The letter should have been addressed to my father but was handed to me, maybe because I'm considered to be an Indian on my mother's side. We decided not to act on it in case it was a trap…"

"His actions don't make him seem like someone who's willing to negotiate," Saint-Jean pointed out.

"I know the man," Smethurst protested. "He's greedy. The main purpose of his expedition in the Baye des Chaleurs is to line his pockets. He'd do anything for money and to divert trade from the French… Make him an offer, you'll see."

In the end, they had no alternative, and the solution was obvious. They had to visit the invaders on their ships before they left the Baye des Chaleurs for Halifax.

Saint-Jean spent as little time as possible with the slippery snake MacKenzie. He earned the latter's full attention when he brought out the emerald from the island treasure. Saint-Jean told him a necklace of precious stones would be his if he freed the Acadians. MacKenzie risked facing a firing squad if he returned to Halifax without any prisoners, but he planned to tell his superiors that the ship's condition and the early freeze-up prevented him from fulfilling his task. That way, he could free 452 Acadians. However, the 335 unfortunate prisoners he planned to deliver to the Halifax and Fort Beauséjour prisons were not as lucky. Of course, he kept the leaders of the resistance as captives: Olivier Blanchard, Armand Bugeau, Jean Cormier, Joseph Dugas, Michel Doucet, Pierre Gaudet, Jean Gauthier, Joseph Guilbeau, Paul Landry, Paul Le Blanc, René Terriot, Joseph Richard… Most had been captured with their boats outfitted for privateering. In Saint-Jean's view, as long as just one Acadian from the Baye des Chaleurs was still held prisoner, the battle had not been won. From that moment on, he began questioning the wisdom of his decision to stay in Ruisseau with his clan.

During this time, a few fishermen who hadn't heard about MacKenzie's raid were on board the Sikitoumeg exploring the fishing grounds between Tracadie and the Tabusintac River, not far from Miramichi. Zacharie Douaron, sweetheart of Anne, one of Françoise's daughters, was among them. He was back from a journey he'd made to flee the deportations and find members of his family. The journey had taken him first to Ile Madame, then to Ile Saint-Jean and, from there, to Quebec, Restigouche, Gaspeg, and Caraquet. His rough-and-ready crew also included Marie, Françoise's other daughter, with her sweetheart, François Gionet, René and Mathilde, as well as Lentaigne and a Mi'kmaq nicknamed St. Peter of the Rock because of his attachment to the church. As a young child, he had been cured of smallpox by baptism when his mother plunged him into a basin of holy water. He wasn't the first native to believe in the therapeutic virtues of baptism. Ever since, he had worn a small bag around his neck, which held, he said, a letter from Jesus Christ to the Pope exhorting the native peoples not to trade with the English nor buy brandy from them. St. Peter of the Rock, who could be quite a stickler about his beliefs, pointed out with a mischievous wink that the "bull" did not prohibit trade with the French.

When the English arrived, René and Mathilde were alone on board Douaron's ship since the rest of the crew had decided to help themselves to some of their catch and set out to find a sheltered spot in some cove along the coast to make a fire and then cook a fat cod and strings of herring on which they feasted then napped for the rest of the day. This was a common practice among fishermen, who regularly came up with all kinds of excuses for their meagre catch. On shore, Lentaigne was the first to see the dreaded English sail, but although he shouted until his throat burned and blew loudly into his borgot[2] shell, the two lovers were oblivious, as though off in another world.

* * *

When the sad news of their capture reached Ruisseau, the spectre of death appeared in Saint-Jean's eyes. René meant more to him than life itself; he was the one who, as the male child, would carry on the family name, especially since Membertou seemed unready to start a family. Saint-Jean spent his nights tossing and turning and his days muttering, blaming himself for the misfortune that had befallen all the poor souls of the world.

Angélique, too, was a pitiful sight. She kept her head covered with a large handkerchief – called the Norman scarf – that local women often wore; dressed in black, an impenetrable expression on her face, she looked like an old woman marked by suffering. Gallien tried to comfort her, but had neither the proper means nor words. "They'll be signing a peace treaty soon," he assured her. "There have been no deportations to the American colonies since last year. The English need the Acadians to repair the aboiteaux that the tides in the Baie Française destroyed."

His arguments fell on deaf ears, especially since Angélique had read in the cards that there would be a death in her family. Then she had strange dreams several nights in a row during which she left her body and found herself in a damp dungeon where a feverish, cough-ridden René was being held prisoner. Gallien kept trying to tell her it was only her imagination, but she was convinced he was ill and dying.

Membertou decided something had to be done. He gathered together the best warriors – Ferocious Caribou, Foaming Bear, Moaning River, and Raging Tuna. They would walk to

---

2. A seashell that carries sound great distances.

Halifax, one hundred leagues to the south of Ruisseau, in an attempt to free René, Mathilde, and the other prisoners. Angélique wanted to accompany them, but Membertou refused. "Your father needs you."

Three unmarried men decided to join the group – Frigault, Douaron, and Gionet – leaving behind them a worried Josette, Anne, and Marie. They left with Saint-Jean's blessing in late November, their snowshoes, axes, and rifles slung across their shoulder. After hugging the shoreline of the frozen bay for three days, they arrived in a deserted Miramichi. Beausoleil-Broussard, with what was left of his family, was busy roasting a bear quarter.

"Come with us," Membertou insisted. "We're going to sow some destruction in their camp when they least expect it."

"I can't. This spring, I'm going to refloat a small schooner the English damaged..."

In other words, any excuse would do.

"You do know the English have sworn they'll have your hide? Right now, Rangers on snowshoes are surely on a mission to find you."

Beausoleil couldn't deny that fact, and eventually he agreed to follow Membertou with a dozen or so of his own men.

* * *

Despite Angélique's prayers and the shaman's incantations, Saint-Jean died in January 1762. The cards hadn't lied about a loved one's death; however, it was Angélique's father, not her son, who died. When old Saint-Jean's death was announced, the Mi'kmaq started crying "Ou-ay! Ou-ay! Ou-ay!" to summon his spirit. Then they undid their braids and let their hair fall to their shoulders. Afterwards, they sat on the ground together in deep silence, like statues, without saying a word, without even a sigh, never taking their eyes off his body until the following day. Messengers arrived from all over the Baye des Chaleurs. Despite the cold and the distance, a number of people came from Nipisiguit, Bonaventure, and Gaspeg. The people of Bocage[3] came as well. The spokespeople – almost everyone in attendance – paid tribute to the deceased. The praise was unending. For six days, one would have thought Saint-Jean had created the galaxy itself. At daybreak on the seventh day, when Lentaigne, whose grandmother Marie Giraud was Saint-Jean's cousin, had finished his tribute, Angélique declared, "I want him buried now."

Jean-Baptiste complied. No one wanted to see the ceremony last forever, not even the natives, for whom Saint-Jean was next to a god. Despite the frozen ground, he was buried in the small cemetery to the west of Ruisseau. The missionary put on his surplice with its black star, recited the prayer of absolution, and chanted the *De Profundis*. Then Angélique placed on her father's chest the gold cross from the island treasure. She had kept her sorrow and revolt in check thus far, but when they covered her beloved father in birchbark, she broke down. She swore at the Catholic God, the papists, the missionaries, and all their representatives who had taken away the natives' beliefs and, in so doing, their strength. She cursed the white man's war, then stretched her arms toward the wan January sun to pay homage to the supreme god of the Mi'kmaq, begging for protection for her sons. Then she set off into the woods alone, into the snow and the cold, insensitive to hunger and pain, indifferent to her fatigue and the falling snow. She was consumed by something resembling a fever. She fell several times, clawed at trees, and cried out, despair blowing through her like a wintery northwester. At sunset, exhausted, lost, wild-eyed, she collapsed at the foot of a large spruce tree. By the time the moon appeared in the sky, she had regained her wits, but the pain was still there. She thought of Joseph, gone, René, imprisoned and ill; Membertou, far away, perhaps in danger; and her father, dead; and she asked evil Gougou to let her have her revenge.

---

3. They were still in Bonaventure.

Chapter 37

France cedes Acadia, Ile du Cap-Breton, the gulf and river islands, Canada and all its dependencies "in the most sweeping sense, without restriction, and renounces hereinafter any plan to retake them."

> – Fontainebleau, February 10, 1763

Where you stand, where you build houses, where you fortify this fort, where you hope to establish yourself, this land which you now wish to reign over as absolute master, this land belongs to me, I was born of it like the grass, it is my birthplace and my dwelling place, it is my native land: I swear the Great Manitou himself gave it to me to be my land for all time.

> – A chief's declaration of war
> upon the founding of Halifax

For several hours now, the Ruisseau "band" had been keeping watch on the outskirts of Fort Beauséjour. Hoarfrost covered the trees, and the branches chimed in the crystal forest. A black woodpecker hammered at the trunk of a birch tree. Aside from the pecking bird, there was no movement. Silence blanketed the surrounding landscape, in hues of white, brown, and green. Fertile plains were visible, stretching to the bay under the snow.

Beausoleil mused aloud, "Abbot Leloutre spent 100,000 livres here to build the aboiteaux. They would have drained the marshes and made it possible for many families to settle here... To think I fought to the last minute to defend this fort," Beausoleil said sadly.

His reputation was firmly established among the Acadians. A skilful gunman and captain of the militia of franc-tireurs, he had resisted the English troops for years. When Major Scott dropped anchor in the Baie de Chipoudy in November 1758 and laid waste to the houses in his village and the surrounding region, including Coude[1], Beausoleil kept up the fight in Miramichi.

"All we hear about is one defeat after another," François Gionet roared. "Villages destroyed, forts surrendering, useless aboiteaux..."

"Not always," Beausoleil retorted. "During the Austrian War of Succession in 1747, we just about liberated the country when we took the English garrison by surprise during a snowstorm one night."

"That's ancient history," Membertou objected. "They're highly fortified here, and we won't be able to repeat the exploit. We'll have to enter the fort in broad daylight."

"You're crazy!" Zacharie Douaron exclaimed.

"We could disguise ourselves as Indians and tell the English we want to trade with them, just long enough to reconnoitre the place, and when night falls..."

"It's a good plan..." Beausoleil agreed. "That's how we freed some Acadians in Port-Royal four years ago."

He looked defiantly at the fort. The hexagonal bastions now carried barbaric-sounding names – Duke of Cumberland, Prince Edward, Prince Henry, Prince Frederick, Prince William – which only strengthened his resolve to set the prisoners free.

* * *

Mathilde was holding up all right, but René was doing poorly in his cell. Ill and feverish, he had many dreams. His dreams

---

1. The houses stood in what is now Moncton's Bore View Park.

centred around food – a nice, hot barley soup with a big chunk of beef. Outside of his dreams, however, there was never enough meat to allow him to eat to his fill. Just the day before, rats had been discovered in the pork barrels. René dreamt about his father a lot, on the Isle of Jersey with Emilie. Alive and well. The dream was so real he felt he could hear and even touch his father. He asked him for help, and in his dream, Joseph promised that René would soon be free and that he would watch over him in the meantime.

Joseph Gueguen became his protector. Since he spoke French, English, and Mi'kmaq, the English had put him in charge of the prisoners' supplies and provisions. Gueguen made sure René got better food and in sufficient quantities. He also brought rags dipped in animal fat to give them some light. René had recognized Gueguen who, as Abbot Manach's servant, had been in Ruisseau in the fall of 1754 during the abbot's travels.

"I married and had two children."

"But when you came to Ruisseau, your dream was to become a priest!"

"I had an accident during a crossing to Ile Saint-Jean in 1755. A bullet cut off the index finger on my left hand…"

René interrupted him, "But I don't understand… it's not that hard to hold the host and chalice."

"The church is quite inflexible in that regard. A priest has to have all his fingers intact. It was for the best since Abbot Manach sent me to study at the Quebec seminary anyway and, on my return, I met Nanon Arsenault, who became my wife."

"So your descendants were within a finger of never being born," René joked.

Gueguen was encouraged at René's attempt at humour since it meant he hadn't lost the will to live.

* * *

During this time, Membertou gave his warrior instincts free rein. The men in his "band" disguised themselves so well that their own mother wouldn't have recognized them, and they entered the fort without a problem. In the soldiers' eyes, they were just another Indian band come to sell to the commander and officers, a highly profitable trade. Captain MacKenzie was openly delighted to see the Ruisseau representatives since it was the first time the tribe had agreed to trade with the English. He gave them an extra-warm welcome, out of fear, mostly, since he had heard stories of scalpings. MacKenzie wasn't surprised either to see so many natives come to trade since his only thought was for the jangling ecus that would brighten his old age. So he decided to hold a celebration and ordered that brandy be served and an ox be cooked – an animal that had been stolen from the inhabitants of Memramcouk in any case.

The celebration came at a perfect time, for it was Charles Gautrot's and Françoise Bourque's wedding day at the fort. In the absence of a priest to consecrate their union right then, Gueguen officiated before the witnesses Barthélémi Doucet and Pierre Douaron. Although he was relieved at having deceived the enemy so easily, Membertou was a distracted participant in the celebration. He was disappointed to see that most of the prisoners from the Baye des Chaleurs had been sent to Fort Edward and Halifax. MacKenzie kept only the strongest among them to put them to work come spring on the aboiteaux since the English didn't know how to go about repairing them. There was at least one consolation. Nicolas Gauthier, a prisoner in the fort, told him that René and Mathilde were definitely at Beauséjour and that they were just waiting for a chance to escape. The trip would not have been in vain after all. During the celebration, Gueguen, who had met Membertou before in Ruisseau, took pains to tell him how to go about making an escape possible.

* * *

In Ruisseau, although everyone was busy getting ready for winter, the preparations primarily served to help keep their minds off their loved ones. Josette gathered misotte at the Rivière du Sud and brought it back to Ruisseau; Bocage's inhabitants had mowed the hay using a scythe during the last days of autumn and carted it to higher land to make haystacks before leaving for Bonaventure. They agreed to let the hay be used to meet immediate needs. When ice imprisoned the bay, Josette led two oxen along the coast; it was the shortest route to a hangar located down the small Rivière du Bocage, where she could store the misotte. It was a Herculean task that she performed singlehandedly since almost all the men were off hunting. As for Geneviève, she squared off wide, thick beams and boards to be used come spring to repair the aboiteau boxes damaged by the ice.

Angélique spent all winter weaving, diluting her sorrows in the woof of the fabric. It was a productive winter, as productive as her sorrow was great. All the worn clothes she could get her hands on were shredded, carded to make them supple, then separated again and again. She spent many hours at the spinning wheel, twisting the wool and linen she'd prepared into one long thread, then transferring it to the spindle to make into skeins. The wheel turned from morning till night like a mantra, gradually anesthetizing her pain. Peace returned to her soul and slowly the loom produced thick fabric, druggets, and netting with which she made dresses, aprons, and shawls, as though recreating a world of harmony from shapeless matter. She soon reached the stage where the material was to be dyed. Some women only used black and green, the only colours they could find; others added red threads ripped out of English fabric. But thanks to her knowledge of herbs and barks, Angélique could choose among all the colours of the rainbow. Although Jean-Baptiste was busy with his preparations for fishing, he sometimes kept his sister company. Now, she let herself be comforted by a look, a gesture, a smile, where she hadn't before. Sitting by her side, he made her a hat and a pair of leather moccasins that would hold her in good stead in the cold, snow, and rain. Pierre Gallien also came to see Angélique when he was in Ruisseau, spending more time than he needed there, as far as Jean-Baptiste was concerned.

At spring breakup in 1762, Membertou, René, and Mathilde returned to Ruisseau. All their efforts and hope had managed to free only a handful of prisoners since most of the Acadians were not kept in Fort Beauséjour. There was also a fly in the ointment: Beausoleil had let himself be taken prisoner to allow Mathilde to escape, a sacrifice worthy of the man. After a long winter spent at her loom, Angélique was ready to fully experience her joy. As for Frigault, Josette gave him a hero's welcome. It should be said that her belly had grown and that the world would soon be graced with a newborn. Her cousins Anne and Marie weren't as far along with François Gionet and Zacharie Douaron, but they were nevertheless terribly excited to see their men again; the light shining in their eyes spoke volumes. That night everyone danced around a huge bonfire. The Acadians from Haut- and Bas-Caraquet as well as those from Port-Royal and Papôg threw themselves into the quadrille, the cotillon, and much more intimate dances in the undergrowth. Dance – an ever-present part of native life – was for them a sacred rite.

All night long the tam-tam articulated the rhythms of the earth and the lovers' heartbeats. The scent of spring was in the air; nature reawakening to the smoke of grass fires, plaster pipes, and peace pipes. Tobacco was part of every rite: celebrations of peace, war, rejoicing, even the calming of hunger pangs. The celebration made a more intimate meeting of two peoples possible that night. Delirious with happiness at finally being back with his own people, René pulled out of his bag the cruets from the Beaubassin church that Gueguen had given him in Fort Beauséjour and poured some wine for each member of his family; then he raised the cruet, sending a mute prayer to his grandfather resting in peace not far from Ruisseau.

In May, Josette gave birth to a son they named Pierre. As was customary, he was bathed in Ruisseau Creek, then given oil to drink from the seacows Jean-Baptiste fished off Miscou. All necessary precautions were taken on the spiritual plane as well. Alexis Landry came from Bonaventure with Raymond Boudages, come to check on his fishing post at Caraquet. Boudages was married to Esther, the daughter of Grand'Pré's notary LeBlanc. Alexis baptized the child in a lay ceremony, a frequent occurrence at the time, as was the white mass he celebrated right afterwards, during which the congregation sang the *Kyrie*, the *Gloria*, and the *Credo* in the great outdoors. After mass, the women taught the children their catechism.

Landry went to visit his meadows and aboiteaux at the Rivière du Sud. He hoped to return to Caraquet once the peace treaty was signed, as did Léger, Poirier, and others. He surveyed his land, checked the earthen embankments which served as dykes, and made sure the aboiteaux were functioning properly. One of the valve gates was broken, and he replaced it with one of the boards Geneviève had prepared. That same summer Parisé, who had notions of physics as well as solid training as an officer of the king's regiments, is said to have suggested he use the principle of Archimedes' screw to irrigate his land above the hillock. Through a spiral screw revolving inside a culvert running downhill, the force of the river current could be used to raise the water by stages. Child's play! Gabriel Albert distinguished himself by finding a water source using a willow branch, a method true to the ancient tradition of water divining. Then, that summer, he built himself a house in a spot known as Petit Marais, between Bocage and Ruisseau.

To make up for the lack of a source of fresh supplies since the Restigouche post had distributed the last of its provisions the previous year, Jean-Baptiste and Gallien perfected their fishing technique: they tied one end of a long net to a buoy close to shore and the other to the schooner, then turned the ship in ever-smaller circles to create a giant fishtrap. They were also able to capture seacows, whose oil was used as a substitute for butter.

* * *

Would England keep Canada? That was the question on the mind of every inhabitant of New France. Certain London sugar merchants wanted to keep Guadeloupe, taken from the French in 1759, in exchange for Canada. Some of the most perceptive intellectuals in England considered that a French Canada was the surest means of ensuring the loyalty of the

Anglo-American colonies because it would limit their expansion. But most English would rather hold on to what they already had. The Anglo-American colonies were fiercely opposed to seeing New France returned to French jurisdiction. In France, Canada was not popular with either the public or the court. Other than the sugar islands, which were more popular than snowbanks, France's negotiator Choiseul was asking for mere crumbs: a few counters in the West Indies and Africa, where the trade in black gold offered profitable prospects. The timid protests raised by the chambers of commerce of Saint-Malo, Nantes, La Rochelle, Bordeaux, and the other cities that earned income from Canada's fisheries did not wash, despite the vigorous arguments that had been presented over decades by Frontenac, D'Iberville, De la Galissonnière, and Bougainville to name but a few, who claimed that if Great Britain took possession of North America, it would have such a hold over trade and the seas that it would rank first among the world's nations.

New France's future was discussed in the evenings around the campfires that burned timidly from Port-Royal to Gaspeg in the most isolated locations. Dotting the bays and mocauques[2] were the flickering yet tenacious flames on which meals were made, fearful hearts warmed, and light and colour added to the darkness. Flames that burned in the most impenetrable and camouflaged of places, as though nature itself had come to the refugees' defence.

The Acadians held their breath the space of an incoming wave when France dispatched a small fleet, a parting shot in its effort to take back Canada. In the summer of 1762, a few French vessels took over the town of St. John's, Newfoundland as well as a few English vessels. The English were panic-stricken, especially in Halifax, and fifteen hundred Acadians held prisoner in Nova Scotia were sent to Boston. The Massachusetts general assembly would not let the prisoners disembark. Instead, they made them wait for three weeks in the harbour, then sent them back to Halifax like so much unwanted merchandise! The to-ing and fro-ing was all to no

---

2. Marshlands.

avail since the French fleet was not large enough to confront the English ships waiting near Louisbourg.

When news of the French victory in Newfoundland reached Ruisseau, rumours of peace were already circulating. France finally decided to cede Canada in exchange for Guadeloupe. On November 3, 1762, French, English, and Spanish diplomats signed the first drafts of the treaty that was ratified in Fontainebleau on February 10, 1763. There was no precedent in the history of white civilization for such total abandonment of a colony by a mother country. The treaty specified the absolute nature of the conditions agreed to by France, which ceded Canada and all its dependencies and granted eighteen months to settlers to emigrate where they saw fit. Those who stayed could practise the Catholic religion insofar as it was authorized by the laws of Great Britain. Those same laws had little tolerance for Catholics and their allegiance to Rome! France was entitled to keep two small islands as shelter for its fishermen: the islands of Saint-Pierre and Miquelon off Newfoundland.

"This is incredible," René exclaimed when he heard of the treaty. "Nothing, not a line, not a word to safeguard the rights and customs of the people living here."

"At least the Canadiens kept their lands, their property, and their laws," Alexis Landry said sadly. "There is no provision for us, it's as though we didn't exist. We're not even sure we can keep our fields of rocks and our marshes!"

"How can we prove our entitlement to our former land without any records?" Joseph-Jean said sorrowfully.

"We should have allied ourselves with the English," Gabriel Albert muttered. "At least they defend their citizens' rights."

He would certainly have sworn a blue streak if he'd heard Minister Choiseul proclaim, "I can even go so far as to say that Corsica is more useful in any case than Canada ever has or would have been." Choiseul was the man who negotiated to keep a few islands in the Caribbean in exchange for New France and Acadia. Coincidentally, his fortune came from the Caribbean!

Finally giving in to an insistent Pierre Gallien, Angélique agreed to a marriage, and the wedding date was set: March 17, 1763. Angélique was some ten years older than her future spouse, but her radiant expression and generous curves belied that fact. Gallien was the one who looked older than his age because of his greying hair, which did, however, lend him a certain presence – a considerable asset in his long process to win, if not Angélique's heart, her hand. After years of hesitation, she had made up her mind. *Joseph has been gone for close to three years. Thirty thousand hours without love is a long time. It's not as though I can bring him back to life... Pierre is not the love of my life, but I care for him... He's gentle and patient...* she told herself.

On the wedding day, the tribe's shaman lauded Angélique's ancestors, going all the way back to the year one thousand and the Viking chief. To hear him speak, all her ancestors had been gods, kings, and heroes; each had lived an extraordinary life, given wise council, and been unequalled as hunters. In compliance with the tradition, Angélique gave her thanks and made a vow to the moon and the stars. She assured the Mi'kmaq that, from that time on, the region would become a hunters' paradise. Adopting the same tone, Gallien improvised a song telling of his exploit when he killed a sea monster several years earlier, a kind of aquatic gougou that, according to his story, was bigger than Ile Caraquet. Jean-Baptiste gave no speeches, which his sister interpreted as a sign of his lack of enthusiasm, even though she knew he understood her needs.

There was no missionary to join the newlyweds, but there were many witnesses to their union. The absence of a missionary didn't bother the Mi'kmaq, for whom it went without saying that a mismatched couple would separate without a scene. The saying went, "One shouldn't marry just to be unhappy for the rest of one's days." Such wisdom had humanized the missionaries, who until then had been prisoners of their own dogma. It didn't bother the Acadians either, for they had seen "marriages of convenience" take place for several years by then. But to give the event a more official stamp, François Gionet had drafted in his finest handwriting a marriage contract on birchbark, which the couple signed.

Then all the guests were invited to the wedding feast featuring products of the sea (smelt, rocklings, small codfish) caught through a hole in the ice, oysters gathered using wooden rakes, and game from the forest served with marsh plants and samphire. Violins, flutes, and spoons were brought out to enliven the wedding with music; brandy flowed freely to loosen spirits, while the guests sang songs from France and told each other hunting and buccaneering stories. The sad drunks among them were able to weep or worry about their loved ones while surrounded by solicitude.

René sulked on the wedding night as he lay on his bed of seaweed. It was Mathilde's turn to comfort him. She managed to distract him so well that he brought out his collection of ancient javelins and silex arrowheads to show her, forgetting about Angélique and Gallien cuddling by the fire in the quilt the tribe had offered them.

Chapter 38

The Acadians of Georgia wrote to the Duc de Nivernois in 1765:
By mutual consent after such a lengthy wait, they (the Acadians) throw themselves on your mercy, seeing in you the person who will set them free... We beg you to have our children brought back to us, our children who were taken from us and sent to scattered plantations where they were sold by English gentlemen: an unworthy practice...

A proposal made by Jacques Robin, whom Abbot Leloutre had met at Elizabeth Castle, provoked quite a bit of controversy in Ruisseau in the spring of 1763. He sent a request to the governor of Nova Scotia for a concession in Miramichi for his fishing operation and addressed the following request to several Acadians:

...to all Acadians without resources in Halifax, Boston, and New York at present, and to all the French without resources in Cap Breton and elsewhere in northern America, I would be delighted if all the aforementioned people would agree to go to Miramichi where I will give them good land in sufficient quantity and the means of making an honest living at their trade whatever it may be, since I need carpenters, locksmiths, seamen, coopers, labourers... and I will advance you the money needed for you to settle with...

When Jean-Baptiste received the letter, he interpreted it as a sign that a distant emperor had deigned to notice his status as lord in his own land, and he was thoroughly flattered. *This is my opportunity to build a cod empire*, he thought.

Guessing at his thoughts, Angélique pointed out, "Robin will be the great lord and you'll be his servant!"

"Maybe, but don't forget that many exiles won't come back otherwise."

"I know that, but Robin isn't serving your interests. In a way, you have become the band's chief since our father's death, and Robin wants to make use of your influence."

"He could bring out new settlers."

"The cost would be too high. It takes close to a generation to adapt to life on this continent. Here he has seasoned labourers within easy reach."

Angélique and Jean-Baptiste weren't the only ones having a lively discussion on the matter. The Acadians who had carried on the agricultural tradition felt threatened by the massive return of fishing Acadians – the never-ending conflict between land and sea. "After all," they said, "Robin establishes the price for the fish we sell him and for the products we need that he sells to us. Under that kind of system, he can keep people living in poverty for a long time."

Another letter sparked a great deal of curiosity in Acadia. The Acadians had never received so much mail! The Duc de Nivernois, France's ambassador to London, invited them to return to France if they so wished, promising highly advantageous settlement conditions. The debate was on again in Ruisseau, Petit Marais, and Bocage's Petite Rivière between those for and against the offer; anyone who had spent time in France after being freed from London prisons did not want to return.

"We won't adapt. There's no room. You spend all your time paying taxes for the tiniest plot of land. There are too many laws. If you're a peasant, the lords rule. Everything is complicated. Everyone has his or her station or place," predicted a man named Blanchard.

"You can't be serious," Parisé exclaimed, "Do you really think we'll be freer here to do what we want under English rule? Worse yet, there's nothing saying the English will grant us any land."

Another factor further complicated the debate when news spread of a royal decree whereby the English authorized the Acadians' return home but not their taking possession of their former land. The glimmer of hope was not much more real than the colour of the wind. They also learned that the Halifax Board of Trade had rejected Jacques Robin's proposal in a response drafted by Governor Montague Wilmot. Alexis Landry put in words what others were thinking, "It's because they fear French influence in the Gulf." From all this, the Acadians inferred that yes, they could return to live, but certainly not in the best locations such as at the mouth of rivers, and that the least cultivated land would be reserved for them. It was also clearly spelled out that the Acadians were only entitled to come back in small groups.

"I know what their strategy is," Gabriel Albert explained. "They want to make us weaker by scattering us through the marshlands between the English villages."

The events didn't stop the Baye des Chaleurs' Acadians, who settled along the rivers, creeks, capes, coves, and lagoons. Several began building half-timbered homes out of wood and cob; the latter was a mixture of oily clay and chopped salt hay from the meadows of the Rivière du Sud that was bleached with lime and used as mortar. The first dwelling of its kind was built by a certain Dugas, who was inspired by traditions from northern Normandy.

As soon as the peace treaty was signed, nothing could stop the return of the exiles, who had been shunted from one side of the known world to the other for seven years, treated like they had the plague, unloaded like livestock in the middle of winter in American colonies that weren't expecting them, and considered a public menace by a population hostile toward anything French or Catholic or remotely linked with the natives. Almost half of the sixteen thousand or so exiles had died or gone missing. When the authorization to leave their land of exile came, several thousand left limbo to return to live along the coasts of Acadia.

They poured in from all corners: from those who had been declared *persona non grata* in Virginia and turned back to England through those who had slaved away in the cotton fields of Carolina to those who had survived malaria in the sugar plantations of Saint-Dominique. The exiles in Boston's slums had lived only for the day when peace was finally declared; several of the men and women who had gone looking for their families were made to pay fines and suffer beatings or prison sentences for having left the zone they'd been assigned to. A group of Acadians deported to Carolina had spent almost the whole Seven Years' War in flight in one old, rotting tub or another. They first ended up in Virginia, where they were sold another floating coffin to replace the raft-like craft in which they'd been travelling. With it, they were able to reach a deserted island in Maryland, where they spent several months repairing the boat. Few survivors remained by the time the old tub reached the Saint-Jean River! In Georgia, others who had been treated like black slaves on the cotton plantations went looking for their children who'd been sold at auction, hoping France, through the Duc de Nivernois' diplomatic efforts, would intervene!

The fate of those who had landed in Pennsylvania was no better. After being parked like slaves in the port of Philadelphia for three months, they'd been scattered throughout the colony. The patriarch LeBlanc, despite many services rendered to the English, died in near anonymity with 116 of his children and grandchildren still missing. And the latest news on the unfortunate Acadians in Philadelphia came when an English merchant requested that Philadelphia's legislative assembly pay for his coffins – used for Acadians. Acadians who left Maryland to return to their country were no more fortunate. They disappeared into huge forests and left only the murmur of the wind to speak for them.

Agapit Vigneau had made three trips back and forth between Halifax and the American colonies. He eventually turned up in Ruisseau, near death and spitting blood because of a poker blow to the ribs administered by a farmer in the state of New York when he asked for his wages. As the farmer chased him off, he added, "If it hadn't been for fear of the law, I would have finished you off like a frog."

The refugees came home by whatever means they could find: on foot, in oxcarts, on horseback, riding a donkey, on rafts, or in schooners or canoes. Those who were too feeble to come travelled home in their minds. The giant Anatole d'Entremont carried his aging father on his back, like the Trojan prince Aeneas carrying his aged father Anchises to the place that was to become Rome. Babies clung to their mother's breasts, old people clung to the horizon. Lines of refugees, like spokes on a wheel, converged on a central hub, returning to a familiar land, to the smell of salt meadows, an ocean tasting of life, and maple syrup. They looked for mothers, brothers, fiancés. Their way was dotted with small crosses as their exhausted companions in misfortune fell. En route some left behind loved ones, who, like Ariadne's thread, showed the way, or who slept for eternity in kelp-shrouded, rotting ships. So the pariahs of a period of white man's history, having known prosperity and opulence, ended up resembling shaggy-haired, stinking beggars.

A small number of exiles decided to go to Quebec or France. Others remembered Governor Vaudreuil's bold idea, before Montreal's surrender, of setting sail for Louisiana with 2500 men and 250 canoes, and left for that region. For several, it was on Joseph Gauthier's schooner instead of by canoe that they reached Louisiana, unaware that, by a secret clause, the French had ceded Louisiana[1] to the Spaniards. A few years later, other refugees would settle in what was then the Malouines[2] with Bougainville. The nobility and great merchants made a beeline for France, leaving behind them a ravaged region, a people in rags, and villages and towns razed by enemy fleets all along the Atlantic coast.

* * *

---

1. One-third of the area of the current United States, on the right bank of the Mississippi River.
2. Today's Falkland Islands.

Father Bonaventure Carpentier came from Bonaventure to bring some spiritual comfort. A group of Acadians met at Ruisseau to ask themselves whether it was better to stay or to go. Mathilde lit a candle in the centre of a Mi'kmaq mat. Angélique opened the book of runes from the Viking oracles, the great priests whose essential message, like the oracle of Delphi, was, "You will find the answers within. Know yourself." From the embroidered leather bag his father had given him, René pulled out the twenty-four disks carved out of seashells polished by countless waves. The symbol on each disk represented a path, destiny. Slowly, he set each disk on the mat. The total silence in the big tent was eloquent in and of itself as though, at that precise moment, it alone held the truth. René took Mathilde's right hand in his and together they closed their eyes and reached out for the disk that would show them the answer they had within and predict their future and that of their people. Angélique's book showed that the disk they chose symbolized taking root and growth. Everyone present decided to stay in Ruisseau; they all felt they saw the candle flame burn brighter, a symbol of an Acadia that would forever be alive.

Afterword

The poetry of the sea, my mother's gentle disposition, the stories my father invented to transport us into worlds of fantasy, those first seeds sown in my child's imagination served as my landmarks along the way. Our rich history did the rest.

I still have trouble understanding why our literature, unlike those of France and the United States, has rarely touched on historical fiction. I have tried to close that gap somewhat by choosing to write about the richest period in our history – the years 1740 to 1763, when the French empire in America came to an end, an era that broke with the past, offering adventures and myths that have ramifications even today. I tried to raise a corner of the veil by showing the confrontation between three cultures – the French, English, and native cultures.

It is always difficult to speak about one's ancestors. I tried to do so respectfully, highlighting their beauty and goodness. Often, I only had a name or a snippet of information to go on so I had to come up with traits, defects, qualities, emotions, and a physiognomy, all that without the help of a picture or curriculum vitae! If by chance a word, a sentence, or a paragraph pertaining to someone who once existed seems offensive to the reader, I am sure the fault is that of the fictional characterization.

This novel is based on historical facts, which I tried to respect insofar as possible. Joseph, my ancestor on my father's side, arrived in Ruisseau (Bas-Caraquet) circa 1740 and wed Angélique, the Métis daughter of Gabriel Giraud known as Saint-Jean. Saint-Jean had lived with the Mi'kmaq for some thirty years by then. The couple had five children; the novel only refers to René, Geneviève, and Josette.

Since Joseph's origins are impossible to trace, it is not inconceivable that he could have been the illegitimate son of one of the dukes of Brittany; why not even a king! Certain characters are fictive: Membertou, Emilie, Jehan, Angéline, Tristan, the priests Minelle and Ignace de la Transfiguration, Tjigog, Aglaë, and most of the native characters. René was born several years after the date shown in the novel. He did wed Mathilde. However, the latter did not arrive in America with the Duc d'Anville's fleet, and Joseph-Jean and Anne were her real parents. The Joseph-Angélique-Emilie love triangle is entirely a product of my imagination. However, when Angélique was widowed, she did indeed marry Pierre Gallien.

The important events are true to history. I did take certain liberties, however. For instance, it is probable that certain Acadians mentioned did not take part in the Restigouche battle or were not all on the *Corsaire Acadien*. Likewise, none of Wolfe's fleet ran aground in Caraquet and, since Tjigog is a fictional character, he certainly did not save Lentaigne's life. There is nothing to preclude imagining that a Viking ship could have run aground on Miscou. As for the fabulous treasure and the cave with native paintings, there is no saying for sure they did not exist or are not hidden away someplace on Ile Caraquet! Another detail of note: as this novel went to press, we learned that research by the historian Fidèle Thériault reveals that Camp de l'Espérance in Miramichi was probably not located on the pine tree island but on terra firma. Moreover, other research has shown that, contrary to what was thought up until now, Berryer, Minister of the French Navy, made many attempts to help New France.

There will always be those who find fault with certain finer points: some will say that such and such a fabric was not worn at the time, others that hunting took place either farther to the south or north, or earlier or later in the year, or that such and such a cannon used smaller cannonballs… I did, however, try to focus on the historical record and how it could have been experienced by a family living on the Acadian peninsula.

I strove to highlight, as does Robert Sauvageau in his history book on Acadia, the heroic acts which show the lively resistance in Acadia, contrary to the image that has been handed down over the years of a people resigned to the deportations.

Finally, in her book entitled *Le vaisseau fantôme*, Catherine Jolicoeur analyzes at length the phenomenon of the phantom ship without finding a plausible explanation. The former mayor of Bas-Caraquet, Théophane Noël, has, however, made an interesting hypothesis. In the spring, during the spawning season for herring, a long white line can be seen out at sea when fishermen catch huge quantities of herring. Until the 1960s or so, the surplus from that catch was either used to fertilize the ground or rotted in a pile onshore. Gases were emitted that contained phosphorous, which might explain why people saw images on the sea. But why a ship on fire? No one knows. The herring haven't spawned in the bay since the 1960s, which coincided with the arrival of the large factory ships that are destroying the seabed. It should be pointed out that the practice of fertilizing the land with herring was abandoned with the arrival of those ships since they disturbed herring spawning habits. Since that time, no one has ever seen a burning phantom ship again!

Acknowledgments
(to the original French edition)

I would like to single out André Vanasse for his invaluable assistance and pertinent comments, as well as Johanne Falardeau for her remarkable job of copy-editing, and Diane Martin for additional proofreading of the text.

I owe a special debt of gratitude to my son Alexandre, who regularly asked, "How is your novel coming, Papa?" Finally, it would take too many pages to name the many francophones of America and Europe who helped and encouraged me. Nevertheless, I believe that without the support of the people from our region and all their good vibrations, this novel would never have seen the light of day.